CRIMINALS

MIKE KARPA

MUMBLERS

Published by Mumblers Press LLC, San Francisco CA USA

LCCN: 2021945502 | ISBN 978-1-7362444-0-1 (e-book) | 978-1-7362444-1-8 (paperback)

For Joanne Underwood, who believed.

1

THE BORDER

Conner rolled his shoulder blades against his airplane seat, shifting the hashish he'd banded tight around his ribs, and still he itched. What kind of idiot was he? Some white-toothed chatterbox in an airless Bangkok drug alley tells him the packaging will fool the airport dogs and Conner believes him? And now here he was, planted in a window seat flying straight, no doubt, toward Japanese jail at five hundred and fifty-five miles an hour.

A soft warning bell sounded overhead and the fasten-seat-belts light went on as a female voice announced the plane's descent into Tokyo-Narita in Thai, Japanese and English. Beneath Conner's yellow business shirt, the plastic buckle of the belt was snagging against his skin, daring him to unbuckle it.

"You okay?" the guy next to him asked.

Conner glanced at the man. White. Medium build. Dark haired, like Conner. Perhaps a few years older. He was awfully good looking, but Conner couldn't risk interacting with anyone. Conner nodded. "Fine." His shoulders cramped and the too-short strap drove into a space between two ribs he hadn't known was there. He felt like a penned-up calf on slaughter day.

The guy stuck out his hand across the empty seat between them. "Matt." He had a rich, rumbling baritone, a Midwest American accent straight off TV. So unlike Conner's old-school L.A. drawl—more Okie than Valley Girl—that English-school owners found so distressingly unintelligible.

Conner shook Matt's hand. The guy's grip was firm, his hand warm. Conner wanted to hang on to it for a week.

"You work in Tokyo?" Matt asked.

"Ikari Bank." Something about the word *bank*, Conner had found, killed conversations, and as much as he liked hearing that resonant voice, he needed to smother this interchange in its crib.

The guy straightened up in his seat. "Survived the great 'crash' of 1990, did you?" He made quotation-mark signs with his fingers, as though he didn't believe the stock market had plunged by half. "We're partnering with Ikari. I'm at the American Embassy, on contract." He laughed. "Working with the Ministry of Finance, liberalization, that sort of thing. What are you in? M&A? Commercial paper?" Matt crossed his legs, letting one leather-clad foot stick out into the aisle.

Ah, *gaijin* salaryman, Conner thought. Tokyo was still crawling with these educated American fortune seekers, despite the meltdown. Not aimless chuckleheads like himself but kids who did things like intern, interview and tell amusing stories about . . . well, who knows what. Conner wasn't "amusing." He had prepared a story about selling traveler's checks for Ikari, but now sat in awkward silence because he couldn't carry the lie very far and the guy had a firm grip that he wanted to feel again.

Matt's foot caught the skirt of a Thai flight attendant as she hustled up the narrow pathway to her station. He jerked his head in a very small bow and lifted his hand in a slight reverse karate chop of wordless apology. It was an effortlessly Japanese gesture for an American and made Conner kind of enviously hate him. The flight attendant turned to smile at Matt, her teeth as deep white and perfect as the Bangkok drug dealer's. Matt's dark green eyes sparkled back.

"Damn, Skippy," he whispered to Conner as she sashayed up the aisle. "Sexy," he growled, pitching his voice low.

Conner exhaled, shrinking his lungs to relieve the bite of the strap. To come out or not come out? Conner watched the woman dip to pick up a stray headset from a seat cushion and noted that he *did* feel a spark of excitement as he looked at her. Maybe it was time for a different sort of coming out. "You know, I guess she is."

"You guess?"

"I'm new at this."

Matt looked at Conner. Conner could see his mind was trying to figure out what Conner had just said.

Conner's ears buzzed, blood pressure rising. If he could risk carrying drugs customs, could he not risk a little honesty? It was the nineties now; times had changed. "Always thought I was just gay." His throat stumbled on the word *gay*, so laden with power. "But I'm going out with a woman for the first time." Ah, Katie. *Going out* definitely wasn't the phrase. Katie didn't think much of Conner; they only had sex, really, which was about the last thing he'd ever expected. But he liked it. Quite a bit.

Matt shifted back in his seat. Not a good sign, but sometimes it took people a moment to get over the surprise. Matt recrossed his khaki-sheathed legs and drummed his fingers on his knee.

The buckle of Conner's chest pack crabbed into his back, a fingernail on a fleshy chalkboard. He internally thanked Matt for taking his mind off it for so long. He'd picked up the pack in an open-air Bangkok market yesterday. It was emblazoned with an already peeling Louis Vuitton insignia and the proud statement, *Happyness of life is satiety. My shoes.* It sounded like something Conner would have come up with.

Matt glanced at him, but nervously. Never mind. Conner wasn't sure what he thought of himself either. Sleeping with a woman hadn't made him any less attracted to men. But Katie had made a move one night, and he'd wondered if anything had changed since high school. It had. So, was he going to be a different person now? The experience now had him thinking: was he a person, or just a bunch of behaviors? Hello, I'd like you to meet my friend Conner. He's a behavior.

Conner stared out the window as the coast appeared. The outskirts of greater Tokyo were just visible at the edge of the wintry brown countryside outside Narita. Somewhere out there was Mount Fuji. Lots of people saw it on the approach but Conner never had.

The wing flaps rose and the engines began to scream, setting off a scream inside Conner as well. Shining beads scrawled across his oval plastic window. All it took for Conner to land in prison was for one Japanese policeman to look at this scrawny twenty-five-year-old in a pin-striped suit and butter-toned shirt and ask, Is he stupid enough to lash a kilo of hash to his chest?

The plane dropped.

Thump. Touchdown. Thump again, the final touchdown, a soft, cracking sound of settling plastic, and then the engines really howled. Conner clutched the arms of his seat and looked at green-eyed Matt.

Matt batted his ticket folder against his leg, hair-topped knuckles tapping his solid thigh in a forceful pattern.

The plane slowed and taxied past the surrounding forests and rice fields to the terminal.

Showtime.

Now Conner had to ignore Matt, ignore the strap, and slough off his anxiety. He and his ex-boyfriend Arata had worked out how he'd do this. In a few minutes he would head up the jetway into the terminal, transit Passport Control and Customs, and walk right out that automated sliding glass door to freedom. Conner would carry himself like a clone of Matt, adopting a haggardly bright-eyed, I-have-business-all-over-Asia demeanor. What had Matt said? He worked with the embassy, Ministry of Finance something. Conner couldn't remember any of the lingo, or even the tone, usually the thing he nailed on one hearing. Wait a minute, Matt was *partnering*. No, *we're* partnering. *I'm* at the embassy. *Liberalization*, that sort of thing. Conner had it. He'd trail Matt, let Matt warm up the customs inspector so the inspector would see only a couple of law-abiding-ish young American assholes trying to make a bunch of money in the business world.

It was a plan.

The plane rolled across the dewy tarmac and stopped. A jetway melded to the body of the plane with a polite sucking sound. Cool late-winter air flowed into the compartment as people began standing, lowering bags from overhead bins. Conner remained seated. He tightened his tie and looked out at the huge terminal building he'd last seen five days ago.

Narita. Tokyo. For weeks before he'd left, it had been gray, neither raining nor snowing, and it was comforting somehow that it still was. He put his palm to the cold window plastic. He liked being in Japan. People didn't pry, they weren't violent. They were nice to him. "Hi," he whispered at the airport buildings, quietly, so Matt wouldn't hear. "I'm back."

Matt pulled a briefcase out from overhead.

Conner breathed in, ribs rising, lungs expanding. He felt unconstricted for the first time in hours. He could pull this off. Yes, he could.

Matt pushed out into the aisle without a backward glance. Conner pulled down his black carry-on, letting a few groups of people go ahead, and buttoned his suit jacket. He wanted to open up a discreet distance between himself and Matt, since Conner had seen a baggage tag on Matt's ticket folder but had checked nothing himself. Matt moved toward the exit. Conner squeezed into the aisle and deplaned.

The passengers fanned out as the windowless corridor widened. A faint smell of bleach hung in the moist air. Up ahead, Matt overtook a tall woman who looked half-Asian, half-European, and they marched side by side over the linoleum-tiled floor, yellow health questionnaires in hand. Conner, watching each step they took toward the guard at the health station, registered Matt's muscular ass bunching and noticed the shift of the woman's softer cheeks, accentuated by her black high heels. What was it that made one attracted to one gender or another? A visual shape, an imagined touch, an association of strength or tenderness? Conner imagined her sitting astride Matt, facing him, his hands on her ass, clutching her skin as she moved over him, hands grasping at his chest as . . . .

The health station guard slapped down a form, snapping Conner back to reality.

Sukebe! You lech! Conner berated himself.

The guard was looking straight at him.

Wait a minute, Conner thought. I'm not in pain. He allowed himself a quick glance down. His pouch of hash leaned out against his shirt and tie like an open fuse box. His heart did a flip. The blasted buckle must have broken. Piece-of-shit flea-market knock-off. He could feel it drifting over his side. The only bathroom was now behind him, and pivoting back would draw too much attention. He pinned the straps between elbows and torso and cinched the pouch to his chest.

Conner smiled at the guard, trying to draw the man's attention to Conner's face. The buttoned jacket should help hide the shirtfront bulge. He looked the guard in the eye until the man looked away. Conner handed him the yellow health form, which informed travelers that if they got sick after arriving in Japan, it was the fault of germs they had brought in with them. He walked past the guard and headed for Passport Control.

Conner got in the same line as Matt and waited for the feel of an official hand on his shoulder, but there was nothing.

The woman and Matt were now both just the right distance ahead of him. She tucked her long hair forward over one shoulder. The Passport Control officers were seated in their booths, but had not started processing people. Conner huffed a breath. Three more hours and he would be at the bar delivering the hash to Arata.

Conner began to relax, stupidly happy at the thought of seeing Arata. Stupid because Conner was not doing this out of guilt, which he had good reason to feel, but because he still wanted to be with Arata. What was the point of missing an ex who had dumped you, especially when you were seeing someone else?

Conner set his carry-on down. His tensed arms clamped the pouch to his chest; his armpits were sweaty. He looked past twenty heads of straight dark hair to the officer in his booth.

The green *Residents* light above the booth went on.

Wait, how could Matt and the woman be in the residents line? Well, the tall woman looked possibly half-Japanese, so that made sense, but Matt? This Conner could not have foreseen.

Conner moved to the end of the other very long line. He scanned the other passengers for someone to trail behind, but everyone in his new line was Thai, dressed casually in short sleeves for color and comfort. And why not? Japanese thought Thais were all criminals to begin with. Conner was in trouble.

The orange booth light was now lit, but the square-faced Japanese officer was on the phone. Conner sucked sweat off his upper lip, tasting salt. The officer occasionally looked up, but was careful not to engage the single file of foreign eyes. One aisle over, the tall woman was already picking up her stamped passport from her officer and walking down the stairs toward the baggage carousels. Soon Matt's officer handed him back his passport as well and off he trotted after the woman. Going, going, gone. This was going to be one of those days when you wake up in vibrant sunny Bangkok and go to bed in an antiseptic Japanese jail. Well, at least it would be clean.

A very young blue-uniformed man came out with a stamp pad and the square-faced officer accepted the first olive-colored Thai passport. The line began to move.

Conner pushed his carry-on forward with his foot, flexing his shoulders to keep blood flowing to his arms as they tired of cinching the pack to his ribs. At length, Conner handed his scuffed navy-blue US passport to the officer. The officer inspected Conner's multiple-entry visa.

"You've been to Thailand twice this year."

"Business. I sell traveler's checks." Conner twitched a kind of homeless smile. "We're partnering with Ikari Bank. Liberalization, commercial paper, that sort of thing."

"Ah, Ikari Bank." The officer hesitated, hanging onto the

passport, looking on edge, adrenaline pumping. Oh shit. The officer licked his lips.

"Is real estate still safe?"

Conner breathed a sigh of relief. The guy was grieving for his lost portfolio balance, like most of the country. "They don't call it *real* for nothing!" Conner offered. He'd heard a chipper accountant in a bar use that line.

The officer stamped the passport and handed it to Conner. "Thanks."

"No, thank *you*."

Conner felt back on his pace. He'd nailed the lingo *and* the tone, if not the smile. Now everything depended on how professionally the joker he'd bought the hash from had wrapped it. Conner felt alive. This was way better than trying to tutor grammar he'd never learned to twelve-year-olds heartily sick of afterschool *juku*. He glanced at the wall clock. The plane had been on the ground an hour and a half. He jogged down the stairs to Baggage Claim, prepared to see the last Japanese passengers already exiting the customs stations, but the baggage carousel was empty, absolutely motionless, a long gleaming steel pyramid surrounded by a sea of empty-handed people that included, at the far end, both the tall woman and Matt.

Conner felt a rush of euphoria. This was going to be easy after all. When Arata sold the kilo, Conner would tell him they were even. Conner would land a real job, a real visa. Granted, he'd struggled since grade school to decipher the shifting jumbles of letters on pages, but he wasn't the kid who'd hyperventilated in a bathroom stall at LAX five years ago, trying to get up the nerve to go someplace he'd never been on the advice of a bump-faced Marine from Camp Pendleton he'd jerked off in a bus station. He had skills now, maturity. Japan was the best thing that had ever happened to him.

Conner approached Matt and the woman and pretended to check the numbers clicking over on the connecting-flights board, giving himself an excuse to linger. The woman now shifted her long silky hair neatly over her shoulders. Matt smiled at her and nodded silently to Conner, friendly enough now.

Conner nodded back, arms taut. See, it just takes people a minute to adjust, that's all. The carousel jerked into life and began coughing up bags.

"I don't know what took them so long." Matt forced a bit of laughter.

"It's the Kuwait invasion," the woman said, her accent thoroughly Californian. "Every time there's trouble in the Middle East, baggage handling slows down." She retrieved a wheeled bag.

Matt nodded his agreement ruggedly as she walked away. Conner looked beyond her to the weir of inspection platforms between them and freedom.

Matt grabbed a tan bag from the rotating carousel and walked to the same customs station as the woman. Conner got in line directly behind them and thought businessy thoughts. On the opposite side of the station, a stocky priest in beige robes and shaved head hoisted suitcases onto the steel platform.

The woman was quickly cleared. She waved goodbye and walked through the sliding glass doors, another person Conner would never see again. For some reason, Matt wasn't heaving his suitcase onto the steel platform. That was odd. Sure, they sometimes waved people through with a cursory glance, but he was *supposed* to put his case on the platform.

Conner didn't care much for the law, but following rules calmed him.

Matt handed the inspector his passport and a pink form unfamiliar to Conner. The inspector, too, seemed puzzled by it. He stared at the cover of the passport and opened it to the first page, checking Matt against his photo.

Conner's arms burned with fatigue.

The priest on the other side opened his bags on the platform and stepped back, flipping an unlit Mild Seven cigarette through his fingers as the customs man went smartly through his luggage, clearing him.

The inspector hadn't even touched Matt's case, but was still laboring over the damned form, slow as cold honey, as though drawing things out deliberately. The agent sucked breath in skeptically through the corners of his mouth. Conner rubbed the toe of his shoe over the green line that said *Wait Here* in English and Japanese—that much he could read. Underarm sweat was now seeping through his jacket.

Three black-uniformed police came out of the office at the far end of the customs hall. A dog handler followed with a big black lab. The inspector shot a glance at Conner. The man's big eyes, nose and cheekbones seemed to stretch his face. Conner's insides were melting. The delay was for Conner. He'd been spotted by the health station guard after all. He could still feign a bathroom emergency, flush everything in the Baggage Claim restrooms. He was so stupid to be doing this, but he still couldn't bring himself, even now, to let Arata go down in flames. Strangely, he felt himself wishing that Matt was already through, as though it mattered if Matt saw him take a fall, as though Conner had to be a credit to his particular collection of sexual desires.

The policemen stopped in front of them.

Now that it was about to happen, the idea of actually being

arrested came as a surprise. The doorway was right there. Conner could lunge past the uniformed guards, lose himself in the waiting crowd.

The policemen's shoes scuffed against the tiled floor in front of Conner's station.

"Open your bag, please," one said in English. He had a thick head of silver hair and looked like a captain. Conner looked at him, but the captain was looking at Matt. The black dog pointed at Matt's suitcase and barked.

"No," said Matt.

He was talking to Matt?

The captain reached for Matt's suitcase. Hot damn.

Matt put his hand on the case. "My father's a vice-consul," he said in good Japanese, way prettier than Conner's rough-and-tumble version of the language, learned in bars. Matt drew himself up to full height. He was three or four inches taller than the captain.

"You're not a dependent," the captain said. "Not anymore."

He knew Matt?

The captain deftly pushed Matt's hand away from his bag. Matt shoved him. The two junior policemen moved between them.

"Take your hands off me," Matt yelled. His Japanese was damned good.

In a flash and flurry the captain grabbed the suitcase while Matt yelled, "My father's a vice-consul." The biggest policeman and the inspector wedged Matt against the steel platform with a muffled bang. The other policeman snapped on wrist restraints as the dog wagged her tail.

The captain snapped open the suitcase. Conner leaned over. Little single-wrapped baggies of pot were sprinkled brazenly among underwear and shirts, like the guy was Paul McCartney or something.

"Holy shit," Conner said, a bit too loud.

The captain ran his eyes methodically over Conner's face. Conner felt ready to crack—Yes! I'm guilty too!—but the captain closed the bag and motioned the other policemen to follow him. They towed Matt off. Matt's head drooped to his chest, like the air had gone out of him. The dog handler remained. Conner's sides were soaked with sweat. The four men got smaller and smaller and were gone.

"Boy howdy," Conner said in English to the inspector, who was breathing hard from his part in wrestling Matt to the platform. Conner slid his bag toward the inspector to begin an exaggerated display of compliance. Arata had suggested he make a show of it, overwhelming the inspector by opening every last zipper down to the waterproof compartment inside his shaving kit. Conner leaned and tugged on the first zipper.

His pouch slipped.

The inspector pointed at Conner's chest. "What's that?"

Conner's yellow shirt bulged toward the man. Conner damped down a nervous smile and counted to five. "Oh, this?" He chuckled dryly. "It's my passport pouch. Saw some German guys with them and thought it was a great idea, but the damn thing was made in Thailand, and, well, it broke already."

The inspector raised his black eyebrows and peered closer. Conner puffed his chest out a little so he could show the inspector the outlines of the square pouch without divulging its thickness. "You'll never get your pockets picked," Conner said, "but they sure get scratchy when you sweat." Conner undid two shirt buttons and revealed a corner of the thing through the opening.

The inspector nodded. "Yeah, those are a good idea. But you should buy a Japanese one. They're made better." He called the dog handler over. The dog sniffed Conner and his carry-on, but showed no interest. Score one for the vacuum-sealing abilities of Thai lowlifes. The inspector glanced briefly inside Conner's bag, patted it and motioned Conner through.

Conner grabbed up the bag. The automatic doors opened. He walked between parallel aluminum rails that divided the crowd of faces into two eager masses, waiting for family and friends, and out to the sidewalk of the arrivals loop, where airport buses sat idling for their hour-plus journeys into points around the city proper. He pulled the pack out through his open shirt. The buckle had snapped completely in half. He tucked it away in his shoulder bag and took a deep breath. The diesel-scented air flowing freely into his lungs felt excellent. He was home again. He was in Tokyo.

2

THE BURBS

Tokyo was only an hour away by train, but for Marika it might as well have been the other side of the planet. When she'd left her rural home for college, she'd dreamed of living in Tokyo, but here she was in the suburbs, head pounding, as her dentist husband, Isamu, sprawled snoring next to her on the futon. Her eyes felt bloodshot. She was upset with herself. She'd let herself be cajoled into last night's outing to his favorite club. Yes, she'd set the alarm so she could feed the two neighbor dogs they were dog sitting, but she'd neglected to turn it on. Now it was past one. The Akitas were docile and patient, but had to be starving. She made herself get up.

Marika walked into the kitchen but found no dogs, though she could see Isamu had cracked the back door open. She poured kibble into the dogs' bowls and checked there was food in her cat's dish, up out of the reach of the Akitas. She looked out the kitchen window for the dogs. An ant colony seemed to be settling on the pine tree just outside.

"Puffy," she whispered to her cat, trying not to wake Isamu. "Puffy," she whispered again, throat scratchy and raw, hoping

Puffy would pad in on her soft feet, but the cat was apparently out of earshot.

Isamu had lured Marika to the club last night by promising to talk seriously about moving his mother back to the family house in the country, but he had really just wanted Marika's company while he drank whisky-and-waters and gambled away half their monthly profit. Perhaps he was incapable of making a decision. Over the last month it had been getting difficult even to lie in bed next to him. Marika now listened for the sound of him getting up. It would be like him to get up as soon as she did and follow her into the kitchen. He loved her, he loved her, blah, blah, blah.

Marika got out the instant coffee, wanting to calm her throat with hot liquid, but heard the dogs outside. A bowl in each hand, she shouldered the back door the rest of the way open.

"Good morning!" a strained, high-pitched voice warbled at her.

Marika pivoted on her heel, nearly spilling the kibble. Isamu's mother was bowing at her very low—too low, as women her age always seemed to do, as though competing for a national title in submission. Marika recovered her equilibrium and returned the bow, blood throbbing in her head as she matched and exceeded Mother's angle.

"Good morning, Mother."

"I noticed you got home late so I came over and fed the animals this morning." With her furry bun of silver hair, she looked like a little mouse, small enough to squeeze her soft-boned body through any crack that would give her access to Isamu's life.

"Thank you," Marika forced herself to say. The two dogs were lying side by side on the grass behind Mother, seemingly content. Marika admired the way they seem to require so little from humans.

"You know I don't mind," Mother said. "The poor creatures."

Marika looked at the woman. She wasn't that old, sixty-five at most, but she acted eighty. Her hands wavered with a slight tremor, at least until she needed to do something; then she moved with vigor. Marika had first noticed it with Mother's oil painting: she dabbed the brush around on the palette, applying a bit of blue, a bit of green, a bit of white and then slowly moved the wildly jumping brush toward the canvas. Marika had expected stuttering strokes of color to slice the otherwise realistic seascape, turning it into something abstract like a Domoto Insho painting, but at the last moment the old woman's muscles steadied and the stroke went on the canvas with a decisiveness Marika found disturbing.

Isamu's mother began walking toward her, smiling.

Marika felt the urge to scream. She backed away. "Have you eaten?" she asked Mother.

The woman bent over to pick up an old red leaf that had fallen from a maple, leaving it bare. The yard was much cleaner now that Mother was living in the house next door.

Marika set the dog bowls down. "Mother, have you eaten?"

The older woman looked at her. What did she see, Marika asked herself. Not the beautiful marital complement Isamu saw. A *paa-fuu* bubblehead? An incompetent?

"Yes, I heated up a lovely salt-grilled mackerel for my lunch. It was delicious. Thank you." She handed the leaf to Marika and walked past her into the house, as though it were her own. Marika leaned against the stair railing, twirling the leaf in her hands as her head throbbed. She pulled a cigarette from her jacket pocket and lit it.

The yard was carefully planted with maples and moss, like

many in suburban Inudani, and the house was spacious and comfortable. The freshly painted exterior sparkled bright white beneath its glossy blue-tiled roof, with bristling rows of thin yew trees that were already two feet above the wall enclosing the lot. In five or ten years they would completely seal off the house from the outside world.

"Marika!" Isamu called.

Now what? Marika thought, but she yelled "coming," trying to sound pleasant. She stubbed out the half-smoked Mild Seven and went back into the house.

Isamu, wearing only his underwear, was looking through the white cabinet over the kitchen sink. His mother was nowhere to be seen. Marika wondered if the two had talked, what they'd said. He rattled through the bowls and china they'd received at their wedding reception nine years ago but never used. When she looked at his body, she saw the sallow flabby man he would become in ten years rather than the softening but still attractive thirty-one-year-old he was at the moment. His spirit had already made the jump.

He slammed the cabinet door and glanced at her. She was supposed to ask him what he wanted.

She waited.

He opened the cabinet that held the glasses, cups and plates, and closed it immediately. Marika leaned against the steel sink beside him. She heard rustling paper as he pawed more carefully through the spices, onions, coffee filters, teas. He was getting close.

She twisted to the sink, put her hand under the plastic sieve that caught wet garbage, and emptied it into the appropriate trash can. It was full. Trash day was still two days away so she mounded it evenly over the top.

He glanced at her again. She looked back, the word "What?" on the tip of her tongue, but would say nothing till he asked. He went to the other side of the sink to open the cupboard there, the one he'd been looking in when she'd entered the room. His hair looked dirty and was sticking up in back. She added water to the kettle and put it on to boil. He went back to the sundries cabinet again and peered into it.

He wanted the instant coffee, of course; she knew it and he knew she knew it. It was sitting out on the table in plain sight, where she'd set it after taking it out. He'd figure it out in due time. She decided to take a shower. She pushed herself away from the sink.

"Marika!"

"What!"

"Where's the coffee!"

"On the table!"

He glared at her, embarrassed. Nothing made him as mad as embarrassment. He was thinking of some way out now, some way to blame it on her. His mother would help him with that.

Marika looked around, listened. "Where's your mother?"

"Groceries," he said. "There's no food here."

The refrigerator was brimming with food. But of course, with the exception of her beloved mayonnaise, his mother didn't consider Western food quite real. Only cows should drink milk, she always said, like she was some Meiji-era throwback to the last century, when Japanese people didn't quite believe foreigners drank the fluids of other species. "I'll make her a cheese omelet when she gets back."

Isamu glared at her.

The kettle began to whistle and when Isamu grabbed it, Marika ducked out to the bedroom. She could hear him clattering in the kitchen. She shucked off her clothes and put on a robe. He yelled "ouch," as though he'd spilled water on himself, but Marika knew it was a ploy to get attention. She stepped into the bathroom and switched on the water.

The room began to cloud as steam overwhelmed the little ceiling fan. Marika dropped her robe and stepped in the shower. She filled her mouth with water from the showerhead and swallowed. Wetting down her long hair on first one side, then the other, she worked in vanilla-scented shampoo from top to bottom. The wet mass hung like a dead thing. She rinsed out the shampoo and then lathered again to get out the smell of smoke from last night.

"I burned myself," Isamu said from outside the bathroom door. His voice had that uncertain, surprised quality that meant he was telling the truth, as though he only expected people to believe him when he was lying.

She began rinsing out the shampoo. "Well, come in and run cold water over it."

He opened the door and stuck his hand under the tap at the basin.

"And rub on some of that stuff I wash my face with. It has alcohol." She stuck her head under the shower nozzle. "Takes off the heat," she yelled.

She remembered how he used to be happy and open. They had talked for hours and he had patiently tolerated her inarticulate attempts to express herself: why it was so important to her to come to Tokyo all the way from Yamaguchi, how the most important thing was to be a full person, whether you were a boxer, a prostitute, a *soba* server, to have a dream and pursue it. Even a politician. A politician! he'd snort, and, not understanding his contempt, she would feel dumb. But that was okay. She didn't fully understand herself, often feeling she borrowed the thoughts and dreams of others. She nevertheless trusted she would one day fashion the secondhand thoughts into something of her own. And in those days, he had genuinely listened. She felt herself opening up to him again with the memory, loving even his childishness, and remembering this, she wanted him to hold her like he used to.

She heard him wince again loudly and the longing grew stronger. In spite of herself, she loved him most when he was pathetic. Maybe she had somehow trained him to whine.

Marika turned off the water and pulled open the shower curtain. She was clean. Isamu held out a towel. The back of his hand was reddish, but didn't appear to be blistering. Marika stepped into the towel and his arms and he wrapped the towel around her.

"Your hand," she said.

"I wasn't looking. I was so mad," he said. "I'm sorry about last night. I'll talk to Mother today." The door was open and the steam was now billowing out into the bedroom. The top half of the mirror was clouded.

Marika leaned into him and he embraced her. It had been so long since he had touched her with affection. And a long time since she had returned that affection. But maybe the warmth would be there if she gave it a try.

"You silly thing," she said.

He ran his hand over her wet hair. "You know I love you," he said.

He leaned down to kiss her and she closed her eyes and let the towel drop. It had probably been a month since they'd been intimate. They'd reached a point where every touch seemed to summon anger in either him or her over a previous touch denied. She felt a little of that now, but she pushed the sensation away. Marika opened her eyes. In the mirror was his mother, peering at them from their bedroom.

Marika screamed.

His mother screamed.

Isamu jumped.

"Get out." Marika grabbed up the towel. "Get out of my house."

"Mother?" Isamu said. "What are you *doing* here?"

"Well, why do you leave all the doors open?" Mother said.

"Get out!"

"Marika! She's my mother!" Isamu said.

"Well, what is she doing in our bedroom?"

"There wouldn't be a scrap of decent food here if it wasn't for me," Mother said.

"And if I had the right food you wouldn't sneak about my house like a rat?"

Mother seemed to shrink into the wall and Marika felt flustered. She shouldn't have called the woman a rat. But she deserved it. Isamu turned his shoulder toward her and stared at himself in the sweating mirror. His rib cage rose and fell beneath the soft white fabric of his undershirt. "Apologize to her," he said.

At first Marika thought he was talking to his mother, but then he turned toward Marika. Of course. Her face flushed.

Mother began shuffling about in the bedroom. Marika stood on the already cold plastic floor, overwhelmed with hopelessness. Was it too selfish to want him to defend her? She swallowed. "I'm sorry, Mother," Marika said. What she'd said was extreme; what else could she do but apologize?

She adjusted the towel around her and turned to Isamu. "Please ask her to leave and we'll talk later." This had to be resolved. Marika didn't like being angry all the time.

Isamu nodded and escorted his mother into the bedroom as Marika shut the bathroom door. She could hear them discussing the burn on his hand as he dressed. She looked in the mirror. Her face was a wreck. Her eyelids were so puffed up from last night's smoky air she could barely see her eyes. She swabbed her face with the alcohol, but it made her feel drier. Why did they say this stuff was good for you? She heard Isamu and Mother leaving as she toweled off. The front door closed and they were gone.

Marika finished dressing and went into the kitchen. She sat at the table with Isamu's coffee, half-filled and untouched, surrounded by a cold puddle where he'd spilled the hot water. She read the newspaper. Hours went by. She put the paper down and the water raced into its dry fibers. She took the dogs for a walk.

It was getting dark. Isamu had not come home. Marika fed the dogs. She turned on the long fluorescent light that hung over the table. It made the kitchen look like an annex to Isamu's dental office. Marika took a sip of the cold coffee. They were talking about her. Mother was filling his head with thoughts. Why couldn't he come back and talk to Marika first? Saying what she thought was not very Japanese of Marika, surely, but it hardly made her a monster. The old woman had been watching them caress, with Marika standing there naked! Mother knew exactly what she was doing. It was unacceptable.

A fly buzzed in from outside and landed on the table. Marika looked at it more closely. It was a fat winged ant from the colony on the pine tree. She was getting so accustomed to the ants they didn't even bother her. She would have to do something about them; and soon, before she started liking them. Another landed on the table, then another. She shut all the windows in the room. Where were they coming from? She looked up at the light. It was now crawling with silent ants. They seemed to be multiplying as she watched, climbing over the fixture. There were hundreds of them. She picked up the damp newspaper and swatted them. A scattering of dead ants fell to the table with a handful of live ants, their abdomens wiggling. She jumped back. This wouldn't work. She turned off the light, opened the window and sat a bit away from the table, waiting for the ants to fly through the open window toward the streetlight outside, but in the thin dark she could see them crawling over the clear plastic and white metal overhead, occasionally dropping to the table. She wished Isamu would come back and take this hopeless feeling away. She turned the light back on. There were more ants than ever.

Marika went to the closet and brought back the hand vacuum cleaner. She closed the window once again, plugged in the vacuum and began vacuuming the ants from the swinging light fixture. The clear plastic dust receptacle began to fill with ants. She could see them struggling inside. Some of them were actually flying within the little chamber. She vacuumed one side, then the other, then the top, the chains from which the lamp hung, the sides again.

Her arms tired. The ants were almost gone, but new ones seemed to appear now to take the place of the old ones and she couldn't get them all. Where were they coming from?

She turned off the vacuum and sat at the table, watching. The light fixture turned black once again. She followed the path of the ants. They were flying in through the kitchen ventilator fan. She pushed the lever to close it. It was stuck. She pushed harder, but it wouldn't budge. She hit it with the vacuum cleaner and the lever broke completely off, locking the ventilator open.

It was fully night now. Isamu still wasn't back. Something was wrong with the man, deeply wrong. She was his wife, they'd argued, and he was over at his mother's, unable to say no. Marika shuddered as a cold breeze drifted across the room. No one had forced her to marry Isamu; it had been her eager choice. And yet, if she stayed in this house any longer she would go mad. She put the vacuum cleaner away and went to the bedroom closet for her suitcase, as she'd imagined doing so often. She packed a few outfits and a sweater and clicked the suitcase closed. She wandered through the house, gathering her cash card and all the cash she could find, then walked to the main road and caught a taxi to the Inudani train station, where she caught the first train north, to Tokyo.

3

THE BAR

Refreshed by a quick hot soak and change of clothes at his rooming house, Conner felt a buzz swell within him as he emerged from the depths of mammoth Shinjuku Station, Tokyo's western hub. He had pulled it off, and a day early to boot. Arata would be impressed, and soon Conner would be free of the crime tucked into his shoulder bag.

An early evening crowd of women and men carried plastic umbrellas upraised against late winter drizzle as they walked beneath the giant Studio Alta video screen. Conner wove through them, in love with Tokyo. Wide Shinjuku Road blazed red, green, blue and white for blocks.

He turned down a tiled, tree-lined pathway toward the thicket of tiny bars called Golden Gai, where Arata's place, Giotto, was tucked like a slice in a loaf of bread. The alleys grew dark, tight, deserted. He reached a bar with a rock facade. A dirty white cat ran across his path and around the corner. Conner stepped inside.

The barkeep, Fumie, was the sole person in the tiny establishment. She stood behind the counter sautéing eggplant for the night's bar snacks. Conner tried to hide his disappointment. Though she, not Arata, was the reason Conner had started hanging out at Giotto, she had frozen Conner out once he'd begun spending nights at Arata's in-town crash pad.

"Hey, Fumie." Conner tried to sound friendly. He plopped himself on one of the stools, the only seats in the place.

She looked up, brushing bangs away from her wide brown eyes, and turned off the flame. Her expression clouded. "Arata's in Niigata visiting family." She gave the black countertop a violent swipe. "You said you were coming tomorrow."

Conner felt his stomach drop. He couldn't off-load the drugs. And of course she was annoyed. Conner had diverged from the plan the three had carefully devised. But he'd woken in Bangkok, hash under his pillow, knowing he couldn't spend another night on a bedbug-ridden pad beneath the faded pink peonies of a terry-cloth blanket that seemed to have been washed in mud. He'd shoved enough baht across the Thai Airlines counter to get on an earlier flight and now he hardly had train fare back to his room.

Fumie tossed her cleaning rag in the sink. "Well, better early than late, I guess. The *yakuza* are really not forgiving of lateness." She locked eyes on him. "You know I'm not kidding, right?"

Conner ducked his head in a slight bow of apology and thought about what the yakuza would do if Arata couldn't come up with the money. Sever a pinkie? No, wait; severing a pinkie was a self-inflicted expression of gangster loyalty, not a punishment. It was sometimes hard to tell the difference. Conner watched Fumie go about her work, fiddling with pots and pans.

"What?" she said. "It's creepy, having you watch me."

"I should have called. It's just . . . I really, really want this to be over."

She gave him a look, like this was new information. Had she expected him to blithely take up smuggling as a profession? She set a beer glass on the bar in front of Conner and a bottle of beer next to it, which she opened but did not pour. In Japan, friends always poured for each other, so not pouring was a statement. Come on, Fumie, he thought, pour for me.

She tucked a few blank whisky bottles onto the shelf above the mirrored wall behind the bar. Other labels bore customers' names scribbled in black marker.

Conner sat still, not touching the bottle of beer. Come on, Fumie.

She opened one of the snack jars by the phone and filled a small dish with *arare*, a mix of little rice crackers, that she slid over to him. She leaned forward and filled his glass. "I don't hate you, you know."

Tension rushed out of him. He felt like he'd been holding his breath for days and now could let it out.

She sighed, dramatically. "It's just that *you* got him into this whole mess. You got me into it, too."

That seemed a little bit of an exaggeration, but he let it slide. "So, it's not the . . . you know . . . him and me?"

"No!"

He was not entirely sure he believed her. "Have you met his wife?"

"Once or twice. I don't think she really approves of the bar, but maybe she's just afraid of what she'll find."

"She already knows he's gay, Fumie." Conner popped a rice cracker in his mouth.

"He told you that?"

Conner nodded. "He came out to her *before* they got married. It's one of the things I liked about him, though I don't get why his wife would go ahead and marry him."

Fumie tilted her head. "Well, she'd know he was honest.

And he's smart, attractive enough, likes being part of a family. I wouldn't do it, but I can see why she might."

"Then why doesn't she come down here?"

"Knowing he's gay and meeting his latest boyfriend are two different things."

Conner felt tightness in his throat. Latest?

"Plus, it's a long way to Utsunomiya," she said.

Well, that was the truth. People could fight over love, honor and money, but a long commute trumped everything.

Fumie put down her knife. "If you really want this over, then you're not going to like this bit: Arata said you have to go again or the bar will go under."

Conner looked at her, shocked. It was just supposed to be the once, to get Arata square with the world. Conner's thoughts drifted back to Matt's black hair, straight nose. Except for the green eyes, Conner could have been Matt's brother; his younger, plainer, gray-eyed brother who always got the smaller piece of pie. The police captain had sounded like he'd been after Matt for a long time. The captain had also studied Conner so thoroughly he'd be sure to remember him.

Fumie cocked her head at Conner as though seeking confirmation he'd heard her.

Could he go again? He did not want to, but this *was* ultimately his fault.

Back in those first heady months, when Conner was staying most nights with Arata in the crash pad, Arata had glumly reported one night that a man had tripped over the heat-exchanger piping on his way out of Giotto and claimed to have injured his back. The next day the man had sued Arata for damages. A message came in from a shady fellow with a punch perm: sell us half your business or you go to trial. The judge is in our pocket.

The punch-perm guy was yakuza, Arata had said.

You mean gangsters are not just in the movies? Conner asked. He had never expected yakuza to be part of his life. Even in the movies they were hard to take seriously. The last yakuza movie Conner had seen culminated with a young Japanese nun, the heroine, mowing down the gangsters, machine gun blazing, to save her convent and avenge her murdered parents. Or something. His Japanese wasn't quite good enough to really follow a whole movie. Arata explained that the yakuza had been demanding protection money for some time, but Arata had successfully resisted. This was their next move.

Like any good American, Conner urged Arata to fight it in court. He envisioned an articulate, crusading lawyer. Even if the bad guys had the judge in their pocket this round, he said, we can beat it on appeal. Arata listened. He had not been eager to surrender his life's work. And they were both in such good moods, sleeping together five nights a week, having more sex than either of them had ever had in their lives, and finally having it just the way they wanted. That kind of thing will do wonders for your morale, and both were seeing things through a haze of bleary joy.

Arata hired a private detective to prove the man was faking his injury. Initial reports had looked promising—the guy was working a full-time construction job. Being bold with Conner had paid off, so Arata decided to gamble again.

They presented their evidence, but the guy showed up with his leg in a cast, X-rays of a cracked vertebra and fractured femur, and a suave doctor who testified the X-rays were the guy's. The judge barely listened to Arata's pleas. They lost.

Arata set his lawyer to work on an appeal, but it had yet to be scheduled and apparently could take a decade. Ten years. Court delays were a big source of leverage for the yakuza. Arata realized what a horrible mistake he had made. Conner wished he'd never opened his mouth. Until they won the appeal, Arata would have to pay the man a goodly sum each month, and even his detective was saying the broken leg was genuine, although the healing was not as advanced as it should have been. The formerly profitable bar began losing money. Then the stock market crash cut Arata's savings in half. Arata raced to sell his house in Utsunomiya before property prices followed stocks into the abyss and moved his wife and daughters into a nearby apartment, which, though comfortable, was a decided step down that set the neighbors gossiping.

Arata shut down his and Conner's relationship like a business gone sour. Conner tried to convince Arata that things would get better, but Arata was firm. It was over. That was that.

He accepted Arata's decision. It didn't even feel unfair.

Now Conner watched Fumie line up clean glasses on the bar, wondering if they were friends again. She was right—he owed Arata—but surely one trip was enough. Conner was determined to put on his one suit and interview for teaching jobs again.

The thought made him feel heavy inside: standing in front of a room of men and women in their twenties and thirties, some who believed mastering English conversation would help them get ahead, some who enjoyed being more international, but all expecting him to work some change in them. And then the dread of having to open up the textbook. All the preparation, the memorizing of words laboriously identified in advance, the fear that a student would ask him about the next chapter and it would become apparent that, under pressure, Conner not only struggled to read Japanese, he could barely read English.

Conner fingered the plastic-wrapped kilo nestled in his

shoulder bag. Matt had botched it, while Conner had breezed through, even with his broken chest pack. His success now made him feel powerful, special.

Fumie set a final glass in the row and looked him in the eye. "Will you go again?"

He felt a pull to feel that excitement again. At worst he'd go to jail. He somehow knew he could handle that. Other people would be in charge. He wouldn't have to think about anything. His Japanese would improve tremendously, kind of like the world's most serious home-stay. It's not like he had somewhere else to be.

Did he really have so little to risk? How could he have gone so far from home and still have his world be so small?

4

THE FRIEND

Marika knelt on the living-room *tatami* of her friend Eriko's apartment, clutching the phone to her ear, Isamu on the other end of the line. She was afraid to speak, as though Isamu could spin her words to trap her. So she listened to him jabber on. About how his mother had lent them the money for the down payment on their house and the dentistry practice four years ago. Both were really hers. And he couldn't move the practice now that it was established.

"Say something," he said.

"I don't like you."

There was a silence. "We have a good life together."

Marika covered the telephone mouthpiece with her palm, certain Isamu could hear her panicked breathing. She'd never done anything in her life like leaving him. Should she go back? If she could summon the patience to put up with her mother-in-law, she could outlive the woman. Mother was about sixty-five now. If Mother would promise to die by eighty, could Marika last the fifteen years? Marika heard Eriko making the family dinner in the kitchen, the next room over.

"I'll ask Mother to move," Isamu said.

Surprised, Marika asked, "Really? When."

"Immediately! Well, soon. She has her flower arranging class with the Ikenobo *sensei* that she'll want to finish before ..." His voice trailed off.

"Which is more important to you, her flower class or our marriage?" Marika asked quietly, trying not to let the thinness of the room's paper door impose her life on Eriko.

"The class is a once-in-a-lifetime thing for her. It'll be over in six weeks. She says that ..."

"This is once in a lifetime, too," Marika said, her voice rising. She heard Eriko bang something metal on the side of a wok, a chair pull away from the kitchen table.

"I know, but Mother says ..."

"This is not about her! This is about you!"

"But she says ..."

"Some dark night I'm going to run your mother down in a truck, I swear!" Marika yelled into the phone. Her fist clenched around the receiver's neck.

"She ..."

Marika slammed down the phone. Was he that stupid? She took a deep breath. Eriko had probably heard every word she had said. She picked up the phone and dialed Isamu back. It was busy. She hung up and dialed again. He picked up the phone immediately and said, "Forget about my mother. I'll make her move. Just come back. I love you."

She said nothing. He did love her, in his way. At the very least he valued her. She was a pretty and charming wife; everyone said so. He had the fancy name, but she had the looks. She had been considered something of a catch, despite her humble background.

"Marika?"

She cupped her hand around the mouthpiece. "I can't,"

she whispered. "I can't go back to Inudani yet. I need to think, and my mind won't settle when I'm there."

"I can't live without you. I really can't."

"Don't be silly." She heard Puffy meow in the background.

"I won't send you any money," he said.

"What? Why not?"

He said nothing. She tried to imagine what he was doing —smoking a cigarette, lolling the fluid of his blistered hand from side to side.

"I don't need much." Her mind scrambled over other ways to get money. A good job would be hard to land for a thirty-year-old married woman.

"I called the bank. Your cash card won't work."

How could he do that when she was a signer on the account? She should have withdrawn the limit when she used the card last night. She should have withdrawn everything else first thing in the morning. "Why did you do that?"

He said nothing. She waited.

"What will you do for money?" he asked triumphantly.

"I'll become a prostitute." She dropped the phone into the cradle.

It burned her up. She tried to see it from his side, but was unable to grasp why he thought pressuring her over money would get her to move back in. It was like dealing with a Martian, or one of the Ultraman aliens from the planet Baltan, with their lobster claws constantly opening and closing nonsensically.

Eriko called from the kitchen. "Are you all right?"

Marika heard the crackle of food hitting hot iron as Eriko cooked dinner for her four-year-old daughter Chieko, herself and Marika. Eriko's husband, Yuuske, would eat at the office and be home late. Thank God. Marika wasn't ready to face him over a meal. Last night, after a short but heated discussion, Eriko had cajoled Yuuske into swearing not to tell Isamu that Marika was there, but he and Isamu were good friends from when they had all been in school together, so who knew how long he would adhere to his promise.

Marika stood up, slid open the paper door and stepped into the kitchen. "I'm fine."

Chieko was sitting at the table, leaning her chin on the tabletop. She looked intently at Marika. Marika smiled. Eriko stood facing a hot wok on the two-burner gas stove, a drop of sweat beading at the tip of her button nose, stirring vegetables with long, thick, cooking chopsticks. Plastic bottles of condiments balanced on the rim of the stainless-steel sink.

When Marika had called Eriko last night from Tokyo Station, their conversation had consisted of a series of silences: the first after Marika apologized for the lateness of the hour, then again after she asked if she could stay a night with Eriko and her husband, then again after she told Eriko why. Marika had handled everything "wrong"—each silence of Eriko's had begged for a polite retreat from Marika—but Marika had no choice but to persist and so the last thing Eriko said was, "Of course you can stay."

Marika pulled a chair away from the kitchen table and sat down, putting her elbows on the table, her chin in her hands. "I'm sorry I made so much noise."

Chieko plopped off her chair and went to stand next to her mother, holding onto Eriko's dress.

"Oh, don't even think about things like that. You have enough to worry about." Eriko stirred the sizzling vegetables and tossed in a handful of fast-cooking white mung-bean sprouts.

"Like money," Marika said.

"Really?" Eriko stroked Chieko's hair. Eriko saw Marika

watching and smiled. "Well, you can stay here as long as you need. Right, Chie-chan?"

Chieko nodded once sharply and said a clipped, emphatic *Yes*.

Marika suspected she looked wistful watching Chieko, who was so adorable Marika wanted to pick her up.

Eriko wiped her other hand on her flowered apron, leaving a long smudge of soy sauce. "It's been years since we had any real time together." She wiped the sweat off her forehead with the back of her wrist. "And I'll deal with Yuuske." She tumped the hot vegetables into a serving bowl. "I just don't want you to be unhappy."

Marika sat up. "What do you mean?"

Chieko climbed up onto the chair opposite Marika.

"We're not so young anymore, you know," Eriko said.

Of course. Eriko was assuming Marika wanted a divorce, which meant Marika might be giving up any chance for children. Funny how Eriko's mind went to divorce immediately. But then again, she knew Isamu. Marika laughed.

"What?" Eriko said. "What are you laughing at?"

"I don't know." Eriko was right that no man worth having would date a thirty-year-old divorcee. "I always thought I wanted children. We did try. And I like children, I do. But I don't exactly ache to have one."

"Well," Eriko said crisply. Water hissed as Eriko turned on the tap to let it stream onto the hot surface of the wok. Had Eriko taken what Marika had said as criticism? Eriko could be touchy.

Marika sprang up and began washing the wok while Eriko silently dished the rice. After she'd had Chieko, Eriko had drifted off into that sorority that looked on the childless as incapable of understanding the profound meaningfulness of their lives. Marika scrubbed stray food bits off with a plastic brush, thinking that, honestly, she found that whole attitude smug. She strongly suspected that parenthood was as overstated as everything else that was supposed to be transforming, like love, like sex, like marriage. It amazed her how little these so-called transformations had changed her, and to the extent they had, she quickly forgot things had ever been any different, so she felt unchanged.

Chieko picked a hot bean sprout out of the bowl and popped it into her mouth as Eriko arranged hot croquettes on the rice with her cooking chopsticks and drizzled *tonkatsu* sauce on them.

Mariko ran rinse water over the wok. "I'll start looking for an apartment. I'll bet my brother will lend me money. He's never liked Isamu. And then I'll get a job." It had been years since she'd worked, unless she counted doing the accounting for Isamu's dentistry practice and filling in as a hygienist. Too bad she'd never gotten properly certified. "Of course, it would make more sense to get the job first. Salaries must have gone up. Isn't there a labor shortage?" Marika dried, oiled and hung the wok on the wall. Divorced or not, she was still a good worker. Someone would value that.

Eriko cocked her head to one side and sat down. She mixed vegetables into Chieko's rice. "Life doesn't wait for you."

Marika frowned. "I can't think clearly when I'm around him. And he's there *all* the time! You can understand that, can't you?"

Eriko looked at Marika and then at Chieko, patting Chieko under the chin as though that were an answer. Once, it would have been, but things had changed. Marika had changed. Perhaps, in leaving Isamu, she'd found her transforming experience. She was moving from the land of the childless to the land of the divorced woman.

Well, she had always wanted to travel.

5

THE HOSTEL

Conner applied downward pressure on the glass door of his rooming house in the Kanizawa neighborhood, twenty minutes by train from Shinjuku. The gentle pressure kept the door from rattling against its wood frame as he slid it open. It was nearly three a.m. and the two-story building was dead quiet. Officially called Hideo's Maison by its owner Hideo, the rooming house had been dubbed ("affectionately") by a since-departed Kiwi wag as "the hideous mansion," which had since evolved into "the mansion"—confusingly, since in Japan a "mansion" was a modern apartment block in a concrete reinforced building and this was anything but. It was, rather, one of the cheapest places to stay in Tokyo, outside of *minshukus* for day laborers that didn't take foreigners.

Conner tried to push off his loafers with his toes but lost his balance. He'd had three or four beers, and was beyond tired. He sat down on the edge of the spacious *genkan*—the indoor area for people to take their shoes off—and dropped first one shoe, then the other. He leaned back onto the dark cedar floor of the big prewar building and closed his eyes. He

roused himself before truly falling asleep and padded in his
socks to the common room across a hallway polished by
decades of shuffling slippered feet.

Another mansion guest, Carmen, was seated on a bench
by the communal table, rosy cheeked as she smoked a
cigarette and stared into the wisps of gray floating before her.
The roots of her platinum blond hair were dark. She had her
glasses off and blinked nearsightedly as smoke drifted into her
big hazel eyes. Like Katie, Carmen worked in a hostess bar,
passing nights in idle innuendo with sexually frustrated businessmen.

"Is Katie back?" he asked.

Carmen shook her head. "When'd you straggle in?"

"This afternoon. Want a smoke?"

She waved the cigarette at him.

"No," he said, "I mean a real smoke."

"Fair dinkum?" she said, in Aussie jargon that no longer
threw him. Translated to *for real*, as he understood it. "In
Japan?"

He nodded and pulled out papers and the little chunk of
hash he'd separated for Katie. She had said she liked hash and
Conner liked having something to offer. He pulled a cigarette
from Carmen's pack, used the tobacco to mix up two fat joints,
and offered her one.

"I've given up drugs for Lent." She tapped her cigarette on
the ashtray, even though there wasn't much ash on it.

"Are you Catholic?"

"Baha'i."

The sliding glass door rattled loudly on its rollers.
Someone else was getting home late. Stocking feet shuffled
over wood. The thick cardboard door swung into the common
room and a woman about Conner's age, in a red silk jacket and
black knee-length skirt with gold brocade, looked through the

door. She smiled and entered, swinging her long blond hair behind her. "Hey, Conner's back," she said.

Conner grinned. "Hi, Katie."

Her clear green eyes and delicate nose reminded Conner of Matt. They were two of a kind, only Katie would never end up in handcuffs. She'd been a lumberjack in the bush back of Prince Rupert, British Columbia, for God's sake, toughing it out in a lumber camp for two summer months, the only woman among fifteen beer-swilling, chainsaw-wielding guys. Conner would never have had the nerve.

She walked through the room into the kitchen and came back with a beer. She put the beer on the table and her handbag on the bench, tossing her red jacket onto it. Underneath she was also wearing red, a vermilion silk vest/blouse thingy. She looked as though she was going to lean over and kiss Conner, but instead pulled out a cigarette.

"He's got something besides tobacco to smoke." Carmen tapped her ciggie. "What, marijuana is it?"

Conner drew the joints from his suit jacket pocket. He handed one to her. "A Marlboro plus hash. Brought in a little bit from Bangkok."

Katie whistled. "What, to sell? Where do you sell something like that?"

"It's just a little bit for personal use," he said, smiling.

"We better smoke it in my room," she said. "You know how Hideo is. Let me get something to eat."

"I'll meet you there," Conner said, anxious to lie down.

Carmen waved goodbye as Conner trundled off to Katie's first-floor room down the hall. The red double futon was still out from the morning. A good Japanese would have rolled it up and put it in the wide, deep closet made for just that purpose. Conner would bet Fumie put her futon away every day. He knew Arata never did.

Conner sat on the futon and leaned against the cardboard sliding door of the closet, glad now to be spending the night with Katie, with the prospect of honest-to-god sex, rather than upstairs in the room he shared with his straight roommate Rob. Conner lit up the first joint and smoked a little. He'd forgotten that hash was tasty. The room was quite small, only three mats—roughly six feet by nine—and the futon stretched nearly from wall to window.

Katie shook his shoulder. He'd fallen asleep sitting up. He blinked awake and took the smoldering joint from her hand. She'd nearly gone through half of it and the smoke filled the room. She had also undressed. Her body was toned, and her long arms and legs looked strong enough to saw down trees. Her long rounded breasts moved side to side as she unbuckled and pulled off his pants. Yay! He might not respond much—or at all—to the sight of those breasts, but he loved the feel of them and the way her nipples hardened under his touch, the way she moistened up under his fingers. And the feeling of being inside her could not be beat. Imagining it he was hard already. After the horrors of high school he'd been convinced he couldn't have sex with a woman, and yet here he was.

He passed back the joint and shed the rest of his clothes. He closed his eyes as Katie finished the cigarette. She nudged him awake again. She straddled his middle and started moving her wet crotch over him.

"Oh God, Katie." He was barely able to say more, but did manage, "condom."

She rolled it on him and pulled him into her. She was doing all the work, moving with the same purpose and control she had when they went dancing, as though confident her body would do exactly what she wanted it too. It felt *great*. He chuckled. He'd finally done something that would make his parents proud. He laughed out loud. She smiled languidly and rocked over him. He moved his hand downward and rubbed her where she'd showed him, angling his hips the way she liked, lengthening his stroke. Time slowed. He remembered his fantasy of Rugged Matt and the long-haired woman at the airport and came fast. At least he thought it was fast. Maybe it was slow. Maybe this was his imagination, his hands on her hips, her leaning down, kissing him, rounding her hands over his shoulders. Maybe he was still in Bangkok.

"I was in Bangkok this morning."

Katie looked down at him as though trying to find a double entendre. "I like Bangkok."

She kept moving, trying to keep him hard, or maybe unaware he'd come. He had to remember to make more noise next time. He was so wasted. He yawned. "You're so nice," he said. There was a stand-up electric fan in the corner that had a broken neck. The fan blades faced the floor. Katie was Canadian. Carmen was Australian. His roommate Rob was American. Some tribe we are, he thought.

"Hey, don't fall asleep," Katie said.

It was barely light when Conner awoke. The thin white drapes glowed in the early sunlight. Birds were singing. He had the satiny futon to himself. He stretched, naked under the covers, enjoying the feeling. Exulting, he thought, this was called. He wondered where Katie had gone. Maybe for coffee. They could have coffee, then do it again. He got hard. He sighed contentedly, staring at the open closet door. It took him a moment before he noticed how clean it was. It took a minute more before he realized it was empty. Katie's clothes were gone. All of them. His clothes were gone too. Maybe she was doing the wash.

Then he saw his bag was gone. Oh no, he thought, don't let

it be true, but he instantly knew it was. *Where do you sell something like that?* Her question suddenly had a different ring to it. No, no, no. He must be wrong. He looked behind the curtains, in the ratty white cardboard box Katie used as a nightstand. He scrambled around the corners of the little room. Nothing. In the closet only a red silk robe. Had she taken his clothes by mistake? He looked under the futon, lifting it over his head, shaking out the covers. His wallet was there. His passport was there. His hash was gone. All of it. Goddammit, even the second joint.

Conner sat staring at the worn tatami of the floor. He ran his hand over his hair and blew out an angry breath. He pulled on the red silk robe, tied it around his middle and went out to the common room. Carmen was making an uncommonly early breakfast.

He sat down on the bench beside her. "Early gig?"

Carmen nodded. "Teaching."

"Have you seen Katie?"

"She left."

"She left?"

"Took her bulging backpack and walked out the door."

"You mean *left* left?"

"Two hours ago. Well before six a.m., apparently. Hideo's pissed because he let her get away with not paying rent for almost a month. I wish I had Katie's gift of gab."

With a two-hour lead she could be anywhere in Tokyo. He hunched forward and clutched the robe tight around his shoulders, rubbed at his gritty eyes. "You're not making this up, are you?"

"Sorry, honey. Didn't she tell you?"

He felt like he was back in high school, the subject of hall gossip, exposed to the world. She'd been sleeping with him for over a month now. That was supposed to mean she liked him, right? "Motherfucker."

Carmen turned to face him. "You've seen enough people come through here, Conner. The ones like Katie never stay anywhere too long."

He shook his head and clutched the robe to his throat like Norma Desmond. "She took my hash, too."

Carmen laughed. "That's a Conner story if I ever heard one."

"Go ahead, kick me while I'm down."

"Want some eggs and bacon? You can have this. It's still hot. I'll make myself some more and bring out the Kewpie mayo. In the squeeze bottle."

"No, thanks." His stomach boiled and his skull felt like it was shrinking, ready to press his brains out of his ears. Kewpie brains. Maybe Katie had planned a short vacation and his hash was actually still in the room somewhere.

Naw.

Carmen pushed a slice of pinky bacon through bright yellow egg yolk and then looked up at him, as though trying to conjure up a smile, though all that came to the surface was a wrinkling around her eyes. She seemed embarrassed. Boy, he must look pathetic.

"Never mind," he said out loud.

This was supposed to be it: Arata would be bailed out. Fumie friendly again. And he himself would have five hundred thousand yen in his pocket. Fifty crisp, brown, *ichiman* bills, each ten thousand yen. He would have been willing to share with Katie. And the kicker was, without Arata to sell it for her, she wouldn't get anywhere near that much for it.

Hideo came in from the shared kitchen. He was probably forty, but his round young face and goatee made him look more like a guest than the owner of a thriving business.

"How was Bangkok?" Hideo asked in crisp, clear English, sounding upbeat. He was good with languages, perhaps because he'd grown up bilingual in Japanese and the rather endangered language of his native island down south.

"A hell of a fucking lot warmer than Tokyo." Conner instantly regretted the tone. Hideo was nice to him.

Hideo started to pick up breakfast dishes someone had left. Maybe one of the German guys. People from neat countries, Conner had noticed, could really turn into slobs when they left home

"What's wrong with him?" Hideo asked Carmen, indicating Conner with his chin.

"Oh, he's just learning how to swear. You know how hard that is." Carmen stacked the dishes for Hideo with one hand, a cigarette burning in the other. "And he lost some hash."

"Hash?" Hideo glared at Conner. "If you bring any drugs in here, I will throw you out so fast your head will spin." Hideo snapped his fingers. "Out. I'm serious."

"No drugs," he said. Now it was even true.

"You're smarter than that, Conner," Hideo said.

Conner felt ashamed. Hideo was always better to him than he deserved. If Conner were anyone else Hideo'd probably have just kicked him out. "Sorry," he said. And he felt it too. He would have to tell Fumie. Arata would be more than pissed. And as a bar owner he knew all the wrong people, too. Arata, Arata, Arata. Mr. Sexy Shoulders, handsome and capable. Fuck him. "Goddammit."

"See?" Carmen said.

Conner grumbled. He'd swear if he wanted to.

"I have to go," Carmen said, "but you can use my food to rustle up brekkie when you get hungry." Carmen took her dishes to the communal kitchen, washed them and left.

It wasn't even seven-thirty. Conner stared at the table for

fifteen minutes, intending to go back to bed for a couple of hours, in his and Rob's room. He wondered where Katie would go. He stuck his hands in the robe pockets. In the left one he felt paper. He pulled it out. It was a big brown ichi-man. Ten-thousand yen. Roughly seventy bucks. Katie had left him a tip. Gee, thanks.

He stared at the table. Despite the lumberjacking, she was no country girl. She'd stay in Tokyo, he felt sure. And he'd find her.

6

THE AGENT

Marika stood outside the locked door of a down-at-the-mouth rental agency near Kanizawa Station, waiting for the agency to open. Her heart pounded. The closest she'd come to living on her own was when she'd been roommates with Eriko her second (and final) year of studying accounting in college.

The glass door was almost entirely covered with taped-on pink paper squares—ads for apartments listing room sizes, whether there was a bath, whether the floors were tatami or carpet, the walking distance to the nearest train station, and, of course, the rent. Between the agent's fee, rent, deposit, and non-refundable two months of key money, it was six months' rent just to move in. A week ago, most of these would have looked affordable to her, but not now. She scanned up and down, multiplying the thick black numbers by six, contemplating all the zeros and peering through the slits between the ads at a middle-aged man who sat at his desk doodling.

The agent caught her eye. He came over to unlock the door. Marika looked away. She couldn't do it. She pivoted and walked toward the station, breaking into a kind of run, her long hair and full-length black leather coat fluttering behind her.

She bought a train ticket from a machine, lit a cigarette and paced outside the ticket gate. She felt foolish, but even after getting that first lungful of smoke she was still scared. It had been bad enough when she had tried to use her cash card that morning and the machine confiscated it. Then, on the phone, her brother had said she was being irresponsible for leaving Isamu, which surprised Marika—when had he turned so traditional?—but he'd agreed to wire her money once she had a new account, so he was supportive in the way that mattered. Her father had seemed half-convinced she was losing her mind. If he could have seen her running down the street, he would have had no doubt.

Marika inhaled deeply, holding in the smoke as long as she could. How could she explain how intolerable all those one-sided conversations had become, Isamu really saying to her no, no, no, hush, hush, hush. Did he even want her there? That's all life was anymore: wondering what he wanted. Tense, constant watching. It might have been acceptable to spend her days anticipating his desires, trying to give him what he wanted, but he himself did not know what he wanted. She knew what she wanted. She'd read that the many mountains and small valleys of Japan meant there was nowhere one could see the flat horizon on land, the curve of the earth appearing as a straight line. That's what she wanted: to see the vastness of the earth. That would go over well. Father, I'm leaving my husband because I want to see the vastness of the earth.

Her cigarette had burned down to the filter. She dropped it through one of the round holes on the steel top of the station's ashtray. She thought of Isamu's triumphant tone telling her he'd cut off her money and of her father's incredulity. They thought she couldn't manage on her own. It sounded absurd, but look how she was acting. Were they right? She had to know. She walked back toward the rental agent and slid open the glass door.

"I'm looking for an apartment."

"Welcome," the man said, bowing his head with a quick, heron-like jerk.

"Welcome," his wife echoed from a perch in the corner. Marika hadn't noticed her from outside. She seemed to have been struck into life by her husband's speech, a human version of the mechanical cat beside her that also welcomed Marika, with waving paw.

The man indicated the chair on the other side of his scratched-up desk. Marika wheeled the rickety chair out and sat down. She looked around. Everything in the shop needed an upgrade.

"With or without a bath?" he asked.

"With, please." She didn't want to go to the public baths if she didn't have to.

The man flipped through a book of listings. "What sort of rent were you thinking of?"

"As little as possible," she said.

"But with a bath," he said.

"That's right."

He lit a cigarette and flipped a few pages forward, then a few pages back. Marika liked him better with a cigarette in his mouth. "Here's a six-mat that's only three minutes from Kanizawa station."

"How much?"

"Fifty-two thousand."

Times six. She flinched.

He looked her in the eye. "It's the cheapest you'll get with a bath. And it's really close to the station."

She'd noticed much cheaper places, including a three-mat room—barely room to lie down in—with no bath. Once she got a low-paying temporary job she could earn enough for that, easily, but she'd also have to pay her brother back. Could she get a settlement from Isamu? She knew alimony would be a pittance; that is, if she won any at all.

"Shall we go take a look?"

Marika nodded.

The agent grabbed a key and Marika followed him to the door. As they left, the wife called out, "Thank you for coming," and bowed quite low in her chair, pressing her hands and her chest to her thighs. Marika bowed and glanced back as she closed the door. The woman remained folded in half, which Marika found irritating.

They walked. The agent unlocked the door to a third-floor apartment and showed Marika in. The six-mat room was old and dark, the closet doors and walls dingy. A train roared by outside. The wooden kitchen floor was buckled and stained in one corner by a square of rust, probably from a small refrigerator. Companion rust spots crept along the creases of the steel countertops like lines of ants. She pushed off her shoes and stepped up into the kitchen. The windows were a rippling, fogged glass embedded with wire mesh to prevent shattering in an earthquake. One was cracked.

"The tatami is new," the agent said.

Indeed, the yellow-green straw of the mats glistened. She breathed in. The room smelled like a field of grass. She imagined herself there and felt happy. She could cover up the stains. A curtain would hide the cracked window. It would be all hers.

She unlatched the cracked window and slid it open. The smell of wet garbage flowed into the room. She looked down and saw bins.

"You can hardly smell it with the windows closed," the agent said.

Marika thought of Inudani, the scent of cedars on the ocean breeze that blew in from the beach, walking distance away. Isamu sat there now, in the white two-story house with its carpeted Western-style living room, tatami rooms, guest bedroom, garden, kitchen, cabinet after cabinet and he didn't even know what was in them. And here she was, aspiring to garbage. The sad part was that she could live with the smell—the agent was right about the window—but she didn't even have that imagined temp job yet. And of course, temp jobs expired. A week or two without a paycheck and even this rent would be too much.

She looked at the view, ignoring the garbage bins. Over the neighbor's small trees, less than half a kilometer away, she could see the tall unpainted concrete of Eriko's building, one of two identical towers. She scanned the porches of the complex till she found Eriko's—six floors up, three balconies over—with its little washing machine and red plastic clothes wheel. She pictured the multicolored clips hanging from the clothes wheel—blue, yellow, green, purple—and Chieko's small socks dangling in the breeze beside Yuuske's white briefs. She imagined Eriko and Yuuske looking down on her apartment, watching the light in her window at night, perhaps seeing her dark shape walking, Eriko saying "poor thing" and Yuuske grunting assent.

The agent looked at her, expression open, friendly, hopeful, even if life didn't seem to be providing too well for him. He ran a hand over his salt-and-pepper brush cut. "What do you think?"

"I'm afraid this won't do."

He nodded, smile slowly broadening. Marika felt embarrassed as she realized he expected her to opt for something grander, more suited to someone wearing a full-length leather coat. But she no longer lived the life that went with it. Was it kinder to leave him with the truth or with hope?

Marika would leave him with hope. "I'm sorry, but this really won't do." When she returned for the three-mat apartment, no bath, paid for with borrowed money, the truth would come soon enough for both of them.

7

POETRY GIRL

Conner twisted on his futon, pretending to sleep as his roommate Rob dressed for his nine-to-five. The beer had given Conner a headache. Or the hash had. Or the prospect of telling Arata he'd lost the hash had.

Conner opened his eyes a slit, but only a slit; he didn't want Rob to ask how things had gone. Rob slipped into his slacks, shrugged his shoulders into a dress shirt, and knotted his tie. Rob had a lean, sporty build and often sat at the little table by the murky window in tank top and running shorts as he went over papers from work. Conner would find other places to put his eyes. Rob was the first straight guy Conner had encountered who had known Conner was gay and still treated him with that physical disinterest that straight men casually bestowed on each other. It made Conner feel brotherly toward him. It also made Rob seem sure of his place in the world, like one of those cool people in high school who seemed to grow up faster than everyone else. Rob had kind of inspired Conner's smuggling endeavor. Like Rugged Matt, Rob had brought in a few illicit packages back in the day, when his parents had been missionaries in Atsugi, so he was the only person Conner had told about the hash. Well, besides Arata and Fumie. And as of this morning, Katie, Carmen and Hideo. So basically, everyone he knew.

Rob brushed back the slight wave of his dark-brown hair and checked himself quickly in the small mirror by the closet door one last time.

The wood frame of the door slid along the groove in the sill as Rob opened it. Conner listened to the hush of Rob's socked feet as he used the sill to push into the toes of his house slippers. The door slid closed again and the slippers buffed over the cedar floor toward the stairs, the door and Rob's high-paying job at an American consulting firm.

Now Conner opened his eyes. He stared at his own sweaty suit, hanging from a nail hammered into the doorframe. At least Katie hadn't stolen that. He'd need it dry-cleaned before he could get that teaching job. As if he could ignore the hundreds of thousands of yen Arata had staked him to buy the hash, not to mention the profit that was supposed to keep Giotto afloat. Conner groaned and headed for the bath to consider his next move.

AN HOUR LATER, dressed, fed and armed with a plan, Conner was at Kanizawa Station. It would be many hours before Arata arrived at Giotto, giving Conner time to search for Katie. The prospects of finding her were actually pretty good. Katie didn't speak Japanese, so she probably wouldn't leave Tokyo. The city was massive, but a tall, strikingly blond gaijin would stand out like dandruff on black leather, and there was most definitely a gaijin circuit, at least one for English speakers. If possible, he would search her new room—wherever she landed—while she was out. If he found her, he'd cut a deal. Offer half his cut, say. That would be better than her other options. The only hash he'd ever seen or heard of in Japan was the stuff he'd brought in. She'd have a hard time unloading it.

Conner transferred at Shinjuku and went to the first place she might go, the Satsuki Guest House in Ikebukuro. She had stayed there before she'd come to Hideo's, he remembered her saying once. But the manager at Satsuki Guest House hadn't seen her. Conner went to Geshuku Okubo in Shin-Okubo. No luck. He went to Hotel America. Hotel America said try Tachibana House in Shibuya. Tachibana House gave him a whole list of other guesthouses where a gaijin could stay for less than two-thousand yen. The length of the list made his stomach churn—the circuit was bigger than he'd known.

Traveling the trains was burning through his ichi-man tip in a hurry, so he stepped into a phone booth, bought a phone card from the machine and called his way down the list. No one had seen her. Tired, he sat down on the ground in the phone booth.

The phone beeped at him to remove his phone card. Thirteen, fourteen, fifteen beeps. Would Hideo really kick him out? Nineteen, twenty beeps. The booth was plastered with small color ads for prostitutes, brightly printed in pink, green and black with glossy pictures of women trying to look seductive. Obviously to some people they *were* seductive, but he didn't want to have to look at them. He had counted thirty-nine beeps when a wrinkled old man in a cloth cap rapped twice on the door wanting to use the phone. Conner grabbed his card and pushed out past the man toward Shibuya Station.

It was getting dark. The sweet smell of sugar caramelizing on roasting chestnuts blew over from the vendors under the railroad bridge in their stalls with red-and-white striped awnings. A train on the Yama-no-te ring line rumbled south. Conner walked with the crowd through the first floor of Tokyu department store into brightly lit Shibuya Station, following familiar currents of people up stairs, over bridges, through shortcuts so narrow they seemed like tunnels, merging and separating till he reached the north ticket gates for Japan Railways, the JR.

Right about now, Arata would be arriving at Giotto, expecting Conner to show up with his load. If only Conner had stayed the extra day in Bangkok, he could have gone directly from the airport to Arata and sat on the damned heat-exchanger till Fumie opened. He thought about standing Arata up, but remembered something Edward, his first gay friend in L.A., had said more than once: Bad news travels fast. Better they hear it from you.

Running away was *so* appealing, but time had proven Edward right about, well, everything. Conner groaned out loud and decided this time he'd try to be mature. He could run away next time.

He caught the northbound Yama-no-te train to Shinjuku, trudged with the commute crowd off the platform and oozed slowly with the clots of trench-coated men and women squeezing downstairs through the ticket gates into the vast underground expanses of Shinjuku Station, past newsstands, fast food joints, and the store selling *omiyage*—souvenirs— from other parts of Japan for those needing evidence of a faked trip. It no doubt had innocently forgetful customers, but Conner always thought of it as "the adultery store."

At Shinjuku West Entrance, a massive opening cut down from the ground level roadway brought the night sky through two stories of roadways swaddled in concrete down into the bowels of the station. It was a disconcerting effect that always left Conner wondering where ground level was. Conner stopped to look at the sky. The signs and windows of the banks and discount stores were too bright for him to see stars, or even the moon, but he knew they were up there.

A shaft of electric light shone onto a high-school-aged girl standing in a dark-blue and white uniform. Her hands gripped a white, hand-written sign hanging from her neck with some Japanese words—My something—and a price. A stack of white photocopied booklets lay at the girl's feet. Her face was expressionless and the traffic of commuters flowed as far away from her as it could manage, creating a ten-foot circle of open space.

Conner picked up a book. Poetry. As far as he could make out, they were linked poems, like a mini play. It was perhaps the sort of thing aspiring actress Fumie might enjoy. Besides, the girl looked so alone.

"What is your book called?" he asked her.

"*Death of an Old Woman.*"

In English, poetry was the easiest thing for Conner to read, especially if the lines were short. It was the only thing he read for pleasure. "Are they any good?"

"No," she said in a monotone.

"I'll bet they're really good."

"So far everyone who reads them hates them." She sounded proud.

"Strong stuff, huh?"

She said nothing. She wasn't going to make it on her sales skills. "How much?"

"Three hundred yen."

Conner dug three coins out of his pocket and bought a copy. He'd already spent close to two thousand out of Katie's tip. Without his cut from the hash, he was in financial trouble, same as Arata. He opened the booklet and looked at the first page.

"You won't like them," the girl said.

"I already don't."

She smiled.

He headed back into the station toward Giotto, reading as he walked. He could puzzle out enough to make it interesting. Apparently, poems kind of worked for him in Japanese, too. If only the whole written world consisted exclusively of signs and poems, he'd be golden.

He stayed in the underground promenade and passageways for about half a mile before trotting up a staircase. It was cold once he left the teeming station and underground shopping malls, and he wished he had the coat Katie had stolen instead of his rancid suit. He crossed the brightly lit boulevards and turned into the alleys leading to Golden Gai. A trim bald man with a graying beard and a stained white apron was washing down a plastic mat in front of the bar next to Giotto. Conner could hear water running in a sewer under the street. He opened the door and went in. He was the first customer again.

"Arata's not here," Fumie said.

"Hooh boy." It had been a long couple of days.

"It's only eight o'clock."

Fumie was right. It was early. He shouldn't blame Arata for his own antsiness. Or Fumie. He pulled out the book of poems. "Say, Fumie. Read these. What do you think?"

Fumie took the book. "*Death of an Old Woman*," she said, reading the cover. Conner looked over her shoulder at the characters for "old woman." Complicated. She read the first poem, and flipped through the rest. "They're about what you'd expect. *Death* and *poem* is a kind of hackneyed pun."

"You don't like them?"

"See this here?" Fumie held the book before her and began reading in her stage voice—she was constantly auditioning, but good parts were hard to come by. She gave the poem the best of her dramatic skills.

Caught in the uniform of death
I stand transfixed,
falling backward,
into the armless dust of the playground,
the hard crumbling concrete.

My skull cracks.

My classmates shout in answer to
their chanted names,
Murakawa, Murazawa,
Murata, Murata, Murata.

It was great to hear Fumie read it to him, not only to fill in the missing words, but to reveal the overall sense of it that he had only half-guessed.

"See, now, everyone in high school is the same," Fumie said, "but she wants to be different. I'm guessing she's a high school student, right?"

"She was wearing a blue sailor uniform," Conner acknowledged.

"High school students all write like this, especially girls. How do you make the images fresh when everyone's experience is the same?"

Conner took the book from Fumie. He kind of liked the poem. It didn't seem bad enough to warrant Fumie's criticism, or its author's. Most high school students really wanted to be the same, in his experience, not different. Conner was different, the only out gay kid, and not by choice. No one had wanted to be him, no use pretending otherwise. "Did you like high school?"

"I didn't finish." Fumie wiped the counter again with a wet cloth.

"Me neither," he said, though Edward had hounded him into doing his GED a couple years later.

She got Conner a beer and this time poured a glass for him.

Conner took a sip. "Fumie, I have a problem. We all have a problem."

She looked up.

"My hash got stolen."

She leaned back and crossed her arms, as though shielding herself. Her face grew angry. "And it wasn't even enough to save us. Now what are we supposed to do? What are you going to tell Arata?"

Conner shrugged. "I don't know."

"Do you have any more money? Can you make another trip?"

He pictured Matt being led off by the police in handcuffs. He shuddered.

Fumie began snapping the heads off a handful of green bean pods. She slammed the headless bean pods into an orange plastic colander. "This was supposed to work."

"I don't see why you're so angry."

"Conner-san," she said. "That money you took was mine. Everything Arata had after he sold his house went to the yakuza or key money for the new apartment. If the bar goes under, I have to go back to harvesting apples in Aomori. You're not the only one who doesn't fit in at home."

"I'm sorry," Conner said.

She waved at him—doesn't matter.

"Fine. I'll go again. Can you lend me any more?"

"I don't have it, Conner. You need plane fare. You have to eat, right? And a place to stay. And then you have to buy the stuff."

"Well, I'm already looking for Katie. I've eliminated a lot of possibilities."

"Who's she?"

"She stole it from me. I'll get it back from her."

"How?"

"I'm trying to find out where she lives."

Fumie shook her head. "Look for her where she goes for fun. That's one thing you learn working in a bar: they run out on their jobs, their wives, husbands, children, their lovers . . ." she caught Conner's eye ". . . but people are loyal to their fun."

"There're a lot of bars in Tokyo."

"But she doesn't go to all of them, does she? If you don't know where she goes, ask someone." Fumie put the bean pods in a pan with an inch of water and set them on the stove, but didn't turn on the flame. She took out a plastic bucket of cucumbers, already peeled, and began slicing them in half and then into quarters.

Conner began thinking. Katie loved to move. There was a bar with a dance floor she'd liked in Shinjuku Ni-chome, not far away. "Here's Mimi." He'd been there with her a few times. Ironically, it was a gay bar, although much frequented by straights as well. It had kind of a bisexual atmosphere that had given Conner a convenient way to think about himself when Katie came on to him one night he'd been out with mansion friends, trying to forget Arata. Katie had thrown herself into the music, moving exuberantly, athletically, with complete control over where her body was in space. She'd been surprised to find Conner could move, too. Hey, I do have some talents beyond identifying accents and mimicking tone of voice, he'd thought. He remembered how they'd come home from the bar together and she'd coaxed him into her room. He'd been nervous at first, afraid to get naked with her, remembering his one traumatic experience with a vengeful girl in high school—she who shall not be named—but Katie had liked his wiry body, which surprised him, and her touch made him feel good. He became excited at her excitement. Men and women both got aroused the same way, it seemed. And then how wonderful it had felt to enter her that first time, to be inside her, connected. And how easy to suddenly feel better about himself. He was suddenly one of "them," the tribe who ruled the world. Arata who, again?

"I've thought of a place she goes, but it's too early." Conner gestured at the cucumbers. "I'll help till Arata gets here."

Fumie gave him the bucket and a knife. She pulled a plastic bag of eggplants off the floor and began slicing them crosswise. Her knife seemed alarmingly sharp. Conner wondered what he would do if she turned on him. He'd never thought of her as dangerous, but her money was riding on this too. She turned and looked him in the eye, dispassionate, as though sizing up a side of beef for sale. Conner turned his eyes to the cucumbers before he even realized he'd done so.

8

TRAVAILLER

Marika sat on the tatami in Eriko and Yuuske's living room, an ancient copy of the job-listings magazine *Travailler* open on the top of the *kotatsu*. The red bulb under the kotatsu's low tabletop providing a cozy warmth. More of the advertisers were still around than Marika had expected. Many had jobs open, but the wages they offered were quite low. If anything, the going wage had dropped since the magazine was current. And the jobs were temporary, so there would be no summer or winter bonuses to make up for the low pay, no matter how long the job lasted. She shivered and tucked her legs under the kotatsu's blue flowered quilt.

Eriko rattled breakfast bowls in the kitchen.

Marika found an ad seeking an "office lady" that listed no salary. After the low salaries, that seemed promising. She punched out the number. Before long a receptionist had Marika on hold listening to a tinkling rendition of the Song of the Volga Boatmen.

Eriko came into the room and put the thick business comic Yuuske had brought home last night into the recycling stack by the television. Marika imagined Yuuske reading about the adventures of lecherous businessmen as he hung from a subway strap. "How's it going?" Eriko whispered when she saw Marika with the phone to her ear.

Marika tilted her head and whispered back, "Nothing yet. I'm on hold."

Eriko waved goodbye and left the room.

A man came on the line. The job was full time, but paid a measly ¥525 per hour, was temporary, furnished no train pass allowance and only offered a ¥100 raise after six months. Marika calculated the monthly salary. She would be struggling even in the three-mat room.

"Hello?" the man said.

"How do you expect anyone to live on that?" she asked, unable to restrain her dismay. She should never have quit school when she got married, but helping Isamu with his practice had seemed such a smart choice.

"Our office ladies, you see, well, they're single, live at home. They really sock it away. As spending money the pay's quite good," he said.

Eriko came through carrying a small basket of wash and slid open the glass door onto the balcony.

"Hello?" the man said.

"I'm sorry to bother you." Marika hung up. She remembered the real estate agent seeming to think the dark apartment was beneath her. She should sell that leather coat.

Eriko began filling the washing machine on the balcony from the hose. Marika flipped to the end of the book and glanced at the ads for club hostesses and bar girls. They advertised three to four times as much. Isamu's club in Roppongi had an ad. What if she worked there? Spinning the roulette wheel in the back room. Pouring whisky. Isamu would come in and she'd come greet him in a slinky dress.

What are you doing here? he'd ask. Would you like your usual whisky and water, sir? she'd reply. Marika! He'd yell. To whom are you referring, sir? My name is *paa fuu* girl.

"Something funny?" Eriko called from the balcony.

"I found an ad for a hostess at Isamu's favorite club."

"Oh, don't do that," Eriko said.

"It *would* be funny, though," Marika said, wondering what options Eriko thought she had. "Can't you just see the look he'd have on his face when he saw me? And these others pay terribly."

"Still! Those girls are . . ."

"Not like us?" Marika laughed again and Eriko stuck her head in the doorway looking stern. Eriko's attitude was old-fashioned. Working in a hostess bar didn't scar you for life. And it beat the alternatives. A picture came to Marika's mind of the old drunken men of Shinjuku Station who slept on cardboard on the underground Metro Promenade. She saw herself among them, pawing distractedly at the tangles in her hair, laughing madly to herself at an inner joke, only the joke was really on her. She flipped back to the front section and found a receptionist ad for a photo shop that offered ¥750 per hour. Not bad. She punched out the number on the speaker-phone.

"Hai, Realism Photo!" a bright woman's voice said over the speaker.

Marika quickly picked up the handset. "I'm calling about the job you have advertised."

"We're located in Shinjuku Station right by the West Entrance for Japan Railways," the woman said. "It's the busiest part of the station, so the work is tough. It's only half time. Is that okay?"

Better than nothing, Marika thought. She arranged to go

by for an interview that evening. Marika held the phone in her hand, staring at it as it beeped.

"I got an interview." Marika said. "Tonight."

"It isn't at a club, is it?" Eriko asked.

"No." Marika half-swallowed the word.

Eriko looked at her as though she were lying, as though she expected Marika to work in club, simply because she was pretty.

"No, it's not." Marika pushed an encrusted spot of food off the Formica top of the kotatsu with her thumbnail. She knew what job she wanted: one where people saw her, not looked at her.

9

THE BOYFRIEND

The Giotto front door creaked. A man in a gray suit with a square face and bushy eyebrows stumbled in and careened toward the bar. But it wasn't Arata.

"I'm drunk," the man announced. He grabbed the first bar stool. He didn't look very drunk, for all the stumbling. He looked official and policemanly and Conner was suddenly glad he didn't have the hash. The man blinked at Fumie. "Fumie-san, right?"

She nodded and smiled tightly. "Kuwano-san, welcome." She poured the remains of Conner's beer in his glass and hissed, "Go! I'll fill Arata in."

The bushy-browed man stared at Conner, as though he'd heard Fumie's urgency.

It was tempting to have Fumie break the news to Arata, but Conner again heard Edward's voice in his ear: Best he hears it from you. Fumie flicked her eyes at the door. Conner stayed put.

Fumie moved to the front end of the bar and started talking to Kuwano, forcing the man to face away from Conner to hear her. She told him about a new play she had been cast in, which was news to Conner. Way to go, Fumie. Kuwano wrinkled his nose as though he were about to sneeze and turned, looking Conner over.

Fumie mouthed 'Go,' and launched into lines, presumably from the new play. "Am I crazy?" she declaimed. She grabbed bushy-browed Kuwano by the lapels. "Am I crazy?"

Kuwano backed away, straining the fabric of his jacket. "Yes!"

The door creaked again.

It was Arata.

He was dressed in a dark suit and trench coat, as though he'd come from a business meeting, although the cut and cloth of his suit beat anything you'd find on a salaryman. He wouldn't be buying any more of those. His prematurely salt-and-pepper hair looked clean and shiny. He bowed crisply to Fumie and, the perfect gentleman, said good evening to the man. Kuwano said good-evening back in loud drunken tones of instant familiarity. Arata introduced himself to Kuwano as the master.

Conner waited at his stool while the three bantered. Arata hadn't looked his way yet. Arata already had Kuwano laughing at a joke that Conner had heard him tell several times before. Conner sighed and turned to stare at the posters for past or upcoming plays at the neighboring playhouse, plastered on the wall behind him, including one prominent poster of a bare-breasted Japanese woman with pointy nipples. Conner checked his reaction to see if the Katie effect was being transferred to other women. Uh, nope.

"Hey."

Conner jerked his head up. Arata was next to him, smiling. Smiling? Of course. Arata thought he was going to be paid up with the local yakuza for another couple of months. And maybe he was happy to see Conner.

"I'll take you to that new bar I told you about," Arata said. "Market research."

"Oh. That 'new bar.' Sure, let's go. Bye, Fumie-san."

Fumie waved goodbye and Conner and Arata left, watched by Kuwano.

They walked in silence to a blue Mercedes parked in the alley and stood next to the expensive foreign car. Conner wondered if it was Kuwano's, meaning he was a yakuza advertising his criminal effectiveness.

"They didn't get you, I guess," Arata said.

"Oh, customs?" Conner shook his head. "No, I made it through both airports."

Arata stood with his hands in his pockets, shoulders filling out his tan trench coat. Conner felt the need for a least a hug. He ran his hand over the blue hood of the car instead. "There's some bad news though."

"Oh, what's that?"

Conner paused. The pause stretched into full-blown silence. "It was stolen from me last night."

Arata looked stricken. "Hey, not funny." His brow narrowed, then went slack. "Conner?"

Conner said nothing.

A series of expressions passed over Arata's face—surprise, anger, disgust maybe, then a blank look Conner couldn't interpret.

"I'm sorry," Conner said at last.

"I can't keep on like this. Everything's turning to shit. I can buy us a little time, but it's going to cost me. You know they will also go after you, right?"

Conner swallowed and looked at his pinkies, waiting to be sacrificed.

Arata said something Conner didn't catch. It felt like a curse. "I wish I'd never . . ."

Never what, Conner wondered. Left Niigata? Gotten married? Listened to me? "I'm sorry."

"Oh, stop apologizing. You just sound weak. That's why you get robbed." Arata grabbed Conner's arm. "*Never* apologize."

"I . . ." Conner bit off the word 'sorry.' ". . . *stand transfixed in the armless dust of the playground*?"

Arata looked at him as though he were insane. "Wait, was it yakuza?"

"No, a Canadian," Conner grumbled.

"*Nikkei*? If he was Nikkei he might still be yakuza."

"No, this person was Anglo."

"Well, be grateful for small blessings."

"I'll get it back. I'm going to go find her now."

"The Canadian is a woman?" Arata raised his eyebrows.

"Trust me. I'll get it back."

"You better."

Anger welled inside Conner. Scolded *and* threatened? But at the same time Conner thought of how many times he'd apologized to Katie, often for things she wasn't even aware of, like not being able to correctly read a note she left, like not getting aroused at the mere sight of her naked body, like needing to be touched by her to feel a connection. Arata had a point.

Conner took a deep breath. "Well, she doesn't know how to sell it."

"Hm." Arata laughed.

He was laughing at Conner? And yet, wasn't Arata right again? Katie could figure out where to sell it. Conner was suddenly glad to no longer be dating a thirty-six-year-old guy, eleven years his senior, who knew so much more about the world than he did. Conner was seized with a scorching desire to return to L.A. and find someone who was A) male, and B) his own age. He could, like, *totally* do that. He turned to go. "I'll call Fumie when I get it."

Arata stepped forward and grabbed Conner's arm. "No, call me."

Conner shivered at his touch.

"If you find her, don't do anything. Just call me. I'll make sure we get the stuff from her."

"Are you that close to the yakuza now?"

Arata's face stiffened. "If I were going to join them, I would have done so a long time ago."

"That probably would've been better." It seemed so ironic. He'd advised Arata to fight the yakuza and now they'd become criminals themselves. But then, as gay men, they were innately criminal in most jurisdictions of the world. So, fuck the law. Conner turned to go.

"Wait," Arata said. "I'm going with you. To keep an eye on you."

"Not necessary."

"Look. I shouldn't have laughed at you. It's just that I remember what it was like to be twenty-five. It makes me want to keep you from having to go through everything I've been through, to . . . you know . . . protect you."

Conner's mouth was open. He couldn't believe his ears. He closed his mouth.

Arata touched Conner's sleeve. "We'll go together." Arata looked around. The little alley was deserted and cold with the night air's charge of moisture. "Maybe I'll even give you a kiss." He gave Conner a quick dry peck on the lips. "Let's go find her."

Conner scowled at Arata, feeling not guilty but resentful that he was expected to be grateful for this nothing of a kiss. Arata looked away. Conner stared at the back of Arata's head. Conner had been so looking forward to seeing him, but being in his presence had nothing in common with Conner's solitary imaginings. Conner's resentment continued to build until he wasn't sure it was actually Arata he was resentful of. Arata stretched out his neck; he was getting twitchy. Conner was a bit twitchy himself. Whatever Conner was feeling, he wouldn't figure it out that night.

"Come on, then.

They walked in silence out onto Shinjuku Road and headed for Here's Mimi.

The bar was smack in the heart of Shinjuku Ni-chome, the gay area of Tokyo, not too far from Golden Gai, but so very different. The bars in Ni-chome were mostly dance places, not drinking holes where alcoholics roosted on stools after work, playing match games and preying on bar snacks like egrets watching for frogs. Ni-chome was bright, the dark of night buzzed away by brilliant neon shaped into squares, circles, triangles, Japanese writing, English writing—for clubs, drinking places, restaurants, pachinko parlors.

They climbed the two flights of stairs to Here's Mimi. A mirror ball threw whirled diamonds onto the orange, graffiti-splattered walls and the checkered black-and-white linoleum tile of the empty dance floor. House music pounded away, synthesized vocal and melodic fragments layered uneasily over a stuttering beat that snuck up on you from behind. The place was not even half full, but then it usually didn't get going till after twelve, when the last trains of the evening were gone and anybody still out was either catching a cab or staying up all night.

"Wow, it's dead," Arata said. "How do they stay afloat?"

"No lawsuits, I guess."

Arata winced.

"Besides, it's only eleven. They just opened."

Conner scanned the little tables that hugged the dark

walls of the small room. A few were occupied, but he didn't see Katie's blond hair. They found a table and sat down. The graffiti was in English and Japanese, all in the same thick black magic marker. Conner had decided it had been purposefully added to give the bar an American air of urban decay. In Japan things didn't happen, they were made to happen. The master of the bar, a tall, smiley, mustachioed gay man of about thirty, waved to Conner. Conner waved back. The master had always been friendly. He liked Conner, and Conner liked him. It occurred to Conner he was technically single. He should ask the master out. He was a good-looking fellow. Although maybe Conner should aim even younger.

Arata looked up and down the six-high stacks of brown cardboard Asahi beer boxes, then over at the man. Conner thought he caught a look of jealousy in Arata's eye, which seemed gratifying. In a maddening way.

"Different sort of place," Arata said. "It draws a crowd?"

Conner nodded. "It's packed on weekends." He was surprised Arata hadn't been there, but Conner had learned, back in L.A., that big city gay life held so many nooks and crannies that some had no overlap whatsoever. "Be right back."

He went over and bought two bottles of beer, chatting with the master and running his hand over the wood counter flirtingly close to the master's hand. Let Arata wonder. Conner paid and returned to Arata. The place was filling up, the music getting louder. He nursed his beer.

"I'm going to dance so I can keep an eye on the door," Conner yelled over the music.

Arata yelled "Sure," as though Conner had invited him. He draped his trench coat over a chair and set down his bottle in the exact center of the table. They moved to the dance floor, shifting in time to the now almost industrial beat of the endless song. It was fun to watch Arata dance, in stiff, serious movements Conner had never seen from him before. It fit the music, surprising Conner, perhaps the way he'd surprised Katie.

Arata moved to the far side of the dance floor, away from Conner. Conner moved toward him. Arata moved away. Okay, right. Conner felt his lack of sleep catch up with him. He left the dance floor and finished his beer. He wanted another. And when was the last time he ate? He watched Arata dance in the growing crowd. Here's Mimi had filled up. Now Conner had to squeeze between dancers to get across the floor.

He got a beer and stood by the bar, watching the door while Arata's head emerged and disappeared in the crowd of dancers like a seagull floating on a rough sea. A blond woman came in, but it wasn't Katie. Conner swallowed. While he was staking out this place, Katie would be out trying to find a buyer. If she thought he was looking for her, this was the last place she'd come.

He took another swallow, finishing the second beer. His tongue felt swollen. After everything he'd drunk and smoked last night, the beer tasted strangely flat.

He saw someone with a head of long blond hair enter the bar. It was the right shade, but with all the people in the way he couldn't really tell if it was her. He moved toward the door. It *was* her. Incredible. She robbed him one night and went out partying the next. Conner pivoted over the edge of a table and pushed his way through the crowd over to her. He couldn't believe how mad it made him just to see her.

"You ripped me off, you fucking worm!"

"Hi, Conner." She faked a smile and placed her arm on the shoulder of the tall, brown-faced Japanese man who'd come in with her. She was wearing a buckskin jacket with long fringes on the arms. She leaned close to Conner's face and said, "Hi," again in a raspy voice. He imagined her sitting on a tatami somewhere with this coiffed man smoking hash.

"Where is it?"

"God, Conner, you're totally drunk." She turned toward her companion. "Let's go."

"Katie, you robbed me!"

Katie turned on her heel and walked out the door. Conner looked back at Arata. He was still dancing, oblivious. He might as well have stayed at Giotto for all the good he was. Conner scuttled down the stairs to the street after Katie and her friend. Katie was walking quickly away toward the subway station. Conner broke into a run and caught up with her. "Katie, stop!"

She turned to her friend. "Call the police." Her friend took a step backward, looked at Conner and ran.

Conner realized he needed to switch gears. Yelling at her would get him nowhere. Cutting a deal was the best plan. "Katie, listen for a minute."

"Look!" she said, and when, like an idiot, he turned to look, her hand lunged at his eyes. Conner jerked away before she made contact, but then Katie's knee slammed into his groin. She brought her boot down hard on his foot. He bent over, pain shooting throughout his body. She kneed him sharp in the face once and Conner felt himself spinning to the pavement, as though his body was not his own. She kicked his neck and buried the pointed toe of her shoe deep in his stomach. Conner flailed after her leg as the entire contents of his stomach seemed to roar up through his throat, but she was too fast. He rolled to one side. He felt a blow on his forehead and then nothing.

10

THE INTERVIEW

Realism Photo was a very small shop, hardly more than a booth, squeezed between the JR West Entrance and a shop that sold souvenirs from around Japan. If she and Isamu were to stay together another five years, no doubt he'd be shopping there for stale Satsuma *sembei* to substantiate a pretend trip to Kagoshima, or somewhere else suitably distant. Marika walked up to the Realism counter and looked inside. A short, stocky woman was writing down the name and address of a frumpy man at the counter. The woman looked up at Marika and sighed.

"I'm here for the interview?" Marika said.

The woman reached over and unlocked the door with one hand. "Come on in. Betchaku-san . . . he's the boss . . . is already here. Let me just finish this." She went back to her form.

Marika stepped into the booth. The roar of passengers rushing out of the JR for the Keio and Odakyu commuter lines filled the air like fog. The back wall was divided into pigeon holes stuffed with packets of pictures sorted by first syllable of family name. The customer left and the woman tucked his film packet into a bin.

"I'm Futatsugi." The woman nodded a brief bow, not taking her eyes off Marika. She smiled. "Call me Rei-chan. Everyone does."

"I'm Shirayama." Marika returned the bow, after a snap decision to use her maiden name. "Marika."

"I hope you take the job. I've been alone here for ten days and I'd love company. It only pays ¥750, but the boss might give you ¥800 since you're pretty. He's odd, but you won't have to work with him much."

A narrow white door opened at the left of the booth and a man's round head peered through the crack. His eyes blinked behind square black wire-frame glasses that looked too stylish for him.

"This is Betchaku-san," Rei-chan said.

"I'm Betchaku," the man said.

"Shirayama," Marika said. "Very pleased to meet you."

"Please." He indicated his office.

Marika bowed again and looked into the office. It was half as wide as the outer booth and she wondered how she was supposed to get in there.

Betchaku opened the door wider, and Marika could see a little desk had been fashioned from a wood plank painted white. "There's room," he said.

"Hai." Marika bowed again quickly. She squeezed past as he leaned back to create a space, his stomach pressing against the buttons of his white shirt. Marika sat on a small stool by a trashcan at the rear. She held her legs up by resting only the balls of her feet on the floor, but her knees still touched his rough brown trousers. He closed the door, quieting the noise of the foot traffic, the trains, the warbling bells.

"You're interested in the job, then?" He leaned against the

door, rubbing a palm over his pant leg as his eyes darted around the room.

"Yes, I am," Marika said. "Futatsugi-san said it was part-time?"

He nodded. "Twelve to four, Monday through Saturday. ¥750 an hour. You can have the job."

"You don't want me to take a test or anything?" Marika's thighs were already tiring from holding her legs out of the way. She couldn't move without touching his pants.

"No." He wet his lips with a quick movement of his tongue, apparently unaware this made him look like a lizard. "You have a nice face. Customers like that and you were the first to call. You'll do." He unearthed a small stack of forms from the side of his desk and pulled one out. "Just write your name and address on this form."

His eyes focused not on her eyes but on a point just above her shoulder. Marika couldn't decide if he were creepy or merely shy. "¥750 an hour?"

Betchaku shifted his legs toward the door and Marika quickly moved her legs to the other side of the stool before the space closed. Her calves were cramping. Betchaku blinked, as though frightened of her. Why should *he* be frightened? He was the one blocking the door.

"It's hot in here with the door closed," Marika said, "isn't it?"

He looked at the door, but didn't open it. "¥850, then." He still wouldn't look at her. "Will you take it?"

Marika followed his eyes to his wall calendar. Every date was blank. Marika looked back at him and his eyes darted away. The pay was better than anything else she'd seen. And Rei-chan had promised she wouldn't have to work with him. "Yes," she said. "Thank you very much." She started filling out the form.

"Great!" he said. "Great!"

He jumped up and opened the door. The haze of noise flooded the office. This was apparently her cue to leave, so Marika stood up with the form in hand and squeezed by him out into the booth. "Come tomorrow at eleven-thirty and I'll personally show you what to do." He closed the door, sealing himself in his office.

Marika took a deep breath. Up at street level the fall air had been cool, but down here in the station the breath and body heat of hundreds of thousands of commuters warmed it to a stale closeness. Still, it felt fresher than the office.

"I took the job," Marika said.

"Wonderful! It's simple. Just take the film. Get the customer's name and address on the bag, put in the film, drop it in this bin and give them a receipt with the finish date. I'm so glad you'll be here."

"Is he . . . okay?"

"He's harmless. Just a little . . . you know," Rei-chan whispered, pointing to her head. "He's fine. Don't look so worried."

Marika forced a smile, a nervous quiver of the lips. She filled out the form, using Eriko and Yuuske's address, and handed it to Rei-chan. "He's paying me ¥850," Marika added.

This didn't seem to faze Rei-chan. "I'm so glad you'll be here."

Marika forced a smile. She began to feel depressed. Handing the form to Rei-chan had felt like leaving Isamu. She remembered the first night they'd moved into the house, lying together on the fresh dry earth where later the garden would grow, looking at the sky, heedless of the dirt. It had been a clear night. They'd been married six months. Everything had happened fast and it had been wonderful. A beautiful wedding with both of their families, a honeymoon in Saipan, the excitement of building a new house that would also someday house Isamu's dentistry practice. She had looked at the clouded moon. He'd taken her hand. My life is starting now, she'd thought. But in the end that life hadn't gone anywhere. It was going to be hard to start over. Alone. Even when they'd fought, at least she hadn't been alone.

"It'll be fine." Rei-chan smiled at Marika.

Marika squeezed a smile back. "Okay, I'll see you tomorrow." She waved goodbye and headed for the Odakyu line, fighting her way through the stream of people transferring from the JR to the Keio.

A bubble of space opened in the flow near the base of a flight of stairs. Marika entered it to rest for a moment. A high-school girl in a sailor uniform stood in the center of the bubble with a sign around her neck that read "My Poetry." The skin under her eyes was dark and she stared vacantly, steadily, into the onrushing river of salarymen and office ladies.

The commuters caught her unwavering gaze and fanned away, creating the island of eerie calm. Her hair was badly cut, a hacked-off attempt at a short cut. The girl was obviously a little "wound to the left"—nuts. At her feet were photocopied books bearing the title *Death of an Old Woman*. Marika had made a similar book of poetry when she was the girl's age. Whatever had happened to that book? She felt sorry for the girl. "Hello," she said.

The girl turned her somber expression to Marika. Her gaze softened and the island of space began to collapse.

A woman bumped Marika from behind. Marika grabbed a copy of the book and was swept by the crowd toward the Keio line before she could pay the girl, who closed her eyes and was buried by the crowd.

11

BUTCHERS

C onner lay still and tried to keep from breathing. Vomit clogged his throat. He opened his eyes, telling himself to be calm, that he wasn't going to choke. He coughed to clear his throat and spit onto the pavement. Now he let air in as slowly as his starved lungs would let him. He coughed and breathed out again, a rattle, clearing his throat.

Two women and a man walked out of the restaurant at the corner. The man glanced down the street at him briefly, but didn't come over to help. Conner couldn't believe how fast Katie had moved. A taxi drove by on the street beyond the restaurant, the driver slowing at the sight of the threesome. Another taxi drove by, tapping its horn once. Two guys in white aprons and black rubber boots chatted at the back of a truck about ten meters from Conner. Both had smears of blood across their aprons. Butchers.

Conner sat up.

He put his hand to his forehead and looked at his palm. It glistened red under the bright streetlight, like one of Fumie's Aomori apples. He managed to get his feet under himself and stood. The foot Katie had stamped on hurt like a mother-fucker, but his balls didn't ache much, despite the uppercut from her knee. He felt queasy, but life wasn't too bad if you could still stand on your own. He leaned against a concrete telephone pole and straightened his back. He really didn't feel in too much pain, considering. He touched his forehead again and the top of his head. It was still bleeding. He felt calm, at ease, as though the world had been restored to order. Why was that? A drop of blood pooled off his nose. He wiped his face as clean as he could with just his hands and teetered back upstairs to Here's Mimi, gingerly favoring the stamped-on foot.

Arata was still dancing by himself on the crowded dance floor, swaying almost imperceptibly back and forth, a zombie on quaaludes. Conner walked over and sat down by what he thought was Arata's beer. He ran his tongue around his mouth. No broken teeth. Now he felt horrible. Now it was too much. That was the thing about pain: as soon as it started you wanted it to stop. And once it was gone, he'd forget he'd ever been in pain. He'd heard that once, anyhow.

Arata saw Conner and worked his way out of the crowd. His already big eyes widened as he saw Conner's face. "What happened?" He pulled out a handkerchief and gave it to Conner. Conner wiped at his forehead.

"It's cut, isn't it?" Conner asked.

Arata nodded a few times rapidly.

"I tripped." That's what you were supposed to say, right? "I tripped, fell down the stairs, got hit by a taxi and then run over by a garbage truck. But I feel okay. Zippity doo dah."

"You're not making any sense," Arata mumbled, then added something drawn out in his Niigata dialect Conner didn't quite catch.

Conner looked at the handkerchief. "I threw up." He swallowed. It tasted horrible. He picked up Arata's beer. "Can I have this?"

Arata said, "Sure."

Conner took a mouthful from the bottle to rinse his mouth. He swallowed and offered the bottle back to Arata, but Arata waved his hand rapidly at Conner in refusal. Conner's head hurt. His head always seemed to hurt. Why did his head always hurt? He tried to remember why. Oh yeah, Katie had kicked it. Friend Katie. He wasn't as drunk as she'd thought, but if he'd been sober this wouldn't have happened.

"At least I'm not hung over," he said.

"You should see a doctor," Arata said.

Conner tried to imagine where he could find a doctor at one in the morning, a Japanese doctor who would silently blame him for everything that had happened to him. Or not so silently; Japanese people were not shy about cheerfully telling foreigners everything that was wrong with them. Now he waved his hand no at Arata. Finding a doctor who'd see him was way too much trouble. The top of his brain felt as if it was swelling. Maybe his skull was shrinking again. Lucky his brain was so small. Everything seemed to be getting smaller. The stars were moving closer. In a flash Fumie was sitting before him on a barstool reading poems to Rugged Matt. *My head hits the hard dusty concrete. Murata, Murata, Murata.* Arata was helping him up by the shoulders, half-dragging him out of the bar. Conner kept meaning to walk, but his feet just seemed to stumble behind him. Arata waved down a cab and bullied the driver into taking them. They got out of the cab and Arata dragged Conner up the iron staircase to the forbidden territory of Arata's crash pad.

12

THE FRIEND'S HUSBAND

Marika could see Yuuske reading the evening edition of the newspaper at the kitchen table as she bent forward in the apartment genkan to nudge her shoes off by the heels.

"I'm back," she said, announcing herself.

"Welcome back," Chieko sang out from the living room. Eriko was nowhere to be seen.

Yuuske looked at Marika over the top of his newspaper. "Welcome back," he said more brusquely.

"I just had a job interview with a kind of creepy guy," Marika said, stepping up onto the kitchen floor.

Yuuske turned a page of the paper and his chair creaked. "Did you get the job?"

"He offered it to me."

"You didn't take it?"

Marika shook her head. "I gave them my application, but I don't know if it's going to work out. It's only part-time. It won't be enough money."

Yuuske half-snorted and scratched his ear. Yesterday he had wanted her to go back to Isamu; now he sounded like he just wanted her gone. They used to be friends. Had he always been so impatient? The door to the living room, where she slept each night, was open, and the television was on low. Chieko's dinner dishes were on the table. Marika began to gather them up.

"Eriko will do that." Yuuske's brow crinkled.

"I don't mind."

"She said you were looking at jobs in clubs."

Marika stacked the last bowls in the sink and began scraping the leftover food into the plastic sieve for the wet trash. "They're in the back of *Travailler*. They pay much better." And what business is it of yours anyway, she wanted to say.

"I can't believe you're seriously considering degrading yourself like that."

"Who said I was?"

"They're all run by Koreans, Chinese and yakuza. Completely under the table. They're into sex, drugs, all kinds of things. A lot of girls think they're okay nowadays, but believe me, they're not. I've been to them. Do you want to get pulled into that? At your age?"

Marika turned on the gas to the water heater above the sink and clicked on the pilot. She didn't exactly disagree with Yuuske, but he was definitely exaggerating, and being lectured made her feel what a long day it had been. She turned on the faucet and hot water spurted out the spray nozzle with a whoosh as the gas lit. Marika rinsed down the dishes. A key turned in the red metal front door and Eriko came in.

"How did the interview go?"

Eriko slipped off her shoes, stepped up into the kitchen and dropped two white plastic bags of groceries on the clean wooden floor. She knelt by Yuuske, short-cut hair swinging forward as she began stocking the little refrigerator with fresh meat and vegetables.

"They offered me the job." Marika soaped the dishes.

"Fantastic," Eriko said. "When do you start?"

Marika looked at Yuuske. He looked back at her with a challenge, but said nothing. He returned to his paper. "Tomorrow, I suppose," she said.

Marika waited for a comment from Yuuske, something like, Are you sure it's good enough for you? Years ago, in Marika's first year at college, Yuuske had taken her bowling with a bunch of his friends. He'd gotten completely smashed and asked her to a love hotel in front of his friends, one of whom was Isamu. His friends had been almost as embarrassed as she had, and Isamu had taken her home. Yuuske had been quite apologetic the next day, blaming it on the drink, and his friends had ribbed him relentlessly for most of the next year until even she thought it was funny. Marika wondered if Eriko had ever heard the story. Yuuske had been an athlete and a good bowler. Unlike Isamu, he still looked athletic, his tailored trousers showing the solid muscles of his thighs.

"Isamu called tonight asking if you were here," Yuuske said.

Marika gasped. Surprisingly, she felt afraid.

"Don't worry," he said before Marika could say anything. "I lied for you."

"I'm sorry to make you do that," Marika said. "I'll be out of here soon. Now that I have a job." Not that she could live off it. Marika suddenly felt like she was back in Shinjuku Station, the roar of people filling her ears, making her lightheaded. She looked at the dish in her hand and was swept by a feeling she'd seen the thick blue-and-beige-striped bowl before. She'd been through all this before. Grasping the bowl, she'd been standing here years ago, washing dishes, Yuuske at the table holding a newspaper, pouring his own beer from a silver can of Asahi, Eriko kneeling beside him, hand dropping to her thigh as she pushed herself up, walking toward Marika, Chieko watching *Doctor Slump* on TV, Isamu not knowing where Marika was, a moment trapped permanently in time. Or maybe it really had all happened before, endless repetitions of the prosaic fabric of life, doomed to be always the same. If Isamu knew she was here he would come, bully her, yell at her, force her back so she could leave again and again and again, until even he acknowledged that the marriage would never work.

Marika stared Yuuske in the eye, trying to get him to turn away as Betchaku-san had when she'd stared at him, but Yuuske only smiled and stared back, as though he knew what she was doing, as though he recognized the game and had played it every day at work with his colleagues until he was a master. Marika was so far behind in the game of life she could never catch up. His smile grew and grew until finally he chuckled and it was she who looked away.

"Excuse me," Marika said

She stacked the rinsed dishes in the corner of the sink, put on her shoes and stepped out. She walked to the late-night bookstore at the train station and bought the current issue of a job-ads magazine, in which she found the name of a club, Stardust The Moon, in Akasaka. She called the number. She was connected to an older woman who asked her what she looked like. She said simply "pretty." They told her to come by the next day at five.

13

THE CRASH PAD

Arata was snoring on the futon beside Conner, just like the old days, meaning last year. Conner's torso and face ached. His foot throbbed. And the hot sunlight angling through the kitchen window was blasting through his eyelids. He blinked.

Conner felt his temple. It was bandaged and taped. He was wearing only underwear. He imagined Arata undressing him last night and cleaning his wounds. His morning erection stiffened further. He barely remembered the journey to the apartment, clinging to Arata's shoulder, but was glad to be there. Arata could have just as easily had the taxi take Conner back to the mansion.

Arata appeared to be sound asleep, facing Conner. The opaque sliding glass panel between the kitchen and the tatami room gave Arata a hint of shade. His thick shoulder poked out beyond the *kake-buton*, the top futon, and his lips were slightly open. Through the gap where their bodies held the kake-buton up, Conner saw a nipple pressing against Arata's white undershirt. He brushed a finger over Arata's shoulder. Arata did not respond.

Conner slipped out from the futon and hobbled to the sink, keeping his weight off the foot Katie had attacked. Opposite the kitchen window was a familiar brown stucco wall caged in by water pipes and electrical conduit grown black with grease and diesel soot. Being there reminded Conner of something he'd lost track of over the last year of longing, guilt, and elaborately nursed resentment: they'd been happy. And maybe that was what really bothered Arata. Conner had shown Arata how empty his sham marriage was. Conner wanted that happiness back. How ironic that Katie had gotten him into Arata's bed when for almost a year he himself hadn't been able to. It almost made the beating worth it.

Almost.

He breathed in deeply. Ouch. He would have expected his stomach or groin to really hurt, but neither was too bad. He breathed slowly, testing his limits. He inched up his arms. His neck and sides were very sore. She must have kicked him more than he remembered, and in different places, perhaps after he'd lost consciousness. Did she hate him? He would *never* do something like this to her. To think he'd actually slept with her. And liked it. He remembered being twelve and thirteen and how much he'd wanted to be like his friends, to not be the hidden target of their free-floating scorn. Sleeping with a girl had seemed the be-all and end-all. But he was who he was, so he'd distanced himself from friends and focused on staying hidden until he could move away and start his real life.

He raised his arms slowly higher, above his head, stretching his arms and shoulders and filling his lungs, bit by bit. He contracted his belly till a gap opened between waistband and stomach. His morning woody was hanging on, despite the pain. Well, Arata *was* sleeping right there, and Conner *was* standing at his sink nearly naked. Conner didn't want Arata to see his desire. Their usual pattern was for

Conner to be eager, Arata to slow things down, Conner to offer, Arata to make his selection. Conner catalogued the subway stops on the Marunouchi line to redirect the blood from groin to brain. Shinjuku, Shinjuku San-chome, Shinjuku Gyoen-mae, Yotsuya, Akasaka. Was that the right order? He'd seen it too many times to remember. He dropped his arms and exhaled.

He blinked back tears. Shit. His ribs were so tender. Maybe something was broken, splintered, torn loose.

Arata rustled in the futon, behind him.

Conner couldn't turn around yet. His erection was somehow persisting through the pain. He continued his mental subway journey. Yotsuya, Akasaka, Kokkaigijido-mae. Always fun to say. Kokkaigijido, the Diet building, Japan's parliament. Oops, he'd left out Yotsuya San-chome. And it was Akasaka Mitsuke, not Akasaka proper. Akasaka proper was on the Chiyoda line. Was there an actual "akasaka," a "red hill?" His woody was fading. He rolled his shoulders, gently flexing sore neck and back. He sensed Arata's eyes on him and became hard again. Argh. He was hopeless, perpetually flooded with desire. He tested his sore foot, pressing his weight into the floor, and the surge of pain again brought tears to his eyes, taking care of the woody, pronto.

Arata stopped his rustling.

Conner peeled back his temple bandage and inspected his cuts in the mirror hanging on a corroded chain above the sink. The cuts were minor, except for one wet three-incher from his eyebrow almost to his ear. He might need it stitched.

He washed his face and reattached the bandage. If Katie had only listened, he was sure he could have cut a deal. It was a win-win for her. But how would he find her now?

Arata rustled again.

Conner looked.

Oh ho ho. He'd shed his undershirt. That was a message. But he'd rolled away from the light so his back faced Conner. Conner had held that smooth back many nights when they'd lain together after sex. Arata had covered Conner's hand with his own and opened up about how he'd dreamed of moments like this, how at twenty he'd been pressured by everyone to marry his wife, the same old story.

Eyelids heavy, Conner slipped between the kake-buton and the warm, cozy *shiki-buton*, the mattress futon, setting his head on the pillow.

Arata moved his leg backward, brushing Conner's. Coming from Arata this was an ardent invitation. Conner snuggled against Arata's skin and slipped his hand onto Arata's chest. Arata stroked Conner's hand and this time Conner allowed his erection to grow, to press against Arata's ass, settling into the crack between his cheeks. Arata eased his underwear off over his hips and then reached back to feel for Conner's cock. Conner slipped his own briefs down and Arata pulled Conner's cock forward and down, clamping it between his thighs. Conner let out a small moan and pressed tight against Arata's back, wrapping his arms around him. As long as Conner held Arata close, his ribs didn't hurt. Conner's pre-come was now moistening the inner sides of Arata's thighs. It was a pale shadow of Katie's bountiful lubrication, but it still felt glorious when he moved. Conner wanted desperately to be inside Arata, but had no condom. Arata always said that didn't matter, but safety mattered to Conner, Edward had drummed that much into him. Still, couldn't it be okay, just this once?

Arata twisted his neck around to kiss Conner. Their mouths met, tongue touching tongue, lip to soft lip. Arata ran his hands through Conner's hair and stared into his eyes as Conner ran his fingers down Arata's chest to his hard dick, fat and silky smooth. Conner gripped harder and stretched forward, to better kiss Arata's open mouth despite the awkward angle. His mouth was sweet. Arata kissed him quick, a series of fast pecks.

"I'm sorry," Arata said.

Conner laughed. "You said to never apologize."

"It's okay when you have reason to," Arata said, neck still twisted toward Conner.

In other words, it was okay when Arata did it. But Conner didn't want to argue. He ran his finger down the ridge on the underside of Arata's dick to shut him up. Arata moaned and flopped around so they were face to face. Conner inserted his dick back into the space between Arata's thighs he'd slicked up so nicely. Arata ran his hands over the dusting of fine hair on Conner's butt as Conner pumped Arata's legs, and tried to work Arata's erection, squeezed awkwardly between their bellies. His speed grew with Arata's moans. Conner was already close. He could feel the beginning waves of orgasm.

Arata pushed away and jumped out of the futon, slamming Conner's ribcage in the process.

Conner curled into the kake-buton, feeling as though his skin had been pulled off. Burning waves of pain raked over the sides of his torso where Arata had pushed. Arata was talking but Conner couldn't hear. Conner clenched his eyes closed and gasped. This was what it had felt like when Arata had broken up with him, so suddenly, without the warning of a buildup of complaints, after Conner had gotten used to thinking he had a boyfriend, a partner, someone he'd spent most nights of the week with for almost a year.

And then nothing. It was as though Arata was two different people.

Conner held himself, ribs pulsing with pain, the air sucked out of him.

"We can't do this," Arata said.

Conner sat up, slouched forward and gripped his pounding head, unable to get words out.

Arata stood over Conner, one arm across his chest, hand just below his nipple, as though about to play with it. "This is no good." His wide nostrils flared wider with his still-deep breathing, and his penis, darker than the rest of his body, quite dark except for its glistening pink head, was still reaching toward Conner, foreskin stretched away to nothingness.

Arata tossed Conner's clothes onto the futon. "You have to get that hash back, you understand. You have a lot to lose too."

"Arata, it's just a bunch of drugs. Us, that's what's real."

"What's real is people trying to take away my livelihood. They've already got my house. I refuse to lose more."

He imagined Arata with a missing pinkie or two.

"Conner, there are things you don't know. You are not my favorite person at the moment, but still, I don't want you to get hurt."

Like this didn't hurt? Conner picked up his shirt from the tatami. The blood dotted and streaked across its white fabric made him queasy.

Arata knelt beside Conner. "I should have sent you home, but I'm greedy and stupid." He placed his hand on Conner's chest, circling his finger over one of the swirls of black hair that ringed Conner's nipples. His hand dropped down to the centerline of fuzz from Conner's navel to his groin. Talk about mixed messages.

Arata broke off with a moan. "You have to go now."

"No argument from me," Conner managed.

Arata's eyes avoided Conner's. Arata began pulling on clothes.

Conner sat for a moment to let his head clear, pulling the

futon over his naked legs. His head hurt. Katie had kicked him in the head; he remembered that much. He closed his eyes.

Arata nudged Conner's shoulder and Conner opened his eyes. He'd fallen asleep. Arata was dressed in jacket and slacks. "You okay?"

"Okay enough, I guess."

"Forget what I said. I'll go. You sleep. That makes more sense," Arata said. "Feel free to take a shower. Just don't be here when I come back tonight. And close the door when you go. It locks on its own."

Conner nodded. He knew all that. He'd done that many times as Arata had scurried off to wifey. Arata checked his hair in the mirror and left. Conner went back to sleep for an hour, then showered and left. He didn't bother to put the futon away. That much Arata could do. Or not.

CONNER WALKED out to the street, hungry. Arata had always claimed to have an understanding with his wife, but Conner now wondered if this understanding was something conveniently unspoken, along the lines of "she must know." Conner had thought he loved Arata, but he didn't feel that now. Then again, if it were solely lust driving Conner, wouldn't he have had the sense to leave? There were other guys in the world, like the master at Here's Mimi. He remembered his dick pressed against Arata's butt crack. He'd wanted in. He'd wanted to slick his precum all over Arata's hole and slide inside him, skin to flesh, condoms be damned, lifetime of safe sex—waiting watching testing—be damned. He wanted to escape the fear of having physical functions ripped away one at a time until you suffocated in a miserable and inexorable death. He'd wanted to connect without death hovering over him. To come inside Arata, to have Arata come inside him.

It was an unachievable fantasy. There was still no treatment and no cure, and Conner didn't think there ever would be. Arata seemed to figure being Japanese was enough to protect him—a form of insanity or racism, Conner wasn't sure which—but Conner had always protected them both, ever alert to the specter of death alive in the room, in the world.

Conner looked up and down the street. It was completely unfamiliar. He'd taken a wrong turn. He looked about and saw it was almost spring, the plums pushing out their white blossoms a little early this year. The pink cherry blossoms wouldn't begin for another month. Tall buildings hid any horizon and the sky remained stubbornly overcast, gray. Much of it was smog. Tokyo shared that with L.A.

He walked out to the next larger street and got directions to Shinjuku San-chome Station from a plump young woman in a mom-and-pop grocery store.

He walked up a hill toward the station through a wooded neighborhood that was probably very expensive, considering it was inside the Yama-no-te line, the above-ground line that ringed the big, beating heart of Tokyo. It was late morning and sunny, but no one was walking the street or shopping in the lonely little shops on the way to the station.

He found the station, and bought a ticket and an *an-pan*. He sat on a bench on the Shinjuku-bound side and nibbled hungrily at the sweet red-bean paste stuffed inside its bready shell.

Arata knew what he wanted, and it wasn't Conner. So, better for Conner to clean up his mess, get his money and stay the hell away from Giotto. He wasn't going to find Katie at her hangouts, not now, but he would find her. He envisioned the scene. Hi, Katie, I need my hash now. He would handle it smoother this time. He wouldn't be drunk. He wouldn't call her a worm. He would offer to sell it for her, split the proceeds fifty-fifty. She would smile. You do everything anybody asks you to, don't you?

No! That wasn't how it would be. It wasn't. However it would be, that wasn't it. He would find her, wrap this thing up. It occurred to him that maybe he'd come to Japan for answers. And that Arata, telling him to leave, then running his hand down Conner's belly to grip his cock, and then telling him again to leave, had somehow supplied that answer. But what was it, exactly? That it was time to go home? After five-plus years it was easier to stay than to go—how would he survive in L.A.?—and the idea of returning to America frightened him. So maybe that was his answer: if he didn't overcome his fear, he would be trapped in limbo forever.

14

THE MAMA-SAN

M arika clung to a white plastic ring on the Marunouchi line as the subway train rattled out of Shinjuku toward her interview in Akasaka Mitsuke. It was just before five and the subway was filled with salarymen returning to work from afternoon appointments. At each stop Marika moved in and out between subway car and platform to allow people to pulse off and on. Only three days since she left Inudani and already she was on the road to wrack and ruin, as her parents would see it. And Isamu, and Yuuske, and Eriko. Rei-chan, at least, was encouraging. She had tugged and smoothed Marika's black dress to help her get ready as they chatted at the end of the overlap of their shifts between three and four. Rei-chan had smiled approvingly at Marika's outfit and wished her luck at Stardust The Moon, giving Marika the confidence to go through with this. The subway burst briefly above ground into fading sunlight at Yotsuya Station to reveal green, wooded hillsides topped by mid-level office and apartment buildings, then burrowed back into the earth as it approached Akasaka Mitsuke.

Cool evening air brushed Marika's face as the escalator,

crowded with purposeful people, took her up out of the station and into a wide noisy plaza. The space was massive. Two stories high and piercing the tall building built over the station, it blurred the distinction between inside and outside with openings onto the streets on either side of the building. A bit of moisture hovered as she read the directions to the club she'd taken down over the phone. The name of Yuuske's company, Ikari Bank, was emblazoned across the top of the notepaper.

Marika looked up at the blockish New Akasaka Towers before her. It was difficult to tell what sort of establishments the dirty white building might contain. A "hostess" could be anything from a waitress who offered a bit of polite small talk, to a purveyor of raunchy banter and teasing touches, right on down to a freelance prostitute or even, she had read in a recent issue of *Focus*, virtual sex slaves, positions reserved these days for desperate young girls enticed from the Philippines or Thailand by dazzling sums of money they would never receive. Those girls worked mostly in Shinjuku, though. Akasaka, even with its pachinko palaces and seedy past catering to Korean War GIs from America, was quite a bit more upscale. After all, it was close to the Diet building and that meant political get-acquainted sessions, liberally if not democratically splashed with money.

There was no one in sight when Marika opened the hand-carved door to the Stardust The Moon on the seventh floor. The little entryway was paneled with promisingly expensive mahogany. A large potted palm spread its green fronds beside a podium sporting a sparkly gold light fixture.

"Excuse me," she called out, politely. There was no response. She called out again louder. "Excuse me!"

A smooth-faced man in a black dinner jacket walked briskly to the podium. "How may I help you?"

"I've come for an interview," Marika said. "I called yesterday."

He looked her up and down. "To be a hostess?"

Marika nodded.

"Come this way," he said. "Just to let you know, you'll have to wear something more current than that to work here, dearie."

He spun round and walked into the club. Marika followed, clutching her oversized bag to her chest. The interior of the club was as posh as the entry, with plush beige couches and matching stools around little round tables. Soon it would probably be filled with businessmen. And perhaps a few junior politicos; she doubted senior politicians frequented places this accessible to the public.

"This way, princess," the man said, sounding playful rather than sarcastic.

Marika entered an office and sat down to wait, holding her back straight, her legs together, her hands resting on her knees as she pursed her lips forward into what she had been told was a gentle, becoming pout. A stupid look, yes, but if pretty and stupid would get her a job she'd be pretty and stupid.

The office was far larger than Betchaku's. Any thigh-touching would evidently go on outside. An older woman entered, the *okami-san*, Marika guessed, ruler of the house. Her stiffly wrapped peach-colored kimono completely contained her body shape, giving her the appearance of a fat tube of cream rinse. She crinkled down onto the chair opposite Marika and moved a hand upward along the line of her dyed black hair as though smoothing its swirls and curves, though they were already shellacked into unquestioning submission. Perhaps she wanted to reassure herself that everything was still in place. She scanned Marika with a few quick glances.

"Marika-chan, right?"

"Yes, we spoke on the phone."

"How do you look with short hair?"

"Young. Like a high-school student."

"Hmm," she said. "Please take off your coat."

Marika pulled off the big black coat, glad she'd worn the leather.

"And hang it up there." The woman's silk kimono rustled as she pointed to a coat rack.

Marika hung up the coat, aware that the okami-san was evaluating her movements.

"Now sit down."

Marika sat down.

"How old are you?"

"Twenty-five," she said, instinctively dropping five years.

"What are your clothing sizes?"

Marika told her.

"Kneel for me."

Marika knelt.

"You'll do nicely. Keep the long hair and wear a bit more make-up. What you've done is nice, but you need more color around your eyes. Blue eyeshadow. Watery blue, a little more toward garish. But only a little. And red lipstick. What kind of clothes do you have?"

Marika described the two things she'd brought from Inudani that might be appropriate. The woman suggested one for the next night and recommended that Marika procure a greater variety.

Marika swallowed, throat dry, thinking, *How?*

Shiny was good, the woman added. So were bright colors,

but nothing flowery. Men didn't come there for homey. Think elegant, like the coat Marika was wearing.

"Now I try not to concern myself with what my girls do with customers on their own time, but we are a very reputable club," she said. "It's important to understand that anything questionable you may do, keep it well away from here. We have important people who come here, you understand, and you have to get on with all of them."

Marika shook her head and then nodded. No, she wouldn't; yes, she understood.

"Here you serve drinks, entertain the customers, and so on. Be their favorite. Keep them coming back. We need you to start tomorrow."

Marika nodded. "Hai."

"Good. You are lucky to get this job. I've interviewed seventeen girls."

Marika knew the woman was right—she was lucky to have been born with looks that won jobs, husbands and ¥100-per-hour pay hikes for nothing—but she felt like a baby seal about to be clubbed.

The woman rapped the desk once sharply. "Ai-chan!" No one came. The smiley man walked by. "Shin-chan, tell Ai-chan to come in here."

"Immediately," he said.

Less than a minute later a striking, slightly built woman came in. Her sleek, dark eyebrows arched over wide eyes and high cheekbones. Her full round lips parted as she said, "Shin-chan said you wanted me?" She stepped into the room, her movements fluid and graceful. She seemed a few years younger than Marika. And far more attractive. Marika wanted to touch her.

"Marika will be starting with us tomorrow. Show her

around a little before we open, to get her ready for tomorrow." The okami-san stood and briskly rustled out of the room.

Ai-chan peeked around the corner after the woman and then turned back to Marika. "Don't believe a word she says," Ai-chan said. "Shin-chan is great, but Mama-san's a nightmare."

"You call her *mama-san*?" It sounded like something out of a sixties movie. "Not okami-san?"

"Not to her face. *Never* to her face. To her face use her last name, Shiomi-san."

"And why's she a nightmare?"

"She's a schemer. And she's hard to read. Especially since the stock market crash. It makes me nervous."

"Terrific," Marika said. "Should I keep looking for a job, then?"

Ai-chan shrugged. "Mama-san's not really that bright, so if you keep your eyes open, you'll probably be fine. I'll show you the ropes. First rope: pouring yourself a glass of Hennessy and drinking it behind the counter with the maître d'. He's Shin-chan, the guy you just met. He's a sweetheart. A homo, naturally. Come on. I'll show you everything."

15

THE OTHER FRIEND

It was five o'clock and Conner sat at the table in the mansion's common room, watching the American guy across the table, a white, former junior-college professor, scan job ads in the *Japan Times*. Tokyo was brimming with qualified Americans competing for teaching jobs; so much so that it was getting really hard to get a gig without a college degree. Some of these people had masters degrees, teaching credentials, even experience. Plus, they could read.

Despite his throbbing ribs and foot, Conner had made good use of the day since leaving Arata's—dropping his suit off for dry-cleaning, phoning his list of hostels again. He'd come up empty, but in the afternoon he'd grilled Carmen and Hideo about Katie's friends, her jobs, where she'd come from, when and why, and come up with a Lethbridge, Alberta, address from Hideo's registration book and an interesting tidbit that Rob and Katie had been lovers some months ago, something Rob had never mentioned. Everything else that Carmen and Hideo knew, Conner had already heard. In fact, despite what had always struck him as the Arata-like reserve Katie showed in private, it now seemed Conner knew more about her than anyone. He knew, for example, that she'd been in Taiwan for a year studying ink brush painting and that her father had died when she was fourteen and that she had a sister and two brothers. Why had she shared this only with him? Perhaps in her own peculiar way Katie had cared for him. He wondered what would she have done if she *really* liked him. Cut off his head?

The chunky pink payphone rang out in the entryway. Hideo picked it up. "Conner, it's for you," he said in English, which kind of bugged Conner. Conner always wanted to speak Japanese, Hideo English, as though they had to out-practice each other.

Conner shuffled out to the payphone, his sore foot letting him know he'd overdone the walking. He sat down with a grunt. "*Moshi-moshi.*"

"The yakuza know the hash was stolen, Conner. And they are *not* happy." It was Fumie. "Arata didn't tell anyone. I certainly didn't. Did you?"

None of the people Conner had told could possibly be connected to organized crime. But he remembered the scene outside Here's Mimi, with Katie's unknown friend, the taxi drivers, the couples, the butchers. And before that, yelling drunkenly inside the bar, and after, when he'd come back bloodied. He didn't remember what all he might have said.

"Conner, I think that guy Kuwano last night is a policeman. I think that yakuza Benz that's been parked out in the alley every night this week attracted his attention."

"He gave me the once-over, that's for sure." Conner heard Fumie turn on some water. She must be calling from the bar.

She sighed. "I don't want to go to jail, Conner. My new role is big. The crazy girl has so many lines. And I've lent every last *sen* I have to Arata. I can't go crawling back to Aomori. It's so deadly boring you have no idea. Everyone knows me, and believe me, they do *not* have a very high opinion of me: Fumie's too noisy. Fumie lets things bother her. Fumie can't hold her tongue." He heard the slap of something wet and an angry grunt. "They expect me to fail at everything," Fumie said. "I know that sounds like nothing to you, but if I have to go back there I will die."

"No, I get it. Believe me. I'll find Katie. It's only a matter of time."

"Find her now, Conner. April is only eight days away."

"What's that got to do with anything?"

"The yakuza gave Arata a deadline. Which just so happens to be the start of the new fiscal year, when Arata's lease runs out, exquisitely maximizing pressure, since the bar has to pay key money again. And after the stock market crash, selling his house, and borrowing from me, he has nothing."

"Eight days, I don't know . . ."

"Eight days is a lot! You've already had two."

Was it two days already?

"You have more at stake than anyone, Conner. If they find out how Arata was getting the hash they'll never let you stop."

Conner remembered Arata standing naked over him in his apartment. *I don't want you to get hurt.* Arata hadn't meant emotionally. Conner thought of the suit against Arata and his bar, and the plaintiff, with his occult vertebral fracture and broken leg, deliberately broken after the fact. He remembered Arata insisting Conner keep away from the courthouse. In fact, Conner had never actually seen any of these supposed yakuza. Arata had been protecting him all along.

The line was quiet. "Maybe apple picking won't kill me," Fumie said. "I'm scared."

"Well, keep your wits about you and tell Arata that I'll have something for him soon."

"How soon?"

The glass door rattled open and his roommate Rob stepped into the genkan, briefcase in hand.

"Soon."

Conner nodded at Rob, who nodded back. Conner hadn't grilled Rob for Katie info yet.

Fumie breathed. "Take this seriously, Conner."

Rob lost his balance as he pushed off his shoes, and hopped backward.

"*Falling backward, my skull cracks the dusty concrete?*"

Rob looked only briefly puzzled.

"It will, too," Fumie said.

The line was dead. Fumie had hung up. Conner watched Rob go upstairs.

He hobbled up after him, leaning on the handrail to avoid putting weight on his bum foot, and slid open the door to their room. Rob was changing out of his suit and tie. He already had running shorts on. Rob often hurried home to get in a run before daylight ran out. "What happened to your face?" Rob asked.

"Nothing much. Can I talk to you a minute?" Conner asked.

"Uh, sure." Rob straightened his slacks and slipped them on a hanger.

"I heard you and Katie had some kind of thing going."

Rob glanced at Conner, as though reevaluating him. A trace of a smile flashed by. "I wondered if you knew."

Conner shrugged. "What do I care?"

Rob pulled off his shirt and grunted a 'hmm.'

"Does she have any friends in the area, someone she might stay with, that sort of thing?"

Rob pulled off his undershirt and faced Conner in bare chest and running shorts. "Just let her go, man."

Conner tried not to stare at Rob's strong-looking pecs and

straight dark chest hair, the kind that lies flat. Rob's body was in a whole different realm of sexy from Conner's or Arata's, and his lack of modesty sometimes interfered with Conner's cultivation of brotherly feeling. "She can go. I just need to get something from her first."

"You act like a dick when she's around, Conner. Like you're trying too hard. You lose your sense of humor."

Conner sat on the tatami as Rob unearthed a gray-and-blue UCLA sweatshirt out of the futon closet.

"You know what I'm saying?" Rob pulled on the sweatshirt, which of course had the sleeves cut off.

Conner frowned. His foot cramped, as though someone was pulling the bones up through his skin. He grabbed it and compressed. "Rob, I *need* to find her."

"*That's* exactly why you should let it drop. I'm telling you this as a friend."

"Look, I know you're right," Conner said, "and I'm dropping her. She's dropped. Gone. History. But I have to find her. I can't tell you why, but I need to. So do you know anything?"

He tilted his head, flicked his eyebrows. "We only spent a couple nights together. Turns out she's not my type, and I'm not hers. No big deal. If you have to find out about her, ask Carmen."

"Carmen doesn't know anything," Conner said, wondering how Rob could not be anyone's type.

"Sure she does." Rob looked toward the door. He took off his socks, hopping on one leg, then the other. Conner waited for him to say more. "Uh, they work together?" Rob finally said.

"You're kidding."

Rob crossed his arms and looked at the ceiling. "Maybe Katie doesn't work there anymore. That was a while ago."

"Do you remember where this was? Carmen's already left for work."

Rob shrugged. "Akasaka somewhere. That's all I got."

There were thousands of bars in Akasaka. That was miles of walking.

"Katie's so cold, man." Rob looked concerned. "Seriously, let her go."

It occurred to Conner that Rob was the only person who'd expressed any awareness of how this might all feel for Conner. Conner didn't *want* to smuggle, and certainly not for the yakuza. Couldn't this just be over? Yes, Conner felt responsible for his bad advice, but Arata's yakuza problem had predated Conner. Was it maybe enough for Conner just to pay back what Arata and Fumie had invested in this venture?

"If I had seven hundred thousand yen, I'd let Katie go. Can you lend me seventy *man*, so I can get my sense of humor out of hock?"

"That's a lot of money. Who's the mortgage to?" Rob asked.

It was a lot. Five or six thousand dollars. "The wrong people. And I have eight days to set things right."

"I don't have that kind of money. But . . ."

Conner would have bet Rob had that much and more. "But what?"

"I don't know if I should tell you this."

"You should."

"How desperate are you, Conner?"

Conner thought about this. Someone else might say the smart thing would be to leave the country, but he couldn't bail on Arata and Fumie, not knowing he could save them.

"I'm not desperate, Rob, but I am determined."

"Okay," Rob said. "I'm trusting you not to breathe a word of this to anyone."

Conner nodded.

Rob pulled a slip of paper out of his briefcase and wrote down a name and number. He handed it to Conner. "Paul Barkley. He's a friend of my parents from when my dad was chaplain at the Air Force base in Atsugi. He's always into something interesting. He used to be in Naval Intelligence a long time ago, a real romantic. He smuggled his first wife out of Burma in the floor of a van. Now he's married to a Japanese woman with a nice house in Yokohama. He has an office near the Diet building."

"And he'll lend me money?"

"No, but he is the sort of person you need to see to earn seventy *man* in a few days. If you are, as you say, determined." Rob pulled the door open again and stepped into the hall. "See you later. Hot date with a jogging track."

The word *jog* sent shivers slicing across Conner's arch. "You can't tell me more?"

"Just call him." Rob slid the door shut.

Smuggling. That had to be what Rob was talking about, since Rob had smuggled in the past. Maybe it should have surprised him that Rob would have illicit connections, but the other kids of missionaries Conner had met in Japan all seemed prone to rebellion. Why else would Rob stay in a travelers' hostel like the mansion if he didn't gravitate toward a more adventurous kind of existence? There was an excitement to be had from, say, buying plane tickets by mail from a shady Hong Kong operator to bypass Japanese regulations. Or changing money in excess of government controls from "the priest" in Taipei, swapping FEC tourist money for black-market local currency in a van outside a Guangzhou rail terminal, or cadging someone's unused return ticket, bought to obtain a Japanese visa but left orphaned when plans changed. There was a romance in having a total stranger go with you to the airport to check in and hand you their boarding pass. When you sat in that airplane seat, you felt a membership in a gang of clever, daring and resourceful people.

Conner looked at the slip of paper and imagined all the stairs between him and Kokkaigijido-mae, near the Diet building. It was smarter to stay home and ice his foot. But it was only five-thirty. He imagined gangsters pulling Arata into a car, breaking his bones. Nobody besides Americans stopped work at five in Tokyo. The Diet building was only one stop past Akasaka-Mitsuke, where Katie's bar was, and it would be an hour or two before the bars got going anyway. He'd been blustering when he'd told Fumie he could get the money, but maybe there was more than one way to skin a cat.

16

THE GIRL CRUSH

A few minutes before Stardust the Moon opened, Marika emerged from the bathroom outside the club, wearing Mama-san's requested black silk dress, watery eyeshadow and red lipstick. She felt like a walk-on character at Tokyo Disneyland.

"Good morning," Shin-chan said as Marika stepped through the door. It was almost five, hardly morning, but their working day was just beginning. "Mama-san's cranky. But she's gunning for Ai-chan. Say, I like that dress." He smiled, eyes forming half-moons as he showed a lovely set of teeth.

"Thanks. I'll have to buy something new soon." Marika walked into the club lounge, silently thanking Yuuske for goading her into working there. The photo shop tedium of writing down names and making change was such that Marika mourned the hours lost forever and counted the minutes till her overlap with Rei-chan, when she'd have someone to talk to. She thought of the unpaid years she'd spent keeping the books for Isamu's practice, assisting with procedures, nagging him to be more careful with expenses.

She felt a frown forming, a frown she could not afford. She willed it away.

Ai-chan was breaking apart a block of ice with an icepick. Her dress was the same Chinese style as Marika's, only green, and Marika laughed. Ai-chan looked up with wide, young eyes. She had to be the most beautiful woman Marika had ever seen.

"Morning," Marika said.

"Morning." Ai stabbed the pick into the block, shattering it. A large chunk flew onto the carpet. Marika picked it up and handed it to Ai-chan.

"Thanks."

Ai dropped it back into the ice bucket, carpet fibers and all. "Mama-san won't let me do anything important. Apparently because I have high cheekbones." Ai turned her mouth down in a sneer that Marika assumed was an imitation of Mama-san. "What does that have to do with anything? She probably wants you to go."

Ai stabbed at the bigger chunks again and again and again.

Wants me to go where? Marika wondered, edging away from the stabbing

"Not that that's your fault. She's always thought I was a goody two shoes." Ai laughed, though it was more of a grunt. "You know, nobody else gets insulted at being called *mama-san*. Does she think this isn't a hostess club and she doesn't run it?" The icepick scudded into the bottom of the bucket.

Marika looked at the wet shards of ice in the bucket, now quite pulverized. "Yay! It's done."

Ai-chan stabbed the ice one last time, dropping the pick in the bucket. "She still thinks she's twenty-nine and living the glamorous 'international' life, like that life was something more than falling in love with a couple of GIs in the sixties."

Marika looked over her shoulder, expecting to see Mama-san lurking behind a potted palm, but there was no one.

"Hey, a friend of mine asked me to do some voice-overs for a pornographic film. Do you think I should? Maybe then Mama-san would trust me. It's just voice-overs."

"Aren't there a lot of yakuza mixed up in that sort of thing?"

Ai-chan laughed. "Who do you think asked me? I think I'd be good." She started making quiet, pre-orgasmic sounds. "Aan, aan, aaaan."

Marika laughed nervously. She picked up the ice pick and gave the ice a half-hearted thrust.

"Aaaan." Ai-chan rubbed her head and shoulder against Marika's side. Ai-chan's hair shushed quietly against the silk on Marika's back.

Marika flushed. She put her hands around the metal bucket, the cool condensation chilling her. She touched the back of a hand to her forehead. "Ai-chan, I think there's a customer," she said. "Let's not get in any more trouble than we already are."

Ai-chan laughed again. "*You're* not in any trouble," she said. "Not yet. Though your left eyelashes are loose. And call me Ai if it's just us."

Marika hurried to the back bathroom and fixed her eyelashes. She leaned against the door and chuckled, glad that Ai wasn't punishing her for whatever Mama-san had denied her. This was kind of fun. When Marika returned to the lounge Ai was mixing drinks and bantering with a handsome man with a full head of salt-and-pepper hair. The ice bucket was where Ai had left it, the ice floating in a pool of cold water rapidly forming from the too-small chunks. Marika drained it, rinsed it and drained it again.

"Welcome," she heard Shin-chan call out. Shin-chan, Ai-chan, Marika-chan. It was like a bunch of kids in school, the ones the poetry girl wrote about. It was funny how childhood habits endured. At Realism that day, a pair of women had stepped up to the counter to get copies. The one with long hair had closed her eyes and droned through a list of names, like a school roll call, while the other woman kept count on her fingers so they would know how many copies of each print they needed.

Murakawa, Murazawa. Murata, Murata, Murata.

Another party of customers had entered and was being seated—two American men, one tall, black and middle-aged, the other white and a good twenty years younger. The young guy had a fresh cut running from his eyebrow almost to his ear. Needed stitches. Marika downed a shot of Hennessey, tossed another block of ice in the bucket and took the ice over to greet them.

17

THE NEMESIS

Conner stood bathed, shampooed and combed in front of a steel door at the address Paul Barkley's secretary had given him, rotating his hinky foot. It throbbed, but he could hobble around, maybe enough to spend the evening hunting down the bar where Katie used to work should this Barkley thing be a bust. He opened the door.

Conner heard a murmur of voices. What were the right words to get someone's attention? *Moshi-moshi*? Too telephoney. *Gomen kudasai*? Too piano lesson. *Oi! Kimi!* Too Conner. He noticed a cup-sized black-and-white spotted cylinder on the reception counter bearing Japanese writing. Please upside down . . . something. He turned it over.

"Moo." The little canister made a faint, even, cow noise as a bladder slid inside the cylinder. He turned it over more quickly. "Moooooo," it said, more loudly. "Moshi moshi," he added.

"*Haaaai!*" From off to his left the same woman's voice that'd transferred him to Paul Barkley earlier called out. Her harried tone made Conner feel like he was ruining her life.

He tugged his suit to settle it on his shoulders and ran his fingers over his forehead. No bleeding. The woman did not appear. Minutes ticked.

Conner had done a lot of the weird one-offs a gaijin could do to earn money in Tokyo—radio voice-overs, brainstorming ad slogans for soft drinks, reading lists of words beginning with 'L' for a performance artist—but even by those standards this felt murky. The only thing Conner had picked up over the phone was that Paul Barkley was Californian. Based on his flat, standard tones, this guy was from the San Fernando Valley, not hailing from no Oildale nor Visalia, like Conner's family, flotsam from the great migration out of the Dust Bowl.

A young woman with narrow cheekbones and full lips plopped down at the desk, her hair pulled back into a ponytail. "Sorry to keep you waiting. We're up against a deadline."

"Mr. Barkley asked me to come in?"

"Have a seat." She pointed at a table and chairs that carved a small reception area out of the crowded office. "I'll tell him you're here."

Conner sat down opposite a poster. A fair woman in a black, hooded body glove, bright red lipstick smeared on thick pouting lips, slouched aggressively with her arms before her, defending against two pink neon tubes that slashed across the foreground of the poster. At the bottom in blocky letters: "Hatotaka—The future of microwave ovens." Conner imagined himself in that bodysuit. With the cuts on his face, it would look like the microwaves were winning.

"So, you're a friend of Robbie's." Barkley was a light-skinned black man, perhaps in his early fifties, with slightly yellowed whites to his eyes, a high, freckled forehead and a beard. He stretched out his hand with the physical confidence of a strong man, but he'd obviously let his body go.

Conner stood up to shake. "Conner."

"Call me Paul." His grip was firm. It actually made Conner's ribs hurt.

"Excuse my face. It will heal." Conner backed up till Paul let go.

Paul laughed. "You'd be in trouble if it didn't. What happened?"

"I was caught off-guard by a woman I used to think cared about me."

"Ooh, very cold," Paul said. "So, what can I do you for?"

Conner frowned. What could *he* do for *Conner*? Conner looked at Paul, a big guy, suit rumpled by a day's wear. Wasn't this what Arata was always doing to him? Making Conner ask, then implore, then beg, so Arata was always the one making the decision. This wasn't exactly the same, but it wasn't that different, either.

Conner moved another step back. "This isn't going to work out." He might be desperate, but he'd find another way.

Paul laughed. "Whoa, son. I'm just trying to find out a little more about you. Small talk. It's called small talk. And I sense some potential. I can already see you're not like the first guy Rob sent me, who was all tea ceremony, calligraphy, *aikido*." Paul put his arm around Conner's shoulder and herded him toward the door. "Look, we can't talk freely here. And there are some people I'd like you to meet. Come with me."

Had Conner misjudged Paul? At Conner's first sign of resistance Paul was changing his tune. It buoyed Conner. Paul needed him for something, and this time Conner would be the one making the decision. Maybe, even when you were desperate, it was good to not be too desperate.

18

THE MEET CUTE

The club Paul took them to was spacious. A dark-paneled entryway with a large potted palm gave way to glossy reddish woods, polished pink marble, and plush carpets that challenged customers to match the owner's outlay. Paul seemed quite well known by the staff, who handed off tasks: guiding them to a quiet corner, bringing sembei that were several notches above Fumie's corner-store rice crackers, and chatting with Conner until Paul motioned them to leave. Paul then grilled Conner on his life details—single, five-plus years in Japan, currently a few days into a fresh two-month tourist visa with two extensions remaining—while flaunting his own travel history: years in France, Southeast Asia, Afghanistan before the Soviets, Iran before the Ayatollah. He would have been right at home among the rootless cosmopolitans of the hideous mansion, trading tips on cheap hotels, duty-free scams and West African beaches. It made Conner wonder how Paul had crafted a profession out of that motley experience.

Conner sipped the whisky and water that had been set on a round coaster on the smoky glass table in front of him, sparks shooting in his foot. "Rob didn't say what you need." Conner felt a glimmer of hope. Was there was a way to turn all this scamming into something that wasn't actually illegal?

"What can you do?" Paul said.

"Take risks." It just popped out. He thought about his insistence on condoms, his tailing Rugged Matt through the airport, how he'd shown the customs man just the right bit of hash pouch through his unbuttoned shirtfront. Was assessing risk what he was good at? Maybe so.

"Hm. You hungry? They make a mean club sandwich here."

Conner nodded, trying not to look too eager. He was starving.

Paul waved at the dinner-jacketed bartender, who summoned a hostess, who relayed Paul's order out of the room.

The okami-san walked into the room, swaddled in a crackly pink kimono.

"You've come," she said to Paul in a welcoming singsong that sounded reasonably sincere. She seated herself on a stool by their table, legs folded to one side. Her soft brown eyes looked a touch red around the rim, though Conner doubted she had cried twice in the last decade. She winced ever so slightly when her glance brushed over the wound on Conner's temple.

"Shiomi-san." Paul straightened up in his mushy seat, pulling in his gangly limbs. "This is a new young man who may be helping us out."

Conner bowed his head. "Pleased to meet you," he said in his politest Japanese. "My name is Conner."

"Appropriate language." The woman nodded at Paul. "And a clear enough accent. Better than yours." Conner felt uncomfortable at the praise, but Paul actually smiled. Conner was relieved. Not only did he apparently have a useful skill apart from carrying drugs, Paul was pleased about it. "I have someone new, too," Shiomi-san said. "Marika-chan!"

At the table next to theirs, a hostess in a black silk gown was mixing drinks for two Japanese men and a woman, sloshing whisky onto the coasters.

"A little mineral water for these gentlemen when you're done there," Shiomi-san said.

"I'll fetch it now." The hostess excused herself from the other table.

"It's her first day. She'll replace Ai-chan when I fire her."

"You can't fire Ai-chan. She's too breathtaking." Paul took a healthy swallow of his drink. "A veritable Ono no Komachi." He pointed out a willowy young woman in a green silk dress who was distractedly stabbing something. "What do you think, Conner?"

Ai-chan began wiping a tabletop, wiping it very slowly. Conner had no idea who Ono no Komachi was, but knew he was supposed to be impressed with Paul's learning. Ai-chan seemed sad to Conner, although maybe she was just drunk. He did agree she was beautiful, but being asked to say so felt like Matt's interrogation about the flight attendant on the plane: prove you are one of us.

"Ai-chan is so difficult." Shiomi-san winced again. "She's a lez, you know. A lesbian."

"She is not," Paul snorted.

"You're always slow on that sort of thing." Shiomi-san winked at Conner.

The host, drying glasses behind the bar with a white cloth, shot an irritated glance at Shiomi-san. He noticed Conner watching his gaze and smiled, but it was forced. Conner grinned back. The guy tilted his head at Conner before turning back to his drying.

The hostess in black, Marika-chan, knelt beside their table and clunked two ice cubes into the glass Paul had emptied. Her long hair shimmered as she moved. Her face was round and her mouth seemed to be held in a dark-red pucker, like a demure chipmunk. Her silk Chinese gown was slit just past her knee. She leaned forward with the whisky bottle, carefully, hobbled by the gown and high heels. Her balance was going.

Conner put out his hand.

Marika-chan grabbed it to steady herself.

Shiomi-san smoothed back her stiff hair. "Watch yourself, Marika-chan."

"Thanks," Marika-chan murmured to Conner. She nodded an apology to Shiomi-san and poured whisky into Paul's glass.

"You do that very well," Paul said to the hostess. "*Ne*, Mama-san, doesn't she? For a first day?"

Shiomi-san forced out a little grunt and left them. Paul motioned Marika-chan to keep pouring. When he finally said stop, there was so little room left for mineral water it hardly qualified as a *mizu-wari*.

"You're downright beautiful, Marika-chan." Paul smiled.

"I have freckles," she said. "And my eyes are too small."

Conner chuckled.

Marika-chan flashed him a brief grin. She freshened his drink and leaned forward on her knees, sliding the glass back toward Conner. Her hair fell forward and as she looked up her eyes met Conner's and she looked as desperate as he felt. She wobbled again, but Conner's hand was too far away to grab, and this time she plopped to the carpet.

"Ah, *the armless dust of the playground.*" Marika-chan sighed.

Conner looked more closely at her. "*My skull cracks the hard dusty concrete?*"

Her eyes widened.

Now it was Conner's turn to grin. "And then the classmates scream or something . . ."

Marika-chan dropped the pout. "*In answer to their chanted names.*"

Paul's brow knit. "You know each other?"

They shook their heads.

Marika-chan righted herself, balancing on her toes, pout back in place. "I bought the book from a girl in Shinjuku."

"In a high-school uniform with these dark circles under her eyes like she hadn't slept for weeks. Yeah." Conner sat forward on his stool.

Paul seemed more displeased than he should be. Conner wondered if he'd blown it, whatever *it* was. Dang. He'd been getting excited at the idea of making legitimate money off his skills. Paul's office had looked so above-board.

"Thank you for helping me with Shiomi-san," Marika-chan said to Paul. "I'm in your debt."

"Maybe you can pay me back sometime." Paul struggled in his chair, but seemed happy at the idea of someone owing him something. "It's late. Someone help me up."

Weird. It wasn't late, the sandwiches hadn't come, and Paul hadn't paid. Whatever the test had been, Conner had apparently failed, but he gave Paul a hand up. Conner's stomach rumbled as he thought of bacon, mayonnaise, lightly toasted bread and how little he had to show for trekking in to Akasaka-Mitsuke. He should have eaten more of the high-class crackers.

Paul wriggled into his jacket and strode to the door, flanked by Marika-chan and Conner. The host held open the door and Paul exited. Conner lagged behind. To Marika he said, "Hope you don't get into trouble."

She shrugged. "Well, it's my first day, so if I do, I haven't lost much. If you're ever at the West Entrance, come by the little photo shop near the poetry girl. I work there. We can take her for a coffee or something. She needs some perking up."

"I will," he whispered. "My name's Conner."

The elevator bell chimed out in the hallway and Conner limped along to catch up to Paul. The two rode the elevator down in silence.

At street level, Conner scanned the brightly lit signs up and down the road from Akasaka-Mitsuke to Akasaka proper, each one potentially the bar where Katie had worked. Conner stifled a cry of pain as his foot cramped. No way could he canvass bars. What a stupid waste of time. Icing his foot at home and resting would've been smarter. Was there some way to get smarter? And could he manage it by the end of the month?

Conner grabbed his toes to release the tension as Paul hailed a cab. He looked up at Conner, hand on the cab door. "I'm heading to Shinjuku. Want a ride?"

Conner got in gratefully. The door closed automatically behind him with a thump.

Paul leaned back as the driver pulled onto broad Aoyama Road beside the Imperial Akasaka Guest House. He looked at Conner. "So, what do you think of her?"

"Shiomi-san?"

"No, Marika-chan. Do you think she's smart enough to work with?"

"Of course," Conner said.

"Good. I think so too. Can you fly to Hawaii with her the day after tomorrow?"

That had been the point of this exercise? Evaluating Marika-chan? "In return for what?"

Paul smiled. "How does seven hundred thousand yen sound?"

Sounded like the exact sum he'd told Rob, was what it sounded like. And it sounded like smuggling. Oh well. Conner thought back to nearly walking out after Paul's initial manipulation at the office. That had been the real interview. Well, if he was going to do it, he better earn some real money off it. "Make it a million and you have a deal."

"Done," Paul said. "Call me tomorrow and I'll line it all out for you."

Wow, that was easy. Conner could repay Arata and Fumie and have enough left over for a couple month's rent. But it was too easy, just like things with Katie had been too easy. "Why me?"

"I need someone who won't fall apart. You know, when you're out there alone, with no one to hold your hand."

Conner wasn't sure he was that, but maybe Paul was onto something. Maybe Conner's ability to function on his own was a greater skill than taking risks. Conner thought of his "romance" with Katie, how casually he'd fallen asleep with a kilo of hash sitting in a bag he'd tossed onto the floor of her room. He wasn't all that great at assessing risks, was he?

"I don't have to kill anybody, do I?" Conner asked.

"Would you?"

"No way."

"Good," Paul said. "I feel safer already."

19

THE ALLY

As soon as Marika saw the money from her brother sitting in her account the next morning, she called Rei-chan and invited her to go apartment hunting. Marika was nursing a blend coffee—the simplest, cheapest version of coffee on the menu—at the Chateau Parfum coffee house near Kanizawa Station when Rei-chan sat down opposite her with a whoosh.

"I love this area. So convenient. It takes me nearly an hour to get to work from Tokorozawa. Do I have time to get a quick cup?"

Marika had nearly three hours before she had to be at Realism. "Definitely. I'm so glad to have someone else to bounce things off of."

Rei-chan ordered a Vienna coffee from a young waiter whose full-bodied hair hovered above his head. He watched Rei-chan intently as she spoke, as though watching would let him hear better.

When he left, Rei-chan leaned forward. "So, tell me about this husband of yours. Handsome?"

Marika examined Rei-chan's square, earnest face. "Handsome, rich, charming; perfect in every way. You and he would make a great couple."

"*Maa*," she said, leaning away, astonished and happy.

Marika found herself recounting the last few years and her current predicament—camping out in a friend's living room, feeling guilty for disturbing the life of three people who lived in a cramped four-room apartment, and deeply looking forward to a place of her own.

Rei-chan put her arms around herself. "But won't you miss your husband?"

What Marika really missed was her cat, Puffy, but she was embarrassed to say so. "I used to miss having a body beside me when Isamu went off on a trip, but I'm not sleeping in my own bed, so it doesn't feel like anything's missing. I've gotten scared these past few days, at times, but not lonely."

"But that's the same thing," Rei-chan said. "That aching, empty, frightened feeling that your insides are swelling and something could happen and no one would be there with you for it, that's loneliness."

"Is it?"

THEY RETURNED to the same agent Marika had gone to before because she had rather liked him. She described in greater detail what she preferred, and he showed them another, newer apartment in a four-story reinforced-concrete building. It was quite modern, a six-mat 1DK—one living room/bedroom plus a kitchen and dining area—with electronic controls for the kitchen and bathroom water heaters. Rei-chan was sure it would be too expensive, but Marika now had sufficient money for the deposit and enough income to cover it. The agent would get a plump commission after all.

He showed them how to work the plumbing. His graying

brush cut made him look like an ex-navy man. "The tatami's new. Station's not far, right up there around the corner from the Mister Donuts." He pointed out the window and Rei-chan went to look. She nodded approvingly.

Rei-chan came back over to Marika. "You have to have a party for all your new friends," she whispered.

"Sure," Marika said, though all her new friends were already in the room. She opened the window. No wafting aroma of wet garbage. The day was clear enough to just make out mountains in the distance, beyond the immense, chunky sprawl. She would miss Eriko and Chieko, but the farther Marika went from Isamu, the less connection she would have to people like them. Now she was even working in a bar. She would clear over fifty thousand a week, not counting her pay from Realism. She could start paying her brother back immediately.

She wondered how it would be, making new friends. She looked forward to a life that wasn't so quiet. She hadn't spoken to Isamu in days, and it hardly seemed different. On slow days at the clinic, Marika used to take the neighbors' Akitas to the beach. She'd miss that, but looked forward to a circle of friends emerging out of all this nothing that surrounded her. She wondered how Ai and Rei-chan would get along. She had never fit in down there, in the rich suburb. Everything there had been determined by Isamu's life, nothing by hers.

She realized the agent was staring at them. His brow was knit. "The landlady lives two floors down," he said. "Very convenient if you want to get the key today."

Marika looked at her watch. Eriko had offered Marika the use of the kotatsu and an old TV. If Marika decided fast, she would have time to go get them. If Eriko could spare the futon Marika'd been using, she could even sleep there tonight.

She looked around. Her new home. "I'll take it."

. . .

MARIKA LOOKED out from the Realism booth at the thundering hordes of Shinjuku Station, West Entrance. People seemed to be walking faster these days. All of them. Soon something would happen and all Japan would realize it was what they'd been waiting for and break into a run.

The poetry girl was starting her shift, too, placing her cardboard box of booklets on the tiled floor, stringing the sign around her neck and fixing her stare into the crowd. The crowd began to part for her. She must be skipping school every day, Marika thought. Or maybe she was already finished with school. Perhaps the girl was not crazy, but just incredibly astute at crowd control. When the salarymen and office ladies stampeded, however, the poetry girl would be destroyed. With a glance at Betchaku-san's door, Marika left the booth and trotted over to her.

"Hello, I forgot to pay you the other day. I took one of your books."

The girl stared at her.

"*Death of an Old Woman*," Marika prompted.

"It's written about a real woman," the girl offered.

"Did she die?"

"Of course."

"I'm sorry." Poor girl. Marika picked up another copy of the booklet and gave the girl ¥600, nearly an hour's wages.

"I didn't know her." The girl sounded aggrieved, as though some slight had happened that Marika should have known about.

Marika didn't know what to say to that, so she merely thanked the girl and hurried back to the booth before Betchaku discovered her absence.

In between customers, Marika scanned the poems. There

were haiku in the back and longer poems toward the front. Mostly, they were so personal as to be incomprehensible. That man Conner last night had liked them. Well, she liked them too, if only because the poetry girl stood there with them, hour after hour, alone.

Was Rei-chan right that loneliness and fear were the same? Although getting her own apartment had been exciting, the idea of being in it alone that night with her borrowed furniture was now intimidating. Was that loneliness? She thought of Isamu, the beautiful house in Inudani. No, Marika knew what lonely was. This stepping out into the unknown? This was something else.

20

THE CLUE

Conner stretched on his futon, in a position that didn't hurt anywhere, waiting for Carmen to wake up so he could get the name of Katie's club. He heard her telltale heavy shuffle in the hall and looked at Katie's blocky red clock, which he'd taken as a souvenir. Almost two o'clock. He threw on clothes.

"Carmen?" he called through his cardboard door.

There was no response, but he hadn't heard her leave.

The bathroom door opened and shut and he heard the little wooden bolt slide. He got up and went to the bathrooms. "Carmen? Don't leave till you talk to me, okay?"

He heard an affirming grunt. He went into the men's bathroom, lathered his chin and started shaving. His cut was crusted dark red, having reopened during the night. No modeling jobs for Conner—standards for gaijin models were low, but not that low. He moved the scabbed skin back and forth over his skull, satisfying the itch without disturbing the scab. There were a few scratches on his nose. He looked at his dishwater gray eyes and sharp nose in the mirror. His hair was straightish and dark brown, close to black, a less stressful color to live with in Japan than, say, blond.

Conner waited for Carmen in the common room. Now that this thing with Paul had given Conner options, he had a hunch Katie would be easy to find. Fate worked that way, toying with you, giving you things only if you didn't need them.

A fortyish Swiss woman was tugging on a long red braid streaked with white as she watched the television in the tatami half of the common room. The program she was watching looked like a soap opera. A jilted man was apologizing to his female ex-lover. Then a mom was trying to convince her preteen son to stick up for a classmate who was being bullied. The connection eluded him.

He heard racing footsteps on the stairs. The front door opened and closed. What the hell? He ran out after her.

"Carmen!"

"If you want to talk you have to run with me." Her rust leather handbag bounced on her hip as she race-walked toward the station.

Conner hurried to catch up with her. His foot felt okayish. "Rob said you worked with Katie."

"That was a while ago," she puffed. The train bell began clanging at the tracks. "Dammit, that's my train."

"Where did you guys work?"

The red lights flashed and the yellow-and-black-ringed bamboo barrier began descending across the road. The station entrance was on the other side of the tracks. Carmen began to run. Conner ran with her, but the poles were already dropping.

"Where, Carmen?"

The train was visible in the near distance. Carmen ran faster. "I don't know," she gasped.

"What is this, Carmen, the hostesses' code of silence? Give me a name."

The gate descended just as they reached it. The train roared into the station and squealed to a stop, with them trapped on the other side of the barrier.

"I missed my train!"

"No you didn't. Come on." Conner ducked under the barrier and crossed the tracks to the entrance on the other side, quite illegally. Carmen looked up the tracks and followed. Conner fished into his pockets for two silver hundred-yen coins and bought two tickets. The ticket-taker yelled at them for crossing under the barrier. The door-closing bell was warbling.

"Here, Carmen." He handed her a ticket. They charged the ticket taker. He refused to clip their tickets.

"When the barrier is down you have to wait," he said to Carmen and Conner very matter-of-factly. The train doors closed.

"Damn you!" Carmen said in English.

Slowly the ticket-taker clipped their tickets. The train pulled away. "An express could be coming in the opposite direction." He was right—it was dangerous—but still, it would've been nice if he'd let them make it.

Carmen walked toward the disappearing train. She collapsed onto a bench. "My teaching job will make me stay late, and then I'll be late to my club. They said one more time and I'm through. I'm such a fuck-up."

"Another train will come in ten minutes. They'll forgive you. Here, I'll buy you a coffee." Conner guided her to a little restaurant bar on the platform and sat her on a stool. The proprietor plopped cellophane-wrapped handwipes on the counter in front of them and Conner ordered two blend coffees.

Carmen got a piece of paper out of her purse. "I've forgotten or blocked the name of the place, but I'll draw you a map."

Conner rubbed his foot—it had started pounding as soon as they started to run—as she pawed through her purse.

Carmen pulled out a pen. "Do you know Akasaka?"

"Better and better."

"Okay." She drew a couple crooked lines on the paper. "You know where Cozy Corner is, on the Mitsuke end of things?"

"*Hai.*"

"Do you know where First Kitchen is?"

"Fast Chicken. *Hai.*" He sipped his coffee. It was strong and fresh.

"Okay, you go to First Kitchen, keep on down that street till you run into the one that has those pink and gray bricks in the circle pattern on it." She drew a circle at the end of the two lines. It looked like a lollipop. "Turn left, walk about forty feet, go down a flight of stairs by a bakery," she drew the stairs, "and it's the second or third door, a black door." She handed him the map.

Her map looked like an irradiated daisy with the word "bar" at the end of it. As Tokyo street maps went it was pretty straightforward. "Do you remember anything about the name?"

"No, but it's run by a Chinese lady. She likes to be called Michiko. You better not mention my name. She's a real bitch. You know how Chinese people are."

"My mother's Chinese." She wasn't. Conner just said it because of all the times people had made tacky comments about gay people and he'd had to stay mum.

Carmen moved back on her stool and cocked her head as

though reassessing the meaning she gave to his looks. "Okay, I can see it."

People saw what they wanted to. The bell clanged. Another train was approaching.

"Thanks a lot for the map." The train pulled up and he rode with her as far as Shinjuku, where he gave her a hug for good luck before she hurried off in the other direction to make her connection.

Conner found a payphone and stuck in his phone card. 28 units left. He punched in Paul's number. The receptionist picked up the phone and Conner asked for Paul.

"Oh, Conner-san. Hold on a moment. Paul-san's on another line." She left Conner listening to recorded music, a synthesized version of some classical piece he'd heard a million times, usually when Bugs Bunny was up to something. The units remaining on his phone card ticked away. 24, 23, 22.

"Hello, Conner," Paul said.

"You asked me to call . . ."

"Okay, here's the deal. I have tickets for you and Marika to fly to Hawaii tomorrow evening. I'll explain it in more detail later, but basically, I need you to shepherd her through everything. She doesn't speak English, which is perfect, no problem there, but just look out for her. So be at Stardust at five o'clock tomorrow. Shiomi-san will brief you. Then come to the office to rendezvous with me and Marika. Understood?"

"I'll be there, sure, but why are you paying me a million yen for holding her hand?"

"There will also be a packet for you to bring back."

"Got it." Conner felt more relaxed. "And it will be professionally sealed? No telltale leaks? No pesky scents?"

"We're nothing if not professional."

"Tomorrow at noon, then." Conner hung up. And there he was, in the middle of Shinjuku Station, with crushing responsibilities, voluntarily undertaken, and nowhere to go. Too bad he wasn't a junkie; they always had somewhere to go, usually someone else's house through a second-story window.

Katie's former bar wouldn't open for at least a couple hours, but he didn't have any other leads, so he'd go there early to see what he could see. He got on the Marunouchi line and listened to the soothing hum of train wheels on rail. So, he'd agreed to smuggle again. It occurred to him that if he were trying to be smarter, he wasn't off to a great start.

THE AIR WAS cool on the quiet Akasaka streets. Everyone seemed to be in offices, working. Six days till the end of the month, Arata's deadline. If he found Katie today, he'd skip Paul's job. If not, he'd go to Hawaii on Sunday, come back Monday or Tuesday, and pay back Arata and Fumie. Hell, if the yakuza demanded hash, not cash, he could still fly to Bangkok that night and be back with a new kilo.

Bile rose in his throat at the thought; his heart raced. He swallowed. He sweated. Damn. His nerves were shot. Could he even do this?

The very first and only time he'd smuggled into the US had been an errand of mercy. He'd been outed early in his senior year of high school. Suddenly, everyone knew who and what he was and had an opinion about him. It was the late 1980s, and if anyone was supportive they weren't brave enough to tell him, let alone be seen with him. He'd folded under the notoriety and spent the rest of his senior year walking around Torrance, not wanting to bother his distracted, divorcing parents with the fact he wasn't going to school. No one minded his absence. He'd failed his classes and didn't graduate. He started to creep out into public and meet other gay men. He'd been looking for friends, but mostly found guys to have sex with who the next day might pass him on the street and not even say hello. But some were okay, and some were good, and the best of the lot was Edward.

In a West Hollywood bar, he'd met Edward, a tallish, wiry fellow with neatly barbered chestnut brown hair. Edward had invited Conner for dinner and Conner had shown up at the door dressed up for a date and trying to be attractive, but had instead been greeted by a skinny older man with thinning blond hair and thick mustache who introduced himself as Toby. Conner stuttered his hello, wondering who the old guy was. Was this going to be a threesome? Over dinner, it dawned on him that this was a meal, not a date, that Toby was Edward's partner, and that he wasn't more than a few years older than Edward, maybe in his early thirties, rather than forties, as Conner had thought. Toby had wasting from full-blown AIDS.

They had a wonderful time that night and Conner became a regular at their apartment. The duo hosted dinner parties, and Conner discovered there was such a thing as gay society. Men greeted each other with kisses on the lips, drank wine, had friends in common they'd known for years, even friends from other countries. They revealed a wealth of gay history to him. Leonardo da Vinci was gay? Alexander Hamilton was gay? It almost made Conner want to return to high school, just to announce this buried history in class, but the truth was if being outed hadn't driven him away, the way printed words skittered away from him as he stared at them would have. Conner began to drop by Edward and Toby's to help out with things and they were always glad to see him. Conner began to fall in love with Edward, though Edward didn't return the feeling. Conner came to love Toby, too, in a different way. Toby was older than Edward, but acted younger, more light-hearted.

Toby wasn't working, and drug co-payments and a thousand miscellaneous costs kept them short on money. One day, when Toby ran out of the pot he smoked to perk up his appetite and control nausea, Conner decided to do something bold. He borrowed his sister Peggy's surfboard and wetsuit, drove her old Volvo to Mexico, and bought a kilo of pot—which was many, many times larger than a kilo of hash. He drove back over the border with the pot hidden in the wetsuit, still moist and sandy from a quick dip in the Tijuana surf. Conner had dressed like a suburban straight kid. The border police couldn't search everyone and it had worked. Even as a nineteen-year-old he'd been smarter about smuggling than Rugged Matt.

When Edward found out what Conner had done, he'd flipped. Conner had never seen him so angry. He cussed Conner out something fierce and made him swear never to do it again. Conner had promised, a vow now broken. But then Edward had promised to look after Toby till he died and he hadn't, so they were even.

Conner pulled out Carmen's map and soon he was shuffling up the stem of her daisy. Katie's bar was only three miniscule blocks from Stardust The Moon. Conner hobbled sideways down the staircase to the below-ground floor.

A glossy, low-ceilinged hall was walled in marbled pink tile with thick grout joints and lined on both sides with what looked like one-room bars a la Giotto. Neither the second nor third door was black, but the fourth one was, and better yet, it was marked by a small black plastic sign with a cut-out, lit in fluorescent green, of a chrysanthemum, the perfect Japanese symbol for a Chinese owner to hide under. The name was written in English letters: Kiku.

The door was locked. The nearby bars were locked as well. Conner was way too early.

He splurged on a cup of blend at a Mister Donuts across the street and stared out the window at the stairs down to Kiku. He watched for hours, spotting numerous potential hostesses, but every single one of them was Asian. Finally, it was five, late enough to go to the bar.

Conner walked down the stairs and opened the door.

"*Irasshaimase.*" A middle-aged woman at the counter greeted him with the usual welcome.

The bar was dark, with fuzzy black walls and deep purple upholstery on the couches and stools. It was about ten feet wide and maybe twice that to the back wall, but even with two customers and the young hostess mixing their mizu-waris, it looked empty. Conner nodded to the woman at the counter—who had to be the Chinese mama-san Carmen had mentioned—and took a stool by the bar. He ordered a mizu-wari of his own.

As she added water to his Suntory he asked, "Didn't you used to have a blond gaijin working for you?"

"Oh, that one. Very selfish. Always late and complaining I didn't pay her enough." The mama-san's Japanese had a Chinese flavor—not her accent, which was pure Tokyo, but something in the way she clipped her syntax. "I fired her. She's not as nice as Atsuko." She pointed at the hostess chatting with the two men. "At-chan, haaai." She waved at Atsuko, who looked up at the mention of her name and waved back with a coy flutter that didn't match her boyish cropped hair.

"You remember Katie?"

"Oh, *Katie.* I thought you meant the Australian one. Katie quit. Such a nice girl. Quiet."

So, it was Carmen who'd gotten fired. That must have been why she hadn't told Conner about this place. Poor Carmen. Always poor Carmen. "Do you know where Katie lives?"

"*Ne*, Atsuko. Where did Katie live? Somewhere near Kanizawa, wasn't it?"

Atsuko nodded slowly. Kanizawa. That would be the hideous mansion.

"But she moved from there," Conner said.

"Then I don't know."

Conner took a sip of the drink. "Do you have a phone number?"

"Sorry."

"Did she pick up her last pay already?"

"Sorry." The mama-san smiled sadly, as though pained to disappoint him.

"Shoot. See, a letter she was waiting for came. From one of her brothers. It feels like a plane ticket. There must have been a family emergency or something." He took another sip of the drink. He felt bad lying to this woman.

"Oh, from her father, in Canada?"

"No, her brother. Her father died years ago. I hope her mother's cancer isn't back." At least that part wasn't a lie.

"*Ne, ne.* She sometimes calls you, *ne*, Atsuko?"

"Who?" Atsuko said.

"Katie-chan!" the mama-san said angrily. "Her mother has cancer. I know she calls you and your roommate all the time."

"Sometimes." Atsuko's eyes wandered over the ceiling. The two men were looking angry, like rich kids left out of a game after they'd bought admission tickets for everyone else.

"If you hear from her, can you call me? My number is the same as Katie's old number."

The front peak of Atsuko's boyish hair swayed a wee bit with her one crisp nod.

"But don't tell her it's me." Conner stared into his drink and tried to conjure up the jilted boyfriend from the soap opera the Swiss woman had been watching. "She's mad at me.

That's partly why I came all the way down here. To apologize."

"Ah." The mama-san smiled. "Katie's a nice girl."

Conner twisted his glass. Yeah, *so* nice. "I'm sure if I could just talk to her . . ." He finished off the drink and slid his glass toward the older woman.

"Did you have a fight?" She mixed a new mizu-wari.

"Yeah." Conner took the glass from her and drank half of it, trying to look rejected, bashful and in love. "A big one. It was my fault."

"At-chan, what was that club she was so hot about? The one in Shinjuku with the strange name?"

Atsuko grunted discouragingly.

"Wasn't it a number?" the mama-san suggested.

"10 cc?" Conner asked.

"Tsubaki House," said Atsuko.

"The disco?" Conner asked.

"Ah!" the mama-san cried in exasperation. "Not the disco, At-chan. The one she goes to all the time. It's not a number. Something about comedy and tragedy."

"Tragic Grimace?" Conner said.

"That's the one!"

Tragic Grimace was only two blocks from Here's Mimi, but two blocks meant a hundred bars and that might be enough for her to feel safe. If Katie smoked some afternoon hash, her judgment might just be impaired enough to want to go out.

"She talked about that one all the time. What's your phone again? I'll call you if Katie comes by."

Conner told her and she kindly wrote it down. His own mom was fine, but he'd take this mama-san for a mom any day. He checked his watch. A quarter to seven. Time enough to check in at Giotto. Arata and Fumie deserved an update, plus he wanted to tell someone he was leaving the country, so if he turned up missing someone would know to look for his body in a Honolulu dumpster. After Giotto, he would move on to Ni-chome to stake out Tragic Grimace. Maybe having beaten him up so easily the other night, Katie's guard would be down.

"Thanks," he said to the mama-san. He finished his drink and peeled enough from his remaining funds to leave her smiling even as Atsuko glowered in the corner.

21

THE BOX OF FLESH

Marika sat at the counter at Realism, shift three hours old, so ready for Rei-chan to show up. She filled out a receipt for a man with oiled hair and a movie-star face. Poetry Girl was still standing by the escalator, placard hanging from her neck. The girl would be able to see Marika too if she ever looked her way, but in the few days Marika had been there, the girl hadn't once turned her head, to either direction. The girl kept her head tilted to the left, eyes angled down. Her neck muscles must be so strong. Marika gave the movie-star man his receipt and he left.

The door to Betchaku's office opened. He stuck his head out. "Marika-chan?"

"Yes?" He'd gone from calling her Shirayama-san to Marika-chan in just four days. She didn't like that.

"Can you come in for a minute? I have something to show you before you leave."

"Hai." She got off her stool. A vinegar odor seemed to flood from the office, like he'd been eating *gyoza* with his fingers and hadn't washed. Marika looked at her watch. Less than ten minutes till Rei-chan arrived. Marika scanned the crowd for customers. No one was coming to save her. She went into the office and sat on the tiny stool. Rei-chan had promised he was harmless. Betchaku closed the door.

"Shouldn't we leave it open? The customers . . ."

"It's so noisy," he said. "Besides, we'll hear a customer if one comes."

Marika felt distressed. "That doesn't make any sense."

"I live with my parents," he said, rocking back in his chair. Marika tried to figure out if this could be a response to what she'd said. "How is your new apartment?"

He knew already? Marika bowed. "Very nice, thank you." Rei-chan must have called him. Why would she do that?

Betchaku slid a piece of paper over the desk toward her. Marika glanced at it. It looked official. "Go on," he urged her.

She picked it up. It was a receipt.

"It's my gas bill," Betchaku said.

She let her eyes scan briefly over his face.

"I paid it." He seemed proud. She considered why and finally decided that it was proof of his life. Human interaction. She wanted to be polite but did not know what to say. "Um, I hope to receive my first gas bill soon." She stood up. "Well, I should get back to the counter."

"Wait, I have something to show you." He opened the drawer of his desk and pulled out a shoebox. "Maybe you noticed yesterday there was a roll that we returned to a customer without printing."

Marika thought hard. Yes, there had been such an envelope. She remembered the man, on the younger side of middle-age with an oval face so smooth and clear he looked like he'd never had a worry in his life.

"There are certain rolls we're not allowed to print." He opened the shoebox. It was filled with photos. He put a couple on the desk. Marika caught a quick glance of skin and hair and interlocking body parts. She looked away before she could identify them.

"Disgusting, aren't they?" Betchaku grabbed up the photos and touched them, placing a few more before her. The man who'd picked up his undeveloped roll yesterday had not asked for an explanation.

"I hear a customer." Marika stood up and pushed open the door.

"Wait." Betchaku grabbed her leg.

Marika smiled and pulled his hand away from her leg. His fingernails dug into her skin as she pulled his fingers back. She squeezed out into the roar of Shinjuku, closing the door on him. She braced herself for the vinegar wind of his nervous body odor when the door opened, but Betchaku stayed inside. He was not harmless. Why did this have to happen the same day she'd deposited her key money into the landlady's bank account? Even tomorrow would have been better. But if Betchaku knew that, maybe that was why he'd done it.

A pudgy silver-haired lady leaned on the counter with her thin adolescent grandson. Marika pulled down another orange envelope. Another selection of prints to be copied and distributed to friends, colleagues or relatives; she'd handed over so many envelopes to excited customers already. Marika scanned the West Entrance for Rei-chan, who was late. Betchaku's door stayed closed. The grandson pointed out the correct spaces on the form for the grandmother. A man in a trench coat stood behind them, leaning slightly backward with his leather briefcase grasped before him in both hands. Another man stood behind him. What intimacies were they carrying for her?

Rei-chan waved as she walked toward Realism from the Seibu Shinjuku line. Marika waved back; she was supposed to work for another hour, but was ready to flee.

Marika finished the grandmother's form, took the trench coat man's form and worked frantically to clear the line so she could talk to Rei-chan. Rei-chan took the other man's order.

Betchaku opened the door and rolled toward them on his chair. "Marika, could you come in here a minute?"

"There's a customer coming," Marika said.

"I'll cover you," Rei-chan said.

"He's showing me dirty pictures," Marika whispered to Rei-chan. "He grabbed my leg."

Rei-chan looked past Marika toward Betchaku. "She'll be with you in a minute, Betchaku-san," Rei-chan said.

He closed the door.

"Just look at the pictures to humor him a little. I just say, 'Oh, how horrible!' or 'They shouldn't let people do that!' That's all he wants."

"He touched me," she said.

"Tell him to stop and he stops. He doesn't do it often."

Marika just looked at Rei-chan.

Marika tapped her pen against the countertop. "How does he have these photos if we're not supposed to develop them?"

"Some people never come to claim them."

"So then he develops them?"

Rei-chan sighed. "Let me handle it." She opened Betchaku's door. "I'll help you, Betchaku-san."

"I want Marika-chan in here, now."

"I don't want to look at your pictures," Marika said.

"It's important," he said. "This is work!"

"It is not." Marika pulled out an envelope and filled in the date as she looked around for the next customer. How could there not be a customer for a whole two minutes during rush hour?

"You're fired," Betchaku said. "Now try paying your rent."

"Fine." Marika crumpled the dated envelope and threw it at him.

"Betchaku-san!" Rei-chan said. "Let me talk to her." She closed Betchaku into his office.

Marika gathered up her bag. "I'll return the uniform tomorrow. I'd do it now, but I don't want to change here." Marika stepped out of the booth.

"Marika, you can't quit," Rei-chan said.

"I didn't quit. He fired me."

Rei-chan sighed again, deeply. "Sorry."

"That's okay."

"I like you," Rei-chan said.

"Well, I like you too. I'll call you. We'll go out for coffee."

Rei-chan nodded.

Marika walked down to gold-walled Metro Promenade and boarded the Marunouchi line for Akasaka. She had spent all her brother's money on the deposit and the next instant lost her job. Rei-chan saying "he's harmless" that first day should have been all she needed to hear. She told herself she could get another job just as easily, just flip open a copy of job magazine and pick one, and that was probably true, but she kept thinking all the same that all that separated her from a cardboard box on the Metro Promenade was Stardust The Moon, Mama-san, and Paul.

22

THE EYEBROWS

Conner rode the Marunouchi line back to Shinjuku and hobbled underground toward Giotto, Atsuko's glower burning in a corner of his mind. Atsuko must be helping Katie hide. She had been angry as he'd left Kiku because the okami-san was giving everything away. Conner finally had a real lead.

He surfaced east of the tracks in front of the gigantic Studio Alta light screen, which was showing a Madonna video. Quite a few of the bulbs were out, leaving poxy blotches on Madonna's face. He walked down the pedestrian malls toward Giotto.

Conner flung the door open, inadvertently banging it against the dreaded heat-exchanger outside. A bushy-browed man seated at the bar turned to look. It was Kuwano, the same man who'd come in the night after Conner had returned from Bangkok, the one Fumie was afraid of. He was joined by a clean-cut man with a bird-like nose, a good bit older, also in a gray pin-stripe suit far less harsh on the eye than the usual navy-blue polyester of salarymen.

"*Ara,*" Fumie said as he walked through the door. "Look

who's here." She set an empty glass on a coaster by the phone, at the farthest end of the bar from the two men. She grabbed a beer from under the counter and opened it.

"You're going to get your money back," Conner whispered. The men sat only a few stools away. He wouldn't tell her about Hawaii. She'd never believe him.

As she poured the beer, she too whispered, "They've been here two nights in a row now. Would police do that? We'll talk when I close."

"That's hours! When's Arata coming in?"

"Fumie-san's play opens next week," Kuwano interrupted loudly.

Conner looked at the men. They didn't look cheesy enough to be gangsters. They had to be police. Or was that a stereotype?

"Sorry to interrupt your discussion," the one with the beaky nose said.

They couldn't have heard their whispers, could they? Conner raised his eyebrows. "Huh?"

Kuwano raised his own eyebrows, as if unable not to raise them when spoken to. "About some drugs, was it?"

"Some what?" Conner tried to stay calm. He'd said nothing about drugs. "No, really? What did I say?"

"What did he say, Shimoda-san?"

"He said, 'I've got some really good hash'."

Okay, so this Shimoda guy obviously knew something. From whom? A yakuza informant? Hideo? The airport police? "Sorry," Conner said. "The Japanese of me it so bad. You mean that stuff at Mos Burger in morning?"

Shimoda laughed. "Good one."

Fumie went back to the two men and leaned toward Shimoda and Kuwano. "So, the playwright's idea is that my father keeps telling me I'm crazy, even though I'm not. I'm not sure I'm sane so the audience isn't supposed to be sure, either."

"You can go talk to your friend, if you want," Kuwano said.

"I like talking to you," Fumie said. "You should come see the play. It's *so* good."

"I'm sure our foreign friend is much more interesting." Kuwano raised a glass in Conner's direction and raised his bushy eyebrows. "Cheers."

"I'm just drinking my beer quietly," Conner said.

"Oh, your Japanese is pretty good after all," Shimoda said.

Kuwano nodded to Shimoda. "I wish I could speak that well."

Shimoda laughed. "You know, Kuwano-kun, maybe he doesn't know what hash is. If he did, he'd have probably gotten scared and left already. Then again, maybe he doesn't know enough to be scared."

"What do you gentleman do for a living?" Conner asked.

"Adjusters." Kuwano showed Conner a card, which looked quite authentic. "Insurance."

Conner reached for it, but Kuwano withdrew it. "It's my last. Shimoda-san can give you one of his."

"Sorry, I'm out. Do you have a card?" Shimoda asked Conner.

"Soon, I hope." Conner ducked his head in a jerky, apologetic bow.

"Where do you live?"

Conner did not want them knowing that. "In Setagaya." Setagaya Ward was the biggest in Tokyo, probably holding two million people.

"Oh, really? Me, too. What part? I live near Hanegi Park."

"I forget Japanese place names so easily."

"What train line? You remember that, don't you?"

"Either the Keio or the Odakyu. I get them confused."

Between them, the Keio and Odakyu covered the bulk of Setagaya. Conner moved to the bar stool next to them. "Have some whisky, Shimoda-san." He topped off Shimoda's glass from his bottle, which bore the nice, simple characters for Shimoda—lower field—on the label in magic marker. The picture-like nature of characters was often easier for Conner to read than English words. Conner poured a little into Kuwano's glass and stared at him, eyebrows raised, inquisitively.

Kuwano's eyebrows went up.

Conner smiled. "So you aren't detectives?"

"Insurance," Kuwano said.

"If you were detectives, you'd probably arrest me, right?"

"Since you're a gaijin, maybe we'd threaten you to get you out of the country. If you were Japanese we might arrest you. No, I guess we'd arrest you either way."

Shimoda nodded.

Fumie closed her eyes.

"You want gaijin in your jails?"

"Why not? You'd spend most of your time in isolation anyway, not talking to anyone. So, gaijin, Japanese, what's the difference?"

"Well, enjoy your whiskies," Conner said.

Fumie discreetly passed him a note. Conner felt his heart race. What if he couldn't read it? What if he mistook hiragana *chi* for *sa* or katakana *n* for *so* and garbled everything? Conner excused himself and went into the tiny bathroom. The note was written in English, and mercifully brief: *Wait outside. Tell Arata police.*

Shimoda and Kuwano looked at him when he stepped out.

"Hope we'll see you again," Kuwano said.

"Thanks, but I've got a job, so I'm on national health."

"What? Oh, I see. No, I do life insurance. Everyone should

have some. Term life is pretty cheap for a young guy like you. Could be a sweet pay-off. For somebody."

"I appreciate your concern. We'll talk later, okay?"

Shimoda chuckled. "He's so funny," he said to Fumie.

"Isn't he." Fumie closed her eyes, as though fighting off a headache.

Conner slid out the door and hustled down the path almost to Yasukuni Road, from where he expected Arata to come. He looked over his shoulder to see if Shimoda or anyone else was following him. No one. He kept looking just the same.

23

JISU IZU A PEN

Marika stacked white paper coasters ten high on the bar of Stardust The Moon and ran her fingernail down the side to straighten them into a neat column. She could not lose this job. She would not let Ai get her drunk tonight. She knew Ai wasn't trying to get her into trouble, but Marika couldn't handle brandy as well as Ai could. Ai was chatting with Shin-chan at the bar, slowly arranging her tray. The front door opened. The three of them called out "*Irasshaimase*" and Shin-chan hurried over to the front station to greet the evening's first customer.

It was Paul. He was alone. Ai had told her that Paul was a co-owner, and had been for many years. That's why he'd been able to intercede with Mama-san for her. Marika wasn't sure, but she thought she might have lost his sympathy by toppling over and spouting poetry.

Ai grabbed a highball glass. "Paul's mine tonight." She went behind the bar for Paul's bottle.

"Ai, can I have him, please. I have to get back on his good side."

"Nobody's mad at you." Ai picked up her tray and started

walking toward the far end of the club, where Shin-chan was seating Paul. "I'm the one who needs to play obedient."

Marika got up and blocked Ai's path. "Please, Ai. Just tonight. You can have him every other night forever."

Ai lowered her tray. "Mama-san likes you. You're my replacement."

"They aren't going to replace you. You're too pretty. Besides, even with me here, this place is understaffed, and all the customers ask for you." Marika touched her arm. "I got fired from my other job. I can't afford to lose this one too. Please?"

"Oh, all right." Ai handed her the tray.

PAUL SMILED at Marika as she squatted by his table. He settled back in his chair, arranging his long arms and legs at comfortable angles. "How are you doing this evening, Marika-chan?" he asked in his American-accented Japanese.

Marika nodded. "I'm doing very well." Ai was right; he didn't seem angry. And he remembered her name. She poured him a strong whisky. "Mama . . . I mean Shiomi-san is very good to me."

He laughed and reached forward to take the drink. "You can call her Mama-san around me. I call her that." He leaned forward to whisper. "I've known her a very long time. Since just after Korea, if you can believe that. Is she around?"

"Do you want me to get her for you?"

"In a minute. First, I want to ask you a question. In confidence."

"In confidence?"

"I don't want Mama-san to know."

"Oh." Marika assumed a pensive look, as though weighing his question. People were easier to deal with if they thought you were stupid. Then later, when they discovered you had a brain, they were *very* impressed, like you'd learned a new trick, probably due to their beneficent influence. "Well, I suppose so."

He took a sip from the glass Marika had handed him. "Do you speak any English?"

She recalled her grade-school English lessons about pens and books, everything written out phonetically in katakana: *jisu izu a pen, jisu izu a bukku.* "Not very well." She touched the whisky bottle. *Jisu izu a u̟sukii.*

"Well, it's probably better that way." Paul straightened up in his chair. "How has she been lately? Moody? Nervous?"

"Shiomi-san?" Mama-san *had* seemed moody—brusque, solicitous, angry, chatty; demanding and cranky to Ai but more friendly and encouraging to Marika—but Marika felt uncomfortable saying so. "Ai-chan might know better."

"Now, you promised to answer my question," Paul said.

"Oh, was that your question? I thought you wanted to know if I spoke English."

"That was just a warm-up. I want to hear what a stranger thinks of her. Ai-chan knows her too well. Is she okay?"

Marika sucked in her breath. "She has seemed a bit . . ."

"Nervous?"

"Not exactly. It's more . . ."

"Moody."

"You could say so." Marika looked about the room. Mama-san was not to be seen. "She seems . . . inconsistent," she whispered.

"Drinking?"

Mama-san had been drinking quite a lot. "I don't really . . ."

"Marika-chan," Paul said sternly, annoyingly.

"Well, a bit . . ."

"Hmm," Paul said. "Hmm. Is the back room free?"

"It's not booked tonight that I know of."

"Ask Shiomi-san, Mama-san, to meet me there."

"Yes, sir."

Mama-san was at the front station, politely welcoming four guests. Marika waited at her side, where Mama-san pressed her into service to escort the customers to their table. Marika informed her that Paul was waiting in the back room. She seated the four guests and memorized their rather involved first orders—no notepads at a first-class place like Stardust The Moon. She was headed for the bar when she noticed Paul's bottle and glass sitting on his table. Someone really should have transferred them to the back room. She gathered them up on the silver tray and took them to the back room. The door was open. Paul and Mama-san were talking.

"I can't," Mama-san was saying.

"You have to," Paul said. "It'll be at least a day till I can get the tickets arranged. And then another day or two till they get back. And then at least another week till we get the money."

"You can't send them alone! They're strangers."

"How well do we have to know them? It's a simple job. He's experienced and speaks enough Japanese to communicate with her. And she's smart. Have you seen how she plays dumb? It's quite convincing."

Mama-san scoffed. "Didn't fool you."

Silence followed. Was "he" the young American man who had put his hand out for her the evening before? She remembered how his skin had felt clean and moist. Not sweaty, but cool and soft. Sometimes foreigners had oddly long fingers, like space aliens, but he had had very nice hands: short strong fingers, a firm palm, squarish nails.

The silence continued. What were they doing? Marika knew if she moved, she'd be heard. They'd know she'd been listening.

Paul finally spoke. "Don't forget, she looks just like her. Ai-chan could never have passed."

Like who? Who did they think she looked like?

"Just go yourself and forget the sale!" Mama-san said.

"She can't wait. Everyone is selling to pay off stock market losses. Prices are dropping."

"So what? I have problems of my own. I've drained this place dry paying off worthless margin contracts. So you handle it or she handles it. Otherwise, I'll handle it. And I am not in a mood to be sympathetic, not after losing everything I've worked so hard for."

Marika took her chance, before it got quiet again. She entered.

Paul's hand was behind Mama-san's head, gently stroking the nape of her neck.

"Ah!" Mama-san cried, sitting bolt upright. Her eyes were moist. She turned away.

"Paul-san's whisky," Marika said. "I'm sorry."

"Oh, just go away!" Mama-san said.

"She's a good girl, Keiko," Paul said. Mama-san faced away from Marika, toward the wall. Paul pointed at a small table. "Just put it there."

Marika set her tray on the table and turned to go.

"Thank you," Mama-san said.

Marika nodded. "You're very welcome." She rushed to the kitchen, trying to keep the last party's orders straight amid the questions flying through her brain.

And Paul thought she was only playing dumb.

24

THE HEART-TO-HEART

When Arata did appear two hours later he seemed to pop out of nowhere. He looked at Conner, his face hardly registering a ripple. Even with the shoots of white in his neatly combed hair Arata looked years younger than thirty-six. Conner tried to disrupt his composure with a smirk, but got nothing. Conner felt sad.

"I think it's better if we don't see each other for a while," Arata said.

"I'm only here because Fumie wants you to know there are two probable policemen in Giotto. Plain clothes. She thinks they're detectives and I agree."

"Why?"

"They're educated and nicely dressed. They kind of look like you, only more honest."

Arata scowled. The air was cool, and tiny illuminated droplets passing under the streetlights showed the movement of the wind. Little movements also passed over Arata's face—eyes focusing, blinking, cheek muscle swimming under the skin—but Conner couldn't read him. It was hard to believe this suit-and-tie version was the same guy who'd been naked with Conner's hand on his cock two days ago.

"So you've been duly warned. I'm off. I have a lead on Katie. I'm going to find her soon."

"What's the lead?" Arata asked eagerly.

"I have a couple." Conner hesitated. If he put them into words, it all sounded like such a thin chance. "First, I know where she'll be tonight."

"Great. I'll go with you," Arata said.

Strange way to not see me, thought Conner. "Why?"

"So, she doesn't beat you up again, obviously."

Conner looked at him. He was serious. "Thank you for your confidence." He turned his back on Arata and headed up Yasukuni Road.

Arata followed. He seemed more like stalker than protector.

They crossed Gyoen Road, went a block further and turned right. The blue and yellow sign of Tragic Grimace was easily visible a couple blocks ahead. As they reached the stairwell to the basement club the sounds of the Thompson Twins pumped up from below—*Come inside, come inside*. Arata followed Conner down.

The club was half full, the dance floor sporting a few men and women hopping to the peppery pop beat. No House here. The DJ put on The Specials. A quick glance around the room told Conner that Katie wasn't there. This town really was coming like a ghost town.

"You're not going to hang out and wait for her again, are you?" Arata asked him. "That's no kind of lead."

"I was told she'd be coming here tonight," Conner said sheepishly. Or might be. It felt feeble to him too. Everything connected to Katie seemed to make him feel feeble now. It was quite a contrast to the confidence he'd gotten from sex with her, like fucking a woman was such an accomplishment, like it suddenly made him her equal. "I have another lead. This is just something to try till I follow up on it."

"Here's Mimi is barely two tiny, tiny blocks away and you think she'd come back?"

"Trust me. She's not the type to worry—not about me, not about you, not about the yakuza."

Conner walked over to the master to ask if anyone matching Katie's description had been to Tragic Grimace recently. He knew who Conner meant, but she hadn't been there in a few days. Conner traced a path to the back wall of the club. *Pull up to the bumper, baby.* Arata bought a couple of Asahis and joined him. He handed Conner one of the beers and leaned against the wall next to him.

"I thought you were staying away from me," Conner said.

"I need to make sure you do this right."

"You don't think I'm going to find her, do you?"

"I think you have a better chance of finding her than I do."

"Look, Arata, don't you realize I'm doing all this for you?"

"Are you sure about that?"

"It's always been for you."

Arata looked the other way. Conner could see him swallowing. Arata looked back. "I know that, Conner." He swallowed again.

"Arata, let's stop all this dancing around. Leave your wife. It's not fair to her either."

"I'm more of a mess than you realize." Arata fingered his beer bottle. He looked nervous.

"What's she like?"

"She plays a lot of mahjong."

Conner drank down some beer. The music switched to a salsa-flavored number. "Do you have sex with her?"

"Sometimes."

"In between affairs with men?"

"I don't have affairs with men."

"Never?"

"Just you," Arata said.

"So, you haven't replaced me?"

Arata shook his head.

"Then why do you keep an apartment in a gay neighborhood when you're so short of money?"

"Ni-chome is close to the bar. And honestly, I'd love to get rid of the expense. But the trains aren't running when we close. Do you know how much a cab to Utsunomiya would cost? Or am I supposed to motorcycle for an hour after customers have been buying me drinks? Should I turn them down? Plus, I get tired. I don't lie about everything, you know."

"Are you sure?"

"Look, not everybody can just run away from their problems like you did. In Japan you can't do anything unless you are in with someone. You need connections. Homos are outside all of that. I wouldn't own a bar. At best I'd be the barkeep. You think I would live this way if I didn't have to? You think I don't want to divorce her and live with you? I was happy last year."

"Sorry." Conner didn't think Arata would mind this apology. He reached behind Arata's back and grabbed his hand in the dark, where no one could see. Arata held Conner's hand with unexpected firmness. Conner rubbed his thumb over the sinews on the back of Arata's hand. The music switched from Boy George's Hare Krishna number to the Orb's "Little Fluffy Clouds" to the Smiths' "What Difference Does It Make" and still Arata kept sweaty hold of Conner's hand.

"Let's go to my place," Arata said.

"Okay," Conner said. This was more important than Katie.

They walked quickly to Arata's pad. Conner pulled his

shirt off over his head, his ribs complaining, but not enough to stop him. He shucked off his pants as Arata walked to the kitchen to get glasses of water, which he started diluting with whisky. Conner pulled off his underwear and followed Arata. He stood close behind him at the sink, naked. Arata was still completely dressed.

"Can I have some?"

Arata turned around and put his hand to Conner's slender chest, scratching and tugging at Conner's sparse chest hair. He examined the tickle of hair on the back of Conner's neck, at its base. "Like an animal," Arata said.

Conner leaned forward and kissed him. Arata backed away but then this time bounced in close again, kissing Conner deeply. His finger traced Conner's jaw and then looped around his Adam's apple.

Conner unbuttoned Arata's shirt and pushed up his undershirt. Arata's nipples were big, the dark circles surrounding them tiny. His chest was hairless. "Like a kid," Conner said, knowing that would annoy him.

"You're the kid," Arata said.

Conner leaned forward to kiss and bite Arata's crinkled nipples. Conner looked up the slight distance into Arata's eyes.

"I won't stop you this time," Arata said.

Conner straightened up and ran his hand over the soft bristles of Arata's salt and pepper hair, or as the Japanese said, salt and sesame. "Okay, I'm going to believe you."

Arata walked over to the futon and sat down on it. He removed his shirt and undershirt while Conner pulled off his pants and underwear. Arata was erect.

Arata kissed Conner and lunged on top of him, pinning Conner to the futon and rubbing his hands over Conner's chest, which hurt. "You won't tell anyone, will you?"

"Of course not."

"You're afraid of me, right?" Arata said.

"Why should I be afraid of you?"

Arata smothered any further words with his wet lips, tasting fresh and sweet.

Conner kissed him again and again, trying to eat him up. Arata slid down, kissing Conner's belly, dropped down further and took Conner into his mouth. Conner twisted around to sixty-nine Arata. He could feel Arata's hips start to move, thrusting into Conner's mouth. Conner's excitement grew, feeding off Arata's. He tasted Arata's pre-come in his mouth. Without warning, Arata spasmed in Conner's mouth, moaning loudly, not trying to be quiet like he usually did, filling Conner's mouth like he hadn't come the entire year since they were last together. Conner's HIV anxiety soared. Suddenly he was back in L.A.—low risk, high risk, mouth cuts, stomach acids, affairs, lies, obituaries—but he willed it away. It's irrational. You're negative; he's negative. It's virtually impossible to get the virus that way anyway.

But Conner's erection withered away and his dick slipped from Arata's mouth. Not a great performance for a twenty-five-year-old guy. Conner swallowed, hand still clasping Arata's dick. Arata lay on top of Conner for a moment, then turned around and lay by Conner's side. He hugged Conner close, not seeming to care that Conner had lost his erection.

"What you said earlier, about not having affairs with men, was that really true?"

"Of course." Arata blinked. Maybe he blushed.

"But you've slept with other men, right?"

"Only when I was in high school." Now Arata blushed. His embarrassment was believable.

Conner pulled him close. What would the yakuza do to Arata if Conner couldn't come through? Conner didn't want anyone else to ever die, to ever go away. He knew that wasn't possible, that everyone died, absolutely everyone. Still, he wanted to keep Arata out of harm if he could.

"You haven't come yet," Arata said.

Of course Arata wanted him to come, too. It must be tough to have a partner who was laid low by fear and memories. This wasn't the first time.

"I like you," Arata said.

Conner recognized how much stronger "I like you" was in Japanese than in English. His panic melted away. Conner got hard again, and then Arata did too. They made love again and this time they both finished. They lay pressed together, sticky chests bonded. Arata nuzzled Conner's neck. He was a sweetheart when he was like this.

"I hate my life," Arata said. "I hate living with a woman and being a businessman and never having anyone. I can't love her. I can't ever be myself. It's driving me crazy."

Conner kissed his neck. He pulled Arata close. The pounding of Arata's heart seemed to catch the rhythm of Conner's own heart and master it. Conner fought sleep, but now his ribs didn't hurt and his foot didn't hurt and he began to doze off.

Arata began squirming. Slightly at first: a twitch of his arm, a shift of his leg, small and awkward, as though he was trying to suppress it. He wiggled away from Conner.

"Your arm falling asleep?" Conner asked groggily.

Arata got out of bed. "Thirsty," he muttered. He walked over to the sink. Conner heard the water go on and off. Arata stood silhouetted in the moonlight. His stiff bangs spiked out to the front. His body was trim and his shoulders seemed too big for a man his height. Conner got out of the futon and walked over to him, hugging his waist from behind.

"I'm married, Conner."

"You can't help that."

"But it's still true," he said.

"Arata . . ."

"Just let me think. For a minute."

"You got it." If Arata needed to be left alone, Conner could leave him so alone he wouldn't believe it. He went back to the futon and started dressing. He thought about his other lead, Atsuko. He could still get to Atsuko's bar before it closed. There was no way he'd not follow that up. Could he persuade Atsuko to help? Remembering her scowl, it seemed unlikely, but Atsuko knew Katie well; that had to count in Conner's favor.

Arata turned and saw that Conner was dressed. He made no move to stop him. Why should he? Conner thought. He got his rocks off twice, what more does he need?

Arata gave him a strange appraising look without interest, anger, friendliness, hostility. Conner had seen that look in him before, just before he'd decided to let the yakuza take him to court. It wouldn't surprise Conner one bit if Arata called immigration on Conner and got him deported.

"Be patient with me, Conner."

Conner opened the door. "This *is* patient, Arata."

Arata nodded.

The truth was this was the only relationship Conner had ever had that lasted more than a month. Conner had thought he had someone who cared enough to let Conner depend on him, the way Edward and Toby had depended on each other. But Conner wasn't willing to hang around forever begging for scraps. He picked up his coat and left.

He hobbled down the stairs, his foot tender. He ran on it anyway, out into the street with his arms raised. He pulled off his shirt and felt the damp air condense onto his bare chest, droplets of foggy dew clinging to his skin. It wasn't the sort of thing people did in Japan, but so what? It felt good to have water on his skin. He ran through the moist fog. It was like talking to the world, the natural world. Nature didn't care whose laws you broke or who you loved. Nature just loved you. It fed you. Nature might kill you, but it would never be ashamed of you.

Conner slowed to a walk and looked at his watch: one o'clock. He shook out his complaining foot and shivered in the night air. Arata didn't need anyone to save him; he'd save himself. But Conner still wanted to find Katie. She'd robbed him, kicked him in the face and stomach. What made her willing to hurt him just for money? She had slept with him, not just had sex with him but fallen asleep in his arms, wrapped around him peacefully through the night. In some ways it felt more honest than what he'd had with Arata. How could you accept another person's body and passion into your own body and then so casually turn on them?

Conner wanted to ask Katie: When you woke up, not our last morning, but the morning after, when you were alone or with someone else, how did you feel?

Conner walked down the center of the boulevard half naked, shaking. He still had lots to do that evening. The mama-san had mentioned a roommate. Perhaps the roommate would be more helpful than Atsuko. If Conner could find out where Atsuko lived, he could catch the roommate alone. Conner would get his answers. He put on his shirt, buttoned it, pulled his coat tight around him and headed back to Akasaka.

25

THE GOOD GIRL

S hin-chan was cleaning tables. Closing time was approaching.

"Marika-chan," a voice said.

Marika snapped to attention. "Hai." The little gray man's glass was still full, though the ice had melted. Hers was empty and she was wobbly with Suntory. She'd succeeded at first in not getting drunk, but as the evening wore on, everything her customers said sounded like clumsy innuendoes that reminded her of Betchaku and his odious box of photos or all the snide little things Isamu and his buddies said to the Roppongi club hostesses, annoying remarks she'd pretended to not mind.

"Marika-chan," the gray man said. "Come home with me tonight."

Marika smiled at him. "Well, I can't do that, but I can give you a castration."

The gray man laughed and slapped his thigh. "Give *him* one!" He pointed to a taller man just coming back from the bathroom. The two men had been there since ten o'clock and Marika was quite bored with them and trying hard not to show it. It was tough to keep coming up with amusing banter for so long. She had greater respect now for the hostesses of the world.

"It's true," she said. "My ex-husband and I used to volunteer at an animal shelter. He's a dentist, so he did the anesthetic and extractions while I cleaned the dogs' teeth. Castrations are surprisingly easy. My ex and the vets got a kick out of getting a woman to do them. I became quite the master. A few clamps, a little twist and snip, and it's all over. It doesn't bleed much, if done properly." She fluttered her eyelashes. "Would you like me to do one for you?"

"Life would be so much easier!" He laughed so hard his dentures shifted. Marika was starting to like him.

"Marika-chan!" Mama-san was calling her.

"Excuse me," Marika said to the men. She pushed on her knee and rose to standing. "Be right back."

Marika slithered her way between plush walls and potted palms into the back room.

"Hello, Marika-chan," Paul said.

Marika nodded.

Mama-san was seated at his side, but she stood, said, "Be a good girl," and teetered off drunkenly.

"Sit down, Marika."

That sounded like a pretty good idea to Marika. It had been a long day. She sat on a peach-colored stool across the black lacquer table from Paul, back straight, hands side by side, fingertips pressed down, on her knees.

"How would you like to go to America?" Paul said.

"Isn't it a little late in the evening?" Years with Isamu had trained her to sarcasm, which she was now showing to the world.

"I'm serious. How would you like to go to Hawaii?"

Marika examined his face. He looked serious. "Is this a joke?"

"No, a business proposition. I need someone to go pick up some documents. Mama-san can't leave the business, and Ai-chan, well . . ."

This was what he and Mama-san had been talking about in the early evening, something she looked the part for, something that rattled Mama-san. Marika would expect that a woman running a business would need to operate in some gray areas, but no one asked a virtual stranger to fly to another country for business. Much as she needed this job, Marika wanted no part in it. "I'll cover for Mama-san so she can go."

Paul laughed heartily.

"I can do it," Marika said. "I did the books at a dentistry practice for years. I'm very capable."

"That's why I'm asking you. I know this probably sounds strange, but it's completely, *completely* legitimate."

"Why don't *you* go?"

"We need a woman. Come on, Marika, I'll pay your way, and pay you well for your time. Fifty thousand yen. And you'll also get your salary while you're gone. It's just real-estate documents. To be considered legal here, they have to be stamped. It's pretty simple. Think you can manage that? Take our principal's name chop, ink the chop up, stamp her name in red, bring the docs back? The other party is American, so they won't understand how things are done here. They have to witness a woman sign and stamp her name."

What he said could be true. If there was a woman who had to stamp her chop on a document to seal some sort of agreement and the woman couldn't go for some reason and they wanted a woman to carry the chop just so things wouldn't get complicated on the American end . . . Americans wouldn't understand, but it was done all the time in Japan. It was why name chops were registered and so carefully guarded. When she and Isamu had bought the house, his mother had also had to sign on as guarantor. His mother hadn't gone in person, just entrusted her chop to Isamu, who'd stamped all the documents on her behalf. And fifty thousand yen was nearly a month's rent.

Mama-san ambled back into the room, a dark amber drink in her hand. "Is she going?"

"She's fighting me on it."

"Marika-chan! I asked you to be a good girl. Please help us out. We're like a family here."

The money was so tempting. But every instinct warned her this would end badly. Marika thought of a tactful way out. "When do you want me to go?"

"Tomorrow, if you can."

"Oh, I have a lawyer's appointment; I'm getting divorced."

"I thought you weren't married," Paul said.

"*Ne!*" Mama-san looked suddenly alert, curious, even happy. Marika regretted telling them.

"Why do you want *me* to go?"

"Well, heaven's sake, girl. Don't you want to? It's Hawaii!" Mama-san said.

"I'd love to, of course, but with this lawyer . . . It took so long to get an appointment with her."

"Her? There aren't any women lawyers," Mama-san said.

"I found one in Shin-Okubo."

"Look, we need to get these documents filed by the end of the fiscal year," Paul said. "That's five days away. Tell you what. You do this and I'll also pay your first lawyer bill. How's that for a deal, Marika-chan?"

"It sounds pretty good," Marika admitted. She really wanted to start paying her brother back.

"Of course, you'll go," Mama-san said. "You'll love it. So

just go to Paul's office tomorrow and he'll take you to the airport. Six o'clock should give you plenty of time. You're really helping us out," she said. "That will be all."

"Hai." Marika did not know what else to say. She hadn't said yes, but that seemed not to matter. The strange thing was, she couldn't tell if she was being bullied or she'd just had the most incredible stroke of good luck. Still, Marika felt queasy. She didn't trust Mama-san or Paul. She already had to look for a new second job. Or maybe it was just time to go back to Inudani. Admit defeat. Buy a present for Isamu's mother. Yoku Mokus—she loved those—the big tin. Marika already had a reputation for being flighty, which would make a return easier. She would be slightly disgraced by working in a bar, which would give Mother something to lord over her. And Isamu had his good points. He'd taught her a lot: sarcasm, castration. What more could a girl want?

26

THE RACCOON DOG

Conner stepped out of the taxi at the corner of Aoyama and Hitotsugi, within sight of Atsuko's bar, spending fifteen hundred precious yen because the trains had stopped running.

Unwilling to shell out for cheap coffee and a seat, Conner leaned against an outside wall of Mister Donuts where he could watch the stairway up from Kiku. It felt strange that Paul, almost a complete stranger, was going to pay him the equivalent of seven or eight thousand dollars when Conner had less than fifty to his name.

The dark streets were nearly empty. He had expected a long wait—some bars didn't close till the trains started running—but Atsuko came out at a quarter to two. She flagged a cab. When the automatic cab door swung shut, Conner flagged one down himself.

"Follow that cab," he said to the driver, hoping Atsuko wasn't going far.

"Eh?" The driver appeared startled when he turned and saw Conner's face.

"Just start driving and I'll explain."

The driver started rolling while Conner explained what he wanted. The driver stopped. Conner repeated what he wanted. Atsuko's cab was getting away. Conner could still see it, but if it turned, the cab would just be another of thousands of identical yellow post-midnight taxis. The driver acted like he was willfully trying not to understand and Conner knew exactly what was going on: The guy hadn't looked closely enough at the dark-haired man flagging him down and once he realized Conner was foreign? Personality change. It could happen at a ticket window or store counter where a clerk would openly try to fob Conner off onto coworkers, before he'd said or done anything. It could come with an unabashed lecture on the superiority of the Japanese people to, well, everyone. They've tested infants, one language-school owner had told him, and Asian babies are already smarter than white and black babies at six months of age. It's genetic, she'd said. The openness of the assumption of superiority had at first shocked him, then provoked him to think how similar attitudes, though largely unspoken, also seeped through every aspect of life in the US, where people who looked like Conner were the majority. Being unable to hide and being forced to hide were very different experiences, but both were exhausting if you let them get into your head. He'd come to shrug off such treatment as just another thing to live with. But he didn't have time for it now.

"Do it or I'm getting out." Customers were pretty thin on the ground; taxis less so.

The driver relented, maybe bullied by Conner's tone. "Okay," the driver said, perhaps warming to the idea that having a foreigner in his car wouldn't pollute it excessively. "Sure." He began to follow the other yellow taxi. In a movie this would be easier. In real life, it was very difficult. If it hadn't been so late at night, with so few cars on the road, it would have been impossible. The fare on the meter began to rise, already past five hundred. Conner's stomach rumbled and he wondered if Katie had left any food at the mansion. He couldn't survive on beer and whisky.

Atsuko's cab headed west, toward Shinjuku, and then south under the Koshu Expressway into an area he was not familiar with. The meter hit one thousand. Her cab stopped beside a twelve-foot, paunchy raccoon-dog statue, indicating a traditional Japanese restaurant. This one looked especially jovial and cartoony, all semblance of the real-life creature edited away. Even the large testicles resting on the ground— supposed to bring wealth or luck—seemed more like a furry purse than a sex organ. Atsuko got out.

"Go to the next corner," Conner said. "Slowly."

Atsuko paid her driver and went up the stairs.

Conner's driver said nothing, but followed Conner's instructions. They reached the next corner. "Is here good?"

"This is great." Conner paid the driver and walked back toward Atsuko's building, a newish, tan-tiled concrete structure five stories high. The building was entirely dark and quiet. Which apartment was hers? None of the mailboxes had first names, but a few had two surnames. One for Atsuko, one for the roommate? Her lover, probably. He could catch the guy alone tomorrow. A boyfriend. He frowned. He thought of the policemen, Hideo, Rob, Paul. He had such trouble reading straight guys, which was probably why he knew so few of them. He considered whether the taxi driver might have thought him a stalker, but if so he'd nonetheless given him a ride. Conner was going to stick with his gut reaction. If you suspected someone was anti-foreigner (or homophobic), they almost always were.

Conner walked up the stairs and went down the first walkway, listening for signs of life. Nothing. The steel doors and tiny windows were designed to shelter the apartments from street noise. The life of the building's residents—laundry, toys, potted plants—all that would be at the rear of the building.

Which was where Conner should be.

He ran down the stairs and around back just in time to see a light go off. Third floor, third apartment from the right. He went back to the mailboxes. There were five apartments on each floor. He counted over the bank of steel mailboxes: five for the first floor, five for the second, then three more. The box had two surnames. Bingo. Finally, he was getting somewhere. Tomorrow he'd find a way to get the roommate alone. He would have plenty of time before his briefing with Shiomi-san. Tomorrow, he'd find Katie.

27

ELEPHANTS

Marika lay stiff on her futon, alone for the first night in years. A car drove by on Kannana Road. She could hear from the spraying sound of the tires that the rain had stopped. She'd been lying awake in bed long enough for a healthy rain to pummel the city, ease off, and start to dry. She looked at the luminescent green hands of the clock sitting on the tabletop of the kotatsu, borrowed like the futon, like the TV, from Eriko.

Four-thirty.

Marika turned the clock away. She focused on a triangle of amber light suspended in the tall bottle of Hennessy beside the clock. Ai had handed the cognac to Marika at the door when she left Stardust The Moon. No wonder Mama-san was losing money. The triangle shimmered. Marika should be asleep. Drinking cognac wouldn't help; she'd drunk too much already at the club with Ai and Shin-chan.

Marika tried to clear her mind. Thinking about not being able to sleep, about needing sleep, would only keep her awake. She hoped for another car to drive by, noise to distract her.

It was still.

She'd found it easier to sleep at Eriko's. Maybe Marika had been able to hear Eriko and Yuuske and Chieko on some level she wasn't aware of. Maybe their breathing kept the air moving and she had felt that movement, even under the covers in the living room. Elephants, she had read, could hear very low vibrations beyond the range of the human ear. They could communicate in low rumbles across sixty miles of African plains. Sixty miles. They were never alone. Marika couldn't hear anyone in her new building. The walls were concrete, the air stale.

Another car drove by. She turned the clock back toward her. Only ten minutes had passed. Now that she had a room to herself, she missed Isamu. Or rather she missed the low rumbles of his body, any body, just to hear it, feel it be alive, to know someone else was alive and not have to wait till the sun came up to see another human being.

She thought of the elephants again. Two elephants. Two elephants sixty miles apart, rumbling across the grassy savanna. She thought of the young American who'd been with Paul that first night. She trusted him more than she trusted Paul. Anyone who would buy a volume of poetry from that pitiable girl—let alone read it and remember it—must be trustworthy. Was that instinct lonely desperation, or an inborn reaching for connection?

Marika nudged the leg of the kotatsu with her toe and watched the triangle of light shimmer in the Hennessy, like tight Mylar, purple and green. She sat up, poured herself a centimeter of the cognac and turned the TV on with the sound down low. She sipped the brown liquor and watched the small black-and-white screen. The only thing on any of the thirteen channels was a sleazy pseudo-documentary about making pornos that managed to show quite a few breasts. She half-expected to see someone she knew in it. Someone unlikely. Rei-chan, perhaps. Or Betchaku-san, with his voice-overs done by Ai. Aan, aaaan. That was probably just how he sounded.

With her tongue Marika caught rivulets of cognac descending from her last sip. She watched the TV. No rumbles reached her over the broadcast waves of the TV signal, only a desperation that was the opposite of lonely: a desire to be left alone. Marika wanted to be alone. She'd wanted to be alone for some time now. She was happy to be alone. And yet. For the first time she wondered if maybe she couldn't do it.

28

THE DISMISSAL

Conner woke to the buzz of the alarm clock Katie had abandoned. It was Saturday. Rob had gotten in even later than Conner last night.

"Jeez, what time is it?" Rob moaned.

Conner breathed deeply and opened his eyes. "Eight fifty-nine." He felt clear-headed and eager, though physically drained. His foot had survived the forty-five-minute walk home from Atsuko's, during which he'd had time to get a plan in order. He'd track down Katie through Atsuko's roommate, then he'd do this job for Paul. Once his financial problems were settled, if Arata was willing to leave his wife, Conner would stay in Japan. If not, Conner would leave. In the morning light, he realized that would once again leave every-thing up to Arata. Since Conner had promised himself to act smarter, he revised his plan: he'd leave Japan unless Arata convinced him otherwise. Which meant probably he'd be leaving. Was he ready for that? He thought of the previous night's casually foreigner-averse taxi driver. Not a big deal, at all, and yet somehow, it was enough. It was one of many not-a-big-deals. People who didn't want to rent to him, hire him, sit next to him, talk to him, look at him. He was ready to go.

Carmen wasn't eating breakfast when Conner arrived downstairs, but everybody else seemed to be, mostly short-termers trying to make sure they looked like travelers, not tourists. Two German guys in their early twenties were picking at a soupy rice concoction, leather passport pouches hanging from their necks. The elfin, bearded professor was buttering a piece of toast and reading the *Japan Times*. He nodded at Conner. The Swiss woman with the braids was talking to Hideo about ink painting. Hideo was telling her how he harbored a dream of returning to his home island to farm, paint and speak his own language. So this was what it was like to be up in the morning.

Conner found some food labeled "Katie," devoured it and washed up his dishes.

The Swiss woman came up to Conner and tapped him on the shoulder. "Hideo-san wants to see you," she said.

"About what?"

The Swiss woman shrugged.

Hideo was in his corner room doing accounts. His door was open. Conner knelt at the open doorway, putting him level with Hideo's desk. "Hideo-san, you wanted to see me?"

Hideo motioned Conner to come in and finished the item he was entering into his books.

He looked up at Conner without friendliness. He'd heard Katie complain about Hideo being harsh, and he'd seen Hideo be tough, but he'd felt the people Hideo was harsh to generally deserved it. To see that steeliness now turned against him felt humbling. Hideo looked disappointed. Conner remembered Edward's disappointment at Conner's smuggling run to Baja. He'd sloughed it off then, but now he cringed. Why did disappointing Hideo bother him when disappointing Edward hadn't?

"Conner," he said, "this is not going to work."

Conner stared at the black cloth border of the tatami and considered the little aqua speckles in it. What function did they serve? They were so small you would never notice them unless you sought them out. Maybe they were a defect. An attractive defect, to prove not all defects were bad.

"What do you mean?" Conner's heart pounded in his ears.

"Katie was here," Hideo-san said.

"Oh my god, when? When was she here?"

"Yesterday afternoon."

"But I was here then." Actually, now that he remembered it, he'd been around the corner at the payphone in front of the liquor store touching base with hostels and cheap hotels where Katie might be staying. Their payphone took a phone card, whereas Hideo's ancient phone required an endless succession of copper ten-yen coins.

"Do you know where she went?"

"Sorryyy." He dragged it out, presumably to make himself sound more regretful, but he did not sound sincere.

Conner felt like biting off his thumb. "Didn't she say anything?"

"She apologized for not paying earlier. She even gave me a tip."

That was a bad sign. "Did she have a lot of money?"

"Um!" he said affirmatively. "And I know why. She told me."

Conner gulped. "What did she say?"

"She said, 'I stole hash that Conner smuggled in and now I've sold it and I'm moving to Hokkaido.'"

Conner swallowed again. How could she possibly have sold the hash? She might find friends of friends to peddle it to, a joint here and there, but not the whole kilo. "Damn!" Conner said. "Damn!"

"Is it true?" Hideo asked him.

"I'm not going to lie to you."

Hideo looked down at his account ledgers and erased a figure. He didn't look up.

Conner said nothing. There were those damn aqua specks in the tatami again. Not all attractive defects were good.

"You have to leave the Maison, Conner."

"Hideo-san, I'm not going to do it again. It was just one time."

He looked up at Conner, round pupils mirrored in his round glasses. "There's no such thing as *just one time.*"

Conner said nothing. Hideo was right. Conner had smuggled in Baja. And he was planning a smuggling trip to Hawaii later today. But he had to see this through. Could Katie really have sold it all? Conner felt like banging his head against a wall.

"You're paid up till the end of the month. I should just kick you out now, but I'll let you stay that long because I think you are a good person making a bad mistake. Maybe people haven't expected much from you, so you have acted to their expectations. I think you believe you are stupid, but you are far from it. You are intelligent. It is your responsibility to act like it. I know what it's like to want a place where you can belong, but for you, the Maison is not going to be that place."

Conner's gut turned over. "There's always a last time for everything," he said, but Hideo looked down at his books. All it needed was a "dismissed, private" to complete the picture. Apparently, this was a last time. "Okay," Conner said. "Just tell me how much?"

"You're paid up," he said.

"No, I mean how much did Katie sell it for? I just want to know."

"She didn't say. She just said, 'Tell Conner I sold it all.' She seemed happy about it. She's not a nice person."

"Those were her words? 'Tell Conner I sold it all?'"

Hideo nodded.

Conner smiled. He would bet anything that Katie was lying to get at him. "I'll be out of here sooner, if I can. And I am sorry."

Hideo said nothing. Conner got up and closed the door behind him. He left for Shinjuku. He had to track down Atsuko's roommate before meeting Paul in Akasaka. And he had no money for next month's rent anyway.

29

THE HUSBAND

Marika awoke at ten that morning with a splitting headache. Was her new life any improvement on Sunday mornings after gambling in Roppongi with Isamu? She lit a cigarette and clutched her head. Yes, this was better. Falling asleep alone might be hard, but waking up alone was not. She'd lost one job and had doubts about the other, but she had her own apartment, with a month's rent paid. She hated not knowing more about Hawaii, but going would let her keep the job until she got a few more things straightened out. And Paul would pay her first lawyer bill. Life was good.

Marika had in fact looked up lawyers in the phone book at Eriko's and the woman in Shin-Okubo did exist. Marika had just not worked up the nerve to call her.

Isamu. She had known him for a decade. At ten-thirty on a Saturday he would be at the dental office. As would Puffy. She might never see Puffy again. It would be unfair to keep her cooped up in the apartment all day, but if she could just have Puffy she'd let everything else go. Could she really throw away a marriage, and all the work that had already gone into it? She needed to be sure. She needed to see Isamu.

Marika showered and dressed.

She remembered the last time she'd seen him, Isamu asking her to apologize to his mother in the steamy bathroom. She had felt so humiliated. She wanted to see him, but not alone. She punched out Rei-chan's number on the phone.

"Oh hi, Marika," Rei-chan said. "Betchaku-san apologized. Can you believe it? He wants you to come back."

"Oh, don't worry about that. I don't want to go back. I called for a different reason."

"Sure, what?" Rei-chan asked.

"Well, I'm taking the train down to my ex-husband's today to get some things ..."

"I'll drive you," Rei-chan said quickly.

"Really? I called to see if you would keep me company, but if you have a car, I could get some small furniture."

"I'll be right over."

"You're a life saver."

"I can't wait to see what you've done with the apartment." Rei-chan hung up.

Marika looked at the futon, the TV, the open suitcase on the tatami, the almost half-empty bottle of cognac on Eriko's milk-splattered kotatsu. In the kitchen was a frypan and an aluminum saucepan she'd bought yesterday to boil water for tea and cooking chopsticks for instant ramen. What a showplace.

She picked up the phone and punched out Isamu's number.

The phone picked up on the third ring. "Hello?" It was his mother.

Marika's first impulse was to hang up. She did not want to talk to the woman.

"Hello?" his mother said again.

Marika realized she was holding her breath. "Hello," she said. "Is Isamu there, please?"

Now it was his mother's turn to pause. Marika heard nothing, not even the sound of someone putting down a phone.

"He happens to be here, but . . ."

The woman obviously wanted her to identify herself. She knew it was Marika. How tempting it was to just tell the woman that everything was her fault and make her feel it. And how pointless. She was not the cause of Marika and Isamu's problems. "Please tell him he has a phone call."

Now she heard the handset being placed on a hard surface. Marika's fingertips played over the Formica surface of Eriko's old kotatsu, scratching off spots of dried milk on the tabletop. Other people's dirt was always worse than one's own. In the background she heard them talking. His mother sounded angry, though Marika could make out no words.

"Marika?" Isamu said. "Thank you for calling."

"I'm coming down to Inudani today, to get some things if that's okay. You haven't changed the locks, have you?"

"That's great! Of course I haven't changed the locks. But anyway, I'll be here."

"Will your mother be there?"

"I can send her away," he said.

"That will let us talk," Marika said.

"She'll be gone. When will you be here?"

"In about two-and-a-half hours."

"I'll be waiting," he said. "You know I will."

THEY ARRIVED TWO HOURS LATE. Rei-chan had gotten lost on her way to Marika's and then traffic had been dreadful. As summer got closer, more and more Tokyo residents would stream down onto the long beaches east of Inudani. Isamu was standing just inside the yard with several irregular stacks of boxes. Either he'd decided he wanted her to go, or had become smarter and decided to give her some line to run with. A *lot* smarter. Rei-chan pulled into the driveway in her tiny red Honda Boxy, rolling over the gravel to a stop at the driveway gate. Marika wondered what Isamu had chosen to pack.

"Where have you been?" Isamu yelled.

How typical, Marika thought. They were late through no fault of their own and he didn't even bother to ask why. "How nice you packed everything," she said, thinking that he would surely have packed the wrong things. "That's a hopeful sign." She smiled, though it felt false. They were already back to their usual pattern.

He said nothing, but his face was agitated as he looked from Marika to Rei-chan and back. Evidently, he'd expected her to come alone and this didn't fit his plans. She couldn't help but think to herself, what a jerk. She wouldn't need to see him a second time.

Marika got out of the car as Rei-chan pulled the parking brake and unlocked the hatch. Marika moved toward Isamu. He scowled. Marika turned and picked up a box.

"I wonder what's inside," she said.

"Aren't you going to look?"

"So we can argue about it?"

He shifted his weight to his left foot and then back to his right. "Well, what if I did pack the wrong things?"

"Did you pack my clothes?" She put the second box in the car and Rei-chan put a third in beside it.

"Some."

"The toaster? You never use the toaster."

"It's in there."

"Nice. This is my friend Rei-chan. Rei-chan, this is my husband Isamu."

"Pleased to meet you." Rei-chan glanced quickly at Isamu, as though embarrassed to really look at him. She picked up a box. He bowed at her. She skittered off with uncharacteristic shyness. Despite all those customer contacts, Rei-chan was shy, Marika realized. It suddenly made sense that she worked with Betchaku, someone even shyer.

"Will you help us load them?" Marika asked.

"No," he said.

"Can I see Puffy?"

"You have to go inside."

It felt like an order, and Marika knew she wouldn't do it, even to see the cat, who on so many days, purring in her lap, had been her only true friend in the world. She picked up another box and Rei-chan picked up the last. There was room for the small dresser. She needed it, but didn't want to go in. If she had to see Isamu again, they could meet at Chateau Parfum. She would replace anything missing from what he'd packed. "You're sure the toaster's in here?"

He nodded.

"Well, that's it then."

"You're not going to come in to see Puffy?"

"I don't think I should."

"Please? Just come in for a while. She misses you."

"She's a cat, Isamu. She'll forget me." Marika got in the car and closed the door. Puffy surely did miss her; animals were not without feelings. Rei-chan walked around to the driver's side and got in. Rei-chan started the engine.

Isamu stood next to the car. "What'll it hurt to come inside for a minute?"

In better times, if perhaps she had been going off on a ski trip with a friend and he couldn't get away to come with her, he would have leaned over to kiss her goodbye, in front of anybody. Even his mother. That was his good side. Not every Japanese husband would do that, and as she looked up at him, she realized she was afraid. That's why she wanted Rei-chan to come with her: she was afraid that alone, he could convince her to stay. Not force her, convince her. Was she that unsure of herself? If he could convince her, maybe she had reason to stay.

She turned to Rei-chan and whispered, "I'll just be a minute." Marika opened the door and stepped onto the gravel driveway. Isamu smiled as he almost hopped up the path, turning back to see if she was still following, like Orfeo Negro in a movie by the same name they had seen together long ago. He opened the door and held it for her. Marika crossed the threshold.

Dropping her shoes in the entryway, she stepped up onto the floor and squatted. "Puffy," she called, "Puffy." A hand touched her back and she turned quickly.

"She was just here a minute ago, really," Isamu said, standing behind her.

Marika got up and walked toward the kitchen, where the cat's food was. Isamu followed her. She shook the cat food box and waited, but Puffy didn't appear. She looked into the tatami room they kept in the front of the house. The sun was streaming in, warming the straw surfaces of the mat into perfect catnap territory, but the room was empty save for the two of them. Marika waited for him to say something, but he didn't. She sat down on the mat. There was a lovely flower arrangement on a low platform in the *tokonoma* alcove; quite striking, she thought. It showed his mother's touch. The old woman was accomplished. Even Marika genuinely admired the grace of her arrangements and her skill with color.

"If you want to spend a year up there, doing whatever it is

you have to do, I don't mind," he said. "Just tell me that you'll come back."

Marika ran her hand over the edge of the mat, where Puffy had been slowly shredding the straw in an expanding square over the past few months, despite Marika's best attempts to stop her. It had grown since she'd left. She thought she heard Isamu's teeth grind.

"I don't know." She looked at the door, as though the cat would come rescue her. He's offering me a year, she thought. How long would it take to see the vastness of the earth? It made sense to say yes. Whatever she expected to happen to her when she left him had not happened yet, not when she moved in with Eriko, not when she got her jobs, not when she got her apartment. What was the change she was waiting for? She had expected to see it clearly. She looked up at him, waiting for him to move, to say something, to betray with some slight gesture why it was impossible for her to stay.

He crouched down beside her.

"Did I tell you I have dreams of Puffy?" she asked him. "I call her and she dances around my feet."

He shook his head, looking down. He was hiding his eyes. It was time to go.

"Well, Puffy must be outside somewhere. You know how that cat is. Dogs are so much friendlier. I should dream of the Akitas." She stood up. "Where's the small dresser? I could really use it."

He grabbed her hand and held her down.

"Let go," she said.

"You haven't answered me."

"I'll think about it."

"How hard can it be? Just say yes or no!"

"Okay, no."

"Why not?"

She jerked her hand away from him and headed for the entry. There were plenty of reasons why not—because if she promised she'd come back she would not commit herself to a new life, because if she were ever going to come back she needed the freedom of not having to make that decision—but she wasn't about to share that with him, not now that he'd grabbed her. She stopped and turned to the bedroom. There was in fact something she really needed, though she hadn't thought of it till now.

She slid open the closet door. Most of her clothes were still here. She began flipping through the hangers, grabbing only for the most colorful, shiny, slinky, garish clothing. Gold, red, silver, and a black rayon gown that made Isamu nervous because it showed her cleavage.

"What do you want those for?"

"Because I want them." She closed the closet door and strode to the front door.

Isamu huffed. "Why don't you say yes?" He came after her. "Why not?"

"Because you pull my hand, because the cat's not here, because what if a year goes by and nothing changes? Then do I have to come back?" She slipped on her shoes. She pushed open the front door and ran to the car. Rei-chan started the engine.

"Is it Yuuske? Are you seeing him? Is that it? I know you were there."

"Let's go, Rei-chan."

Rei-chan shifted into reverse. Isamu put his foot behind the tire. "My foot's under the tire. Tell me where you're living."

"Let's go, Rei-chan. It's a gravel drive. His toes will survive a Boxy."

Rei-chan looked over her shoulder and backed up.

"Shit!" Isamu yelled out. He hopped up and down and hit

the side of the little car with his hand. "I'll find out, Marika. I'll find out!"

Not while my eyes are black, Marika thought.

Rei-chan shifted into drive and stepped on the gas.

WHEN THEY UNLOADED the boxes at Marika's apartment, Rei-chan offered to help her unpack, but Marika declined the offer. She wanted to unpack alone, so she claimed she was hungry and took Rei-chan out to a late lunch to thank her. They talked until Rei-chan had to go to Realism.

Marika waved goodbye as Rei-chan pulled away from the curb, then began walking back to her apartment. Ahead of her, walking in the crowd, was a familiar head of hair: a little over-long, and fluffy. Was it Betchaku? What was he doing here? Marika followed the man, trying to get closer. He was heading for the station. She pushed against the crowd, which flowed from the station toward the little department store on the way to her apartment. If he would only turn his head so she could see his face or his profile.

She pushed forward. She thought she was gaining on him, but he was short, and hard to follow in the crowd. The man turned a corner, but his face was blocked by a blue-and-white *sake* banner. Marika rounded the corner. He was gone.

She went to the station, but there was no sign of him. If he had been following her it would explain how he'd known immediately when she'd got her apartment; she'd only assumed Rei-chan had told him. But neither Marika nor Rei-chan was working, and Betchaku wouldn't leave Realism in the hands of a new employee. He certainly wouldn't close shop. He probably checked his bank balance every night, fondling the name chops he used to stamp withdrawal slips for tax-free Post Office savings accounts kept under fictitious names.

Marika walked back home and climbed the stairs up to her fourth-floor apartment. It was Isamu's threat to find her that was making her so skittish. He probably *could* find her. But when he did, she'd move. Losing the key money wouldn't stop her. She'd leave town if she had to. She unlocked her apartment door.

She began opening boxes to see what Isamu had decided to give her. The toaster. Her photo albums. A selection of clothing, a snatch of fur—not Puffy, but the collar of a winter coat that soon she would not need. His selection was sensible. One box held her shoes, one her cosmetics. But there was no underwear. Oh, no, that was here, too. He'd thought of everything. There was even a tea kettle, and a frying pan. It was a demonstration that he knew intimately what she needed to live. He had taken great care, perhaps thinking he was obligating her to reciprocate, someday, somehow. There was nothing missing.

Marika put the photo albums on the kotatsu, found a pair of scissors in a box and removed all the photos of Isamu, cutting him out of the ones she wanted to keep. She tossed all the little Isamus in the trash. Now something was missing. As it should be. The obligation dissolved back into her fading past life. Isamu was over.

It was late afternoon. Marika poured herself a quarter glass of Hennessy and drank it as she packed for Hawaii. She felt her good mood slipping away, a cloud of cheer floating down the stairs and into the street to be pulled away in whisps by the crowd of commuters. There was so much to be done in her apartment; she didn't want to do any of it.

When it was time, she put on a bright outfit and went down to the station, retrieving stray threads of good cheer from the crowd as she neared the platform. It was good to be out. It was good to be in the world. The next train was coming in seven minutes. She looked up and down the tracks. Nothing. Across from her on the other platform was a familiar short man with glasses and overlong, fluffy hair. Betchaku. And he was watching her. He waved and smiled, not even trying to hide. The train pulled up. Marika got on and squeezed her eyes shut, trying to damp down the anger seething inside her. The train pulled out of the station and headed into Shinjuku. Beneath her anger, fear was surging. She was flying to Hawaii that evening, but he knew where she lived. Sooner or later, she'd have to return.

30

THE FRENEMY

At ten minutes to four, Conner was seated on a stone bench by a concrete-lined creek from which he watched the door to Atsuko's apartment, nervously checking his watch. He hadn't expected finding Katie would require so much patient waiting. Flowering plum trees bordered the waterway on either side, branches reaching out over the trickle of water. Shiny new skyscrapers stood just visible beyond the roofs of nearby apartment buildings. For hours he'd watched falling petals litter the pathway, the concrete embankments, the black flow of clear water over dark algae.

When Conner had first arrived in Tokyo, scenes like this had appealed to him greatly. Like Los Angeles, Tokyo could be charming on a clear day when its parks, rivers and surrounding mountains stood out, or a drab mass when its vast spread of barely distinguishable buildings was viewed through a smoggy gray haze. From the ground, however, small scenes of old Japan and glittering evidence of new Japan meant surprises around every corner. People had been very friendly to him in his early days. He had found work and enjoyed going out to drinking places to spend his hard-earned money, eating all manner of grilled "*yaki*" food—*yaki-tori, yaki-soba, robata-yaki, tako-yaki, okonomi-yaki*—all the while practicing his Japanese with the many strangers who were more than happy to trade words with him, which he sponged up with glee, trying them in new combinations to see if he could use them correctly.

After a year, and especially after the magical two-year mark, when he could really speak the language, things began to feel different. The first few foreign friends he'd made had by and large gone home, and people started to view him with more suspicion. He didn't have a career. He didn't have a job with a real company. He wasn't married to a Japanese woman. He didn't even date. Why, they seemed to wonder, was he still here?

He'd had his reasons for leaving L.A.: He'd wanted to get away from the obliviousness of his parents, the horror of high school. He'd wanted to get away from the memory of Toby's ghoulish straight family swooping in and taking everything, even Edward's stuff, after Toby died. He had wanted to forget that everyone was going to die. In these last five years he hadn't exactly forgotten that, but he didn't dwell on it anymore. It was ironic. If he was put in the same situation again today, he thought he'd be a much better friend to Toby and Edward, not the scared weenie of a twenty-year-old he was then. He still had his problems, like his blind spot for Arata, but in five years, he knew he had grown up some.

Finally, Atsuko's door opened and she came down the staircase, her face made up with peach lipstick, thick black eyeliner and peacock-blue eyeshadow that looked like it belonged on a sarcophagus. She walked down the street toward the highway and Nakano-Sakanoue Station.

Conner gave it five minutes, walked up to the third floor and knocked on the third door.

"Who is it?" a woman's voice called out.

A woman? "Is Atsuko there?" He smoothed back his hair and stood at the door. He heard the loose chain rattle as the door opened.

The woman stood on the edge of the genkan, leaning forward over it so she could open the door without having to step down barefoot. Her permed hair was tucked behind her ears. Like Atsuko, she was made up, but her bluish-white eyeshadow was applied sparingly. Conner's first thought was hostess, though at a classier club; the less money customers had, the more make-up they got.

"Atsuko's left."

"Maybe you can help me."

"I'm just on my way out."

"It's really important."

She was still leaning forward, holding the steel door open. He put his hand on the door to take some of the weight off.

"It's about Katie."

"Katie?" She frowned.

"I'm trying to find her. To get something from her."

She looked Conner over. He hoped his appearance would help him: He was freshly showered, shaved and dressed to go to Hawaii. His cut was no longer inflamed. His suit fit. He looked as good as he could.

She let go of the door and straightened up. "Talk to me as I get ready."

He slipped off his shoes and went in.

She sat down at a small vanity with a bright spotlight and three mirror panels, rubbed a bit of glitter on the crest of her cheekbones and examined the effect in the mirror. It sparkled as she moved her face side to side under the light. She removed it. Conner watched her eyes move. She didn't so much as glance at him.

She turned off the light, faced Conner and stood up. She took off her blouse and searched the closet for another. Her breasts were fairly large, but she wasn't putting on a display for him. She just didn't seem to think much about being seen in a bra. She reminded him of Rob that way. She pulled out a sheer red blouse. "What do you think?"

"Nice, but it doesn't go with the lipstick."

She put it back and pulled out another, putting it on without asking his opinion.

"I think the police are after Katie," he said.

"Atsuko's the one you should talk to. I hardly know Katie." Her voice was even and calm, as though she were a clerk taking a train reservation, waiting for him to select a seat.

"Actually, Atsuko won't talk to me. See, Katie owes me some money. I have to get it in the next few days."

The woman laughed.

"Is Katie really going to Hokkaido?"

She looked shocked. "What would *Katie* do in *Hokkaido*?"

"Deflower farm boys after English class?"

She laughed again, and nodded. She tucked in her blouse and fluffed out her hair.

"Do you know where she is?"

"No, I don't." She walked to the entry and stepped into the genkan, putting on scruffy black pumps. "She owes you a lot of money?"

"Actually, she has something of mine. I have to get it back."

"What, a camera or something?"

"Something like that."

She looked him over, suspicious. He realized he'd changed his story. Lying was such an effort. "I'm running late," she said.

Conner stepped out of the apartment and she closed the door. He walked with her toward the subway. She clearly knew Atsuko well, calling her Atsuko, not Atsuko-san, not At-chan. They dressed together, were both hostesses, shared a bedroom by the look of it. Conner thought of Ai-chan from Stardust The Moon.

"Are you and Atsuko lovers?"

The woman stopped short at the subway entrance. "Yes."

Conner nodded. "Of course."

"Katie stole this thing from you, didn't she?"

"Yeah. She stole it."

"Atsuko's very protective. Did you sleep with Katie?"

"Yeah," he said, "but I'm gay." He didn't want to get into the complexities of "possibly bisexual."

"Figured."

"Am I that obvious?"

She shook her head. "I'm hopeless at spotting homos. But I know who you are. Conner, right? I'm Kayo. I hope you get your money," she said. "Katie's a bitch."

Conner pulled out a thousand-yen note. He flagged down a taxi. "Take a cab," he said. The cab stopped a few feet ahead of them. Kayo walked toward it.

"Are you sure you don't know where Katie is?"

Kayo laughed and got in the cab. "Not unless you have a whole lot more than this." She waved the bill as she looked up at Conner.

He pulled out a second thousand-yen note, thinking he'd have to walk everywhere if Paul didn't come through. And wondering how he'd eat.

She laughed and shook her head, curly hair bouncing. "Keep it. Call me when you have more." She gave Conner her phone number. "And thanks for the ride, even though a thousand isn't enough to get to Ginza." The cab drove off, taking his best lead so far with it, but Conner smiled. She knew Katie. She knew where she was. And in two days, he'd have all the money he needed to get her to tell.

31

THE MARK

Marika opened the door of Paul's ninth-floor office. "Marika. Good. You're on time." Paul pointed at a reception area. "Have a seat."

A fax machine beeped in the office behind her and Paul disappeared into the office. He returned with a single sheet of white fax paper with a pink stripe down the side. He stood by the table, reading. He was quite a bit taller than Conner, bigger and somewhat darker, though not a lot. Marika wasn't sure if he was black or white. Maybe he was both. She wondered how he'd respond if she asked him. She'd heard that Americans were touchy about that kind of question.

Paul looked at his watch and at the door.

Marika looked inquiringly at him.

He twitched his lips in a quick smile and cleared his throat. He looked like a magician about to perform a trick.

"What kind of papers do I pick up?" she asked.

"A sale contract. Title documents. Before you ask any questions, hang on." Paul picked up the phone and made a phone call. He spoke rapidly in English and then handed the phone to her.

"What?" she said.

"Just take it."

She took the phone. It was probably going to be kidnappers promising not to hurt her mother if Marika would only turn over the plans to the doomsday device.

"Hello?"

It was the woman whose seal she was to stamp. Her name sounded familiar, but Marika couldn't place it. The woman explained how she just didn't have time to get to Hawaii because she had multiple public functions she was obliged to attend, but would Marika please do her this tremendous favor? The woman said she couldn't do a proper signature in English anyway, so whatever Marika signed would be fine. Marika laughed and said she understood: her own signature was childlike in English, devoid of personality. Exactly, said the woman; it was the name chop that mattered. The woman promised she'd be in Tokyo later that week and they would have a delightful lunch together. She was sure Marika would help because Paul had told her what a sweet girl she was. Oh, and please take very good care of her name chop. Whatever you do, don't lose it. She thanked Marika.

"She speaks so elegantly," Marika said. "Is she famous?"

"In a manner of speaking." Paul handed her the fax. "Your itinerary."

She looked at the typing on the page. English. Being required to understand English made her nervous—she'd ignored the language after high school—but this was largely place names, exceedingly familiar ones. Honolulu, Tokyo-Narita. Paul pointed at the first line.

"A Mr. Zakabi will meet you at the airport at 8:15 a.m. and take you to a condominium—the one we're selling, in fact. There you will change into something more . . . sedate. We need you to look like the owner."

"I probably won't fit into her clothes," Marika pointed out.

"Yes, you will." Paul smiled. "Is this all making more sense now?"

"Do I look like her too?"

"You're pretty damn close, considering. You have the same face shape, which is what matters most. We were lucky you finally walked in the door."

"Will I be fired after I make this trip?"

"No, no. Shiomi-san needed someone new for the bar anyway, and you're shaping up fine." He pointed at the second item. "At 1:30 you are meeting Herbert Sauvala and Maxine Marcus at the Halekulani Lounge. They will present you with some documents. You and Mr. Sauvala will sign them and Zakabi-san will take the signed documents. Pretend you don't speak English."

"I don't."

"Of course not." He let out a contented sigh. "This is coming together after all." He looked Marika up and down. "You're going to have to look older. Shiomi-san says you're a whiz with makeup. There are pictures of our client at the condo. After the meeting, Zakabi-san will take you to the airport and put you on the four o'clock flight back to Narita, where I will meet you."

"The same day?"

"Right."

Marika looked at the times and dates on the sheet, wondering how she could make herself look older with make-up. "I'm going to Hawaii for only six and a half hours!"

"Yes, that's right.

"I packed a bag."

"It will be good cover when you come through customs." Paul looked at his watch. "He should be here by now."

"Who?"

"Conner, of course." Paul smirked.

32

GO BACK TO BULGARIA

Conner stood in the quiet lobby of Stardust The Moon as Shin-chan left to get Shiomi-san. Several newspapers lay behind the podium, including a copy of the *Japan Times* that had an account of Rugged Matt's arrest. Conner stumbled his way through the words, which was easier in the moment of unexpected solitude. The police said Matt was likely to spend nine years in jail, which in Japan meant that's precisely what he'd do. Conner imagined Matt's gracefully shaped head shorn clean of that lush brown hair and felt sorry for the dumb handsome lug.

Shin-chan returned, all smiles, and showed Conner to the bar, where Ai-chan was snacking on a small tuna and squid pizza that looked incredibly good. She waved to Conner as he approached and pulled out a stool for him. Conner sat down gratefully.

"I'm Ai, remember?" She had a friendly glide to her voice. She poured Conner a beer a little too fast.

"I remember." Conner sucked at the bitter foam off the top, but some spilled over.

Ai shoved the pizza toward him. "Are you becoming an employee too?"

Conner gleefully took a piece of pizza. "Considering it." The squid was tender, the melted cheddar sharp. His stomach growled in appreciation.

"No, you're not," she said. "You've already decided." She leaned forward laughing, her white teeth flashing for a second before she covered them with her hand. "Uh-oh."

Conner looked over his shoulder. Shiomi-san stood, arms crossed, at the far end of the room. She saw Conner turn, and she forced a smile.

Ai topped off his glass with the last of the beer and took another slice of pizza, one with a big chunk of tuna on the edge ready to drop to the floor. "Drink up," she said. "Back to work for both of us."

Shiomi-san brusquely motioned to Conner. He followed her into the back room, past the paying customers, right-wing party staffers by the sound of them.

Shiomi-san grunted as she sat down. "Can I really rely on you?"

"Yes." Conner felt oddly confident, maybe because he wasn't in jail, Matt was.

Shiomi-san nodded and seemed to relax as she went over the specifics of Conner's run—his contact, where he'd pick up his package, dangers to look out for. "This is business. It's Hawaii, and that's always nice, but it's a five-hour flight there, you're only on the ground for a few hours, and then you're back on the plane. You'll be exhausted when you land in Narita."

Conner nodded. He wasn't looking for fun. "One question. Why is Marika coming? I don't need cover."

"She has her own task," Shiomi-san said. "A big client is getting rid of an apartment building she has there and

Monday's the deadline for the conditional *hakko shosho* and the credit form *soegaki*. You know what those are?"

She could hardly expect Conner to recognize words he likely didn't even know in English—it all sounded like blah blah blah—but he recognized they were the sort of financial words popping up everywhere since the stock market meltdown, often with an undercurrent of muffled hysteria. "I understand *deadline*."

Shiomi-san's eyes bored into him. "Well, we need that before we can blah blah blah collateral blah blah blah to get the blah blah transfer tax into this fiscal year."

OK, she was putting him in his place. If that made her feel better, fine. He'd lived through worse.

She smiled. "Marika doesn't speak English, so you are going to escort her. Two birds, one stone. Now go. He's waiting at his office."

She left.

Conner was suddenly sitting alone at a lacquered table in the back room of a very expensive club. Ai opened the door, covering her face with her hand. She peeked at him between the top of her hand and her bangs. The effect was cute enough to use on TV. "Is it all decided?"

He nodded.

"Hawaii?" she asked.

Normally, he wouldn't consider telling her, but since she already knew ...

"Everybody gets to go to Hawaii except me," she said.

"They do a lot of real estate there, I guess."

"Real estate?" She looked Conner up and down, as though his IQ were encoded somewhere in his clothing. "Stocks were supposed to be a sure thing. Now they say real estate, but if you ask me, it's all a con. But what do I know? As I said, they never let me go." She gathered up the glasses. "Is there something about me I don't know?"

"Not that I can see."

She dropped the whisky decanter on the tray with a bang. She leaned toward him, putting her face in his. "You want some advice?"

"I don't think so."

She clasped Conner's hand, then put her other hand around it.

"Go back to America. Run."

33

THE TRUCE

Marika was glad to see the yellow-purple bruising in Conner's face had faded. He looked much more appealing in a suit and tie than he had in the casual clothes he'd worn at Stardust The Moon. He wasn't surprised to see her, so he had obviously been told more about this operation than she had, which irked her. He said hello to her, then he and Paul started chattering in what she presumed was English; they talked so fast it could have been Swahili for all she knew.

Paul turned back to her. "I assume you remember each other," he said in his heavy accent.

She nodded. Conner said, "Yes." She wondered what his part in all this was.

Paul looked at the blue digits of the clock in the VCR. "It's time. I'll drop you off at the Tokyo City Air Terminal. It's safer to check in and transit customs there because they hand-carry their records to Narita at the end of the day."

They walked down to the taxi in silence. Conner sat in the front seat, but she could see his eyes in the vanity mirror, glancing back at her. Her concealer ought to work on his remaining bruising; their skin tones were close enough. Paul dropped them off in front of TCAT, handed Conner two tickets bundled with a brown money envelope, confirmed they had their passports and left.

"I'm supposed to guide you." Conner picked up her bag. He had a little black one, smaller than hers.

"I can carry it," she said, but he kept it. She narrowed her eyes but followed him into the terminal and waited with him in line to check in. He pushed her bag forward with his foot— annoying, since it was a Tumi—and handed the tickets and passports to the slick-haired man at the counter.

"You've done this before?" Marika said.

"Not for Paul, but . . ."

"I guess Paul doesn't trust me," she said.

"As much as he does me. But you don't speak English."

"Doesn't mean I can't carry a bag."

The clerk gave them back their passports with two boarding passes. "Have a nice trip," he said in English

"Thank you," Marika said, also in English, grabbing the passports. After yesterday's encounters with Isamu and Betchaku, she did not want to be guided.

Conner seemed ready to ask for the passports back, but instead pulled out the envelope Paul had given him, divided the stack of money inside into two equal bundles and gave her one. It was her fifty thousand yen, in advance. "In case we get separated or something."

"He gave you all that?"

"We're not supposed to need it. It's for emergencies. You don't actually need a guide, do you?"

She shook her head.

"Good," he said. "I have another job, anyway. May I have my passport back now? Not having it makes me nervous."

She nodded and handed him his passport and boarding pass.

"Thank you," he said, with the tiniest bit of a smile.

"So, what *is* your job here?" she asked.

He stopped smiling and disappeared into thought for a moment. "I hate to sound like Paul, but I think we shouldn't talk about that." His voice rose at the end of the sentence, as though he were asking a question.

She figured this secret task had something to do with him and Paul both being Americans. Did he think she would report to Shiomi-san?

"You haven't done this before?" he asked.

She shook her head.

"We should get acquainted. We need to trust each other."

She pointed to a couple of plastic chairs in the lounge. He tilted his head in agreement.

They talked about the poetry girl. Marika told Conner about getting fired from Realism, omitting mention of Betchaku's box of photos. He told her how he'd left Los Angeles because neither parent had room for him—Marika figured this was a lie of convenience—and he needed a place to stay, which he'd found at a foreigners' hostel not far from where she lived. She started to laugh, but realized it wasn't a joke. He was living off savings at the moment, he said, but would probably have to start teaching English again soon, even though he hated it. She agreed that teaching sounded stressful—all those eyes on you —but said she'd probably end up teaching too. They laughed. The bus arrived and they got on. She told him about Isamu, Isamu's mother, how she'd left Inudani and was just getting started on her own. He said she was brave and said he thought she was doing the right thing, that if you had to run away, you should never consider going back.

It felt good to hear someone else agree with her. Even Rei-chan, who had certainly helped her a great deal, didn't really understand. Conner, she realized, was the first. She asked him why. He hesitated. Then he told her about a Canadian woman he'd been seeing, sleeping with, he actually said, and how she'd dumped him. He talked about how he had known from the start it wasn't the right thing for him but he'd done it anyway because he wanted it to be the right thing. And then in the end, she'd left him anyway. She was responsible for the cut and bruising on his face, and other bruises she couldn't see.

Marika was glad the woman wasn't Japanese, because she didn't like foreign men who had a thing for Japanese women. There was something about a desire that specific that made you feel dirty, but she didn't tell him that; it was too personal. What she told him was that he should have had his cut stitched, but it looked like he'd get away without a significant scar.

They talked throughout the seventy-minute bus ride up to Narita and on and on at the airport lounge as they waited to board, so that when they at last sat down in their seats and the plane took off, she felt she knew him pretty well. Her previous feeling had been correct: anyone who would buy a book from the poetry girl was trustworthy.

They slept soundly, side by side in their seats, and just after dawn Marika woke to see the first Hawaiian island come into view, bright green vegetation plunging over red cliffs toward the blue sea, with whitecaps marking a stark line at the shore. It looked so much brighter than Japan. She nudged Conner. "We're here."

"That's nice," he mumbled sleepily. It was three-something a.m., Japan time.

"No, you should look. It's beautiful."

She leaned back so he could see out the window. He leaned over her to peer at the cliffs. His cheek was crisscrossed with little white lines where he'd been sleeping against the seat, and stubble was beginning to darken his cheeks and chin. His nose was straight and sharp, his eyes an indeterminate shade she couldn't name. His eyebrows were full and black, his eyelashes dark and long, like a girl's. Hers needed mascara to look like that. His Adam's apple moved up and down as he looked at the sea. He was swallowing. What was it like for him returning to his country? His hand fluffed out the straight black hair cresting over his brow. The plane began descending.

"Are you nervous?" he asked.

She nodded. "What if I do it wrong somehow? I've never even been outside of Japan, except once to Saipan. I don't speak English very well."

"So, you do speak some?"

"This is a pen," she said in English, reverting to the phrase everyone started with in Japan. "It's been a long time," she said, reverting to Japanese.

"It sounds like you won't have to say anything. And I'll be there."

She grabbed his arm. "Thanks." Now she appreciated having a guide. She breathed deeply.

He looked in her eyes. "What's wrong?"

"It's just that I'll be glad when I settle into my place, when I can just have a normal life that's dependable. I can't wait to have a week where I go to work for five days in a row and do laundry on the weekend. I can't wait to get back home and sleep in my own bed." She yawned. Sleeping on the plane was not restful.

He yawned too. "That does sound nice. Weird, but nice."

"Gee, thanks."

Outside the window, the tarmac was rushing up toward the plane. Marika knew Paul and Mama-san were lying to her about something. Despite Ai's warning, the pair hadn't seemed competent enough to be sinister, but with the first bump of touchdown she realized she had launched into the unknown without a parachute. And she'd barely noticed jumping. The plane bumped down again and the engines howled. It was a little late for her to be getting scared now.

34

THE RETURN

Conner's heart began to grind as the plane bounced on the runway. He hadn't realized that America frightened him, but it did. He'd hated being there before, absolutely hated it; he just hadn't admitted it to himself. The plane's tires squealed. Growing up, every day had been a challenge, and then he was out on his own in a world filled with strangers among whom he had to navigate. And when those strangers turned into friends, they died.

The engines roared as they slowed the plane down, shifting the passengers forward in their seats. Conner's valves and ventricles spasmed against each other like a netful of dying fish, yet underneath the terror he sensed a new emotion: a desire to stay. He'd done a lot in the years he'd been gone. His fear and anxiety might be outdated. What would it be like to not need a visa, to work legally? To be able to speak his own language. Maybe it hadn't been America he hated; maybe it had just been the process of growing up.

So, what if he *didn't* go back to Japan? In America, he could meet new people without having to explain himself; he could sit on a bus without having the little old lady next to him move away. OK, that might also happen in L.A., but after years living in Tokyo, it, too, had turned hard on him. Now that he wasn't a stranger there, it mattered more what he did. The desire to stay in the US grew, as though he'd been on his feet waiting tables in hard-soled shoes all day and now a chair was in sight. He could leave Katie, Hideo, Arata, all of them. He had nothing to go back to, really, and every reason to leave.

Marika turned away from the little window. "We're here," she said. She looked excited.

Oh, God. She trusted him now. And he felt the need to live up to that. Fool, fool, he thought. Whether about her or himself he wasn't entirely sure.

Please don't trust me, he thought. Never trust anyone unless they've already come through for you. That had been his motto since Edward. But maybe his motto was backwards. Maybe it was that people you trusted came through. He leaned against his seatback and sighed. He would go back to Tokyo because he had told Paul he would. Oddly enough, Conner's word was good. The promises he didn't keep were to himself. The *never-agains* always gave way to the *this-time-it-will-be-differents*.

"I think we'll be okay," she said.

"I'm sure we will."

35

THE HENCHMEN

Warm air thick with moisture flooded the jetway as Marika walked up toward the terminal with Conner. Marika saw a thin Japanese-looking man in a red and green flower-print shirt nod at them as they cleared customs and immigration. The shirt sagged over his slender shoulders and his glasses were too large. He hesitated a minute, as though unsure whether to rank the Japanese person higher or the man, but then bowed to Marika and said in Japanese, "I'm Zakabi."

Marika bowed back. "I'm Shirayama," she said. "Please treat us well."

Conner also bowed and said, "I'm called Conner," in overly polite Japanese.

Zakabi turned to Conner. "I have a driver waiting for us," he said, to Conner now. "Please come this way."

Marika could tell by the way Conner's shoulders jerked that he hadn't welcomed Zakabi's shift in attention, but she was relieved to relinquish responsibility for a situation she did not understand.

Zakabi spoke to the hulking driver of their sleek, beetle-green

Corolla and they zipped by palm trees, red and orange hibiscus, and dark green, cloud-topped mountains that reminded Marika of a steeper Okinawa. Already the landscape seemed more exotic and larger-scale than Saipan. The Corolla rolled through downtown and beyond to an elegant complex of white beachfront buildings with red tile roofs that looked like they cost a fortune. The driver hoisted Marika and Conner's small bags from the trunk and carried them to a building smack on the beach.

Zakabi removed his shoes and held the door open, eyeing them somewhat warily, as though not confident in Paul and Mama-san's judgment.

"After you."

Marika went through, shucking off her shoes, and Conner did the same behind her. Inside, the air was cool. The white marble floor of the entry ended with two steps down to a large, semi-circular living room, carpeted in a snow-white wool Berber. Marika imagined weekly visits by an expensive professional cleaner. Excitement welled in Marika as she slipped into the luxurious space, ready to assume this other woman's wealth, status and belonging, feeling born to the life.

Zakabi stepped down into the living room as his muscular helper put their bags beside the nearest of three knobby white couches that faced the curtained windows.

"You will find clothes in the bedroom," he said to Marika. "Remember, you're forty-five. Take a few hours to sleep, but leave everything neat. This unit has been sold fully furnished. Be fresh and ready at one." He nodded once and left with his helper.

Marika stepped down into the living room. The carpet was as soft and cushiony as it looked. A wide archway opened onto a glossy, immaculate kitchen. Conner loosened his tie and hung up his suit jacket carefully in the entry closet. He opened the curtains, and Marika saw that the semi-circular wall was composed of floor-to-ceiling windows looking onto a dense private garden.

"Come look." He opened a sliding glass door and stepped into the garden.

Marika heard waves. She stood at the door, stifled a yawn and leaned into the garden. It wasn't large, sandwiched into the twenty feet between the glass and a weathered wooden fence, but it was meticulously cared for. Long, waxy green stems sported unknown spiky blossoms of orange, red and white that towered over soft, small-leafed cushions of green. The manicured shapes and sizes bore evidence of the controlling principles of Ikenobo flower arrangement—dominating central *tai* axis opposed by space-defining axes to the left and right. A gentle mix of perfumes hung in the air. Isamu's mother would approve. There were even sets of garden slippers by the stoop.

"Wow." Conner had found a door in the fence.

Marika stepped into slippers and went to look. She ran her hand down the moist surface of a flat green leaf, warm to the touch. The door opened onto a white sandy beach and the choppy blue of ocean. A light wind took the mugginess from the air. If this were her house, she'd tear down that fence first thing. Conner took off his socks and slippers and rolled his pant legs up around his calves. He stepped out onto the beach. She stepped out next to him. He was a little shorter than Isamu, but put together in a very different way that intrigued her. My God, she should sleep with him. They were in Hawaii, no one would ever know, and she could do a lot worse. The situation was tailor-made, a way to demolish her old life, delivered for her convenience.

"Let's go for a walk," he said.

She kicked off her slippers. "A short one. We don't have much time."

They walked slowly over the warm white sand of the deserted beach. It wouldn't replace the cooler, grayer Inudani beach in her affections—taking the Akitas there for exercise had been her escape from her mother-in-law's mastery of controlling principles—but it was gorgeous. Here, bracketing rocky outcroppings on either end of the beach seemed to open up the ocean, not enclose it, a bit of the earth's vastness also delivered up for her. Weight lifted off her shoulders. He felt the same, she could see; his breathing had deepened, slowed.

They walked over the sand to the closer ridge of stone. She yawned. She had barely slept on the overnight flight. Her giddiness faded. This had been a lovely moment, but she was drunk from lack of sleep. Wow, she'd been ready to have sex with a stranger. Zakabi was right; they should rest. She told him she was going back for a nap.

He returned with her to the condominium and closed the garden gate behind them. He fiddled with a clock radio beside the bed, hung up his dress shirt and pants and curled up under the covers of the king-sized bed, falling quickly asleep. She lay down on the other half of the bed and soon fell asleep herself.

When she awoke, she sensed his body heat through his undershirt. She kept her eyes closed. She did not know if he were awake or asleep. She tried to sleep a little longer, but his presence repeatedly drew her attention. What if I made a move, she thought. I want to, and I can. She was never going back to Isamu. The only thing stopping her was fear. Of what? How he would be when it was over? She'd proven she could launch into the unknown, but this was different. Her heart pounded.

She scooched over and nuzzled her head against his chin

and neck. She told herself they didn't have to go all the way. His warm deep breaths tickled her ears. Their cheeks touched, slid against each other. He was responding. Yes. Her breathing deepened. She ran a hand down his thigh, then back up, ruffling the hairs, enjoying being the forward one. His left hand began gliding over her back. Yes. Then his lips sought hers, and she opened her mouth when they touched. She was so aroused. Their arms wrapped tighter, pulling their bodies together, and then she was reaching between them to run her hand under his undershirt, feel his skin, his flesh. His hand slid up her thigh, under her rumpled dress.

A small noise drifted through her mouth as his two hands cupped her bottom and pulled her to him. He caught her eye.

"You really want to do this?" he asked.

"I am so sure," she said, "it would scare you if you could feel it."

She pushed his undershirt up as far as his shoulders allowed. She could feel firmness through his underwear. It made her wet. She pushed away from him and unzipped her dress. He thumbed aside the strap of her bra and his lips sucked a freed nipple as she pulled the dress over her head. His hands raced over her sides, her thighs, her back. He moved his shoulders, first one then the other, so she could remove his shirt. She looked down at his bare chest.

He gave a flick of the eyebrows and a half smile, as though asking if she approved.

She smiled. Yes, you'll do, bruises and all.

They wiggled out of their underwear and locked together in a tight embrace. He was stiff against her belly, his thigh against her crotch. She rubbed it against him, slicking his leg. A cry escaped her. His hands stroked her arms, her breasts, down her stomach and then inched through her pubic hair to the edge of her labia, right on the very edge, but didn't touch her between, skirting around to her thighs.

She growled.

He laughed and planted his mouth on hers.

She pushed him onto his back and was about to pull him into her but he nudged her back down and moved his head downward. His tongue moved down her belly and beyond. This time he touched her, taking her between his lips, his gentle teeth, extending his tongue down her, into her. The air flowed deep into her lungs and she sighed. Finally, finally, she thought. It was so good to not hold back. It had been months. Bye-bye, Isamu. This was effortless. The problem hadn't been her; it had been them. Her back arched as his tongue worked over her. Then there was his finger, too, reaching into her. She looked down and saw this dark-haired man's pale back and shoulders, one arm climbing up her side to her breast. Now if he only had one more hand for the other breast. She wanted to see his body too. All while he kept doing everything he was doing. She ran her hands over his shoulders. She liked that he wasn't very muscled. "I want you inside me."

He looked up into her eyes. He didn't say anything. He reached over the side of the bed for something. She leaned toward him and took his erection briefly into her mouth as he stretched, searching, in front of her—not her favorite thing, but then again, maybe it depended on whose dick it was. He found what he was looking for, a condom.

Had he planned this? Well, good. She wanted to be desired. She opened the condom wrapper and unrolled it onto him. Then she lay back and pulled him onto her, wrapping her legs around his waist.

She gripped him tight and enjoyed the feel of opening to him, of him entering her. He was so different from Isamu. The angles of his movement were more alert to her, shifting as she shifted, the lead and follow of a dance. She'd thought all men would be somehow the same. She was surprised to find she missed a bit of Isamu's wide-eyed vulnerability—Conner was clearly enjoying himself, but seemed to be thinking, whereas Isamu lost himself in the experience—but she was enthralled with the conversation of her body and Conner's. They were in this together. She dug her fingers hard into his back as he thrust, letting the force of his stroke touch her within, first here, then there, then there. She was already close, so close. This would be fast. It was stronger and stronger and then it was there, intense, long. His breathing grew deeper in response to her moans, and he buried his head in her neck, thrusting harder, grunting low again and again until finally he too screamed.

Conner lay peacefully atop Marika. He felt more confused about himself than ever. If this hadn't happened right now, his experience with Katie would likely have kept him away from women forever. Marika was not like Katie—game but diffident—and not like Arata—fearful, controlling, selfish. Conner couldn't put his finger on the difference. Oh yeah, he had it: she was honest. He sighed, buzzing with relief. There they were, two honest criminals.

He lay in her arms. She ran her hands over his sides—still sore, still complaining—as he pressed her to his chest. This was so bizarre. The first time he'd successfully had sex with a woman, with Katie, he'd been surprised he enjoyed it. It had made him rethink who he was. He had thought perhaps it was just her, but now he knew that was not the case. Was life with a woman an option for him? He could feel the warmth of social approval rain down on him. Physical safety, job prospects, yay! To be part of the ninety-plus percent! To not have respected, upstanding public figures argue he should be beaten to death. Although those folks would still be wanting to murder *somebody*. He thought of Arata, how it had felt making love to him. There was a certain intense excitement from being with a man that wasn't really there with a woman. Could he live without that? When he was with a man, he never thought he needed a woman, but the reverse was not true at all. Or was that simply a reflection of the newness of it? And honestly, would he have made a move if she hadn't? And would he have responded to her move if he hadn't felt the need to keep trust alive by not rejecting her? Should he tell Marika all this? He chuckled. That would be like picking out a wedding dress after the first date. For all he knew, Marika never wanted to see him again.

There was a knock at the door.

Marika rolled out from under Conner and over the side of the bed onto the carpet, lunging for her clothes. She ran into the bathroom and shut the door. Conner slipped on his trousers and undershirt. He raced to the bedroom door and reached it just as it was opening. Conner stopped it with his body and peered around the edge.

Zakabi held the doorknob.

"What time is it?" Conner asked.

"Twelve. I was able to speed things up." Zakabi's Japanese assistant—tall, burly, thuggish—stood on the marbled entryway with hands in pockets.

"We'll be out in a minute," Conner said.

Zakabi stood at the bedroom door as though about to enter.

Conner stepped into the living room, chest to Zakabi's chest. "She's picking out an outfit."

Zakabi stepped back. His eyes narrowed, but he gave an accepting shrug of his thin shoulders, smirk buried in his eyes.

Conner returned to the bedroom and closed the door. He tried the bathroom door. It was locked. Conner explained the situation through the hollow-core door. Marika turned on the shower and replied with an affirmative grunt. Conner grunted back. Conner realized at some level he would never understand the Japanese language. There was so much indirectness and outright evasion that words seemed like an afterthought, as though your attitude toward the words was more important than their mere meaning.

Conner dressed again, properly, glad he'd hung up his dress shirt but wishing Marika wasn't hogging the shower. He felt sticky. He changed the sheets and made up the bed, snapping the bedspread tight, and had Zakabi point him to the laundry room, where he set the used sheets on to wash before returning to the bedroom. He heard water still running in the bathroom. He turned off the alarm clock, which had ten minutes to go before they were supposed to wake up. There would not be time for him to clean up. He shaved his airplane stubble at the sink in the wetbar, wiped the sink down, knotted his tie, and sat in an armchair to wait.

There was a knock on the door and Zakabi entered.

"Still doing her make-up," Conner said.

Zakabi rapped on the bathroom door. "Shirayama-san!"

"Done in a minute!" Marika yelled.

"We have to go."

Marika opened the door. "How's this?" She modeled a well-made but decidedly middle-aged dress, a dark plum-colored fabric gathered at the waist with short sleeves and a white lace collar. Her hair was done up in a bun at the back of her head. Had she darkened under her chin to make herself appear ever so slightly jowly?

"The dress hangs on you," Zakabi said.

"They're all like this."

Zakabi shook his head.

"I'll work on it," Marika said.

"Two minutes." Zakabi went back into the living room.

Conner shut the door. They were alone.

"Did he hear us?" she whispered to Conner.

"I think so. Sorry."

"We'll talk later. How can I make myself look fatter?"

"Pillows? Tissue paper?"

"A towel!" She took off the dress and wrapped a light-weight towel around her middle.

"Wait a minute." Conner riffled through the dresser drawers until he found it: a girdle.

"Excellent." Marika put it over the towel and tightened it and snuggled the dress over it. It looked bulgy, and the bulge stopped too low. She looked vaguely pregnant. She got a second towel, the thinnest material she could find, and wrapped that above the first. Now it looked bulgy in just the right way. Stockier, but still a nice figure. Marika looked through the drawers, inspecting belts. She stopped.

"What is it?" Conner asked.

"You'll never believe whose condominium this is." She was holding a dry-cleaning receipt.

"Whose?"

"Junnosuke Mehita. He's a cabinet minister. One of the minor ones. Transport? No, Construction," she said. "It's a really unusual name."

Conner looked. The name said 'Mrs.' before it and was written in Japanese, two characters he'd never seen followed by the ubiquitous *ta*. "There's a Ministry of Construction?"

"It's notorious for kickbacks. The whole construction industry operates mostly under the table, and the Ministry is the one doling out the big permits. Tanaka got his start as Minister of Construction."

"Well, put it back," Conner said.

Marika tucked the laundry slip inside a sweater and

selected a belt. She looked in the mirror. "This feels so illegal," she mumbled. She motioned him over to the bed.

"Sit."

He sat.

She applied some make-up to his cuts and bruises and smiled at the result. "Been wanting to do that for hours." She reached down to the table for a pen and scribbled a number on a sheet of note paper. "My information. In case something happens," she said. "Let's go, then."

Conner scribbled down the number at the hideous mansion, for lack of an alternative, and handed it to her. Marika picked up her bag, put the slip of paper in it, and went out into the living room, where Conner put on his coat and cinched up his tie. Showtime once again.

37

THIS IS A PEN

When they arrived at the Halekulani, Conner's role ended for the moment. Marika had Zakabi purchase a pair of big, round, half-shaded sunglasses at the gift shop. Combined with the subtle shading under her jawline, she looked like a bulldog with a mostly successful jowl tuck. Zakabi handed Marika a passport, name chop and red ink pad, which Conner watched her place in her purse. She went with Zakabi into the restaurant, leaving Conner to wait in the bar. Zakabi's thug/driver was stashed against a restaurant wall to wait menacingly. Through the tinted plate-glass windows opposite, Conner could see neatly trimmed palm trees and lawn. He ordered a beer and a pupu platter—*damn* was it nice to have money—and copped a stool from which he could keep an eye on the action.

Before long, a man and a woman, both white and middle-aged, approached the table and were introduced to Marika. She stood and shook their large hands stiffly with drooping fingers, which was such an inappropriate politeness it seemed perfect. Marika was good at this.

The two strangers sat down. One ordered while the other

opened a briefcase and pulled out a fat manila envelope, which he passed to Zakabi, who opened it and put its contents in front of Marika. She retrieved the name chop and ink pad and began stamping and signing, as instructed, page after page and then a second copy. Zakabi handed the copies to the woman, who checked them, copied information from the Japanese passport Marika handed her, embossed seals onto both sets, and tucked one copy into the man's briefcase. She returned the other copy to Zakabi and the passport to Marika. The transaction seemed to be over. The waiter came with their meals. The strangers chatted directly with Marika, seemingly in Japanese. The woman's eyes crinkled with laughter.

Conner sipped at his beer and devoured his pupu platter when it came. Empty chairs of maroon leatherette filled the bar. A smoky-glass door opened to the terrace and a gentle breeze cooled the room. Beyond the terrace Conner glimpsed waves breaking on Waikiki. Conner rotated his foot and marveled at the manageability of the pain. It was one o'clock, and everything seemed well.

Or not everything. At the railing over the beach, he saw a familiar reddish face. It was the bird-nosed man, the perhaps-detective from Giotto. Conner couldn't remember his name. Conner followed the man's gaze. He was watching Marika, Zakabi and friends. Watching Marika? The last thing she needed was for Bird-nose to connect her with him.

"Can you watch my drink?" he said to the bartender.

She nodded, and Conner went to buy his own disguise, a pair of reflective sunglasses that completely hid his eyes. He inspected himself in the gift shop's mirror. He was much more formally dressed than when he'd met Bird-nose at Arata's bar, but it wasn't much of a disguise. Conner was still twenty-five— a kid—and looked it. Luckily, since the aftermath of Katie's attack was healing, he had a revised facial shape and, thanks to Marika's make-up job, no cuts or bruises. Conner returned to his drink. The man was gone. A couple names came to mind, Kuwano and Shimoda. Bird-nose was Shimoda, the boss. Kuwano was the junior one with the Arata-like eyebrows.

The two Americans rose from Marika's table. Zakabi rose as well to shake hands. Marika herself then stood, clasping her hands before her as she bowed slightly, a typical educated, middle-aged Japanese woman. She was good at carrying a different set of body mannerisms. No wonder she'd gotten a job at a good club like Stardust The Moon.

The Americans passed the maître d's podium, then crossed the lobby. Shimoda stood near the entrance holding a map. The Americans walked within inches of him. Zakabi, his thug and Marika were coming back to the bar. Conner wasn't going to risk Shimoda seeing Marika with him. But there was no way that Shimoda had flown to Hawaii to catch a one-time small-fry like him, absolutely no way. The connection had to be Zakabi. And drugs. It had to be a lot of drugs to justify sending two cops abroad.

"You don't by any chance speak Japanese, do you?" he asked the bartender.

She laughed and shook her head. With her long blond hair, she looked something like Katie's good twin.

"Can I borrow a pen?" he asked.

She handed him a plastic hot-dog.

"No, a pen, to write with."

"This *is* a pen." She pointed. "Tip's down there."

He scribbled a note to Marika in his childlike Japanese handwriting. *Everything fine. Have tickets. If can't catch at condo, meet at gate 22.*

"Can you give this to the woman in the Imelda Marcos glasses when those three get to the bar?"

She looked toward the three Japanese walking toward them and took the napkin. "We aim to please."

"Thanks." Conner slipped out the back. He had to get Marika away from Zakabi so they could decide what to do. She, at least, was probably safe to fly home.

Unless Conner didn't show and they stuck her with the drugs.

Conner snuck through the shops on the other side of the lobby and stood near a rack of postcards where he could see the drive-up entrance. Zakabi's thug went off, presumably to get the car, while Marika and Zakabi stood waiting next to a taxi, staring at the central fountain. Marika wasn't holding the note, but since they hadn't searched for Conner at the bar, she had presumably gotten it.

Shimoda appeared near the entrance, too, standing right behind Marika and Zakabi. Oh shit, there was Shimoda's eyebrowed henchman, Kuwano. He looked Conner's way. Conner pulled up a big postcard and looked at it. Dear Dad: Up to no good in Hawaii. Your loving gay/possibly bisexual son, Floyd. Yes, Mr. and Mrs. Conner had named their son Floyd. And still they wondered why he'd left the country.

Kuwano looked the other way. Conner seemed to have escaped detection. The thug arrived with a car and Marika and Zakabi got in.

Shimoda and Kuwano got into the taxi and followed them. Conner ran out after them. He looked for a taxi to follow them. Nothing. This had worked last time he'd tried it.

"Can you call a cab?" Conner said to the doorman.

"Certainly, sir." The man picked up the phone at his station and talked. He held his hand to the mouthpiece. "Fifteen minutes?"

"Fifteen minutes!"

"Yes, sir."

"Can I rent a car here?" Thanks to Paul, he had enough money.

"There's a place two blocks down Kalapani."

Conner paced back and forth. Walking down there and doing the paperwork would take more than fifteen minutes. "Ask the cab to come," he said. "Please."

MARIKA WAS ALARMED that Conner had disappeared, but was not as alarmed as Zakabi seemed to be as the beetle-green Corolla sped down the oceanfront boulevard. As soon as the three arrived at the condo he was on the phone ranting and fuming in English. What bad thing did he think Conner was doing? Ai had told Marika that Mama-san needed constant watching. Did Paul think Mama-san needed watching, too? Marika decided he did, and Conner was somehow representing Paul's interests.

Zakabi nodded and abruptly smiled. He liked something he'd heard, and soon the three were back in the car, bags in trunk, driving. Marika didn't have time to change, so Mrs. Mehita would be short one dress, although the old-fashioned thing was unlikely to be one she'd miss.

They next stopped in front of a long, shoddily constructed building occupied by what looked like a variety of small offices. The thug opened Marika's door. "This way," he commanded.

It was getting old, this being ordered about, like a dog on a leash, but she grudgingly complied and soon found herself seated across a desk from a silver-haired, Japanese-looking woman, who checked the stack of documents and Mrs. Mehita's passport again.

"Will someone tell me what's going on?" Marika demanded.

Zakabi turned toward her with a patient look. "We're getting an apostille, which is . . ."

"International authentication. I know what it is. Doesn't the other party have to be here, and didn't the woman at the hotel already do that?"

"No, she was a notary. We need both."

Marika was pretty sure Zakabi was wrong about not needing the other party, but he seemed unlikely to make such a basic mistake. And the woman looked like a professional. She said something in English, which Zakabi did not translate for Marika. The woman compared Marika's face to Mrs. Mehita's passport and placed the thick stack of documents in a green and white envelope. She sealed the envelope and threaded a red ribbon through holes she punched in the sealed end. She handed the envelope to Marika, saying something to her.

Marika looked at Zakabi for a translation.

"Do *not* open it. The apostille is void if opened."

The woman had said much more than that, but Marika felt out of her depth. And if it was some move by Mama-san to counter some attempt by Paul to change the terms of the deal, what business of hers was it? She followed the others to the car. It was a hot day and asking questions hadn't gotten her anywhere so far. She thought of all those unpaid hours she'd worked for a husband who did not listen, all the times she'd had to hound Isamu about expenses to keep the practice afloat. Marika had never hated him more. And she was frustrated beyond measure at the cavalier treatment she got from Zakabi and Paul. And even Conner, disappearing on her with barely a word. That fifty thousand yen he'd given her felt like a tip. Marika was working for Paul and shouldn't have had to depend on charity from Conner. She thought of Rei-chan not complaining about getting paid less due to her looks, or Ai helping Marika with her eyelashes, despite Marika being a rival for an opportunity she wanted. Marika rolled down the window and let the tropical breeze come through, the last bit of her glorious Hawaiian vacation, feeling impotent and hating it.

CONNER LOITERED beside a bank of payphones near Gate 22, with the tickets and his passport. But no bag and no Marika. And no drugs.

A family of tourists wandered by, all in colorful short-sleeved shirts, the youngest girl with a white ginger-flower lei fragrant with nectar as she skipped by. He checked his watch. Where the hell were they? He called the only Mehita listed in the Honolulu phonebook, but got a voice with Japanese-American lilt that no one on Paul's crew had so he immediately hung up.

Conner blew out a deep breath. The cops were following Zakabi, not him, and not Marika. And she was disguised. Everything was manageable, except that Zakabi might give the drugs to Marika. If Shimoda and Kuwano got to her before Conner did, she'd go to jail in a foreign country for a very long time. She and Rugged Matt could be pen friends.

Conner's teeth began to grind. He should have separated from Marika when they landed. They didn't need to go back together. And he certainly hadn't needed to sleep with her. Assuming she could handle him saying no, definitely not a given. He wished that, way back when, he had never urged Arata to take the yakuza to court. If Arata had paid up, none of this would have happened.

And then there she was, walking toward him alongside Zakabi and his bag-toting goon, minus the towels but still in the same frumpy mauve get-up. And waving at him. Of all the lame moves. He trotted over to meet them, looking over his shoulder.

"I saw a narc I know from Tokyo in the hotel," he said to Zakabi, "so I didn't want to be seen with you." He spoke in English so Marika wouldn't know he'd agreed to smuggle drugs. The thought of drugs probably hadn't crossed her mind, so the shock would be profound. He couldn't chance her turning them all in. "Is the package in my bag?"

"A drug policeman?"

"He followed you from the hotel. He was in the taxi behind you. Didn't you spot him?"

Zakabi sucked in his breath. "What does he look like?"

"About my height, black hair—that's both of them. One has bushy eyebrows, fair skin, thirtyish, and a kind of worried look, crinkled brow and all; the other is older, has a big nose, is darker, redder, thinning hair . . ."

"Shimoda."

"Yeah, and Kuwano."

"How do you know them?" Zakabi said, brow furrowing.

"Something wrong?" Marika asked in Japanese.

Conner said nothing.

"How!" Zakabi asked again in English.

"I know them the same way you know them, let's put it that way. Where is the package? I need to know."

"Later. People are listening," Zakabi replied in English. He continued in Japanese. "You two wait in that lounge. Give me your passports and your tickets so I can check you in."

"You're the one they're looking for," Conner said in English.

"Fine. My man will do it. He's new," Zakabi said in Japanese.

Conner balked.

"Conner, do what he says," Marika said. "I want to get home." She gave Zakabi her passport. "And stop speaking English."

Conner got the tickets and his passport out of his chest pouch and gave them to Zakabi. "Don't get caught," he said, sticking to Japanese now. "And hurry. They're already boarding." Zakabi went to have his man check them in, handing the two their carry-ons. Conner and Marika went to a spot in the lounge where Conner could watch the line of boarding passengers. He quickly went through both bags. Nothing.

"What's going on?" she asked.

"Maybe nothing. Did they give you a package?"

She nodded, patting her oversized purse.

"Let me see."

"Not till you tell me what you and Zakabi were talking about."

"I have to see what's inside." Conner noted the long boarding line had begun to move.

"It's sealed."

"Who cares if it's sealed! Just give it to me."

"You sound like my husband."

"Look, I can't talk about it here," he whispered angrily, "but you're *not* carrying it on the plane."

"I don't take orders from you."

The first group of passengers had boarded and the next group of rows was called. Zakabi had left this later than Conner would have liked.

"Let's just dump the envelope, Marika. We have money. We can go to L.A. You can live with my sister. I'll help you find a job."

"What were you and Zakabi talking about?"

"You don't know how dangerous this is, Marika."

She gave him a look, like, how stupid do you think I am?

"Marika, look . . ."

She clutched her purse to her chest. "If Paul wanted changes to the contract, that should have happened before I signed them."

"Marika, please. This has nothing to do with the contracts."

"Don't talk to me, okay? Unless you're going to explain," she said. "Why can't you trust me, after what happened between us? Or is that somehow what this is about?"

Shimoda and Kuwano would be too hard to explain without telling her that he had smuggled hash. That would hardly win her trust. Conner tried to think of a way. Maybe he *should* just tell her everything. A policeman was strolling their way. Some possibly Japanese tourists were sitting within earshot. "Come over here," he whispered.

"If I open the envelope the dates on the papers are not good in court. You know what an apostille is?" she asked.

"Apostille. No." He stored the word away to ask someone later.

Zakabi came back and handed them the boarding passes and passports. Their seats were in a group that had already finished boarding. Zakabi stood between Conner and Marika, keeping a wary eye on Conner.

"Marika," Conner said. "Don't go."

Zakabi escorted Marika to the boarding line. She didn't look at Conner. She got in the tail end of the current group and was allowed on.

"Damn." Conner followed. What else could he do?

～

MARIKA WAS THRILLED to see numerous seats still empty and got permission from a Japanese-speaking flight attendant to change to one in the back sandwiched between two Japanese businessmen. Conner predictably followed her and tried to speak to her privately, but she pulled the call button. The flight attendant came, lectured him, and finally yelled at him to go back to his seat.

Conner returned to his row. Marika sat on the envelope and settled in, chatting with her seatmates, enjoying her lunch.

When she had to go to the bathroom, she stood and looked forward at Conner's row. He was holding a little mirror in the aisle, angled toward her. Was he thinking she'd leave the envelope behind when she had to use the toilet? Good luck with that. She waved at his mirror and gave him a big, fake smile before walking to the toilets, the large green-and-white envelope held above her head, red ribbons fluttering. The mirror did not reappear for the remainder of the flight.

38

THE COLLAR

I t was sunny descending into Narita this time. The yellow-green Chiba Peninsula coast gave way to dark forested spines cradling square brown rice fields dusted with remnants of snow. The fields were punctuated with stiff clumps of dried rice stalks, like hairbrushes with bristles too far apart. The 747 angled side to side as it adjusted its path to meet the runway, touched down, and parked on the tarmac. Conner got off well before Marika, boarding one of the shuttle buses to the terminal before she even came down the stairs.

Once inside he had the advantage. He walked up the stairs into the building and waited behind a partition everyone had to pass. After many minutes, Marika rounded the corner with the last of the passengers. Her purse looked noticeably looser and he decided the envelope was in her carry-on. He fell in unseen behind her and grabbed the handle of her bag. With one quick tug he had it.

"Say one word and the police will have us both," he whispered in her ear.

She turned around.

"Don't react. Wait near the bathrooms. I'll return your bag

and carry the envelope through. Meet you outside." He hurried ahead without looking back.

He headed into a bathroom and closed himself into a stall, thankful that the floor mounting of Japanese-style toilets made low-clearance doors ubiquitous. He pulled the envelope from Marika's bag and ripped it open. He looked inside and between sheaves of papers saw the plastic-wrapped square he had expected. It was the size of a small hardback book, shrink-wrapped in opaque black cellophane and reinforced on all four sides with silver duct tape. It was undoubtedly shrink-wrapped twice or more and washed in solvents between layers. It was roughly the same outline as the hash he'd smuggled, but double the thickness. What the hell was it? He bent it to get a feel for its contents. It made a sound like walking through snow. A powder. Probably cocaine or speed, maybe heroin. Please, not heroin, he thought, although from a practical standpoint it didn't really make any difference. Hash seemed somehow innocuous to him, a legitimate drug, like alcohol. Heroin or cocaine? Not so much. But could this really be enough to justify a trip to Hawaii for Shimoda and Kuwano?

He dropped the package in the rather large hole of the john, a sit-down model, and flushed. The packet bobbed stubbornly on the surface. He pushed it down and tried again. The black square floated gaily. Wishful thinking. The pipe was too small anyway. He could open it, but Shimoda and Kuwano would have dogs stationed to sniff out the least pinch of cocaine or heroin dust that got on him. This was getting nasty. Of course, he had never asked Paul what it was, had he? He'd just said yes. Wasn't that what Katie had said? If someone asks, you just say yes. Carry my drugs? Yes. Have sex with me? Yes. Or had he only hallucinated that after Katie kicked him in the head?

If he abandoned it, they would go looking for Marika when they found it, not him. He dried the package with paper towels, put it in his new chestpack and slipped the pack up under his tie. Damn it was bulky. His suit jacket bulged. He stuck the papers into his own bag, opened the stall door and strode out.

MARIKA LOITERED outside the bathroom Conner had entered, moving her bun up and down, letting the pins scratch her scalp. The *nerve* of Conner snatching her bag. Lending someone your name chop may not be the American custom, but clearly the woman Marika had talked to on the phone at Paul's was the wife of the Minister of Construction. But if Conner wanted to go into a panic, who was she to spoil his fun?

Conner exited through the far end of the barrier screen that hid the entrances to the men's and women's restrooms. His dark hair, hair she now knew was not actually black but very dark brown, was sticking up in back. He dropped her carry-on without looking at her. Marika fumed for a moment, then picked up her bag. He had said to follow. She'd follow.

She walked by him at Passport Control as she headed to the lines for Japanese nationals.

She dropped her bag and handed her red passport to the officer. He flipped through it, reading the reentry card stapled in her passport.

"Why were you in Hawaii for only six hours?" he asked.

There was no need to lie. "I was picking up contract documents for a condominium sale," she told him, "to get the sale recorded before the end of the fiscal year. I spent about fifteen minutes on the beach and was lucky to get that."

He nodded, ripped off the re-entry card, stamped the passport and handed it to her.

"Thank you," Marika said.

She picked up her bag and walked down the stairs to baggage claim. Conner was walking ahead of her casually. This pretense of being strangers was stupid, especially now that he had his precious envelope. She smoothed the mauve shoulders of the hideous one-piece and hurried toward him.

CONNER SAW Marika rushing toward him and panicked. He'd said to meet *outside* Customs. He hustled toward the inspection stations, trying to beat her through. Gone was the calm he'd achieved after clearing Passport Control, without even a question about why he'd gone to Hawaii and come back the same day.

Oh no. Waiting at the line of stations he saw Shimoda and Kuwano. Kuwano's eyebrows went up at the sight of Conner and he motioned to Shimoda.

Conner spun around and strode rapidly to the barrier outside the baggage-area bathrooms. He ran inside and dropped the chest pack and envelope into the trashcan between the men's and women's entrances. Would the detectives fall for it? Of course not. He left the bathroom anyway and walked toward Shimoda and Kuwano. They were running over toward him. He went straight to them.

"Good evening, gentlemen," he said.

Kuwano patted Conner's chest. "He dumped the package," he said to Shimoda

Shimoda raised his eyebrows. "You weren't in there long enough to flush it," he said.

"Flush what?" A meaningless subterfuge, but form was important.

"The stimulants."

That probably meant cocaine or speed, though Japanese use of the word was not very exacting. "What kind of stimulant?"

"Come on. We'll show you."

"Oh, good," Conner said.

Kuwano grabbed his arm and they led him into the bathroom.

"You're ours now," Shimoda said.

Conner managed a strangled, panicky laugh. "At last, I belong."

39

THAT HIDEOUS DRESS

Marika was about to call out to Conner when he turned and rounded the barrier screen for the baggage-claim restrooms. Marika went in the women's side, ready to follow Conner into the men's side if she had to, but when she rounded the corner, he wasn't there.

"Good evening, gentlemen," she heard Conner say on the other side of the barrier. He must have ducked back around. Who was he talking to? Marika stood still, holding her breath.

There was a patting sound and she heard a Japanese man's voice say, "He dumped the package."

Marika peered in the trashcan between the men's and women's doors. Conner's chest pack and the green and white envelope were both sitting on top of crumpled paper towels.

Another man said, "You weren't in there long enough to flush it."

"Flush what?" Conner said unconvincingly.

"The stimulants."

Drugs? Marika almost said it out loud. *That* was why Conner was acting so oddly? How had she not thought of that? The men were police. Marika grabbed the pouch and envelope and went into the women's bathroom. There was someone in one of the stalls but no one at the sinks. The envelope had been opened and was much lighter than before. She opened the pouch. Inside was a square package that appeared to be something sealed in many tight layers of black cellophane. She slipped it into the envelope. It fit perfectly. She pulled it out. She had never seen drugs in her life and now she was holding a good kilo of stimulants in her own hands. Conner had tried to get her to dump it and go to Los Angeles with him. Instead, she'd carried drugs into her country. Marika looked at herself in the mirror. She was looking at a criminal.

Marika could still hear the men outside. She entered a stall and closed the door. They were yelling at Conner. He was quiet though, for once. She couldn't make out what the policeman was saying. She had to flush the drugs.

She scratched at the wrapper. It was thick. She dug her fingernail into it. The plastic stretched but didn't tear. It was only a matter of time before they came in here. If she left the package, they'd find it. They might be right behind her—or right behind her imitation of Mrs. Mehita. If he just hadn't been so demanding, so like Isamu, she would probably have agreed to dump the envelope and go to Los Angeles. She would love to see L.A. But that tone of voice. What a small thing for their fates to hinge on.

The decision came quickly. He'd saved her; she'd return the favor. Marika slipped off the mauve dress and clipped Conner's pouch around her midsection. She opened her carry-on and pulled out her black pants. She slipped them on, pulled on her baggy white sweater and undid her hair, shaking it out over her shoulders. So, it had done some good to pack for a longer trip after all. She stuffed the dress in her bag. Holding herself straight, she walked out of the bathroom.

"Then where is it?" one of the men shouted at Conner. He was doubled over. "I saw a bulge under your shirt, and it's not there now!"

Marika walked by them without looking, shoulder tingling as though about to be grabbed.

"I don't know what you're talking about," Conner said behind her.

Then he cried out. One of the policemen had hit him. Marika was shocked. But with the drugs around her middle, she had to keep walking. Conner cried out again behind her but made no indication he'd seen her. She got in a short line at the farthest customs station. The customs man signaled her forward. She opened her carry-on. Marika looked back and saw the police taking Conner into the bathroom. The customs agent felt through her bag. Conner must have known about the drugs from the beginning. Why had he done it? He'd seemed so nice. The agent patted down Mrs. Mehita's crumpled mauve dress.

"Anything to declare?" he asked.

Was it too late to turn over the drugs? It was the right thing to do. "No," she replied. She clasped her hands together in front of her. She looked back. Conner was gone.

"A lot of times we can't touch them," the customs agent said.

"Who?"

"Gaijin with drugs. The military, children of diplomats. We can go public, but in the end a lot of them get away with murder. But, fortunately, not this guy."

Marika zipped her bag closed. She couldn't bear to look at the agent. "What will happen to him?"

"He'll confess."

"But after that?"

The customs agent shrugged his shoulders. "He'll go to jail for a very long time."

She would never see Conner again. The customs agent patted the sides of her bag as she longed for a cigarette. Marika zipped it closed, picked it up and walked through the automatic doors wanting a cup of hot oolong and a warm futon to curl up in with Puffy. A gauntlet of eyes scanned the trickle of arriving passengers.

"Shirayama-san!"

She recognized the voice. She looked through the crowd and saw Paul's freckled brown face. He was the only person she knew who had more freckles than she did. Paul reached out his hand to take her bag. She pulled the bag back. "I'm fine."

Paul looked at the doors expectantly.

"He's not coming," she said.

"He didn't . . . Did he stay in Hawaii?"

"He was arrested about a minute ago. Let's go."

"Arrested!" he whispered. "Where are the documents?"

"I have them. Let's go."

"Hmm." He looked at the arrivals door pensively.

"There's nothing we can do." She felt helplessness, anguish. "Is there?"

"You can always do something. Question is, what will it cost you?" He pulled down on his polyester tie, smoothing it. He glanced at Marika, his eyes moving reflexively over her body.

"You want the envelope?" she asked.

"We'll get out of here and then you tell me what happened." He pointed toward the parking lot. "I drove," he said. "This way."

They walked to a parking lot cupped within the semi-circle of the terminal building. He unlocked the left door, the passenger door, and she got in. The sides now seemed backwards, just as the American cars had seemed backwards a few hours earlier. Maybe she was really American, born to drive on the right. She put on the tacky sunglasses from Hawaii so he couldn't see her eyes. Paul closed his door and turned toward her.

"Where are the documents?"

"You still want them? Conner broke the seal."

"Of course I still want them." He held out his hand.

Zakabi had assured her breaking the seal would render the documents worthless, but evidently that wasn't the case. Had it been a ruse for her benefit?

Marika gave him the envelope. He looked in the envelope and pulled out the papers, examining them. That's right, my freckle buddy, no drugs, just papers, carefully arranged by Zakabi to hide a package of stimulants. Paul nodded, said "good," and put them back in the envelope.

He cleared his throat. "So why was Conner arrested?"

"I don't know," she said curtly.

"What happened? Tell me exactly."

"You got your contracts. What does it matter? Or is there something you're not telling me?"

He paused. "Conner was arrested, for God's sake."

"Can you do something for him?"

"No," Paul said.

Her heart sank, even though Conner was a drug smuggler. "Then what?"

"Look, you're working for me," Paul said.

He sounded just like Isamu, like Conner: always with the high-handed attitude, never willing to let her in on what was really happening. "I did my job," she said. "Didn't I? Aren't those the documents? Didn't I stamp and sign them like you asked?"

Paul snorted dismissively, but then was quiet.

"I'm scared," she said. "Is that all right with you?"

He snorted again. "Sure, fine. I have the documents." He was trying to sound calm, but Marika heard a tremble in his voice.

"The customs agent said something about drugs—there're going to be more gaijin in Japanese jails." She, of course, had no intention of giving the drugs to him.

Paul shivered. "Tell me exactly what you saw."

"He grabbed the envelope from me, opened it and headed for the bathroom. He dumped it. I got it back. Then the police got him."

"No shit. That son of a bitch." Paul started up the car and pulled onto the road. He muttered something in English and paid to enter the toll road to Tokyo. "Do you work tomorrow?" he asked.

"Huh?"

"At Stardust The Moon."

"Oh, that's right." She had forgotten she had a job. "No, Mama-san gave me tomorrow off."

"Wednesday will be fine. Mama-san will work out an arrangement with you."

Marika nodded. Money. Of course, Conner had already given her fifty thousand.

"I'm going as far as Akasaka," he said. "You can get the subway from there."

"That's better than nothing, I guess." Marika leaned against the door and stared at other cars and trucks pacing them on the highway. She'd have a glass of Hennessy before the oolong tea and sleep for a very long time. With no Puffy to cuddle, just a bundle of drugs.

40

HADAKA NA DENKYU, MABUSHIKUTE

Conner stumbled around the barrier screen as Shimoda shoved the small of his back. Conner glanced at the trashcan. His heart did a flip as he noticed Shimoda following his gaze. Kuwano started poring through the trash. And came up empty handed. What? thought Conner. Where's the package? Did he palm it? Did Japanese cops do that?

Kuwano stared up at him, his hands in the bin. He jerked his head toward the restroom. "Is it in there?"

Conner shrugged. Kuwano went into the restroom. Shimoda shoved Conner again. "All right, all right. Just tell me where you want me to go."

Shimoda shoved Conner hard in the back. "Shut up."

Conner let out a squeak.

Shimoda pushed his elbow between Conner's shoulder blades. "I said quiet."

Conner lost his balance and slipped to one knee. These guys were more fun when they were pretending to be insurance adjusters. Shimoda pulled Conner upright. They watched as Kuwano went through the restroom proper and came up empty-handed. Kuwano went back to searching the trashcan.

A trio of uniformed cops arrived. One spoke quietly to Shimoda.

"You're looking for something he could have strapped around his chest," Shimoda said. "Go over the women's room too in case he went in there. And don't come back without it."

"I didn't have anything," Conner said.

Shimoda drew his arm back.

"Don't," Conner said, covering his face.

Shimoda smiled and looked at Kuwano. Kuwano gave him a flick of the eyebrows undecipherable to Conner and they marched him into baggage claim. Conner sat in silence as they phoned someone from the airport station. The airport police cuffed him, took him to a windowless room with glossy metal paneling and stood him in a line of men, and two women, all presumably in some kind of trouble. The men seemed to be mainly Chinese, but it was hard to tell, since the officers quickly silenced any attempt to speak. They waited, standing, for a good hour, maybe two, with no explanation, as nothing happened beyond yelling at them to be silent. One by one the prisoners disappeared through the door. Finally, it was Conner's turn. Two officers manhandled him into a patrol car and drove him to a police station in the town of Narita. They led him into a small back room and sat him in a chair. Shimoda and Kuwano appeared.

"Do I get a phone call?"

"No," Kuwano said.

"We saw you pull that pouch from under your shirt," Shimoda said.

"Oh, that," he said. "That was just some . . ."

"Some what?" Kuwano leaned toward him. The guy really should trim the errant hairs of his brows. "Some what?"

"Uh, documents?"

"You're not sure?"

"It's confidential."

"Oh, confidential. It's confidential," Shimoda said to Kuwano. Shimoda held up his hands. "So sorry to pry."

Kuwano laughed.

"I want to talk to a lawyer."

"I'm a lawyer," Kuwano said. "You can talk to me. Confidentially." He leaned toward Conner again. "Eh?"

Conner said nothing. Kuwano looked up at Shimoda inquiringly. They had a quick nonverbal conversation of nods and facial twitches.

"Let him rest," Shimoda said. "He looks tired."

"Yeah, me too. Jet lag." Kuwano nodded to a nearby uniformed cop, who took Conner to a cell.

THE METAL CELL door rolled closed behind him and the guard took a seat on a chair outside. The cell was spotlessly clean, but there was no bed, just a stool and a porcelain commode. A single bare bulb mounted on the ceiling burned brightly.

Conner sat on the metal stool and leaned forward, elbows on knees.

"Comfy?" the guard asked.

"Very."

Conner tried to move the stool to the wall but it was bolted to the floor. He sat on the floor and leaned against the concrete wall. The floor was cold.

"Does that light turn off?" he asked.

"Yes."

"Will you turn it off?"

"It stays on."

"All night?"

The guard said nothing, perhaps reluctant to be the bearer of bad news.

Conner closed his eyes.

"Did they beat you up?"

Conner opened his eyes. "Who?"

"Shimoda-san and company."

"They just freshened me up."

"Seems like they did a good job. I can tell you now, you'll get more before you're through. They didn't find anything at the airport."

"Good."

"No, that's bad. Now they have to get you to confess. Japan has a ninety-five percent conviction rate after arrest."

"Have I been arrested?"

"I don't know."

"Oh." Conner closed his eyes and settled into the corner. He could see the bulb through his eyelids.

"You will talk, you know."

"I'm sure."

"You might as well. I mean, why not? Your sentence will be lighter."

"Uh huh," Conner mumbled.

There was a thunking noise. Conner opened his eyes. The guard had started thumping a stick over the bars of the empty cell next to Conner. He and the guard were alone. The bulb light seemed brighter. Conner closed his eyes and lay down on the floor. The concrete was hard and after the hours on the plane his ribs were sore and his neck was remembering where Katie had kicked it. The guard started whistling.

"Are you going to be here making that noise all night?" Conner asked.

"Just started my shift. It sure gets quiet and lonely late at night."

"Get a Walkman."

The guard laughed. "You're very funny. Keep me laughing and maybe I'll turn out the light."

Conner sat up and blinked his eyes open. "Okay." He tried to think of something funny. His mind drew a blank. He was very tired.

"It kind of reminds me of that song," the guard said. "You know the one?" He whistled a phrase and then sang, *"The naked bulb burned brightly."* He smiled. "Before your time."

Not to mention before his country, but Conner had in fact heard it. "With the red lantern and drinking sake."

"Yeah, the boy and girl. They break up in the end."

"Of course. It's a Japanese song."

"So sad."

"I guess." Conner thought of Marika. Shimoda and Kuwano hadn't mentioned her and Conner hoped she'd gotten through. If they checked his itinerary, they could easily find the name of the only woman who was on both flights, and they had seen her at the Halekulani, though dressed as the wife of the Minister of Construction, if that's who the mystery woman was. But why risk the sale of an expensive condo over a packet of drugs? Especially such a modest amount. And if it were speed, wouldn't it be simpler to get it from the yakuza? They manufactured plenty of it in Japan. Conner didn't understand. The contracts looked real, and the condo . . . They had actually stayed at it. It had to be legit. And that receipt. Marika had recognized the name. So, assume the woman really was the Minister's wife. Perhaps a politician's wife might not want to get drugs from the yakuza. Her husband wouldn't want to give gangsters leverage. It made sense.

"Did you think it was sad?" the guard asked.

"Are you going to talk all night?"

He laughed. "It's my job." He ran his club over the bars

again.

Conner pulled his shirt over his eyes and lay down. His bare middle recoiled from the cold concrete. "Great."

"You must have a girlfriend. A Japanese girlfriend?"

Conner pulled his shirt back down and stuck his face in the corner of the neatly painted cinder-block wall.

"Is she good in bed?"

Conner pretended to snore.

"My wife's terrific. Let me tell you about her. Are you asleep?"

Conner felt a rod prodding his ribs, riling a tender spot. "Stop that!"

"I'm telling you about my wife. I don't tell this to everyone."

Conner sat up and stared at him with his eyes closed. "Do tell. I'm fascinated."

WHEN MORNING CAME AROUND, Conner knew he hadn't gotten any real sleep at all. The guard had talked all night—his name was Hongo, Hongo Hiroshi, age 38, Scorpio, blood type O (making him optimistic and easygoing), born in Fukushima, or Fukusuma if you were from the area, and his wife was a tiger in bed—she could move body parts Conner hadn't even known humans had. Of course, so could Hiroshi. Conner would have greeted Shimoda and Kuwano with relief, but at the end of Hongo's shift Conner was taken to a breakfast of rice gruel, a particularly slimy seaweed soup, pickled *gobo*— Conner knew they were basically skinny carrots but they looked and tasted like wet twigs—and a cold piece of roasted salt mackerel. It felt like part of the torture, but Conner knew from experience it was just a traditional Japanese breakfast.

After breakfast he was put on cleaning detail and had to

swab out all the cells, even the empty ones. No wonder they were so clean. He tried to sleep as he mopped, but there was always someone there to keep him awake. By the time Hongo returned at night from the ferocious embrace of his mate, Conner was seeing double, his spine aching from skull to tail and not even Hongo's chatter and prodding could keep him from drifting off into sleep.

"Get up."

He wasn't sure how long he had slept. Hongo had his arms locked under Conner's and was lifting him up.

"Stand up."

Conner stood, aching like he had that first morning after Katie thrashed him. There was another person outside the cell.

"Let's go."

Aided by Hongo, Conner stumbled after the man and was shown into the same questioning room.

Shimoda and Kuwano were waiting for him. They peppered him with questions and tried to keep him awake, but Conner had made up his mind to say nothing in Japanese, not a word. They would do with him whatever they wanted anyway. Then he started to babble—about being a lumberjack, about the photos on Toby and Edward's walls, a little Pueblo ceramic pot Edward had bought in New Mexico from an old woman he called his "girlfriend in Acoma," about the flowers of Honolulu, his sister Peggy's job, gay bars in L.A., gay bars in Tokyo, about how vindictive certain high-school girls could get if you had no desire to sleep with them—but it was only in English. He was too tired to care. He did everything they told him except speak Japanese. Finally, he found himself being given back his passport, the rest of Paul's money and being pushed out the door of the station in the dark of the night.

Free.

He had no idea why. Maybe because they hadn't found the drugs. Behind him Shimoda or Kuwano said "see you later," maybe in English. They worked in Hawaii so they probably spoke English well, he realized. He tried to remember what all he'd said but that was impossible. He recalled how his drunken exchange with Katie seemed to have alerted the yakuza to the hash. Had he now given the police some clue?

He stumbled toward the train station but only made it as far as a small neighborhood park with a ring of round log sections containing a raised, sod-topped hillock, on top of which he fell asleep.

CONNER AWAKENED to the noontime prod of an old woman. "What's wrong? What's wrong?" she cried.

Conner stood up and walked away. The last thing on earth he wanted to do was to be on the receiving end of the lecturing attentions of an *obaa-san*. He found a coffee shop and ordered a *ranchi setto*—a set lunch—that turned out to be loathsome: a swollen spaghetti salad, egg sandwich swimming in mayonnaise and a fat slice of toast so airtight the butter sat in a yellow layer on top. The coffee was watered down the way they thought Americans liked it.

"What day is it?" he asked the snub-nosed waiter.

"Wednesday." The smudged lenses of the waiter's wire-rimmed glasses rested at the tip of his nose.

"Shit," Conner muttered. "What's the date?"

"The thirtieth."

"Damn!" He had a little money now, but not the promised million, and now he'd lost two days. And Arata? Forget Arata. But as Conner sat there, his mind drifted back to him.

"I'm such an idiot," he moaned out loud. Why do I waste

my time on him? Marika had been much nicer to Conner, was a much better human being, but Conner's mind went back obsessively to Arata. Was this love or mental illness? Conner wanted it to end. There was only one more thing he could do now. Talk to Atsuko's roommate Kayo. I dream of Kayo with the long, permed hair. Kayo and only Kayo could tell Conner about Katie. And now Conner had money to buy the information.

"What time is it?" he asked the waiter.

"Twelve-thirty."

"Thanks." Conner sipped his beverage. If this is coffee, bring me tea. If it's tea, bring me coffee. Man, was he tired. It took effort just to keep his head up. There was a yellow payphone on the counter, by a stack of thick comics in lurid but not unappealing colors. Conner sat next to the phone, dropped in a hundred-yen coin—profligate now that he had money—and dialed the number Marika had given him.

"What?" she said drowsily.

"Marika?"

"Conner?" She seemed to come awake. "Are you in jail?"

"They let me go. I'm in Narita."

"Are you leaving?"

"I'm in the town of Narita, not the airport. Can I come by?"

"I'm glad they let you go, but I can't see you anymore." She hung up.

Conner did not have the energy to even feel anything about it. At least he'd let her know he was OK. He blinked his eyes. They felt gritty. He hadn't had a bath since . . . he couldn't remember when, but he'd been to Hawaii and back in the meantime. He rubbed his chin. A couple days' growth, too. The waiter was staring at him, but looked away when Conner caught his eyes. Conner paid his bill and caught a train into town.

41

THE PERIL

M arika felt bad hanging up on Conner—he'd kept her from prison—but she'd saved him, too, and she hadn't left Inudani just to be condescended to all over again, thank you very much. The packet she'd retrieved sat on the table, waiting for her to destroy the drugs or take them to the police. Which of course would implicate not just Conner, Paul and Mama-san, but herself. So she did what any sensible person would do: she ignored the situation.

That afternoon, Marika transferred the bulk of Paul's money to her brother, then went to the lawyer she'd engaged the day she'd returned from Hawaii. Her lawyer, fortunately, was not condescending. Marika got a good feeling talking to her. The woman was frank in acknowledging that the stigma of divorce had real employment consequences, but also pointed out that Japan was big country, so Marika would find lots of people who'd agree she needed no one's permission but her own to leave her marriage. Marika gathered the sheaves of papers to be filled out detailing her and Isamu's assets and took them home. She worked on them all afternoon, making phone calls to banks for account numbers and dates with little success. Every horrid thing came rushing back, making her light-headed. Eventually Marika poured herself a Hennessy, diluted with hot water, like Ai said they drank it in Hong Kong.

In the evening, she called in sick to Stardust The Moon. Shiomi-san begged her to come in, but she was tired from two overnight flights and thinking about her married life had made her queasy.

It grew late. The bottle of Hennessy was empty. Marika descended the steel stairs and wandered out onto the silent little streets in search of a liquor store. All were closed, but one had competing Sapporo and Suntory machines. She stuffed a note into a machine, pressed a button and was soon walking back with a pricey bottle of Suntory whisky tucked under her arm.

She passed a shrine. It looked dark and chilly, but called to her. She hadn't asked any help from the gods recently. Perhaps she should.

Marika bowed and walked under the first stone *torii* gate that arched over the path into the deserted little shrine. She didn't hate Conner. He might in general terms deserve to go to jail, but she'd brought the drugs in, not him. Even apart from the drugs she was a criminal, technically. Although it was common practice to stamp a chop for someone else as she'd done, it was *not* legal. And she'd forged the woman's signature. And she'd deceived the two Americans by dressing up as the Minister's wife and presenting the woman's passport as her own.

She walked under a second, lower, torii. Conner hadn't lied to her; he'd told her it was better not to know. She didn't agree with that, but their moment in Hawaii together had freed her. She was no longer Isamu's wife, not in her own mind. She took a deep breath. She was finally on her own.

The next torii was stone and festooned with a Shinto straw rope and her head barely cleared the lower beam of the gate. She passed between two stone statues of demon dogs, caged in blue chicken wire. One gripped a scroll in its mouth, the other seemed to be on the verge of swallowing a ball.

She walked down the stone path under two red-painted wooden toriis and past the decaying trunk of a tree that had fallen against a larger tree and been left to rot naturally, protected by a barbed wire fence from any unnatural acceleration of the process.

Marika reached the shrine itself, a small wooden building beyond a final scarlet torii of wood. It was spooky, being alone in the tree-cloistered temple, where illumination from streetlights did not reach. Marika felt a presence. The bare ground was beaten down, as though flattened by the pounding of children's feet. She shivered as the ring on her finger drew cold from the glass of the whisky bottle. She'd forgotten the ring was there.

She set the whisky bottle on the ground. Slender red, white and black cloth-covered strands twined around and into a fat rope that hung in front of the shrine. Marika pulled on the thick rope, softly ringing the bell up above to summon the shrine's god. She worked the gold ring off her finger, tossed it into the offering box and prayed for a little luck. She clapped her hands twice to conclude the prayer, gave a final bow to the small shrine and exited into the neighborhood.

The shops were few now. Trees crept out over cinder block walls from private yards into the empty streets. The side streets were dark, but streetlights flooded the main street with yellow so she kept away from the narrow alleys, whose only light seeped in from the larger road.

She looked back. Was someone following? She saw no one. She continued onward. Isamu wouldn't really look for her, would he? And the police didn't even know who she was. Would Paul and Shiomi-san send someone after her? This was paranoia, she decided. But the feeling persisted. She looked back in a quick jerk.

Someone *was* there!

It was Betchaku, running toward her, making no attempt to hide.

Marika ran into the dark, silent alley leading to her apartment. She remembered that bulging box of lurid photos. And here she was, alone. No one would come out of their houses to help her. She looked back. He was far enough away that she could make it to her apartment. She hoped. Her shoes clacked on the pavement. She searched her purse for her keys. Where were they? She reached the bottom of the stairs and stopped for a breath. He was still running toward her.

"Marika!" he cried.

She found her keys and started up the stairs. Her lungs were aching now. Why had she chosen a fourth-floor apartment? She rounded the landing at the second floor and heard Betchaku's shoes hit the steel stairs. She burst up the stairs again and lurched for the door.

"Marika, wait!" he cried.

Marika pushed the key in the lock. It wouldn't go.

"Marika!"

There. The key was in. She turned the knob. Betchaku looked at her from the landing. He caught her eyes. She entered her apartment, slammed the door and turned the deadbolt.

There was no sound.

Marika sat on the rim of the genkan breathing heavily. Her lungs burned. She set down the whiskey, surprised to see it in her hand still. She fumbled through her purse for a cigarette, found the pack and pulled one out, but didn't put it in her mouth. Betchaku was out there, but he wasn't saying anything. Marika stood, pushing herself up from her knees, and looked through the peephole.

He was standing in front of her door.

"I don't work for you anymore," she yelled. "You fired me!"

He didn't move, didn't say anything. She lit her cigarette and smoked. The cigarette was burning down. She stubbed it out in an ashtray. She looked through the peephole. He was still there. "Go away!"

Marika took off her shoes and stepped up into the kitchen. She called the police. She explained the situation to them, but they refused to come. She was in no physical danger and they did not interfere in domestic disputes. They might get involved in a rape, but only to make the rapist pay compensation money. She hung up in intense anger without even trying to reason with them. She took out a carton of oolong tea from the refrigerator and cut the top open with a pair of scissors. Her hands shook as she poured it into the glass. Betchaku pounded on the door. She spilled the tea.

"Open up!" he said. "Open up! I won't do anything bad."

Marika sat on the kitchen floor and sipped at the dark brown tea.

He knocked. "Please, open the door." And then, in a quieter voice, "I love you. You're the most beautiful, elegant . . ." He pounded on the door.

She pounded back. "Go away!" she yelled. Maybe the landlady would wake up.

He pounded. Nobody came to help her.

Marika went back to the entryway, uncomfortable about getting even that close to Betchaku, and retrieved her purse. She opened it and found the slip of paper with Conner's number. He'd said he was close by. She punched it out. It was busy.

Rei-chan lived too far away. She called anyway. The phone rang off the hook. She didn't have Ai's number, and she refused to call Eriko and Yuuske. There was no sound at the door. She crept over to the door and looked through the peephole. He was still there, his enormous eye looking through the peephole. She jumped back. Would he wait until she came out? Eventually she would have to. After all, she'd have to pay her gas bill.

He pounded. She turned out the light. She called Rei-chan again. She called Conner again. Now the phone rang, but he didn't answer. She heard scratching sounds at the door. The door was shaking softly. Don't let Betchaku be doing something perverted, she prayed.

"Come on, someone," she said. "Answer the phone."

42

THE ACTUAL YAKUZA

Conner woke in early afternoon to the shake of a conductor's hand on his shoulder in Ueno, the last stop. He got up without a word and left the train, which was filling up rapidly. If the conductor hadn't woken him, the train would have pulled out again with him on it and he would've been taken back to Narita. He had seen lots of conductors pass sleeping people by, and as he walked up the stairs toward the JR tracks, he thanked the conductor in his mind for the kindness of not passing him by simply because he was afraid a gaijin wouldn't understand *shuten*, end of the line.

By the time he got back to the mansion, he was dead on his feet. He slipped in unnoticed by anyone and crawled up to his room. A square of paper was taped to Conner's door in Hideo's handwriting. He expected another rebuke, a "move-out-now", but it was merely a phone number. Conner shoved it in his pocket, pulled out his futon, and fell asleep on top of it fully dressed.

Hours later, he awoke, feeling like he'd taken all the "stimulant" in that pouch, stayed up for a week and crashed.

He'd taken speed twice back in L.A., but the let-down had turned him off it. Ironically, he'd never really found a drug he liked, unless it was smuggling itself. As he looked around the room, he saw that Rob's jogging togs were out in the middle of the floor, next to his briefcase. They hadn't been there before, he was pretty sure, which meant that Rob had come back, gone jogging and then gone out again. Conner had slept the entire day away. He thought hard. He was pretty sure it was the thirtieth. Two days to April first, the start of the next fiscal year, Arata's yakuza deadline. Conner rolled out of bed, still dressed in his suit and went out to the phone.

He picked up the receiver, reached in his pocket for ten-yen coins and dropped four into the pink phone. It was late, but he dialed the number on Hideo's note. There was no name and the number did not look familiar.

"Moshi-moshi," a vaguely familiar man's voice answered.

"Moshi-moshi," Conner replied. "It seems I had a call from you recently . . ."

"What is your name?"

"Conner." The line went quiet. Conner said hello a few times. There had been no click, so the guy hadn't hung up on him. Conner stuck in more coins as the old ones dropped into the coin box. "Moshi-mooosh," he said into the void.

Conner was on the verge of hanging up when an older man came on the line.

"Listen, you're a friend of Kubata-san's, aren't you?"

Conner didn't recognize the voice, but the man dragged out his syllables the same way the first man had. "No, I don't think so. Who is this?"

"She works at Giotto?"

"Kubata Fumie?" Uh oh. He sat down. "The wonderful actress?"

"That's right. I understand you have a little delivery for me."

"Oh, I see." It was the yakuza. Conner looked at Hideo's message chalkboard for inspiration. He toyed with the idea of hanging up. "Did Arata send you?"

The man laughed. "I think it would be more accurate to say we sent him."

"The delivery was stolen," Conner said. And smuggled hash was so last week. Now speed was all the rage.

"That presents a bit of a problem." It didn't sound like the news was a surprise. Conner stuck in another ten-yen coin.

"I'm trying to get it back." Assuming Katie really hadn't sold it. "Or I can go get some more if you can lend me money for the . . ." As he was saying "trip" he pressed the hang-up button. That way they might think they were disconnected. Unused ten-yen coins clattered down. "Oh dear," he said out loud.

The phone rang again. Conner sat beside it. Ring, ring, ring. It was extremely difficult to sit by a phone in a communal dwelling and let it ring. He patted it on top. "Shh, nice phone. Quiet phone," he whispered.

"Will somebody get the goddamn phone!" an unknown woman yelled.

Conner sat beside the phone praying for it to stop. It did. Conner thought about what to do. One, buy information about Katie from Kayo. Two, . . . OK, so he didn't have any other options. The money he had wasn't enough to get him home to the US unless he could score an unused return ticket, and he'd heard no rumor of such recently. And what would he do in L.A. without money anyway? He was on the verge of being homeless. The phone rang again. Conner watched it ring. "Hush," he whispered, petting it on the head.

Conner heard an angry huff and a door opened down the hall. He stood up and headed for the stairs.

Carmen snorted at Conner's retreating figure in disgust and picked up the phone. "Moshi-moshi." She listened. "It's for you." She thrust the phone at him. "Some of us are trying to sleep, you know."

Conner came back and took the phone, bowing at Carmen. "Sorry." He sat by the phone. "Moshi-mosh."

It was Marika, talking a mile a minute.

"Calm down," he said. "There's a guy there?"

She asked Conner to come over. The guy was apparently standing outside her door. She could see him through the peephole. He'd been there an hour and the police wouldn't come.

"How do I get there?"

She told him.

"I'm on my way." He dropped the handset.

"Conner-san."

He looked up. Two men stood in the entryway, a tall skinny bald man with the deep facial creases of a lifetime smoker and a short fat man with curly permed hair and a nose that suggested insufficient pugilistic prowess. They had opened the glass door without rattling it, quite a feat.

"It has not in the past been our habit to deal with Americans," the tall man said.

"I'm Canadian," Conner lied. "Like the bacon."

"Or Canadians. But see what you can do about that delivery. Think of it as a loan payment. When you're late with a loan payment, the bank repossesses your house. But you don't have a house, do you?"

"Oh, so my life is going into *foreclosure*." Conner felt proud to know the term—take that, Shiomi-san. He'd heard it a lot in bars lately, especially in the post-midnight hour when patrons became philosophical but the tears were yet to come.

"I don't think I like your tone."

Few did, but for once Conner held his tongue.

"Please bear in mind that you're the cause of the problem. Give the material to Kubata-san by tomorrow night. I think you understand how it is."

"Understand how what is?"

"How your life will be if you don't."

"Foreclosed?"

The tall man raised his eyebrows significantly.

"Are you going to beat me up now?"

The short guy looked up at the tall guy. "You want to?"

He shrugged. "Okay."

Conner jumped to standing, springing lightly on the balls of his feet, his fists raised. He was tired of getting pushed around, by Katie, by the police, and now by these goons.

The tall guy laughed.

"What?" Conner said, and then suddenly he was lying on his back with the tall guy standing over him. The guy's fingers opened slightly. He had something heavy wrapped in his hand and Conner thought he might drop it on him. As long as it wasn't on his face. Not his face again.

"Okay," said Conner out loud.

"What's this 'okay' shit?" the little guy said.

Conner said nothing. His face was swelling in new directions now, he could feel it. At least both sides would match now. He lay on the wood floor looking up. The guy seemed to go up such a long way. Conner raised himself onto his elbows. The man's fingers closed on his weapon, ready to hit him again if he got up.

Conner breathed out a heavy puff and thought of lying back down. He got up very slowly, as though if he moved too fast the man would swing at him. The man watched and when Conner got to his feet again, the man knocked Conner down again.

When Conner came to, they were gone. His face was bleeding. This time it was the other side, the same side Katie had concentrated on. "Shit." He needed to learn self-defense or something. After high school he'd focused on protecting his reputation, but apparently his body needed protecting too. He looked at his watch. Only ten minutes had passed. His head pounded. He wanted to fall asleep right there, but didn't want Hideo to find him. He remembered Marika. She needed him for something, he didn't exactly recall what. He got up and walked to Marika's apartment, the instructions a bit knocked about in his head, but still there somewhere, maybe lodged slightly below his left ear. He found what he thought was her building. It had a steel staircase. He walked up, looking for her creep boss, Betchaku, whom she'd described as a short tubby guy with fluffy hair.

The guy was crouching by the fourth-floor railing, hiding from Conner, as though ready to pounce, although the railing didn't do much to hide him. Perhaps he thought he was invisible.

"Hey, you. Stop bothering her, all right! Don't you have any self-respect!" Conner glared at the tubby man, angry that he was bothering Marika when Conner's head hurt so much.

The guy postured at Conner. He was quite a bit shorter than Conner, maybe four inches. Conner wasn't having any of it. He charged up the stairs toward him.

The man looked Conner in the face belligerently, ready to strike, then recoiled as he saw the blood on Conner's forehead and cheek.

Marika opened the door and screamed, Conner wasn't

sure at what. Another door opened downstairs. The tubby man drew back a step toward the railing.

He bumped against the railing and started to fall. Conner reached out and grabbed his lapels. The tubby man's arms whirled as he tried to get away from Conner without slipping over the rail. Conner pulled him back from the railing to the stairs and gave him a kick, heading him down the stairs.

The guy scrambled down to the next landing. "I'll come back!"

"I don't work for you anymore," Marika said. "You're nothing to me."

The downstairs door closed.

The guy scowled and stood there. Conner ran toward him. He scuttled down the stairs, but stopped on the next landing. Conner charged him again and he went down half a flight. Conner ran after him again. He ran out into the street. Conner kept chasing him till he left the building and ran to the main road where he again stopped. Conner stopped. His muscles burned. His face stung. He went back to Marika's stairway. He wiped his face and waited a minute and then looked out. The man came back. Fuck you, he thought. The guy waved at him. Conner rolled his eyes. He felt like beating *somebody* up and he'd finally found someone he could take. Evidently, the tubby man got the idea, because this time he really booked. Conner stepped back into the stairwell. Marika was behind him. She grabbed his arm.

"Is he gone?"

"I don't know."

"Let's give him a minute."

They waited. It was cold. Marika shivered. Conner put his arm around her. He could feel her heart pounding fast in her thin chest.

"I don't need anyone to hold me," she said.

"Whatever." He didn't know the straight etiquette of touch, nor did he much care. He looked out again. The guy was gone.

"He's gone, Marika. I'm going too."

"Come up for a minute," she said.

He didn't want to. "No thanks."

"We need to talk."

Did they? He was so tired. April first was so close. But he nodded and followed her up the stairway.

Conner was more than a little woozy as he crossed the threshold, shucked off his shoes and stepped up from her genkan into the apartment. He lifted the thin blue-flowered quilt sandwiched between the kotatsu table-top and frame and stuck his feet under, bumping the warming contraption under the table. The red lightbulb that supplied the heat was on.

Marika went into the kitchen and brought out two glasses and an expensive-looking bottle of whisky, which she set on the kotatsu. She had also brought a wet rag, which she dabbed at his head, cleaning the new cut.

Conner winced. The damage this time was more painful than Katie's beating. Marika poured an inch of whisky into each glass and took a big sip of hers.

"I wouldn't recommend any mirrors for a while," she said. "You'll need stitches this time." She put alcohol on the rag and daubed again.

Conner cried out in pain.

"I can't stop it hurting." She put down her rag, now streaked and spotted with red. She rooted through a card-board box and handed Conner a white square of gauze. "Apply pressure." He placed it on his forehead and held it firmly in place. Marika sipped her whisky, staring at him. He stared back.

"Let me see."

He showed her the gash.

She came up with butterfly closures, which she applied to his wound.

"I thought you didn't want to see me again," he said.

"I don't approve of drug smuggling."

"I wouldn't expect you to."

"You're not going to apologize for yourself?"

"Why should I?"

"Because you lied to me."

"When?"

"Everything you said was a lie."

"Name one thing," he said.

She sipped at her whisky. "Do you think that if you outfox me with words, we somehow won't be in the trouble we're in? Fine. You win. You never lied to me. But you sure didn't tell me the truth."

Conner hung his head. He could feel Edward chuckling somewhere: Gotcha! "I knew there were going to be drugs from the start," he confessed. "I didn't tell you because I thought it wouldn't involve you. It never occurred to me that you could end up carrying them. That was *my* job. And then when you did, I was . . . I was embarrassed. You thought I was a better person than that. After that afternoon . . . It's too complicated to explain."

"Try," she said.

He shook his head. "In two days, it'll all be over anyway. I just want to start over. I've gotten myself into a mess, but it's not too late to get out. God, when I think of how many years it took to get here, and how much of it happened just because I was a fool." He shook his head again.

"Oh, does *that* sound familiar," she said. The room stayed quiet. Outside there were no sounds. "Sometimes, it seems to me, in life you have so little control over what goes on around you that you latch onto whatever's in front of you. Isamu seemed better than the other men I knew. I think I just got lazy."

Conner nodded. "There's something else I left out, something important. Before that Canadian woman I told you about, and after her too, there was someone else. A man. I think I may be in love with him. That's my only explanation for why I still put up with him." He looked up at her. "Does that shock you?"

"No." She downed the rest of her whisky and then refilled her glass. "Okay, maybe a little." She looked at him as though waiting for him to go on.

"He's not horrible, but he's also not very good to me. I keep saying I'm done, but when I get around him it's, it's like there's so much hope in me, so much desire, that when some chance of getting what I want appears it sweeps me down the drain."

"It really doesn't sound like you love him," she said. "Sounds like anxiety or fear or something. Not love."

Conner was surprised. Wasn't that love, being unable to let go of someone?

"So, are you gay, then?"

"Appears so," he said. "Sorry."

"You don't owe me anything. I'm not in love with you, you know."

He smiled. "Ironically, that makes me happy."

"It shows you're not hopeless, even if you lack sense." She chuckled. So did he. "I'm glad Shiomi-san and Paul-san picked you. At least I'm not in this alone."

She moved beside him and leaned her head on him. He ran his hand over the back of her head. She turned her face toward him and kissed him. He responded.

"Why are you doing this if you're gay?"

"Force of habit? Because I like you? Because we care more

than the rest of them out there and tomorrow may not be kind to either of us?" And because he felt like he owed her something and this was what he had to give. Had that motivated him with Arata as well? Of course it had.

She took another sip of whisky and swallowed. She grabbed his arm and placed it around her waist. It wasn't far from the kotatsu to the floor. She leaned back and pulled him down with her, her hand moving over his back and under his shirt. They moved against each other and he became aroused. He enjoyed being with someone who wasn't trying to work some scheme on him. Her breathing deepened and she ran her hand over his hair. It felt like kindness.

She pulled out the top and bottom futons from the closet and unfolded the two layers beside the kotatsu. She handed him his whisky. He raised it to his lips, inhaling the fumes of the alcohol and downing half of it in a gulp. It tasted good. She turned off the overhead light.

By the red glow of the kotatsu bulb Conner watched her strip. He took off his clothes and crawled into the futon next to her.

Her lips parted and her mouth hovered over his, kissed it. She clasped him tightly, her breasts against his chest, her leg over his. He reached over to his pants and pulled out a condom. She pushed his shoulder to the futon and got on top of him. He ran his hands over her back. It was nice to be wanted.

Afterwards they lay together in the futon, skin touching everywhere, feeling the night outside slink just a little further away. Conner felt safe. Police, yakuza, amphetamines, hash— all would be waiting for him when he woke up tomorrow for his last chance to make things right. But for that moment, he could forget about everything else and sleep, which, wrapped in Marika's arms, he did.

43

THE BETRAYAL

Conner woke with a start. Marika was breathing irregularly, mouth slightly open, the tips of her upper teeth just visible. He touched her shoulder and her breathing steadied.

She turned onto her side. He snuggled close behind her and tried to sleep. The light filtering in through the thin white curtain was once again too bright, though, and he was hopelessly awake.

His eyes felt as though they were filled with pebbles, like after a long flight. And a couple days in jail. He went into the shower. The water heating system was completely electronic. Scalding hot water spurted out of the showerhead when he pressed a red square on the control panel. He pressed the blue square repeatedly until the water reached a comfortable temperature. The rent on the apartment must be considerable. He wondered where she got the key money. He felt a little envious—even the year he'd had a legit job and enough for key money, Japanese landlords wouldn't rent to him. Not one. Conner stood under the hot water for ten minutes, feeling the dirt sluice off. His circumstances came back to him, one by one. Today was the day. He was going to find Kayo. He was going to find Katie.

He dried off and looked at his body in the mirror. It seemed an alien thing, long and pale, accented by swirls of black around his nipples and delightfully asymmetrical patches of red, purple and blue on his face and torso. He was not at all sure he would want to sleep next to something that looked like him.

He leaned closer to the mirror. The cut above his eyebrow was looking pretty abused. It would scar. Well, at least he'd come out of all this with something to show for it.

He made a cup of instant coffee from some powder he found in her kitchen cabinet, catching the teakettle just before it whistled. He brought the coffee back into the tatami room with a jar of Creap creamer and stuck his legs under the kotatsu, pulling the quilt over his lap. He sipped the milky coffee, watching Marika. She started snoring, a restful sound. He turned on the kotatsu lightbulb heater, and his legs silently warmed. He needed to leave, but didn't want to wake her.

"What time is it?" Marika said.

He looked at the clock up on her dresser. "Eleven."

"Come back to bed."

He crept under the covers beside her. She rubbed her hand over his chest. He reached down the smooth side of her body. She moved under his touch. How different women were. Marika seemed to simply enjoy her entire skin. And yet her body didn't really seem fully alive to him, not like a man's body would, its movement drawing his attention from a great distance, awakening greed in him. But still, her body felt very nice up close to him.

Conner lay there thinking over the previous evening. Despite everything, he didn't think he was bisexual, as he had speculated—as he'd hoped—when he was with Katie. He'd just discovered that there was something else he could do. Being able to have sex with someone didn't mean you could love them, let alone live with them, just as not having sex with someone, even a diffident someone, namely Arata, had not meant Conner's love—or other compulsive yearning, if Marika was right—had faded away, even when everything else said it should.

Or not. Maybe all that mattered was what he did. He liked sex with women; he liked sex with men. The latter more than the former, but in the end, what he really needed to be was honest. He was glad he'd told Marika everything. It felt good to have told someone. And luckily, she hadn't kicked him out for being a drug smuggler.

And then it occurred to him: he hadn't told her he was a smuggler.

He didn't think Paul would have. What had she been doing while Shimoda and Kuwano had been beating up on him? Everything seemed to click into place. "You have the drugs," he said out loud. He shook her shoulder. "Marika!"

She opened her eyes and smiled, then saw the look on his face.

"How did you do it?"

"Do what?" she said. "Conner, what's wrong?"

"You must have been right behind me. That explains everything. You have the drugs, don't you? You have the package."

She sat up in bed and swept the hair out of her eyes. "I need a cigarette."

"Did you give it to Paul?"

She fumbled for a cigarette, breasts swinging over the table. "What would he want with it?"

"It's his. It was in the envelope."

"I never saw it in the envelope."

Conner threw his arms up in the air. "Yes!" he cried. "Thank you, thank you." He hugged her.

She stiffened against his touch.

"What's wrong?" he asked.

She turned away. "You're making me remember things I'd rather forget."

"Such as?"

"For instance, why did you grab the envelope from me?"

"I grabbed the envelope because I didn't want you to have to take the drugs through customs."

"How did you know they were in there?"

"Where else would they be? They hadn't given them to me."

"Why not? Were you all setting me up? Was I supposed to go to jail?"

"I saw two drug policemen who knew me in the hotel in Honolulu, so I stayed away from you. Since I wasn't there, Zakabi made you the pigeon."

"How did you know they were narcs?"

"Because, as you know, I've smuggled drugs before and they were already after me. What do you think?"

"I guess I knew that, didn't I?" She shuddered. "It didn't seem real until now."

"Come on, Marika, don't do this. Not after last night."

"That's certainly not happening again."

"Fine. So what?"

His words seemed to sink in slowly. She turned away, muttering "stupid, stupid, stupid."

Now what? Did she expect him to feel more? He had told her he was gay. But one thing he hadn't really thought of until now was that she was not. It probably meant more to her than to him, regardless of what she said. Of course, the flip side of that was she'd gotten something she'd desired; he hadn't, not in the same way. Because that was the truth of it, wasn't it? Having sex with her had been the price of having her companionship, and these after-sex qualms were actually kind of annoying.

"I hardly know you," she said.

"You know me well enough." He ran his finger around the neck of the shimmering bottle of whisky.

She straightened up and lit the cigarette. "I'm not giving you the drugs."

"What did you do with them?"

"I destroyed them."

Conner felt a wave of relief. "Wait a minute. Then why would you say you're not giving them to me? Marika, the police saw me with a pouch. They know what flights I took. They saw you in Honolulu. I put it together. So will they. It's not hard."

"They won't recognize me. I was in disguise."

"They know what flights I took. All they have to do is check both rosters for women's names. Chances are exceedingly high that there is only going to be one that's on both rosters. They're probably on their way over right now. Why else would they have let me go if not to . . ."

To lead them to someone else.

Paul and Shiomi-san. Arata. Marika. That's why they let him go. A lack of evidence wouldn't have stopped them from ensuring he had publicly funded bad haircuts for ten years.

"Except that I don't have a residence register yet. I work under the table using my maiden name. Not even my husband knows where I live," she said triumphantly.

"Except . . ." He stopped. How *would* they find her? They couldn't have followed him there last night. The streets had been deserted. Maybe she was safe after all. And yet Conner felt as if he'd lost an argument that, for her sake, he had to win.

She looked at him, stony-faced. "Look. I'm thirty. I've kept a business solvent for years in spite of having an immature, spendthrift husband. I've run a household and navigated life with a mother-in-law, which is no mean feat. And now I am managing just fine despite my ex-husband confiscating everything that I helped build over the years. Do *not* treat me like a child."

Conner felt echoes of Edward and Toby's situation with Toby's in-laws. Was he the bad guy here? "Are you going to turn me in?"

"No," she said quietly.

"If you're thinking you'll make some money off it, it's far too dangerous now. You're risking years of your life for at most a couple million yen."

"You think I'd do that?" she asked.

"Not really." Conner began putting on his clothes. She was more mature than he was, he'd give her that, but he understood, in a way she could not, how the drugs could reach out and take control of her life. "Marika, if you're not going to turn me in, you *must* destroy the drugs before the police come here. They *will* come here eventually."

She looked at Conner, then away. "Shit, Marika, you can't be afraid of me! Not now."

"I'm not afraid of you."

"Promise me you'll destroy them." Conner looked down at the top of her head. She poured herself a whisky. Really? Another whisky? Why should he not treat her as a child, again? He could make this simple for her. "Where are the drugs?"

"I told you . . ."

"Okay," he said, "I'll find them myself." He went to her bureau and opened it.

"What are you doing?"

"I'm not leaving till I see them destroyed, since obviously I can't trust you to." He tossed her clothes out of the bureau, patting them down thoroughly before heaping them on the floor.

"I'm calling the police." She picked up the phone.

He laughed. "Why don't you call Betchaku instead? He and I can take turns saving you from each other." He finished the bureau and moved to the closet, rummaging quickly through her things. The packet was big enough that she couldn't hide it from him if he searched. She put the phone down. Conner faced her. The closet was clean. He checked under the kotatsu top, putting the glasses and her ashtray on the tatami and then lifting the Formica top up and checking the quilted blanket and the lightbulb/heating apparatus. A good place to stash something, but it was empty also.

He looked under the sink. Nothing.

"Conner," Marika said.

He turned around. She was holding an aluminum frying pan above him like in some bad western. He laughed.

She hit him on the head.

"Ow," he said. She wasn't very strong and hadn't swung with much enthusiasm, but it still hurt plenty. He felt woozy. He grabbed the pan from her and kept his eyes on her as much as he could, holding the pan in front of him like a shield. He wasn't going to make the mistake of thinking she couldn't do real damage. He searched through the rest of the cabinets. Instant coffee, onions, cat food of all things, but no drugs. He went into the bathroom and searched the medicine chest and toilet tank. Nothing.

"See?" she said, a crowing note in her voice that was not particularly appealing. She could be kind of a brat.

Conner sat on the toilet. She stood by the door, arms crossed, steaming. She'd never forgive him.

"Aha," he said.

She quailed. "What?"

Conner went back to the main room. "The tatami."

"Don't you dare."

Conner uprooted all six mats, one after the other, knocking over the bureau and the kotatsu in the process. The room was a mess. And he hadn't found it.

"Hello, police?" he heard from the other room. They probably wouldn't come, but Conner had to admit defeat. He put back the mats. He righted the dresser and the kotatsu. Let her fix up the rest. It hardly mattered now. He stepped into the kitchen and then down into the genkan. He slipped his shoes on. Marika hung up and gave him a glare that would have killed a man with less ability to absorb physical punishment.

"One more thing," he said. "I'm negative. And we didn't do anything risky. So don't go into any paranoid fits about HIV after I'm gone."

The focus of her eyes went slack and she backed away.

"Goodbye," he said, and left.

44

TOO LATE FOR A MOANING

"W hat the hell did you do in Hawaii?" Ai sat down on the stool beside Marika at the mahogany bar and leaned in close. "Mama-san is ready to burst a vessel. If she can find one that hasn't burst yet."

"Mama-san?" Marika said. "She got her contracts. She should be happy after all I went through for her."

"What happened?" Ai demanded.

But Marika wasn't sure what had happened. She stared through the plate glass at the shrubs on the miniscule balcony outside, trying to make sense of it all. Were the drugs for Mama-san? The condo had to be far, far more valuable than the packet of drugs, which ironically, was in Mama-san's office right now, in the pocket of Marika's black leather overcoat.

"They should have asked me to go," Ai said.

Marika scoffed. "It was a disaster. What did Mama-san say?"

"What does she ever say? *That Marika! That Ai! We're going under. Where am I going to get the money now?* On second thought, I'm glad she didn't ask me." Ai started rubbing Marika's back, high up, between the shoulder blades.

It felt wonderful. "Now a little lower." Ai's thumbs shifted downward, to where the buckle of Conner's pouch had bit into her skin this morning. "That's the spot."

Marika couldn't believe he hadn't searched the single most obvious place: her. The drugs had been under the frying pan, so while Conner was searching the bathroom, she'd retrieved the pouch and strapped it on under her sweatshirt. One hug, one touch and he would have known. He may have meant it when he said he'd destroy them, but she was willing to bet once he had the drugs he'd think of some reason he just *had* to sell them to Paul.

She found herself relieved Conner was a homo. Their two nights had been good for her, but she had been getting attached and didn't want that.

After he'd left, she'd gone to Chateau Parfum for a morning set of egg, toast and blend coffee, but arrived too late. She stared out the window at the cold, drizzly street. Marika wanted to give the packet to the police, but then Conner would be in prison forever, and as she thought over the things he'd said that morning, he was changing in her mind back from drug smuggler into poetry lover. Despite the fact he'd ransacked her apartment and was actually kind of arrogant. Crazy. But what else to do? Flush the drugs and throw away the wrapper? Burn it all? Bury it in the park, at the shrine? Throw it in front of an oncoming train. Nothing seemed right. Then it had been time for work. She'd brought the packet with her. It didn't seem very smart to have it so close to Mama-san and Paul, but leaving it at home for the police to find didn't seem smart either.

"Your customer's here," Ai said, kneading her thumbs sharply into Marika's knotted muscle.

Marika jerked away. "*My* customer?" She looked up. Shin-chan was beckoning with his fingers. Come here. She jumped off her stool and hurried over to him.

Paul stood before her, hands clasped in front, damp raincoat draped over them.

"Ah," Marika said.

"Yes." Paul's eyes looked baggy and red. He looked like he'd been through a fight. And lost. In one hand he held a Japanese newspaper. Could he read it? The headline screamed *Ikari Bank in Bankruptcy Talks*. Poor Eriko. If Yuuske got fired, he'd have a tough time finding another job. Kind of like a thirty-year-old divorced woman. Maybe Eriko could work for Betchaku.

"Whisky and water?" Marika asked.

Paul grunted, but Marika did not understand.

"Marika-chan, come in here," Mama-san said from the back room.

"Ah, hai," Marika said.

"Go on." Paul gave her a little pat on the rump. Marika kicked him with her heel and went into the room. Paul followed, rubbing his shin. He hung up his raincoat on the coat rack over hers. Mama-san closed the door behind them and sat beside Paul on the dusty rose love-seat.

Marika stood in front of the rack.

"You did a fine job for us, Marika-chan." Paul indicated a stool by the couch. "Please."

Marika nodded and sat down.

"Marika-chan, you're fired," Mama-san said.

"No, Mama-san." Paul faced Marika, staring into her eyes. "Marika did a good job for us. But tell us the truth, Marika. Or she *will* fire you. Why was Conner arrested? What you said doesn't make sense."

"I told you: there were drugs."

"Who said?"

"The customs agent."

"What did Conner do with the drugs?"

"Well, they caught him at the bathroom. Maybe he flushed them down the toilet."

Paul said something softly in English.

Mama-san screamed. "She'll cancel the condo sale. She'll never buy from us again. I'll never get out from under this debt."

Marika looked at Mama-san closely. She was roaring drunk. Marika imagined a lifetime of drinking, a lifetime of drug use. It would take that to pile up so much debt.

Paul said, "Calm down. She owes us too much. She can't stop the sale." He smiled at Marika. He cleared his throat.

Marika ground her molars together, thinking furiously. If the Minister's wife had run up debts, she must be the addict. But how had they met? The club was essentially a place to peddle drugs—alcohol—legally. What if they'd met the Minister's wife at Stardust The Moon? Marika had a flash of imagination: what if the woman had worked there? It fit. The club had a political clientele. A hostess who married a junior politico, who then rose to become a minister. Twenty years ago, it would have been a scandal. Would the woman still care about exposure? Marika remembered Yuuske and Eriko's attitudes. She might.

"Maybe Conner got them through somehow." Marika wanted to keep them talking.

"Wait a minute. Did he flush them, or didn't he?"

"How should I know?" This was risky. She didn't want them to wonder if she had the package. "I mean, they weren't in the envelope."

"But the envelope was opened," Mama-san said.

"Tell me exactly what you saw." Paul leaned forward. He really was a large man.

"He went into the bathroom and I went after him and then the police got him and I left with the envelope."

"Why didn't they arrest you, too?"

"They didn't see me. We weren't together."

Mama-san looked at her intently. "Marika-chan, if you know where the package is, well, *maa*, we could pay you a little extra something for it. *Ne*, Paul." She smiled, a lifeless ghoul of a smile.

Paul shifted in his seat. He looked at Marika, a cold, hard stare.

"I never . . ." Marika realized what a mistake she'd made, making them consider the police might not have the drugs.

"Five hundred thousand, say? Would that be enough?"

"Who are the drugs for?" she asked.

Mama-san put her hand on Paul's arm and watched Marika. Paul was still staring at her. Marika blinked. "I don't know . . ." Paul didn't interrupt her, and she realized she didn't know what to say. Greed flickered through her. Five hundred thousand yen. She could pay back the rest of what she'd borrowed from her brother. The package was right there in the room with them. It would be gone from her life. Still they said nothing. Marika swallowed. They looked corrupt.

Marika smiled. "They released him, you know."

"Conner?" Paul sat back against the love-seat. "They released Conner?"

She nodded.

"Where is he? Just tell me that much!" Mama-san shrieked.

"I don't know. He wanted to stay with me, but I wouldn't let him."

Paul groaned and Mama-san threw her hands up in the air. "Marika, you're fired."

"No," Paul said.

"Yes! *I'm* the mama-san," Mama-san said. "Even if you and your wife own half, *I'm* the mama-san."

Paul shrugged at Marika. "Sorry."

"I'm sure you are," Marika said. "Well, it's been very pleasant working here. And thank you for sending me to Hawaii. It was beautiful. Do you have my severance pay?"

Mama-san twitched violently, as though about to leap off the loveseat and grab Marika by the throat.

Marika stood up and slowly took Paul's coat off the rack, then her own. "Perhaps later." Marika rehung Paul's coat and carefully draped her own coat over her arm, praying that the package would not fall out. She smiled. "Well, that's that, then." She left the room.

"Marika, what happened?" Ai asked her as she closed the office door.

"I guess I'm the one who gets fired after all."

"You lost your job?" Ai seemed puzzled. "Why would she fire you?" She seemed to be asking it as much of herself as of Marika. She looked unhappy about the situation.

Marika put on her coat. "She's crazy, Ai, and Paul is too. Two used-up, wasted people. You should get out before something bad happens. It won't be long."

Ai nodded. "I just don't know what I'd do next."

"Figure it out fast." Marika took a piece of paper from her purse and wrote down her address and phone. Ai seemed touched. She gave Marika her information as well.

"Good luck," Marika said. She caught the elevator down to Akasaka, jobless, leaving Mama-san and Paul to turn on each other.

45

CALL ME IDIOT

Conner stood at the train crossing near Marika's house listening to a distorted recording of Jesus Jones' *Right Here, Right Now* pour from the little outdoor speaker at Mister Donuts. He'd blown it irreparably with Marika. She didn't understand the danger she was in. What would Rob have done, he wondered. Probably sweet-talked his way through it, charmed Marika with his good looks. Everyone else seemed to know what to do better than he did. They had jobs, places to live, clothes. They knew how to conduct themselves. Why was he always on the outside looking in? It wasn't just the gay thing; Toby and Edward had both had good jobs, good lives. Toby would have said, stand your ground. Fight for what's right. But that didn't apply here. Besides, Toby was dead. Edward was dead. Conner realized he was feeling sorry for himself, a big waste of time. He spotted that twerp Betchaku, who was hanging out by a cigarette machine across the tracks. God, even *he* had a job.

"Go away," Conner yelled.

An express roared by, drowning him out, but Betchaku

looked over at him and smiled innocently when the train passed. Conner walked back to the mansion. Betchaku started walking after him.

"I'm too busy for you to follow me," he yelled at Betchaku, but the guy kept walking after him. Conner ignored him. He rolled open the door to the mansion and sat down by the phone. Betchaku wouldn't have the nerve to follow him in here.

Conner pulled out Kayo's phone number. He had over forty thousand left from Paul's money. Forty thousand was not a real lot, but it should be enough for Conner to buy Katie's whereabouts from Kayo and maybe even the remains of the hash from Katie as a parting gift to Arata. It was still March thirty-first, after all, and would be all day long. Conner dialed Atsuko and Kayo's number.

Atsuko answered. Conner asked for Kayo in a gruff, disguised voice.

"I'll get her," Atsuko said.

"Hello?"

It was Kayo. Conner imagined her brushing her hair out of the way as she put the receiver to her ear.

"This is Conner."

"Atsuko told me all about you."

"I was honest with you." He heard Atsuko yell "hang up" in the background.

She laughed. "Yeah, no one would make up a story like that."

"Listen, I have a sum of money now and I want to *buy* the hash back from Katie. It's enough I think she might go for it. Have you by any chance, uh, figured out where she is? I can pay you for the information."

There was a silence on the other end of the phone.

"Now that you mention it, Atsuko just found out this morning."

"What a coincidence. Where is Katie?"

"Meet me at Studio Alta in forty minutes and I'll tell you."

A VAN of rightists on the turnaround across from Studio Alta was blaring recorded patriotic songs and demanding that Gorbachev return the Northern Territories. It was deafening. Conner was almost a half hour early and starving. He crossed the huge intersection and entered a McDonalds. He looked up at the menu above the counter area. They were having a promotion of "seaburgers," hamburgers with buns pressed into clam-shell shapes. He ordered a lunch special and coffee.

The counter woman pointed at the clock. It was two o'clock exactly. "Lunch special end at two," she said in broken English.

"I knew I should have gotten up ten seconds earlier," he said in crisp Japanese.

She glared at him. "Sir, you can see it's past two."

"It was before two when you said 'May I help you'."

She called for her supervisor. The supervisor came over and joined in glaring at him. With all the trade friction of late, Tokyo had developed an undercurrent of anti-gaijin feeling that hadn't been there five years ago. And he was dishing it back double. He felt like half of a bickering old couple. Yes, the first blush of romance between Japan and America was well over. And here they were, still married.

"Just give me a coffee."

She got him a coffee and he took it upstairs.

The second floor was filled with smoke, the air inside visible. The smoky gray tinting of the windows facing the train tracks looked refreshing by comparison. On the far side of the tracks, a stunted cherry tree was in full bloom, framed by a triangle made by a telephone line, a dead tree of a different variety and a soot-covered brown bank building. Next to him he heard a woman say, "Aren't the cherries lovely?" He wasn't sure if she was talking to him or to herself. Tokyo had become a difficult place, he decided.

He left the coffee and went back to Studio Alta, wishing he smoked so he'd have something to stick in his mouth. He scanned the crowd for Kayo's permed hair. Her apartment was close enough to walk to Shinjuku, but she was a hostess and would probably take the train, if not a taxi. He watched the people coming up the steps from the Marunouchi subway line, two floors underground. A gang of high-school boys and girls coalesced on the sidewalk, the girls pretending to be disgusted by one of the boys' jokes, screaming 'Eeuw, gross, eeeeeuw.' The white fascist van was now proclaiming how much the peoples of Taiwan and Korea had enjoyed being colonized by Japan. The traffic lights turned red and the intersection filled with people, perhaps two thousand black-haired Japanese, and here and there a white-haired old person or a black, brown or white foreigner.

"Conner-san," a voice behind him said.

"Kayo-san." She had come from the direction of the intersection and was dressed in jeans, a white blouse and a black leather cap that accentuated the fluffiness of her perm. She looked far too friendly to hit him up for money. "I can only spare ten thousand," he said. "Will that do?"

"Sure, thanks. That's nice of you."

He pulled out a big brown ichi-man and handed it to her. She folded it and put it in her shirt pocket. She pulled out a piece of paper and put it in his hand.

He looked at it. "Where is this? What's the nearest train stop?"

"Ichigaya, on the New Shinjuku line. You can get it near the Keio."

Conner scowled. Ichigaya was kind of a trek. "This better be for real." He started walking to the station.

"I don't see why you're so mad," she called after him.

Conner stopped and turned to face her. "I'm tired of people lying to me, that's all. If a fellow gay person lies to me, I'll be really pissed."

Kayo's brow crinkled.

"What?"

She bit her lip. "Come on."

"Come on where? I don't have a lot of time."

"Just come on, idiot."

Conner growled but fell in step behind her as she ventured into the street after a taxi. They got in and zipped over to Kayo and Atsuko's apartment. Kayo paid the driver out of the ichi-man and gave Conner all the change.

She unlocked the door. "Okay, come inside then."

Conner stepped up into the apartment. What if Katie was there, sitting at the living room kotatsu, looking up at him as he walked through the door. What would she say? "Oh, hello, Conner. Do you know Atsuko too? Small world."

He stepped into the living room. Atsuko was there, but not Katie.

"What did you bring him here for?" Atsuko yelled angrily. Conner stepped over to a sliding cardboard door, opened it and peered into the bedroom.

"Hey!" Atsuko called out.

The bedroom was in shambles, worse than he'd left Mari-ka's apartment, but no Katie. He felt disappointed. "I thought she was here."

"She was, but she's at a hotel now. She's leaving tomorrow," Kayo said. "Atsuko knows more."

"Kayo, what are you doing?" Atsuko screamed.

"What hotel?" Conner asked.

"You liar!" Atsuko said to Kayo.

"I'm not lying," Kayo said. "If you don't tell him, I will. You said yourself Katie robbed him. It's only fair."

"You never liked Katie," Atsuko said.

"What's to like?" Kayo said.

Conner said. "What hotel?"

"She didn't say," Atsuko mumbled, pouting.

"I don't believe you."

"It's true. I told her you were asking around, so she decided to hide. Otherwise, she'd still be here. She really didn't say," Atsuko said.

Conner looked over at Kayo. "So that address stuff was all a lie?"

Kayo nodded. "Yeah, sorry. It was Atsuko's idea."

"I hate you," Atsuko said. "You always blame everything on me."

"That's because it's always your fault."

"So, you *don't* know where she is?" Conner felt tired.

"Nah," Kayo said. She cleared a place for him at the kotatsu.

He sat down. "Why did you ask me to come here?"

"Tell him, Atsuko."

"She sold the hash," Atsuko said gleefully. "This morning."

"She what? Where?"

"A little bar in Golden Gai."

"Not Giotto."

"That's the one."

"No," Conner whispered. "She sold it at Giotto?" It didn't

seem possible. Giotto wasn't even open. "Are you sure that's the name?"

"Very sure. Giotto was an Italian painter, right? Early renaissance? Innovative with perspective? They had a big article on him in the *Asahi Shimbun* yesterday. Ikari Bank has one. Guess they'll be selling it."

Conner closed his eyes. He felt a clock ticking.

"Here," Kayo said. Conner opened his eyes. She was hunting through papers that cluttered the top of a small desk. She found a typed sheet of paper, and started copying information onto a pad of paper.

"Kayo!" said Atsuko.

"He's not her boyfriend," Kayo said.

"That's not what she said," Atsuko fumed.

"Like you've never slept with a man," she said to Atsuko.

Atsuko wrinkled her nose. "Only to keep my job."

Kayo shuddered, as though fighting off unwanted memories. She handed Conner the notepaper. Atsuko stomped to the kitchen and began banging dishes. Conner looked at the note. It was easy enough to puzzle out. Kayo had written down a flight number and time. Canadian Pacific Airlines, flight 4 bound for Vancouver the next day, April first, at 1:55 p.m. April Fools. "Good luck," Kayo said.

"Thanks. Say, do you know what an apostille is?"

"No idea."

Conner got up to leave. There was a smashing sound as a glass broke. Atsuko said "oops" and then another glass crashed purposefully into the sink.

"Just one more thing," Conner said.

Kayo raised her left eyebrow inquiringly.

Conner looked her in the eye. "Do you think Katie was really a lumberjack?"

"You mean one of those people who cuts down trees?" She

frowned and shook her head. "Sounds like work. I can't imagine Katie working."

Conner nodded. He held up the notepaper. "Why did you tell me this?"

"I like you better than Katie. And maybe I'm tired of people lying to me, too."

Another glass shattered in the kitchen.

Conner cringed. "Sorry about causing a fight."

"That's okay. She gets off on it, actually. In fact, why don't you beat it before she calms down?"

CONNER FLOATED BACK to the hideous mansion, where he would be tolerated for one more night. So, Katie had sold the hash to Arata. It was hard to see how that could have happened. The only thing he could think of was that those two goons who'd knocked him around had tracked Katie down. But then how would Arata become involved? Conner sat at the common table, tracing the grain in its wood surface. The Swiss woman squatted on the tatami section of the room silently rebraiding her long red hair. He asked her if she'd heard of anyone trying to sell an orphaned return ticket out to the US, but she hadn't. It was four in the afternoon and Conner's agenda was disturbingly empty. He had nearly forty thousand yen in his pocket, enough to get him a room in a new hostel tomorrow night, and nothing to do but decide how long to pay for—a night, a week, a month?

The hostel was quiet. It was as though a bomb had gone off: destruction everywhere, nothing moving, no sound to be heard, just him standing in the midst of it, twitching like a severed limb.

Conner picked up a pencil off the table and started flicking it against the tabletop. For better or worse, the yakuza had their hash. He wondered if Arata would lose part of his bar now, or all of it. Despite everything, he would like to see Arata, to say goodbye. Conner could already feel his hand tufting over the short stiff hairs at the back of Arata's neck. His heart raced, then slowed. A hot flash crawled like tiny hands over his skin. He put his head on the table. This was what his Dad would call moping. It was not good.

Conner felt his stubbly cheeks and neck. He hadn't shaved since Hawaii. He gathered up his towel, shaving kit and soap to go to the steaming tubs of the public bath to get clean in a way you couldn't in the mansion's dank communal bathroom. He stood one-legged in the genkan putting on his first shoe.

The glass door rattled open. It was Rob, in shorts and a tank-top, panting from a run, smooth tan shoulders gleaming with sweat. Conner checked his watch. Rob should be at work.

Rob looked at Conner's bathing gear. "I'll go with you. Let me get my stuff."

"I'm going now."

"I'll be quick. I have to talk to you." Rob huffed upstairs.

I'm not obligated to wait, Conner thought. I'm not obligated to do anything. For anyone. But he was curious why Rob wanted to talk to him. Maybe they were planning a farewell celebration, since tonight was his last night. He smiled at the implausibility of it. He'd lived there for years but had never been one of the cool kids. Still, he'd miss the mansion. He sat on the stoop until Rob hopped back down the stairs, bath kit in hand.

They walked the couple of streets to the public bath in silence. They checked their shoes, stepped in the door and paid their two hundred yen. Conner caught a glimpse of a bare-breasted older woman dressing near the entrance as he headed into the men's side.

He and Rob undressed, put their clothes in the little lockers, and went in.

The air was hot and steamy. Conner felt himself relax almost instantly. Sets of hot and cold water taps lined the mirrored walls on either side of the tiled bathing area. Conner grabbed a plastic bucket, walked over to a free set of taps, set his bucket down and took a place on a blue plastic stool in the row of naked men. Rob sat down next to him. Conner did his best not to look at Rob, who, still silent, had just dumped a couple of buckets of water over his head, wetting down his hair, his shoulders, sluicing his dark chest hair downward and slicking it to his torso.

Conner poured a bucket of warm water over his own body. Any brotherly feeling washed down the drain with the water Rob was now pouring over his crotch. The guy was hot. Conner had only seen him naked a time or two. Okay, twice, exactly. Both times from the side. The sight was seared in his brain. Conner started getting an erection. He was simultaneously too relaxed and too wired, as though exhaustion was shutting off the socializing circuits in his brain. Sexual orientation was in the brain, not the gonads, but the body seemed to have a separate mind of its own and Conner's was wide awake and wanting to run a hand over Rob's chest. Conner clamped his dick between his legs, which hid him but also further excited him. He poured buckets of water over his back and thought of Japanese grammar, the varying levels and directions of politeness as expressed in up/down verbs of giving and receiving: *ageru, sashiageru, itadaku, morau, kureru, kudasaru, yaru.* How you give is not how you shall receive.

"How did it go with Paul?" Rob asked Conner, smiling.

Conner's hidden erection faded in a flash. Rob was off work because Paul was tracking Conner down. Which meant Paul knew Conner was out of jail. Conner lathered his stubble.

"It was a train wreck." Interesting that Rob would take time off to run an errand for Paul. "Why?" He tugged the razor down his cheek to his jaw line, hacking the stiff hairs, grown too long for an easy shave.

"What happened?"

Conner rinsed the razor in the bucket. "Who is Paul, really?"

"Probably just who you think."

"Okay, Rob. You're off work rather early today. What do you want to know?"

Rob poured water over himself and began soaping up his left leg. He shrugged and began soaping his crotch, legs wide apart, on display. Conner worked on his chin, trying not to look. He remembered how Rob had stood shirtless when he was trying to get Conner to give Paul a call, as though Conner was such a slave to his libido that a little tease was all you needed to get Conner to do what you wanted. He thought of Arata, of Katie. Apparently, that *was* all you needed.

"Do you have the package?" Rob poured water over himself, rinsing.

"You fucker."

"Oh, come on. I did you a solid." Rob stood up and walked, small wash towel over his groin, to the large communal soaking baths at the far end of the bathing area. Conner finished shaving with a few fierce strokes to the neck, nicking himself. He rinsed off and followed. Rob stepped into the hottest bath and moved to the back side.

Conner made his way over to Rob. "You already search my stuff?"

"You don't have stuff. How can a person not have any stuff after five years in Japan?"

"I have stuff," Conner said, testily. He had that red plastic alarm clock from Katie, for instance.

Rob moved over into the warm tub. Conner followed him. Rob moved to the coldest tub. The surface of the water reflected his upper body, so he seemed to have four shoulders, two heads. Conner followed. This time Rob stayed put. He looked into Conner's eyes. "See how you follow me?"

"See how you run away?" Conner glanced at the medicinal tub, a noxious-looking green stew swimming with brown specks. "You've still got the medicinal bath to run to. And the electrical bath and the sauna."

Rob gazed out at the steam of the washing area, sweating. "I know you probably don't have it, or you wouldn't be here, but you can tell me what you did with it. When did you take it out of the envelope?"

"Jeez, they told you everything," Conner said.

"You had a chance at a real sweet deal, Conner, and you blew it for everyone. Paul's had a single personal relationship for fifteen years. Low volume, high profit. I guess you could call it blackmail, if you wanted. You only go once every three months or so. And after Katie took your hash, you needed the gig. You were desperate. You know it."

Yes, conveniently desperate. Rob's words had a boasting tone. He remembered Rob telling him about Paul for the first time. *I'm not sure I should tell you this. . . .* "Desperate" had been Rob's word, not Conner's. *How desperate are you?* It had all flowed so beautifully, like it had been rehearsed. And the only reason Conner had needed money was because Katie, Rob's ex-girlfriend, somehow had known Conner had more than just a joint of hash, something Conner had told no one at the mansion except Rob.

Had Conner's dilemma been deliberately contrived? "You told Katie about the hash before I went to Bangkok?"

Rob shrugged.

Conner's mind went blank, like it didn't want to think what

it had to, like it didn't want to acknowledge the inescapable. But it was inescapable. His mind put the idea into words: Rob and Katie had together *planned* to rob him. After he'd spent not just Arata and Fumie's money, but also his own buying drugs in Thailand, leaving him destitute. Rob introducing him to Paul hadn't been a coincidence; it had been the objective.

Rob's shoulders rippled the water. Under the water his genitals and pubic hair reached upward like a cluster of traumatized anemones. Rob chuckled. "Look on the bright side: you finally got laid."

Conner didn't know where to begin on that one. But why waste time sharing with Rob how the world looked from Conner's perspective? Perhaps the most painful thing was realizing how he'd idolized Rob, had wanted to be him. "Do you get a kick out of showing me your body?"

"Naw, I get a kick out of watching you squirm back into the closet."

"Go to hell."

"Oh, calm down. I'm on your side, not hers. Katie actually called me to see if I wanted to buy the hash. I said no. I didn't tell *her* about Paul. I gave *you* the chance to prove you could do it. So, tell me. What happened to Paul's packet?"

Conner stood up with a splash. "I'm supposed to be grateful for an audition?" Conner yelled. He was attracting stares. He dropped his voice. "The police were onto Paul, not me."

Conner got out of the tub. It stunned him that Katie had been that calculating, devoting a month to a single crime. And yet, it seemed perfectly in character.

Rob hurried after Conner. "Don't take it so hard, man. We all get taken for a ride, once or twice. It's just money. You'll be able to tell the story for years."

Conner went to his locker and took out his clothes. Rob

followed him, standing next to him silently, droplets drying on his skin, this time no running shorts, no wash towel demurely at the groin, just damp and naked, letting Conner really look at him for the first time. Was this supposed to sway Conner? Sadly, it was working. Conner looked. Dang he was sexy. Conner turned away. He shook his head. "I used to look up to you, Rob." He turned his back to Rob and toweled off quickly. Conner pulled on his underwear and dressed, back still slightly wet.

"It's amphetamines, by the way. Not cocaine."

"Yeah, and it's for some Minister's wife, I know."

Rob's eyes narrowed. "Uh, who said that, exactly?"

"Nobody told me. Dumb as I am, I do have a brain. The Minister of Construction's wife. Charming addict Kyoko Mehita. She's the 'sweet deal.'"

Rob forced a laugh. "No way, man. You're nuts." His Adam's apple bobbed up and down.

Conner smiled. It felt great to finally see Rob rattled. "I couldn't figure out at first why someone would want to smuggle speed in, when that's the one thing that's relatively easy to get here. But the way I figure it now, she doesn't want to buy from the yakuza, right? The Minister doesn't want to give his yakuza backers another handle on him, does he? You did say it could be called blackmail, didn't you?"

Rob looked genuinely worried.

It was Conner's turn to laugh. He was tempted to reach down and give Rob's dick a spongy squeeze goodbye, the squeeze Rob seemed to be daring him to take. But it wasn't about the dick. Okay, maybe it was a little about the dick—it was an awesome dick—but instead Conner leaned over and kissed him goodbye, the way all the guys had done in L.A. It felt a bit like home.

Rob jerked away, pushing Conner.

Conner laughed. "You could get a reputation, kissing a man naked at the public bath."

Rob looked around the room to see who was watching and blushed.

"Yes, wouldn't that be horrible." Conner laughed. "See you round."

46

THE FLYPAPER

Marika toed the yellow plastic bumps that warned blind people of the proximity of the subway platform edge at Shinjuku Station. Until the moment Paul and Mama-san had offered her five hundred thousand yen, Marika hadn't believed that Conner would've destroyed the drugs. But it wasn't as hard to turn down dirty money as she'd thought. He might be as much a pawn in this as she was, though he would probably be too proud to admit it.

She opened her handbag. The cellophane-wrapped package was nestled inside. She'd washed and bleached it. Now she really had to destroy it. She exited the ticket gate, walked up the stairway and wandered the underground promenade. There was a trashcan in front of the McDonalds. Putting on a pair of light-brown leather gloves to avoid fingerprints, she tossed the package in the can and walked to the Odakyu line gates. Simple. She bought a ticket and ventured to the edge of the platform. Safe. The package would be burned or buried in a landfill somewhere, able to harm no one. And even if someone found it, she or he would in all likelihood turn it over to the police. There was no way it could be traced to her. She had bleached it clean before she'd left the apartment that afternoon.

But then the ridiculous idea came into her head that someone might indeed chance upon it, maybe even a child. Maybe even eat it. Die from it. The idea was paranoid and impossible. No one would eat it.

Except maybe a derelict. Or a child who thought it was sugar. Marika pictured the poetry girl writhing in agony in the middle of Metro Promenade. Ridiculous, she thought. No one was that stupid. But the poetry girl kept writhing in her mind. The train came. The poetry girl turned blue. Marika walked out through the ticket gate again and up to the trashcan. She stared at it. She needed a cover story. She went into the restaurant and bought a seaburger, the bun pressed into a clamshell shape, and a melon soda. She shouldered the glass doors open and stood by the trashcan with her order. She looked around. No one was watching. She tossed the seaburger in the trashcan.

"Oops," she said, clapping her hands to her cheeks.

She reached into the can and felt around. She found the seaburger, but no drugs. She pulled out her hand. Her glove was streaked with yellow, red and sticky brown.

"Yuck." She stuck her hand back in the can.

"Is something wrong?" Sure enough, a sweet-faced young McDonald's worker was standing beside her.

"No, no. I just dropped my seaburger in the trash by accident." Marika rummaged around.

"I'll get you a new one," she said.

"Waste not, want not," Marika said, coming across a French fry. She pulled it out and waved it at the girl. "They're really good," she said. "Have one."

"I'll just get that fresh one," the girl said, smiling plastically as she retreated.

Marika sniffed the French fry. It smelled warm and probably was really good, but she dropped it back in the trash. She swirled her hand rapidly in a circle. There! She pulled out the now-greasy rectangle and quickly tucked it into her coat.

"Here you are," the girl said.

"Oh," Marika looked up. The blue-uniformed girl was bowing a tray toward her. Marika took the seaburger. "Thanks," she said, smiling big. She hurried off.

"Your soda!"

"Not thirsty anymore." Marika jumped around the corner, bumping into a flustered man. "Sorry." She zipped around a woman's bulging shopping bags and into a public restroom. She ran past the first, open stall into the far one, tucked safely in the corner. She slammed the door and leaned against it, heart pounding as if she were back at the airport. Outside, shoes shuffled. A policeman? Impossible.

Marika pulled the package out of her coat and waited. That scuffing sound again. Someone was out there. She pulled at the duct tape. The wrapping squeaked noisily. Marika stopped. The restroom was so quiet, only that same shuffling was outside her door. That person was still there? Something was odd. Marika's heart was pounding furiously. She *knew* that first stall was open. Marika tucked the package in her purse and cracked the door open for a peek. A hand ripped the door wide.

"Excuse me!" the woman said.

It was the woman with the shopping bags she'd pushed past to get in. Marika stood aside as the woman plunged, smiling, grateful, into the stall. Marika had little choice but to get out and let the woman close the door behind her. Marika looked at the other stall. Out of order. Broken door.

She sighed. The drugs were cursed. She wished she'd let Conner take care of them. She cleaned off her glove and looked in the mirror. Her smeared makeup made her look like Mehita-san again. She felt terrible about hitting Conner over the head with the frying pan. After talking to Paul and Mama-san, Marika had the sinking feeling he'd been telling the truth all along. That put everything in a new light: Conner taking the package. Conner getting arrested. Even Conner ransacking her apartment. At that point he'd come clean about everything, but she couldn't switch gears that fast: lying smuggler to honest . . . something. Well, not that honest. She still had trouble with it. But the police *had* been waiting at Narita, probably for her. And he *had* chased away Betchaku. Had she even thanked him? Well, she'd slept with him, so there was that.

Marika walked through the brightly lit promenade, eating the burger as she searched for another bathroom. She felt calmer now, but it was so noisy she could hardly think. The clatter of foot traffic pounded in her ears. She could feel the smudged foundation on her face. She remembered talking about make-up in Paul's office before the trip, and Paul handing her black bag to her as she left the office. "It will be good cover when you come through customs." Good cover. Like her seaburger. Paul had planned to have the two of them come through customs together with the drugs so they'd look less suspicious. And never even told her. Whereas Conner had meant to go through on his own. Would she ever see him again to tell him she believed him? They could get rid of the drugs together. He'd know some tricks, she was sure.

Marika called Conner's number and asked for him. A Japanese man answered. Conner wasn't there and the man didn't know when he'd be back, but he was moving out tomor-row. No, he didn't know where Conner was moving to, but if

Marika didn't want to wait for him to get back tonight, she might try a bar on Golden Gai. A bar called Giotto.

47

THE REALIZATION

"You're off the hook," Fumie said as Conner barreled through the door of Giotto.

"Yeah, I know. The yakuza got the hash and nobody bothered to tell me."

"Conner, it *just* happened. This morning."

He snorted. "You're a couple of shits. You know that, right?"

Fumie leaned over the counter and looked into Conner's eyes. "We knew you'd be okay." She shoved a stack of CDs at him as he sat at the bar. "Pick one."

He shoved them back. "I've heard them all."

"You're free now," she said, drying a glass. "You don't have to get the hash, see Arata-san, anything. You've come out even in the game."

"As if. I want to see him."

"He doesn't want to see you. He told me specifically." She wiped another glass dry.

"Call him," Conner said.

"He said he doesn't want to talk to you."

"I have money now. I want to at least pay you both back."

She looked at him for a moment, then turned away. "Take the money and go, Conner. You earned it."

"He'll want to take advantage of me. Call him."

"If you knew everything he'd done, you'd go and never come back."

"I thought you were the one always telling me what a nice guy he is, how he got you this life."

She threw up her hands. "I'll call him, if you want." Fumie talked to Arata briefly on the phone. "There's a country and western restaurant down the street from here, a block from Shinjuku Road. He'll meet you there in half an hour."

"Thanks."

"You'll come out the loser."

"Will I?"

CONNER WALKED down the stone pathway away from Giotto. In his way he'd been proud of the sordid little life he'd put together over the past five years. He'd always made do. He'd succeeded at smuggling. It took a certain attitude to pull it off, something you couldn't fake. It was a foolish accomplishment, sure, but it was real. He'd been so wrapped up in fear and depression when he'd arrived. And now? He wasn't fearless by any means, but he was never depressed, and he could do difficult things. Next time, though, the difficult thing, whatever that turned out to be, would be something worth doing for its own sake, not to prove something to himself, not out of guilt, not out of obligation. Maybe some legitimate import business, like he'd imagined Paul having. He could use his skills, make that a reality, enjoy it, even. He turned onto a sidewalk and walked until he was at the large wooden doors of the country and western restaurant.

The restaurant was spacious, with high-backed wooden

booths, a few tables and a long bar. Conner stepped up to the bar and asked for a *chu sawa*.

Arata soon walked in, ordered a beer and motioned Conner to join him in a booth. He didn't look as competent to Conner as he used to. In fact, he looked a little bit like a puffed up, soon-to-be-middle-aged bar owner. Conner sat down across the table from him.

"I knew you'd come," Conner said.

Arata grunted affirmatively. He ran his hand through his salt-and-pepper hair and looked impassively at Conner, every feature so familiar. Conner wanted to punch him.

"You don't have to give me the money," Arata said.

"I'm not going to."

Arata bristled. "You do owe me."

"You got your hash and sold it. Technically, you owe *me*."

Arata straightened his tie. "Then why did you want to see me?"

Conner licked his lips. "Did you send two guys to rough me up?"

"Two guys roughed you up?"

"Look at my face, you shit." Conner didn't buy Arata's dumb act. Between that "yakuza" phone number Hideo had written on the note, Carmen's feckless and trusting nature, and the fact that Katie and Rob were a team, Conner now had a pretty good idea what had happened. Someone had given Katie that number. And if those two guys were actual yakuza, Katie would have gone to them. But she'd gone to Giotto. Before it opened. She'd gone to Arata. There were no yakuza.

"I swear, Conner, I did not send them."

Conner watched Arata drain his glass of beer. Was it all lies? Conner remembered the feel of Arata's body next to his, his skin alive with warmth, and wanted to hold him close. The idea also repelled him. Why was he still drawn to Arata? It was like the way he'd idolized Rob, only far more potent. Conner stared at the TV above the bar.

"It doesn't matter now anyway. You're not going to see me again. I wanted you to know that I know you sent those guys." Conner couldn't stand to look him in the face and say it. "All this time, I just wanted . . ." But what *did* he want, really? To make things right? To be in love? To earn the respect of Edward and Toby, watching him from the afterlife, by recreating what they'd had?

The TV droned. Conner looked at Arata, raising his eyebrows, trying to get Arata to supply an answer.

Arata reached for the Asahi and started to fill his own glass. His hand began to shake. Conner was supposed to be pouring, if they were friends of any sort. Conner grabbed the bottle and finished filling the glass. He put the sweating bottle down. Arata picked up his glass and drank half.

Conner looked at his smooth high cheeks. Arata's brow suddenly furrowed.

"I lied about the yakuza," Arata said. "About the lawsuit. I mean after I lost." He grew quiet. "I made a deal."

"I know that."

He shook his head. "It was a different kind of deal than you think." Arata finished his glass of beer and poured himself another, his hands still shaking. "Conner, I'm sorry, I'm so sorry. I wish I hadn't done it."

"Tell me."

"I gave them half the bar."

"You mean because the hash was late?"

"No, I mean after we lost in court. They never saw the hash. I sold it to someone else to make money. The yakuza don't know a thing about it and never did." He cleared his throat. "There is no deadline."

"Does Fumie know?"

He shook his head. He looked ashamed. "I lied to her, too."

"I could have been thrown in jail ten times over, Arata. Why?"

"Because I'm not a loser, damn it. I can't be poor. That's supposed to be my reward for marrying her, but now I've lost my house and half my bar and gained nothing, absolutely nothing. I was so mad at you. I thought you deserved it. Conner, I'm sorry. I've lost everything. I don't want to lose you too."

Conner sat very still, like a piece of stone. He'd waited for those words so long. It felt nothing like he'd expected. He felt so very different than he had in Bangkok, just ten days ago, almost a different person. Did Conner even want this prize?

He did not.

He got up and left. Arata followed him out. Conner shivered on the sidewalk and pulled his jacket tight, phrasing goodbyes in his mind as the door swung closed behind them. Pachinko balls roared inside the parlor next door. The bells and whistles and incessant clacking burst louder whenever a customer stepped through the automatic doors. Arata looked up and down the street, the sparkle of the pachinko marquee reflected in his eyes. They stood together on the sidewalk, both shivering now. Reflections of pink light jumped over Arata's forehead.

"Come on," Arata said. "Please."

Conner laughed. The crash pad. Arata was asking him to go. It felt good to be asked, in actual words, to hear Arata say *please*. It felt like victory. "If you want," Conner said, like Arata was a trick, some random guy he wanted to have sex with. What would it be like to have sex with this guy, freed of the compulsion to serve him? It might be worthwhile to find out.

·   ·   ·

IT WAS fun to pretend Arata was some anonymous hot guy, to touch him, undress him, run his hands over his smooth chest, exciting to pull him close, to kiss him. To have this stranger peel back Conner's pants and take his dick into his hand, then mouth. "Slowly," Conner said, feeling Arata's lips on the hardening head of his dick.

It was so quiet. Conner ran his hands over Arata's waist, his firm butt, under the bright fluorescent light. But he couldn't pretend Arata was just a trick. There was magic in being with him. It was a humiliating, unfriendly magic, but Conner wanted it anyway. He kissed Arata's neck and shoulders. He pulled out a condom, his last.

"Here."

"I've told you, I don't need this," Arata said. "I'm Japanese."

"I don't care if you're a fucking Martian; if you don't put it on you don't put it in." Conner had used condoms every time he'd ever had sex, and he wasn't breaking that streak now.

Arata put it on. Conner bent over on his hands and knees. He wanted sex, but he didn't want to see Arata's face. He felt Arata lube him up and enter him. It hurt for a moment, then Arata began thrusting and it hurt more. "Wait," Conner said.

Arata didn't let up.

"Will you fucking let up for a minute till I relax! You're ruining this." But there wasn't much to ruin, just a threadbare fantasy, leaking vitality through innumerable rips and tears, a fabric that could no longer hold anything.

Arata stopped moving. They waited a moment as Conner's muscles relaxed.

"Okay," Conner said.

Arata resumed his motion slowly, and gradually it felt warm and stimulating as Arata moved inside him. This was when he'd always felt closest to Arata, this or when he was inside Arata, when their bodies were bonded. It had been at least a year since anyone had been up in there. It had been at least five years since anyone besides Arata had been up there. It was not the sort of thing you did with just anyone, not for Conner at least. Edward had said the same. As with everything else, Edward had been right. How had he gotten so wise at only twenty-eight? When Edward died, he had been barely three years older than Conner was now. When Conner had last talked to him on the phone, he should have heard it in Edward's voice, the pop and bubble of fluid in his lungs, the overlong recovery from each cough. Edward had said it was just a cold. Like everyone else, Conner had been worried for so long that Toby was dying. Edward was supposed to be the healthy one. He was supposed to take care of Toby till Toby died. That was the way it was supposed to be. Edward had promised. Toby's sister and brother-in-law, flying in at the last minute and thinking themselves heroes, were so focused on Toby circling the drain they hadn't noticed how sick Edward had gotten. And Conner had been so irritated by the grasping pair he'd been staying away. Three days in the hospital and it was over.

If only Conner had gone over to the house during those last days or even called, heard the change in Edward's voice, Edward might still be alive, even now. Conner would still be in L.A.

Edward, you promised, he thought. Even if I wasn't there to notice, even if Toby was too drugged on morphine to notice, even if Toby's fucking in-laws were too self-absorbed to notice, you yourself must have known how serious it was.

You knew.

You knew I loved you. And you let yourself die.

Arata groaned. Conner kept his hands on the tatami as Arata clutched Conner's waist and pumped against him. Arata leaned close over Conner's back, arms grasping Conner's chest, weight leaning into Conner. He felt the movement of Arata inside him, the life inside him. And it felt damned fine. He didn't want time to go on. But his body did. It was a man's skin pressed warm against his, a man groaning behind him, a man's hand around his excited cock, and Conner couldn't keep from coming, spurting tightly onto the golden tatami, hearing in the spaces of their breathing the soft wet sounds of come landing on straw. And a moment later Arata thrust and groaned and squeezed Conner's ribs so tight he thought he would die.

They fell to the tatami and lay together, Arata hugging Conner from behind. Arata kept his arm wrapped around Conner's chest, babbling some rationalizing, self-justifying nonsense, his cheek on Conner's neck as his erection remained stiff inside Conner. Now Conner listened to Arata's voice, not his words.

Conner remembered the phone call he'd received just before the guys came to beat him up. At first he'd thought the voice was Arata's, but then thought it wasn't. Listening to Arata now he knew why he'd thought it was Arata. It was the phrasing, the drawn-out vowels. He could feel the Niigata dialect hovering.

Of *course* Arata had sent the two guys to beat him up. They weren't yakuza. Nothing could ever repair that damage. Conner contracted his sphincter, pushing Arata's dick out of him. It was enough.

Arata kissed Conner's back. Conner felt his eyes watering. It's stupid to cry, he thought, utterly stupid, and he buried his face in the pillow. He'd thought Katie had screwed everything up, but it hadn't really been Katie's or even Rob's fault. It had been Arata's, for lying, for being greedy. And Conner's, for confusing Arata with Edward, with Toby, with the other good people he knew, like Marika, like Hideo, like Kayo and

Carmen even. For hoping too long. But now he knew that, really, it was not such a crime to pretend that things were, or would be, better than they are, not such a crime at all. Edward had only done what he had to. He'd gone ahead to be with the man he loved.

Conner pressed Arata's flawed arm to his chest and kissed it. He forgave Edward, forgave himself, forgave Arata, and felt light, weightless, knowing for everything there is a last time, and this, finally, was it.

48

THE UNBEAUTIFUL

Marika had heard of Golden Gai. It had apparently been famous in the high-growth days, about the time she was born, but its glamour had faded considerably and she didn't know where it was. She asked people for directions as she wandered through Shinjuku and was directed into Kabuki-cho. Here? she thought, as she wandered among the movie theaters and sex clubs. But as she got closer, she was directed out of Kabuki-cho to a small, narrow block of alleys. She walked down a street of eerie quiet till she found a sign reading "Giotto." She opened the door.

"*Irasshai*," a tall woman called out.

Marika quickly scanned the dark little room. Conner wasn't there, just the tall, short-cut woman working the bar. Marika sat down and ordered a beer. The woman gave her a dish of *miso-kyu*—fresh, crisp cucumber spears to cut the beany tang of the purple-brown fermented miso paste. The woman changed the CD to some strange astral music Marika had never heard before.

"Do you know an American named Conner?"

The woman pulled a swizzle stick from a cup. "And you are?"

"I'm just a friend of his." And maybe not even that.

The woman leaned forward on the black counter and looked at Marika like she was from the planet Baltan. "He's never mentioned you."

"I haven't known him long, not even a week." And slept with him twice. Boy, would Isamu be surprised. Boy, was she surprised.

"I've never known him to have any woman friends, except me." The woman laughed nervously. "I'm his buddy. Used to be, anyway."

Did that mean she knew Conner was a homo? Marika hadn't fully believed that, for obvious reasons, but apparently it was true.

Marika looked up at the grubby bottles lining the wall behind the bar. What a seedy place. "What happened between you?" Marika asked.

"It's personal," she said.

Oh boy. Attitude again. Marika grabbed up her purse to leave. "If you see him, tell him Marika was looking for him. To apologize."

"Wait, *you* want to apologize?" The woman poured more beer into Marika's glass. "To *him*?"

Marika looked her over. This was the first of Conner's friends she'd met. She seemed interesting, though a bit strong. "I hit him over the head with a frying pan." Marika laughed. "I thought he was lying to me. Well, he was, but then he told me the truth." She laughed again. "I never hit anyone before in my life. Not that he didn't deserve it."

"I don't think he'll be coming around anymore, actually." She sounded resigned, possibly guilty.

Marika pulled out a thousand yen to pay for the beer, which she hadn't touched. "Maybe that's for the best."

"Look. If it makes any difference, he was sort of tricked into it."

"It?" She didn't want to give any secrets away. "The, uh, customs thing?"

The woman nodded, and explained how her boss had maneuvered Conner into "it" the first time. Marika didn't buy it. People didn't trick you into doing something that important. Risking twenty years of your life was something too big for even the most misguided to miss.

Wasn't it?

A bushy-browed man entered the bar and sat at the counter a couple seats down from Marika.

"Don't say anything," the woman whispered. She wiggled her fingers at the man. "Kuwano-san, good evening."

Marika looked over at the man. He bowed jerkily at her. "Good evening," he said to Marika.

"Good evening," Marika said. "Who's he?" she whispered to the woman.

"I think he's police."

She looked again. Oh, no. She recognized him from the airport. He was definitely a policeman. It made perfect sense that he would be here; that's how Conner knew him. Marika had walked not two feet away from this man outside the bathrooms at the airport, and not in disguise either, but looking very much as she did now. And like then, she had the cursed drugs on her. Everyone wanted them but her and she couldn't get rid of them.

"Your boss not here yet, huh?" the policeman asked the woman.

"How much do I owe you?" Marika said, still clutching the thousand-yen note.

"You're good," the woman said.

"Well, see you later," she said. "And thanks."

She left Giotto and hustled her way through Kabuki-cho toward the station, worried the policeman might be following her. She turned around. He was nowhere to be seen. She went into the mostly unused pedestrian tunnel under the JR tracks. Its dingy yellow walls glared under the artificial light and smelled faintly of smoke and urine. She hurried through to the other end and waited in the misty evening air.

Kuwano-san's face did not appear. He would have to come this way; it was a good kilometer around if you burrowed through the station to get under the tracks. She waited longer. Still he did not appear. Marika breathed a sigh of relief. So many people had been watching her—Eriko, Yuuske, Betchaku. Mama-san, Shin-chan and Ai. And Conner, watching her pour hot water into whisky, touching her with his shifty gray eyes. She had always worried too much about what other people thought, like that subterfuge with the seaburger. She could have reached into the trash and no one in Japan would ever in ten thousand years guess she was searching for a package stuffed with drugs.

She pulled the package from her purse. Standing on the only quiet sidewalk in Shinjuku, she wrestled open the last few twisted layers. White powder spilled from the rent plastic. She shook the powder out onto the dewy street. The cars would destroy it for her, the gentle waters of the first *tsuyu* of spring would sweep it all away. The powder slipped out. Who was to say it wasn't a bag of corn starch? Elated, she flung it straight up into the air. White powder snowed down on her hair. She caught the package and ripped it wider. Now people were staring. This was too much, even for her new, liberated self. A burly businessman with a face like a snail grunted something unintelligible. To hell with him, and everyone like him. She was so tired of people thinking they knew better than she did how she should behave.

She leaned over the railing and twisted the little package back and forth over the street until there was nothing but a dirty empty wrapper in her hand and a little snowy white dust frosting her hair, shoulders and eyelashes. Then, through the tunnel walking toward her she saw a familiar Shinjuku face. Betchaku. He trudged slowly toward her. She licked the powder from her lips. It tingled.

"Marika," he said. "I can't stop thinking about you."

Marika laughed. She couldn't help herself. And as she laughed Betchaku stood there looking forlorn. She wanted him in jail, but she also felt sorry for him. "I'm sorry, Betchaku-san. But whatever would we talk about?"

He shifted from side to side. "I'm helpless," he mourned.

"Betchaku-san. You're no more helpless than I am. I'm just not right for you. And I don't like you. You can't follow women around and tell them you love them. And you certainly shouldn't push nasty pictures at them. Do you actually think anyone would like that?"

"It's not sexy?"

"Not at all. Listen, Betchaku-san. Throw away the pictures. And if you like a woman, ask her to dinner. Ask Rei-chan. She might like to go. No, maybe not. But you can find someone. It's not impossible, if you treat her like a friend."

"But I can't find anyone beautiful like you."

"What's so special about beautiful?"

He stood there, stony-faced, unbeautiful.

"Treat other people with respect. That makes *you* beautiful. And if you ask a woman out, and she doesn't want to go, please, don't follow her home."

He looked at her, crushed and exposed, the picture of humiliation.

"Okay?"

He stood motionless. She waved goodbye and left him standing there, his face slowly decaying into a scowl, at the mouth of a yellowy tunnel just steps away from a small fortune in white euphoria being ground to slush under taxi tires.

49

FISCAL NEW YEAR

Nine o'clock on the morning of April first, Conner rattled open the glass door at the mansion, coming back to get his things. He hadn't bothered to wake Arata when he left. The guy had paid people to beat Conner up, so there wasn't much point in a verbal see-you-later. Conner squatted beside the phone and punched in the Canadian Pacific phone number Kayo had given him. Katie's flight to Vancouver was on time to leave at 1:55 that afternoon. Check-in was two hours previous. That didn't leave a lot of time.

He trotted upstairs and wedged a brief goodbye note into Carmen's door. He thought of what Hideo had said about the expectations of others, and what Fumie had said about people in her Aomori hometown assuming she'd fuck up. If you could live up to expectations, perhaps you could also live down to them. It was something to think about. He wrote Hideo a quick note—*Thanks for everything. Sorry I screwed up. Gone to Narita.*

It was good. Let Hideo and Carmen think he'd left the country. He would, too, as soon as he could somehow boost his remaining yen into enough for a budget two-week advance-purchase ticket home. He thought of the many travelers he'd met, and felt a pang at giving up the world of connections he'd built up over the years.

Rob was asleep too. Conner quietly packed his black bag and realized how little he had after being here so long. Rob had been right. Clothes, an alarm clock, and *Death of an Old Woman*. Everything fit in his bag except Katie's red silk robe. He left the robe draped over Rob's sleeping form. Wear this in remembrance of me. He closed the door and left.

FROM THE WINDOW of the nearly empty limited express to Narita, Conner watched the cold gray clouds that seemed to hover continually this time of year. Outside, Tokyo rolled by—blocky, nondescript buildings, grimy steel freeways, and here and there the dark green of a park, a snatch of glinting river or the occasional modern architectural gem. He slept.

The Narita Airport train station was new, long, and paneled in white marble. Very ritzy. Signs in English invited the traveler to be inspected, as though there were the option of declining.

A short, stocky policeman motioned Conner forward. "Passport and ticket," he said.

Conner handed his passport to the man. "I'm picking up a friend." Security had remained tight since the era of farmer protests and radical leftist bomb attacks, before Narita had opened, and without his little blue passport he wouldn't be able to get in. Even Japanese had to have government-issued picture ID, which was harder to come by in a city where few drove.

The officer grunted. He had a mole on his nose and gave Conner the cold Japanese stare he hardly noticed anymore. It was past time for chatting anyway. Beyond the steel inspection stations stood a crisp row of policemen, hands hidden behind their backs, ready to stop him forcibly if they had to. Conner's officer pointed in the direction of the airport, and Conner walked through the vanguard and into Narita.

The airport building was huge, a spacious cavern. Katie could be anywhere. She might even have come on the same train as he and he wouldn't have known. Conner scanned the hordes. The terminal was very crowded and there were many non-Japanese, but most were Southeast or South Asian so a tall woman with long, straight blond hair should still be possible to spot. He went up the four flights of escalators to the departure floor.

Korean Air, Varig, Alitalia: black signposts with big green-lit numbers marked the six aisles of check-in counters. He walked till he found Canadian Pacific. A giant departing-flights board clicked over as the flight information was updated. Conner checked for the Canadian Pacific emblem. Vancouver. The flight was listed. It was still on time.

He walked to the departure lounge bar, bought a coke and a sandwich and found a spot near a potted palm that gave him a good line of sight to the Canadian Pacific counter.

Three days before, he had been arrested four levels below the barstool on which he now sat, but here he felt safe. No one cared what you took away from Japan, so long as you paid for it. A woman's voice echoed down in Japanese and English from the enormous ceiling of black metal lattice: "Departing passengers on American Airlines flight 34 please proceed to passport control now."

A blond head bopped down the aisle toward him. Katie. She still had great eyebrows. Hey, maybe Conner was an eyebrowsexual. He conjured Kuwano's face and felt a certain excitement. He might be onto something.

Katie didn't seem to see him. She put two spiffy, matching bags on the pre-check-in X-ray conveyor and went to the other end of the machine, waiting for them to appear through the black rubber curtain. She picked up her bags—bags that Conner's efforts and drug users' desires had paid for—and walked to the Canadian Pacific line.

She was so close; if he called to her, she would hear.

She got in line behind a group of Filipinos with mounds of cardboard *balikbayan* boxes addressed to Manila. Each box was at least four cubic feet and they were piled five high. Finally, Katie eased her bags up to the front of the line and leaned toward the clerk, smiling at one of the Filipino men. Conner saw her mouth say something, attempting to charm him, and then he smiled and lifted her bags onto the scales for her. She had the touch. If you didn't know her.

The clerk took Katie's passport. The passengers in line were all watching her, now, as she flicked her hair like a pony. The clerk handed Katie her boarding pass and pointed toward the stairs down to Passport Control, smiling. She tucked her boarding pass in the outer pocket of her carry-on. The top of the pass gleamed white and exposed, marked by a colorful band of green and red.

"Departing passengers on Canadian Pacific Airlines, flight 4, bound for Vancouver, please check out customs and immigration now." The way the voice said *now* was commanding.

At the top of the stairs to Passport Control, she stopped at the airport fee machine to search her purse for the two thousand yen she needed. Conner walked up behind her and quietly slid the boarding pass out of the pocket of her carry-on as she leaned forward to feed her bills into the machine. He looked at it. Katie was short for Caitlin. Caitlin Morgan. He slipped the pass quietly into his jacket pocket. It was as easy to steal from her as it had been for her to steal from him.

"Hi, Katie," he said.

MARIKA WOKE WITH A CRUSHING HANGOVER. She hadn't drunk much—the glass on the kotatsu still had a centimeter of whisky—but she had smoked cigarettes manically and called Conner every half hour last night, partly to thank him, partly to tell him she'd destroyed the drugs. He hadn't called back, though, and at some point, she had fallen asleep. Now her hair stank of smoke. Marika squeezed her eyes tight and called again. The same Japanese man answered the phone. There was a clunk as he put down the phone to go check on Conner. There was a scraping sound and Marika heard the man's breath again.

"He's already left," he said, sounding pensive. "All his things are gone."

"Gone?" Marika looked at the clock beside her. A quarter to ten. "Do you know where?"

"To Narita, I think."

"He's leaving the country?"

"Sure looks like it."

"Thanks," she said, "thanks very much," and hung up. She would go after him. A picture of Isamu and Eriko, irate and disapproving, flashed through her mind—you are going to say goodbye to a criminal?—but the picture faded quickly.

She showered, popped a couple of aspirin, flung on the clothes she'd worn the night before and rushed out the door, stopping only for the passport she'd need to get through Narita security. She caught a train to another train to another train to Narita.

As she passed through the barbed-wire barricades and airport police inspection, she felt a tickle of fear. The several days with drugs had left her skittish. But the drugs had been destroyed and the crime canceled out.

She squeezed between two black-uniformed cops and rode a few escalators up into the terminal building. She went up to the departure floor and scanned the departure board but had no idea where Conner was going. There was a flight to Los Angeles, but it didn't leave for another five hours. Marika walked up and down the terminal. The flight board information clicked down methodically above her.

KATIE TOOK her ticket from the machine and turned around.

"Hello, Conner."

She smiled at him, her lips opening slowly to show those even, white teeth. She looked so good and seemed so friendly, Conner couldn't help smiling back. It was a big smile.

"Are you going somewhere?" he asked.

"Yeah," she said. "You?"

Conner nodded. "Going to visit the folks."

"You have folks?"

"And a sister, too." Conner grinned. "I must say, you're about the last person I expected to see here." Conner kept grinning. She knew it was all lies. But it didn't matter.

She laughed. "Did Atsuko tell you?"

"Kayo. I've been looking for you pretty hard."

"I sold the hash."

"I know. I'm sure you got ripped off."

"Four hundred."

"Arata paid you four hundred thousand?" *He* was supposed to have gotten five. "Four hundred thousand?"

"And I smoked some."

Conner laughed. "You're lying. I can tell now. You got two

fifty, tops. Two-hundred, more like. You were robbed." He laughed again.

Katie turned to go. "Hey, I've really got to run. My plane's already boarding."

"You have a minute. I just have one question."

Conner stared her in the eyes.

She stared back.

Conner held his gaze. He had planned to ask her how she could do it, how she could lie in wait for a month, turn on someone like that. Now, it just didn't seem important. She could do it because she had decided other people don't matter. She probably didn't even know she felt that way. Conner looked her over. He wanted to remember her. Her eyes flickered over the departure hall.

"Well, what?" she asked. "You want to know if I took your hash? Of course I did. You want to know why? For the money. Or is it some stupid ego thing? Did I *care* for you?" Her voice was filled with a sneering quality that was supposed to make Conner feel small but instead sounded childish. "What?" she said.

"Were you really a lumberjack?"

"Hardest job I ever did," she said. "Sweaty, lonely, long days. How else do you think I got these guns?" She flexed.

"I knew it. No one else believes you, you know." Conner felt absurdly happy. "How much money do you have?"

"How much money?" she said incredulously. "How much money?"

"Split it with me. Set things right. You messed me up big time. Sure, I was already messed up—smuggling hash was a deeply stupid thing to do—but you sure didn't help. It's only fair."

"I don't have any to spare."

"Can't you find a little soul in there somewhere? What's wrong with you anyway?"

"Jesus Christ, Conner. No one can answer a question like that. Some woman's waving at you." She picked up her bag and turned.

Conner felt a tug at his arm. He turned. It was Marika. "Well, hi," he said.

"I found you," she said, breathless. "Goodbye. I came to say goodbye."

Conner turned back to Katie.

She had opened her bag and shoved a handful of money at him. "Here, take this, stud. No hard feelings." She hopped down the stairs.

"Don't you want to go after your friend?" Marika asked.

"No." Conner watched Katie run down the stairs. "She's not my friend. She's the one I told you about who robbed me. And she's not going far." Conner looked at the money. About fifty dollars Canadian. Gee, such generosity. That would buy him a week's Happy Meals. Katie's head disappeared down toward Passport Control. In about ten minutes she would discover she had no boarding pass. "Let's get out of here. Up there, the observation lounge. We have something to observe."

They raced up the stairs to a small corridor of restaurants by the observation lounge, the highest point in the terminal.

Marika pulled Conner over to the side of the corridor. "I destroyed the drugs last night."

"I'm glad. I knew you had them."

"I grabbed them from the trash after you got rid of the pouch at the airport. The packet was first in the frying pan and then on me when you wrecked my apartment."

Conner laughed. "Clever."

"I talked to Paul and found out you were basically telling the truth. I think the drugs were for Mrs. Mehita."

"I think so too."

"And I am guessing she was once a hostess at Stardust and that's where she met her husband, the future minister, which she doesn't want anyone to know. I mean, these days, who cares, but she's older. Shame dies hard."

"Interesting."

"You would have destroyed the drugs, right?"

"Today, for sure. Yesterday, sixty/forty odds for me destroying them. You were probably right to keep them from me."

"That makes me feel better. Did that frying pan hurt?"

"Heck yeah." How odd it was to see her at this point. "Guess this is goodbye."

"You're not really leaving, are you?"

He nodded. "It's time. As soon as Katie comes up those stairs, I'm going to slip around behind her and clear Passport Control. They never check IDs against boarding passes."

"Why not stay here? I don't want to be your lover or anything, but I think you're my first real friend in Tokyo and I don't want to give you up."

Conner wavered. Stay here? He'd trashed Tokyo for himself, but everyone he cared about was here: Marika, Hideo, even Carmen. And what would he do back in the States? Sweep up late nights at El Pollo Loco? He had been not quite twenty-one when he left L.A. He had had little experience in the adult American world. He could give Katie back her boarding pass. There she came now, up the stairs, conveniently blond. If she turned, if she knew where to look, she could even see them.

"Oh, no," Marika said.

Conner followed the line of her finger to Katie and beyond.

Police. Shimoda and Kuwano. Coming toward them.

"So much for that plan," Conner said.

Marika grabbed his arm. "But it's *her* boarding pass. The police won't know to flag *her* on their computers. I bet they don't even enter the passport numbers from those paper cards till evening. This close to boarding you can probably breeze through Passport Control."

She was right. He hadn't bought a ticket, so he wasn't on any manifest. But it was such a rushed goodbye.

"Marika . . ."

"Go," she said. "Run!"

"Okay then. Wish me luck." He took off as she went up the last few steps to the observation lounge.

Conner raced through the bright, Formica-tiled passage and hopped the railing to land on the down escalator in the center of the building, looping around both Katie and the police.

He checked his watch. Take-off was in another thirty-three minutes. Conner looked up at the board. The flight was listed as *On time*. He could see Katie arguing with the Canadian Pacific clerk. She'd dropped the charm. She was being herself now and it wasn't working. He reached the stairs down to Passport Control, bought an airport departure fee ticket from one of the machines and went downstairs.

The lines were horrendous. Thirty-one minutes to go. Conner pushed to the front of the line and held out his passport and the boarding pass as he scribbled the flight number onto the departure card stapled in his passport.

"My flight leaves in thirty minutes." He pointed at the boarding pass.

The passport officer looked at the time and flight number and took Conner's passport. "Sorry," Conner said to the woman behind him. She smiled, and he thanked her.

The officer opened it to the first page, looked at Conner's face. "Floyd Conner."

Conner nodded.

The man stamped his passport and he was through. Officially out of Japan. He moved to the center of the large open area beyond the passport stations. Duty-free shops lined the walls of the passages to the gates. Red Dunhills and cognac. He took a deep breath.

The only record he'd come through was the departure card the officer had ripped from his passport. They would have to go through all the stacks from all the stations to know he was in here. A policeman stood by the plexiglass walls of the lounge balcony fifty feet above. Conner ducked, but there was nowhere to duck to. Another policeman. But, of course, they weren't looking down where he was. He was home free. There was Shimoda. And Kuwano.

And Marika.

Kuwano had her by the arm. Oh, shit. Why were they taking her in? If they'd seen her going through customs at Narita, they would have grabbed her then. They hadn't seen her in Hawaii except in disguise. They couldn't have identified her from seeing them together today, not at the distance Shimoda had been. But they might have followed him to her apartment. He must have led them to her. He could see less and less of them as they walked away and Marika seemed to shrink into the ground until nothing was left but her head and then that too was gone.

MARIKA SAT in a small windowless room of the airport police station. The black-and-white spaniel sniffed her coat again and pawed.

"It's definitely there," Kuwano said. "Amphetamines all over her coat. It's enough to convict."

Shimoda nodded. "Good. So, tell us, Ushirone-san. Where is Conner?"

"My name is Shirayama."

"That's not what it says here." He held the red passport in front of her face. The gold sun pattern on its cover was mesmerizing. He handed the passport to Kuwano.

"That's my husband's name, not mine." Marika reached down and petted the dog. The dog wagged her tail. Kuwano jerked his head toward the door and one of the uniformed policemen took the dog out. Another placed Marika's leather coat in a thick plastic bag and took it away. Kuwano flipped through the passport.

"Shimoda-san, Shimoda-san, look at this." He seemed on the verge of dancing. He shoved the open passport before Shimoda's face, pointing to the entrance stamps in her passport. "The dates! Think about it. We have to give that guy Betchaku a reward."

"So, it was you," Shimoda said. "What were you doing in Hawaii?"

Marika shrugged half-heartedly. She looked around the windowless room. It was a little dirty. The airport seemed a lot more than thirteen years old. Betchaku must have talked to Kuwano the night before. She could picture it: he probably picked up the drug wrapper, took it to the Shinjuku Police Station and they connected him with Kuwano. And Kuwano had recognized her from her visit to Giotto. Betchaku was an irredeemable creep. She shook her head. They hadn't known she was in Hawaii, so they would never have arrested her if she hadn't gone to the bar yesterday. To apologize about a frying pan. She wished she was back in Inudani safe with

Isamu. Could she summon tears? They'd probably lighten up on her if she cried.

"How do you know Zakabi?"

"He was introduced to me by a friend."

"Who?"

"What's going to happen to me?"

"Who introduced you to Zakabi?"

She couldn't believe it had come to this. "I don't want to go to jail." She willed her eyes to tear up but was too frightened. "I really don't."

"Look, we know you are playing a small role. If you help us get the people behind you, we can go easy on you. But we do need names. Names and times."

Something told her that she and Conner would be the only ones to go to jail if she told them about Paul and Mama-san. Those two had the Minister of Construction behind them. She thought of how the cops hadn't come when she'd called about Betchaku pounding on her door. "Can you give me a hint?" she tried.

"This is not a joke!" Shimoda yelled at her.

Marika was scared. Conner had never said what happened to him during those two days, but he'd arrived at her door with fresh cuts and bruises. She bowed her head. "Excuse me." Can I just go back to Inudani and forget this ever happened? she thought. She pictured Isamu again, irate. But why shouldn't he be? He was no prize, but Marika had known that when she married him, and went ahead anyway. Marika had lied to him. She hadn't loved him, not even then. She wanted to go back to Inudani, but only to apologize to Isamu, to let him move on with his life.

Shimoda leaned close. "Why don't we take this from the top?" He snapped his fingers. Kuwano gave him a thick enve-lope. Shimoda placed some photos on the table. Her sitting down to dinner at the hotel in Hawaii in that hideous dress. Her with Zakabi. Her with the two Japanese-speaking white Americans in Hawaii. "Now, what were you doing in Hawaii?"

"That's not me."

"Get a woman to search her," Shimoda commanded.

"There's nothing on me," Marika said. "I swear."

Shimoda leaned back in his chair and asked Kuwano for a cigarette. Kuwano uncrossed his arms and passed Shimoda a short Hope. "You'll get full detective for this, Kuwano-kun," Shimoda said.

"Yeah, and you can go into politics." Kuwano smiled and nodded quickly.

Shimoda laughed. "You kidding? I'll die a policeman."

Marika scuffed her feet over the gritty floor and stared at the door, half-expecting to see Itami Juzo step out and say "cut" so she could collect her paycheck and go home. But instead, a wrinkled obaa-chan came out and directed her into another room.

"Disrobe," she said.

Marika slowly stripped, placing her shoes and clothes on the table.

"Everything," the woman yapped.

Marika stiffened, but took off her underwear and shivered. "Stand here."

Marika moved under the light and stood barefoot on the cold tile hoping this would be over as soon as possible. The woman began going through her clothes, piece by piece.

CONNER PACED BACK AND FORTH, ready to tear his skin off. He had to do something. He thought hard. He could get to Marika by going out through Arrivals. This would be the briefest trip on record. Departure at one twenty-five, arrival at one twenty-seven. Technically, he would have left Japan without leaving Narita. He hid his bag, cleared flight security and ran down toward the gates, intending to hop from one moving sidewalk to the other. But when he got to the sidewalks, he found a floor-to-ceiling Plexiglas barrier between them.

"What the hell?" The barrier hadn't been there when they'd flown three days before. Okay, Plan B. He could blend in with arriving passengers. He ran the rest of the way out to the gates. A flight was coming in and he could see passengers walking toward Arrivals. But they were cordoned off from the departing passengers by makeshift barriers and large numbers of policemen. There was no way he could get through.

"What happened to security here?" Conner asked a policeman.

"It's the War," he said.

"What War?"

"In the Gulf."

"What war in the Gulf?"

"Bush invaded Kuwait. Don't you read?"

Great, Conner thought. Where's peace when you need it?

"Canadian Pacific flight 4 is now boarding," the woman's voice announced from above.

There was a bank of telephones on the far wall. Conner ran to them. He pushed a thousand-yen bill into the telephone card machine. "Come on, come on." A telephone card oozed slowly out of the machine. He slipped it into the telephone and dialed Paul.

The receptionist picked up the phone.

"This is Conner. Give me Paul, right away."

"He's in a meeting."

"Do it now!" he yelled.

There was a silence on the line.

"Moshi-moshi." Paul's voice sounded short and irritated.

"This is Conner. I'm at Narita. Marika's been arrested. If you don't call your Minister's wife and get Narita Police Central to release Marika, I'm going to turn myself in and tell them everything."

"I don't know who you're talking about."

"Kyoko Mehita, wife of Minister of Construction Junnosuke Mehita. The one who buys amphetamines and sells Hawaiian condos to pay for them. The one you're blackmailing."

Paul went silent again. "What are you doing at Narita?" Paul said.

Shit! He wasn't going for it. "Perhaps I'll call my yakuza friend to tell them what a wonderful sales opportunity they've been missing: a politician's wife with an expensive habit. She's a little strung out at the moment, I'd bet."

"What the hell are you talking about?"

"They've arrested Marika. They know me. Marika worked at Stardust The Moon with Mama-san. That's easy to prove. They can back up my confession easy—subpoena Rob, my landlord, Ai-chan. Everyone. You'll be in jail a lot longer than I will."

He heard Paul breathe. But then Paul said nothing. Conner sensed him about to hang up. Fuck!

"I don't think Mrs. Mehita will be too happy when the press learns she used to be a hostess at Stardust The Moon."

"There's really no point in you calling the police, Conner. Let them have her."

Yes! He'd as good as admitted it. "I've already gotten myself arrested for Marika once. Remember how stupid Rob said I was?"

"Where is the package?"

"Marika destroyed it. From now on if you want it, you have to get it yourself."

"I'll think about it."

"Think fast. If I don't see Marika walking toward Passport Control in . . ." He looked at his watch ". . . fifteen minutes, I'm turning myself in. There's a policeman standing next to me right now. Do it." Conner hung up. There was nothing to do now but wait. The phone beeped at him, reminding him to take the card. Conner pulled out his card. Paul might make the right phone call. Or he might call Narita Police Central and tell them to look for a certain Floyd Conner in the departure area. Conner went back to Passport Control, leaned against the barrier, and counted the seconds of what might be his last fifteen minutes of freedom.

"You may dress now," the old woman told her.

Marika grabbed up the bundle of her clothes from the table and held them to her chest. The search had been astonishingly and uncomfortably thorough, and all for nothing.

"Are you going to put them all on at once?" the woman asked, watching her.

Marika set the clothes back down on the table and began dressing as the old woman watched. Nothing grandmotherly about *her*. The old woman escorted her out to Shimoda and Kuwano.

Shimoda pulled out the chair and motioned toward it. Marika sat down and stared at the floor. She couldn't bear to look at Shimoda. She felt like he had seen her naked. Shimoda put his hand under her chin and pulled her face up. Marika looked away. Shimoda slowly turned her head till their eyes met.

"Hawaii," he said.

Marika failed again to bring water to her eyes. They were not going to go easy on her. Well, she'd never been a crier. "I was picking up some real estate documents."

"That's better," Shimoda said. "Now, did Zakabi-san meet you at the airport?"

Marika tried to look down, but Shimoda held her chin in place. She felt like a dog.

The door opened. "Captain, sir," a uniformed policeman said.

"What?"

"It's the National Police Agency on the phone. The Criminal Investigations Bureau."

"What do *they* want?"

The policeman cocked his head. "They wish to speak with you."

"I'll call back."

"It's the Director, sir."

Shimoda let go of Marika. "Wait here," he told Kuwano. "Don't do anything. Don't anyone move. Don't anybody say *one word*! Just wait. Like statues."

Shimoda slammed the door shut behind him. He yelled something. Marika looked up at Kuwano. Kuwano stared back at her impassively. Marika returned the stare. There was more yelling outside. Shimoda again. Then it was quiet. Shimoda did not open the door. The uniformed policeman shifted his weight from one foot to the other, then back. Kuwano looked at the ceiling, not as impassively as before. Finally, the door opened.

Shimoda stepped in. "Let her go."

"What?" Kuwano gulped.

"It's decided."

Kuwano looked down at the floor. "All of it?"

Shimoda nodded. He looked fiercely at Marika. "You're to go down to Passport Control."

Marika jumped up and bowed her head briskly. Passport Control. "Thank you." She moved to the door.

Kuwano seemed on the verge of tears. "Criminal," he whispered accusingly.

Marika stopped. "I didn't know there were drugs involved. Honestly."

Kuwano shook his head.

Marika grabbed the doorknob and turned it. She pulled the door open. "Look, I was naive. The guy who sent me was Paul Barkley. He works in Akasaka." Shimoda looked up. "Also, the okami-san at Stardust The Moon, in Akasaka Mitsuke. Her name is Shiomi. I don't know her given name. Zakabi works for them."

Shimoda stared at her. "Not much we can do with that now, is there?"

"I'm sorry."

"But maybe better luck tomorrow, eh? Thank you," Kuwano said.

"Not at all," Marika mumbled and she let the door slowly swing shut behind her.

Once outside the police rooms, she was disoriented. She asked a policeman where Passport Control was and followed his directions at a half-run. She skittered down the stairs and there, by a barrier in the far corner, was Conner. She ran over to him.

He breathed something in English. "I don't believe it," he added in muffled Japanese she could just make out through the barrier

"You're leaving?"

"The flight's already boarding."

"I'm going with you."

"Don't be ridiculous." He shifted his weight nervously and sucked in his lip. "I can't be your boyfriend."

She laughed. "Don't be such an egotist."

"Marika, it was great, really it was . . ."

"I'm not asking you to marry me, stupid," she said. "I'm getting out of this place with or without your help. I need to see the vastness of the earth."

Conner cocked his head and held out a wad of money. "It's Paul's Hawaii money, and what I got from Katie." He tossed it over the barrier. "Canadian Pacific to Vancouver. Flight 4. Top of the right-hand staircase. Come back through the crew line. Run!"

Marika ran up the stairs and pushed her way to the front of the line. She piled Conner's money and everything she had in her pocketbook onto the clerk's desk. "A ticket to Vancouver on the present flight."

"The 1:55?"

Marika nodded and got the remainder of her part of Paul's money out of her pocket. The clerk looked at his watch. "It's 1:40 now. You can't possibly make it." He pointed to the departure board. "See?"

The numbers clicked over. Delayed. The new time was 2:30.

"Meant to be," Marika said.

The clerk chuckled. "Still tight, but can't argue with that. Baggage?"

"None."

He counted out the money he needed and gave her back the rest, a few thousand yen and some blue stuff with English writing and a picture of a woman on it. "Here's your ticket. Better hurry. They may actually leave at two-thirty."

Marika took the ticket and money, paid her airport fee, and raced downstairs and past the long passenger queues to the line for flight crew. "My flight is leaving in fifteen minutes," she said.

The officer looked at her boarding pass. "Passport." Marika handed it to him. He opened it to the first page, looked at Marika's face. "Ushirone Marika."

Marika nodded. Ushirone. How strange she was still married.

He stamped it and handed it back. "I'll tell them you're coming." He picked up a black phone.

Marika grabbed her passport, thanked the man, and rushed through the turnstile and flight security. And this time the police weren't waiting for her. Just Conner. Conner and a jet.

∾

CONNER GRABBED HIS RETRIEVED BAG. He was amazed she had made it. "Come on."

They sprinted around the corner, ignored the clogged moving walkways and ran to the gates. Two flight attendants at the Canadian Pacific jetway waved, holding the plane for them. They got on board. The door shut behind them.

He looked at Marika. She looked at him.

"You can go back, you know. See Canada for a few weeks, go home."

She laughed. "My apartment's in shambles, I'm married to some strange dentist, and I'm flying to Canada with no clothes and a small amount of money in all the wrong colors, but I'm not going back!"

They found their seats and strapped themselves in.

The plane backed away from the terminal building and began to taxi down the tarmac. Conner looked out the window. It was five years since he'd first seen that sight, Narita on a gray day. He thought of Arata, in Conner's imagination still sleeping where he'd left him. How alike they were, in one way at least: both had been faced with a choice, and both had fled from themselves. Conner had used Arata to distract himself from his losses, instead of accepting that those losses were now part of him. And sometime back, when it had come time for Arata to choose his right life, his nerve must have failed him. It was understandable, maybe unavoidable, given all he had to lose, but it was still sad. Given the choice, Conner would rather die like Edward than live like Arata. But that was not the choice before him, and he finally knew enough to be grateful.

The plane jumped into the air and cleared the clouds. He looked out the window. In the north was a single mountain. Not Fuji. In five years, he'd never actually seen Fuji apart from photos. This was some smaller, unnamed mountain. It was not as large, but equally beautiful, and greener. It was his mountain. He turned to Marika. "Hope this works."

"I'm not worried," she said. "If Canada's anything like America we'll be fine. I've been to America already, remember? And there was one thing I found there no one ever told me about."

"What?"

"Everyone speaks Japanese."

Conner rolled his eyes and Marika laughed as the last hint of the Japanese shore dropped under the horizon behind them, and the airplane headed out over the silvery ocean, to Canada.

THE END

ACKNOWLEDGMENTS

The road to this book was long enough that it became a historical novel in the process. Many people helped me on the way, but the first person who ever read my work and urge me forward was Laura Schiff, my teacher at Foothill Community College. Without her support, this book would not exist. Likewise, my longtime writing group, the Mumblers, whose love and support have meant and still mean everything: current members Jan Stites, Wendy Schultz and Melinda Maxwell-Smith, as well as former members Tarn Wilson, Jacqueline "J." Bautista, Leticia Wiley, and Julie Klinger. And especially Madelon Phillips, who is no longer with us and is sorely missed.

Another who worked with me on an early draft was Brent Spencer, from the Stanford University Continuing Studies Fiction Workshop. And from the writing group that developed from that same workshop, special thanks to Tracy Guzman, who stopped me from giving up more than once. Also, Tom Berman, Ann Nussbaum, Gail Howard Clark, Kim Maxwell, Marc Vincenti, Lisa Greim and Stephie Choi (with apologies to anyone I've forgotten).

Thanks also for crucial feedback and support at crucial junctures to Cynthia Karpa McCarthy, Eddie Sher, Eleanor Learmonth, Stephen Miller, Mark Unno, Jerome Carolfi, Alex Davis, Emily English Medley, Chris Lombardi, Jim Vestal and finally Ann Close at Knopf, the first publishing professional to take this book seriously. And big thanks to my current team: illustrator Hitoshi Shigeta, cover designer Maria Oglesby and editors Susie Hara, Stuart Horowitz and not least, David Groff.

Many people also provided inspiration and scurrilous tidbits. Thanks especially to Mayumi Watanabe, Setsuko Fujisawa, George Novinger and Frank Moorhead, and of course the whole office crew. Yoshimura-san and Kikuchi-san, I can't believe you hired me. Kuu-chan, Suu-chan, Same-chan, thanks for indulging me and even making me brave the terror of 電話当番. Yutaka, Miyuki, Masa, Hiroko, Hidehiko, and way back when, Nakamura-san, Asakawa-san and Hideous Creature. ご厚意をありがとうございました。心の底から誠にありがとうございました。この小説を嫌いになっても嫌いにならないでください！

And of course, my family, especially my parents and siblings, for putting up with me. And my husband, Tom Duffy, who not only provides love and support, but also reads everything, and whose judgment, sense and skill I value immensely. And, of course, our buddy Mookie. If everyone had a whoodle in their life, the world would be a better place.

ABOUT THE AUTHOR

Mike Karpa lived in Asia for eight years, including four in Japan. His fiction, memoir and nonfiction have been published by and can be found online in *Tin House*, *Foglifter*, *Tahoma Literary Review*, *Oyster River Pages*, *Sixfold* and a number of other magazines. He lives with his husband and dog in San Francisco.

Made in the USA
Las Vegas, NV
14 March 2024